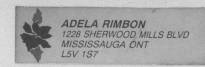

"Men live to bellow, but I expected better from you.

Still," Megan rushed on, "'twill do you no good. I am immune to shoutin'. I *will* tend your wound." Despite her brave words, she peered shyly at him through a fringe of spiky lashes. Her midnight-brown eyes were nearly black. Dark, mysterious pools that drew him, heightened his awareness of how close they were to one another. So close her breath whispered across his cheek. Rosemary and lemon. Sweet. Seductive.

Ross inhaled sharply, his senses filled with the smell of her skin, the texture of her hair, the pinkness of her tongue as it crept out to moisten her lips. What would it be like to touch...to taste? The air around them thickened, but it wasn't the coming storm that made it sizzle; it was desire. A need that turned his blood to fire, his body to stone...

Dear Reader,

This month brings us the long-awaited return of popular author Suzanne Barclay, who was described by *Romantic Times* as a "master storyteller." Her January title, *Lion's Heart*, is the beginning of a new medieval saga featuring the Sutherlands, a clan of Scottish Highlanders.

Also this month, we are very pleased to have Curtiss Ann Matlock back with her new historical Western, *White Gold*, the unforgettable story of unlikely partners who must face countless dangers and their own growing attraction on the sheep trail west.

Our other titles this month include well-known Harlequin American Romance and Superromance author Muriel Jensen's *A Bride for Adam*, the story of a mail-order bride who is forced to keep the secret of her own sons from her new family, and *For Love Alone*, a tale set in the time of Henry VIII, from Barbara Leigh, the author best known for her medieval, *To Touch the Sun*.

We hope you will keep an eye out for all four titles, wherever Harlequin Historical novels are sold.

Sincerely,

Tracy Farrell
Senior Editor

Please address questions and book requests to:
Harlequin Reader Service
U.S.: 3010 Walden Ave., P.O. Box 1325, Buffalo, NY 14269
Canadian: P.O. Box 609, Fort Erie, Ont. L2A 5X3

SUZANNE BARCLAY

Lion's Heart

Harlequin Books

TORONTO • NEW YORK • LONDON
AMSTERDAM • PARIS • SYDNEY • HAMBURG
STOCKHOLM • ATHENS • TOKYO • MILAN
MADRID • WARSAW • BUDAPEST • AUCKLAND

ISBN 0-373-28852-2

LION'S HEART

Printed in U.S.A.

Books by Suzanne Barclay

Harlequin Historicals

*Knight Dreams #141
*Knight's Lady #162
*Knight's Honor #184
Lion's Heart #252

*The Sommerville Brothers

SUZANNE BARCLAY

Scotland has always held a special place in Suzanne's heart. Possibly because Scottish blood runs in her veins. Sutherland blood. Small wonder that Clan Sutherland figures prominently in her trilogy set in medieval Scotland. While the scenery isn't as dramatic as the Highlands, the house she shares with her husband and their two dogs is situated in New York State's mountainous wine-growing region. When she's not writing, the author makes miniature furniture and needlepoint carpets.

To my grandmother,
Arline Sutherland Reed,
who first awakened my interest
in our Scots heritage

Prologue

The Scottish Highlands
July 1358

The sun nudged over the horizon. Peering warily through a bank of ominous clouds, it shed a few pale rays of light on Curthill Castle. Though it was early, soldiers crowded the walls of the fortress built centuries ago high atop sheer black cliffs that formed a natural barrier against attack.

"Look sharp, lads. They'll come soon," muttered Curthill's captain. One shoulder braced against the tower walls, Archie Sutherland rubbed eyes that ached from a night of watching and—

"There. 'Tis a ship!" the lookout called.

Archie's exhaustion vanished. This was it. The moment they'd been planning for ever since word had come that Lionel Carmichael had sailed north with a shipload of soldiers. He glanced seaward long enough to spot the tiny black speck that would grow into a real threat before the hour was out. "Send aloft a flaming arrow to alert *The Hawk*," he snapped at the hovering man. To the piper he bawled, "Sound battle stations. I'll return soon as I've informed m'lord the ship's been spotted."

The shrill, unearthly shriek of the bagpipes summoning the Sutherlands from their beds drowned out the thud as the drawbridge settled to earth and Archie streaked out from the castle. The need for haste overcoming good sense, he raced along the steep trail that wound down the cliff face to the town huddled in its lee. Doors and shutters flew open as he pounded past the wood and stone houses, but he paid no mind to the voices crying for news of the enemy who had twice attacked them in the past ten months.

Nor did he pause until he reached the narrow strip of rocky beach where the fishing boats had been drawn up for the night. At his approach, the thirty milling men-at-arms in Highland battle dress of chain mail and saffron shirts came to attention. Reining in his mount, Archie leaped to the ground and made for the richly dressed man warming himself before a small fire.

"Carmichael's ship comes, m'lord," Archie panted out.

"Ah." Anticipation flickered across his lordship's sharp, cunning features. Tall and whipcord lean beneath the silken surcoat and French-style body armor he wore despite his Highland breeding, he turned toward the sea. Pale eyes narrowing, he searched for and found the black shape set out against the rapidly lightening horizon. His pulse quickened to match the restless churning as the water sucked at the shore. Soon Carmichael and all who followed him would sleep beneath the dark brine, a fitting end to any who dared upset his plans. To Archie he said, "Did ye signal my ship?"

"Aye. Everythin' has been done as ye ordered, m'lord. The archers stand ready on the cliffs. As soon as Carmichael enters the harbor, *The Hawk*'ll sail 'round from the cove and attack his ship from the rear."

A thin, cold smile acknowledged the response. "Givin' old Lionel Carmichael the surprise o' his life?"

"'Twill be like shootin' fish in a barrel." The captain's nasty chuckle matched his leader's. "I'd give my share o' the next haul to see Carmichael's face when he realizes Curthill's nae just an unprotected fishin' village."

"Nay. It's much more than that," the lord agreed, glancing over his shoulder at the drear little huts that hid so much...the townspeople and the work they did in the dead of night. "Things ha' worked out nicely," he murmured mostly to himself.

"But they'll nae keep on that way does Carmichael make good his threat to kill us all off." The captain hawked and spat onto the stony ground. "Why could he nae be satisfied wi' our claim that his son's death was a huntin' accident?"

"The Carmichaels are close-knit. Likely it makes nae difference to the old man whether Lion's death was an accident or not. He wants blood...Sutherland blood...in payment for the death of his beloved heir," his lordship sneered.

"Well, we'd best stop him this time for good and all. We were lucky *The Black Hawk* happened to ha' put into port wi' a load of plunder, or we'd ha' been fightin' the Carmichaels wi' just the castle garrison and yer mercenaries."

"Agreed. We canna afford to ha' Lionel Carmichael sailin' in here every few months and oversettin' our plans. If we dinna vanquish him this time, I'll complain to the king. His majesty had a full report of poor Lion's death at the time. He knows we regret the unfortunate incident," his lordship drawled, pleased with the way that had worked out, too. With the twang of one hunting quarrel, he had eliminated the young knight who'd become a problem on two fronts...one business, the other personal. "King David was so moved by our plight he said he'd outlaw the Carmichaels did Lionel persist in his quest for revenge."

"What if the king sends men here?"

"And what will they find?" the lord inquired silkily, flashing the guileless smile that had led so many people to underestimate him. "A few villagers plyin' their honest trade."

"And a storage buildin' crammed full of things ye'd just as leave the king didna know about."

His lordship snorted. "Ye're carryin' on like an old woman. Two years we've been at this, and none the wiser. Not even Megan Sutherland, who thinks she kens everythin' that goes on at Curthill Castle and in the town."

"She's been duped same as the rest of them. Hasna a clue as to what's really goin' on here." Archie snickered. "Young Lion suspected somethin' was afoot, though."

"Suspected. He never got close enough to actually find anythin' before we shut him up. And we'll do the same to anyone else who comes sniffin' around here, thinkin' to spoil this sweet business of ours," the ruler of Curthill growled.

Archie grinned wolfishly. "Aye, m'lord."

Chapter One

The Scottish Lowlands
Carmichael Castle

"Laird Lionel has returned." Though softly spoken, Owain of Llangollen's words caused his lord's head to snap up from the tally stick he had been studying.

"Is Da unhurt?" Ross Carmichael asked, brilliant blue eyes darkening in alarm.

"He is whole." Owain stepped into the counting room. "But his head is not as high as when he left to go *huntin'*."

"Huntin'." Ross clutched the notched stick so tightly his knuckles turned white. "'Twasna red deer my sire sought when he went north," he growled. "'Twas Sutherlands."

"Likely," the Welshman allowed.

"Damn. What if word of this reaches the king?"

"It may not. 'Tis two weeks' hard march at least from the Sutherland lands on Dornoch Firth to Edinburgh."

"But only four days by ship...which is doubtless how Da went since he's gone and returned so quick." Ross's expression turned grim. "Damn Da and his thirst for vengeance!" He threw down the tally stick and exploded out of the chair in a rare show of rage. "He promised my mother and me he wouldna go after them again."

Stalking to the arrow slit that served as the room's window, Ross braced his hands on the stone wall. The last rays of the setting sun cast his proud profile in sharp relief, wide forehead, aristocratic nose, stubborn jaw. His tall muscular body shook with the effort it took to control his rage. But control it he did. Likely 'twas the years of seeing his sire rant and rage that caused Ross to govern his own passions, Owain thought.

That his young lord was cool and logical...for a Carmichael...was one reason Owain had left his native Wales to serve Ross. But Laird Lionel's obsession with punishing the Sutherlands for the death of Lion, his eldest son and heir, tried Ross's patience as nothing else could. "A father has a right to avenge the death of his son," Owain ventured with soothing Welsh wisdom.

Ross was having none of it. "If King David hears of this, he'll put us all to the horn...as he threatened the last time Da hied off to the Highlands *huntin'* Sutherlands."

Owain grunted in agreement. It was not worry for himself that goaded Ross, but fear for his mother, six siblings and his clansmen. Ross took his new responsibilities as heir seriously, no matter that they had been thrust on him unexpectedly when Lion had been killed ten months ago while at Curthill Castle to wed Siusan Sutherland. "Mayhap if ye went to the king...explained to him that..."

"Explained what?" Ross demanded, whirling on him, eyes blazing with a fire reminiscent of his sire's infamous rages. "That Da willna believe 'twas an accident? That despite what the witnesses say, he thinks Eammon Sutherland killed Lion and willna rest until the sea runs red wi' Sutherland blood? Even if it means outlawin' all of Clan Carmichael." Ross sighed heavily, raking a tanned hand through the thick black hair he'd inherited from his sire.

"Mayhap after this latest defeat he'll let you send someone to Curthill to spy on the Sutherlands and learn the truth."

Ross snorted. "Da brushes aside every suggestion I make." That hurt, but not nearly as much as the fact that though Ross had been back home from the war in Wales for four months and Lion had been dead for ten, their father had yet to officially install Ross as his heir. "Da isna interested in the truth, just in killin' as many Sutherlands as possible."

"Aye. Grief ofttimes brings on such madness."

"I should chain him to his bed until it passes, or his thirst for vengeance will drive all of us into early graves," Ross growled, digging both hands into his hair this time. "As soon as I've seen he's all right, I'm goin' to Curthill myself."

Owain was across the room in a heartbeat, his agitation evident in the way he grabbed Ross by both shoulders, stopping just sort of shaking him. "This madness must be catching. What can ye hope to gain by putting yerself in harm's way?" he asked.

"The truth."

"The truth." On Owain's lips it was a curse. "Do ye think Laird Lionel will be satisfied if ye drag back the poor fool whose arrow went astray and ended up in Lion's back?"

"I hope so."

Owain shook his head. "I doubt it will be so simple. The laird's grief is a huge, monstrous thing."

As big and unending as his love for Lion had been. Ross sighed heavily. "The truth is all I can offer him. If it isna enough to stay his madness, then I'll lock him in the tower."

"Ross Carmichael, how dare ye?" exclaimed a young voice.

He turned and saw his eleven-year-old sister standing in the doorway, arms crossed over her flat chest, the violet eyes she and Lion had inherited from Lionel aflame with fury. "Elspeth, you dinna understand," he began, holding up a placating hand.

"I came to tell ye Da was home, and find ye plottin' treason. Traitor!" She whirled and fled the room.

Ross exhaled sharply. "Now the fat's really in the fire. I suppose I best go after her before her tale makes matters worse." Still he took the time to lock the precious tally sticks and the ledger that held the records of the crofters' rent payments into the strongbox. Keeping the accounts had been his duty from the time he was eleven, for neither his father nor Lion had had the time nor the head for clerical duties.

"Should ye not be going after her?" Owain asked.

"I willna arrive red faced and pantin' like a lad caught filchin' apples." He had his pride. Too much, Lion used to say, warning that Ross's stiff neck would one day be his undoing. Ross sighed again and set about thinking how best to diffuse the laird's anger. Matching wits with his volatile sire was something he'd once enjoyed, but the heart had gone out of the contest after Lion died. Because beneath the struggle of wills there was a wealth of pain and guilt.

If only he could go back...change the things he had said and done that fateful day before Lion left for Curthill. But there was no going back...for any of them, Ross thought wretchedly. Nor would there likely ever be peace between himself and his father.

Firmly closing the door on the past, Ross led the way from the counting room, an alcove off his bedchamber set high in the old keep. It had been built as a fort by the first Carmichael laird, and the steps leading down from the tower were narrow and steep, circling tightly so that only one would-be attacker at a time might come up them. He used the time it took to descend the stairs to gird himself for the coming battle.

All too soon, he stepped out into the neatly cobbled courtyard. It was enclosed on the other three sides by the towers added by successive generations of prosperous Carmichaels, thick gray sentinels standing guard over the lesser buildings, the kitchens, stables and chapel. Despite his inner turmoil, Ross felt a spurt of pride as he beheld the small, scrupulously ordered city that was now his birthright. It was as sleek and thriving as any in Scotland. No matter that he had never wanted to rule here, he prized every stone with a fierceness that turned the strenuous duty of running the estate into a labor of love.

In the months since his return from the Welsh campaign, Ross's knowledge of farming and trade had meant fat yields when other clans went hungry. His fair handling of disputes had won his clansmens' respect. Yet every day his father delayed naming him heir undermined his efforts and his effectiveness, Ross thought as he threaded his way through the courtyard.

It yet teemed with Lionel's men seeing to their gear and mounts. Many of his clansmen smiled and nodded in greeting, but the men who had ridden out with their chief frowned or pointedly looked away. When Ross drew abreast of them, Andrew Carmichael growled something under his breath and spat on the ground.

Ross's gut tightened. Damn, he did not want a confrontation with the grizzled knight who had been Lion's second in command. Not because he feared the sword arm of the man who had taught both brothers to wield one in the first place, but because trouble between them could only make matters worse. Already he felt the tension rippling through the crowd, like a summer storm sweeping across the low hill on which Carmichael Castle had been built. Men drew into groups, instinctively choosing sides, and Ross knew he'd appear weak did he let the remark slide. "Do you have sometin' to say to me, Andrew?" he demanded.

Andrew's leathery face went as red as the flaming locks now liberally sprinkled with gray, and his eyes narrowed to angry brown slits. "I said ye looked right fagged from porin' over yer ledgers and such whilst we were gone," he grumbled.

Ross stiffened, more hurt than angered by the blow from a man he'd admired all his life and who, until Lion's death, had been both friend and mentor. The time was swift approaching when he'd have to settle this... mayhap with swords. But not today. Today there was his father to deal with.

"A good thing I'm tendin' to business," Ross snapped. "Else there wouldna be coin enough to arm you for these *huntin'* trips." He dismissed Andrew with a condemning glance, let it wander over the group. Spotting bloodied bandages on both men and beasts, he clenched his jaw tighter. If these men had been injured hunting game, he'd... he'd eat his own horse. "I assume the *laird*'s in the hall," he muttered, and strode off to confront his sire.

"But we did go huntin'." Lionel Carmichael's outraged roar rang off the high vaulted ceiling of the great hall just as Ross reached the doorway.

Within, tension hung heavy on the humid summer air that barely stirred the silken banners trailing from the timbers two stories above the rush-covered floor. The neat rows of trestle tables were packed with curious Carmichaels. Even the figures in the tapestries that brightened the whitewashed walls seemed to turn and stare. Serving maids bustled about the long room, dispensing bread and ale as briskly as hawkers at a bearbaiting.

The bear in question stood before a fireplace large enough to take an entire tree trunk, but empty at this time of year. As empty as Ross felt seeing his sire. The man whose love and respect he'd give anything to regain. *Oh, Da. Why can we not put this behind us?* But he knew the answer to that. 'Twas because bold, brash Lion had been the heart of the family. Without him, they lived in shadow. Forever in shadow.

"The Sutherlands must be punished," Lionel bellowed. Elspeth held the post at his right hand left vacant by Lion's passing. When she spotted Ross, she tugged on their sire's arm, but the laird's attention was all on the tiny woman who faced him down.

"'Twill be a hollow victory if the king outlaws us all," Carina Carmichael reminded him. Despite the fact that he towered over her, she stood before her husband bravely, a red-haired crusader in bright blue silk that matched the eyes she had bequeathed to Ross along with a cool head and razor-sharp mind.

Ross had never admired her more than he did at this moment. She was logical, loyal and as honorable as any man. When God made Carina Carmichael, he'd thrown away the pattern, so all women suffered by comparison. And Rhiannon most of all. Rhiannon, the Welsh witch whose betrayal had cost him dear.

"I ha' the right to avenge my son's death," the laird roared, violet eyes blazing, big body trembling with the force of his anger. Yet none feared he'd strike her with more than the edge of his tongue. For all his bluff and bluster, Lionel loved his mate and had taught his sons that women should be protected and valued, not scorned or beaten as was the way of some men.

Those same lessons had made Ross easy prey for wily Rhiannon, he thought as he quickly threaded his way through the tables toward his parents. But never again. He'd not trust another woman outside his family as long as he lived.

"Lion was my son, too," Carina replied just as Ross reached them, her voice low now, anguished.

Lionel's shoulders slumped. The color anger lent to his fleshy cheeks did not disguise the gray of fatigue and pain. *Oh, Da.* Ross wanted to reach out to his sire and hold him close, but he knew the old man would welcome neither sympathy nor pity...especially from him. Ross gave him the only gift he *would* accept...a fight on which to vent his spleen.

"Well, did you get anyone killed this time?" he snapped.

Lionel went red to the roots of his long, black hair. "Nay. Those whoreson Sutherlands set a shipload of pirates to attack our rear, but we managed to fight clear and sail away wi' naught more'n a cracked mast and a few cuts and scrapes."

"This time."

"At least the lads and I *want* Lion avenged." His father's jaw hardened. "Least we're nae afraid to punish the Sutherlands."

"The only thing you fear is the truth. You willna let me send anyone to Curthill for fear of findin' 'twas an accident after all and the Sutherlands you've attacked naught but hapless victims." Ross's sharp retort caused a collective gasp to sweep the hall. Benches creaked, clothing rustled as their audience leaned closer, intent on the drama.

"Lionel, Ross...upstairs in my solar where we can be private," Lady Carina decreed.

Shooting Ross a final, condemning glance, Lionel turned and stomped from the room, Elspeth clinging to his side like a burr.

"Why must ye push him so?" Carina asked as she and Ross mounted the stairs.

"Because I'd go to Curthill and find out what really happened to Lion. Mayhap then we could get on wi' the rest of our lives," he explained before looking away.

"Ross, ye must stop blamin' yerself."

"How can I? If I hadna been so determined to honor my pledge to fight the Welsh, I'd have gone wi' Lion...mayhap prevented him from bein' killed."

Ross's anguish cut Carina to the quick. Much as she still mourned the loss of her firstborn, her duty now lay with the living, in helping Ross to forgive himself, in healing the breach between him and Lionel. If only they were not so different. Had she been wrong to teach the son of her heart that there were other things in life besides fighting and hunting?

Nay. He was a fine man. Brave and loyal, yet compassionate and intelligent. Intelligent enough to know that much as he, too, wanted to avenge his brother, no good could come of flaunting the king's edict. Ross had been away fighting the Welsh when word had come of Lion's death and had not been able to return until a few months ago. He'd come home a changed man. Harder, colder and more inflexible... especially about matters of honor.

"Lion might ha' been killed even if ye were there," Carina said, but Ross only shrugged. Somehow she must find a way to set things right, she thought as they left the stairway and entered her sitting room. The looms and tapestry frames that occupied one-half of the solar stood idle, nor would the maids below in the hall come above stairs until she recalled them to their duties.

At the other end of the airy, orderly room, Elspeth finished pouring wine from the flagon set out on a table between the windows and carried the cup to her father, who stared broodingly into the hearth. Laying a hand on the carved back of his chair, she glared defiantly at her mother and brother.

"Da, Ross threatened to kill ye," Elspeth taunted.

Carina gasped. "I'm sure he did nae such thing."

"Ha! Then he could be laird all the sooner," his father grumbled, his expression hard and cynical.

"Elspeth," Ross warned, eyes narrowing. "You'll speak the truth, or I'll shake it out of you."

"Oh, very well." Sullen and mutinous, she complied.

"Elspeth, shame on ye for lyin'," cried their mother.

"She canna help it," Ross said. "Women are natural liars." Rhiannon had been a master of the art.

"I resent that." Carina thrust a wine cup into Ross's hand. "Women are nae more likely to lie than a man."

Lionel snorted. "I'd rather ye challenged me to open combat than ran around plottin' to lock me in my own tower," he grumbled, glaring at Ross.

One shoulder propped against the mantel, Ross clenched his wine cup so tightly the Carmichael crest on it bit into his flesh. 'Twas a reminder, if he needed one, that he had a responsibility to protect the clan... even from the foolishness of its chief. "We canna go on like this, Da..."

"'Tis our right to avenge him," Lionel countered. "Even if ye dinna ha' the stomach for it."

Ross gasped, then dragged in a steadying breath. It was not a question of bravery, he knew that; his father knew that...deep down. With a year separating them in age, he and Lion had trained together. Ross was as skilled a fighter as his brother, if more cautious and less eager for the kill. Small good it had done Lion, dead at five-and-twenty with a Sutherland quarrel in his back. "We need to know what really happened to Lion whilst he was wi' the Sutherlands," he began.

"Bah." Lionel downed his wine, leaped from the chair with a speed that belied his fifty years and went after more. Elspeth made to follow, but her mother tugged her down onto the stool at her feet and kept her there despite Elspeth's objections.

Little hellion, Ross thought. She should have been born a lad, for she neither knew nor liked her woman's place in life.

"I think ye are glad he's gone," Lionel bellowed, turning so abruptly that wine sloshed onto the bright carpets that covered the floor. "Ye always envied him his place as heir."

Ross flinched. He'd wanted the truth and here it was, the canker that had gnawed at his father's gut since Lion had been returned to them sewn into a sack. But before Ross's stunned brain could form a denial, his mother was up and moving.

"Lionel, ha' a care for the Oriental carpets that cost ye so dear." Grabbing a rag from her mending basket, she dabbed at the spreading stain. To Ross, it looked ominously like blood...his brother's blood, spilled so senselessly. "H-how ye can think such a thing of Ross is beyond me," his mother went on. "But ye must stop this. It's tearin' us apart." The sight of her bent head, the quaver in her voice surely wounded his father, because it stabbed Ross like a lance. Then her shoulders began to tremble.

"Ah, Carina." Setting his cup down with a thump, the laird of the Carmichaels knelt to his wife. "Nae greetin', lass, ye ken I canna stand it when ye do." He put an arm around her and awkwardly patted her shaking back.

"I am nae cryin'," she said huskily, raising moist eyes to him. "Nae exactly. But Lionel, I canna stand this."

Neither could he. Ross crossed the room in three strides, went down on his knees beside them. "Da. I swear on my soul...on

Mama's, if you no longer think I ha' one…that I never wanted what was Lion's."

"Ha! Ye always loved this castle, these lands."

"I'll not deny that," Ross said, though he knew he probably should. "But I never coveted them. Nay, I had my own plans."

"Lionel, can ye nae see Ross wants what's right for—"

"Right! Is it right that my son is dead?"

"Our son, Lionel," Carina said softly, laying her head on his shoulder. "And nae, it isna right that he was killed. But killin' innocent Sutherlands and outlawin' our clan to avenge his death isna right, either."

"I ken nae other way," the laird said stiffly.

And that, Ross thought sadly, was the crux of the problem. The old ways demanded an *eye for an eye,* but King David had spent the past twelve years a prisoner in the English court and had brought back more *civilized* notions. Ross admired the ideal, agreed it was wrong to exterminate the Sutherlands for an accident. If Lion's death had been an accident. "What we need is proof to lay before the king. At least let me look into—"

"Nay! I want Eammon dead. He got his cursed daughter to enslave my son and lure him to his death. I want him dead!"

And that was that. Ross's heart fell to his boots, but before he could renew his argument, the solar door flew open and Hunter exploded into the room, fair cheeks flushed, dark auburn hair streaming out behind him.

"Da. Ye're home." He bounded over to them with his usual sixteen-year-old exuberance, skidded to a halt beside the kneeling trio. "What are ye doin'? Did ye lose somethin'?"

"A great deal," Ross said grimly. Rising slowly, he watched with bleak eyes as his father assisted his mother to her feet.

"Why did ye nae tell me ye were goin' after the Sutherlands?" Hunter demanded. "I'd ha' gone wi' ye."

"Me too," Elspeth interjected, coming to stand at her father's other side.

"Ye're just a lass," Hunter scoffed.

Elspeth's jaw jutted out. "I can ride as well as ye can and Sir Andrew says I wield a dirk as good as—"

"Elspeth Carmichael. Ha' ye been hangin' around the trainin' grounds again?" her mother demanded.

The little girl immediately looked to her father for support, but he frowned at her, shaking his head. "Ye shouldna be there. 'Tis dangerous and . . . and unseemly."

"Nay. Just because I'm a lass is nae reason why I must stay indoors and learn to sew and cook. I hate such things, Da . . ."

"Is anyone hungry?" Averly sang out, sailing into the room carrying a cloth-covered tray. At fourteen, she was already a beauty cast in her mother's mold. Small wonder she was contracted to wed in the autumn. "Mama set me to fetch the food as soon as we knew ye'd arrived, Da." After setting the tray on the table, she stood on tiptoe to kiss his grimy cheek, then wrinkled her nose. "Ye're filthy. Shall I ha' a bath prepared?"

"Later. 'Twas a long trip, and I'd sit a spell." He looked so tired and dispirited, suddenly, that Ross's heart lurched. More than anything, he wanted to find the man responsible for Lion's death and hand him to his father.

"Come, sit, and I'll play my lute. That should relax ye," Averly said as she led their father to a chair. His grimace was matched by Elspeth's and Hunter's.

"Now that she's weddin' Simon, she's practicin' at bein' lady o' the manor," Hunter mumbled around a mouthful of bread.

"Mama's been lettin' me be her for a bit," Averly said. Lute in hand, she took the stool Elspeth had vacated, ignoring her sister's pained expression. "Ross is teachin' me to do accounts."

Lionel grunted. "He's apt enough at *them*."

Ross briefly closed his eyes as his sire's thrust cut deep inside him, raking open unhealed wounds. How much longer could they go on hurting each other like this before the damage was so grievous neither of them recovered? Something had to give.

"Anne Fraser rides over to take lessons from Ross, too, when she can," Averly said above the tuning of the lute.

"Does she, now? What's he teachin' her?" Lionel's eyes twinkled in pale imitation of his usual teasing.

"Nothin' improper," Averly primly assured him. "Ross is a gentleman. He wouldna do anythin' *like that*."

"Too bad he's nae a bit more *like that*," his father said, frowning again. "When are ye goin' to ask Anne to marry ye?"

Never. As he'd stood in the rain looking down at the men slaughtered because he'd erred in trusting Rhiannon, Ross had vowed never again to let another woman get close enough to harm him or his clansmen. "There's no need for me to wed. You've heirs aplenty should aught happen to me."

His father's expression darkened. "So, Andrew was right. That Welshwoman ha' made ye afraid of lasses, too. Well, ye'd best get past it quick," he grumbled over Ross's choked protest and Elspeth's scathing laughter. "I'm nae gettin' any younger, and I'd hold my grandson afore I die."

And you'll wish he was Lion's son, not mine. "I know my duty, and I'll do it," Ross said woodenly.

His mother sighed. "I'd hoped ye'd find someone ye really loved," she said wistfully.

"The heir to a great estate doesna ha' that luxury," his father snapped . . . with malicious delight, Ross thought.

"Ye didna let my Da's disapproval stand in yer way," Carina replied, her tone suddenly as light and merry as the saucy glance she tossed her husband.

"Nay, I saw what I wanted and took it." The smile he gave the woman he'd kidnapped and wed was warm with pleasant memories.

A spurt of something that couldn't be jealousy squeezed Ross's chest. He wouldn't let it be. Jealousy implied passion, and thanks to Rhiannon he knew how dangerous an excess of lust could be. It seemed the Carmichael blood was tainted with it, for Lion had loved his Siusan that hotly . . . and it had lured him to his death. Fortunately *he* was better able to control his emotions.

"And so should Ross . . . have what he wants."

Lionel grunted and looked away from his wife. "He has what he wants . . . he'll be laird after me."

"Nay, Da, I never wanted that. Not now, not ever."

A scratching at the door intruded, and the steward stuck his bald head into the room. "There's a message come from the king."

Six pairs of Carmichael eyes collided, all filled with dread. Carina gave permission for the messenger to invade her solar for the sake of keeping this news private. It seemed her action was justified, for the man sidled into the room and offered a leather parchment case to the laird.

After examining the seal, Lionel growled, "Ye've done yer duty. Go below and my man will see to yer comfort." When the courier had fled, he handed the roll to Carina.

With trembling fingers, she broke the seal, withdrew the missive and quickly scanned its contents. Seconds later she gasped, her stunned glance flying to Ross. "Oh, my God."

"What?" Stepping forward, Ross took the paper from her lax fingers. He read past the ritual greetings to the body of the message, and his mouth went dry. "The king knows about this latest raid against the Sutherlands. He'd punish me for—"

"But ye werena even wi' me," Lionel exclaimed.

Ross swallowed hard. "He wants a blood bond twixt our families," he got out. "I'm to marry Megan Sutherland."

"The hell ye are." Lionel snatched the parchment from Ross, picked out the words he knew. "Impossible. I won't ha' the spawn of Eammon Sutherland in my family. 'Twould be like takin' a ... a viper to my breast."

"Aye," the others echoed, faces pinched with repugnance.

"I agree." But what choice did he have? Turning away lest his stunned family see the anguish in his face, Ross walked to the window. Through the opened mullioned panes, the garden below was a riot of color: green, red, yellow, white. Two small figures moved along the neat stone path his mother had had put in to separate the beds into blocks. Six-year-old Brenna held the basket while Margaret, aged nine, cut flowers. So young ... so defenseless. Where would they go if they were all outlawed, driven from their home?

In the slums of Edinburgh, Ross had seen the hovels where the poor lived, the cribs where the prostitutes plied their trade, some not much older than Margaret. He could not have that on his conscience, too. "I have nae choice. I will go to Curthill as the king commands."

"Nay." His father came to him, grabbed him by both shoulders, fingers biting in as though he'd never let go. "I willna send another son north to be killed by those bastards."

Much as Ross appreciated the concern stamped on his father's face, he knew that openly flaunting the king's command would be a death sentence for everyone with the name Carmichael. "I can take care of myself."

"If they cut Lion down from ambush, what chance would ye ha'?" his sire inquired with typical lack of confidence.

"Forewarned is forearmed," Ross replied with feigned lightness. "I'll take as many knights as you can spare." And Owain, who'd give his own life to save Ross's . . . because the debt the Welshman owed him went beyond this life and into the next.

"I willna ha' that bitch here."

Ross nodded, holding his sire's furious gaze with his own determined one. "I said I'd go to Curthill." He'd go and ferret out the truth about Lion's death. "But I swear, on Lion's soul, I willna wed into the family that murdered my brother."

"Yer money or yer life," cried the brigand.

"Ye'll get the point of my sword." The lady pulled out her sword and struck him a resounding blow.

The robber shrieked.

The lady hit him again.

The children howled with laughter.

Megan Sutherland smiled as she crouched behind the barrel that served as a stage, the puppet in her right hand thumping away at the one on her left until the thief cried for mercy.

"Now tell us the one where Lady Fiona runs all the way to the castle to summon the knights and save the croft," demanded Janet, the cook's daughter, brown eyes dancing.

Megan smiled fondly, pleased by their enthusiasm. As *seanachaidh* or bard for Clan Sutherland, it was her duty to keep the old myths and legends alive. She'd learned early on that the hand puppets were invaluable in holding the interest of the youngest bairns through the little stories she made up for them and the ofttimes lengthier tales of their ancestors.

Seanachaidh was a title seldom bestowed on a woman. The fact that her father had entrusted it to her still warmed Megan, made up, in part, for his neglect these past two years. Nay, it did not . . . not really, Megan thought, smile dimming. But she was very good at pretending. After all, telling tales was her life.

"'Tis getting late," she muttered. Climbing awkwardly to her feet, she kept her weight from her left leg. As usual, staying too long in one position had cramped the poorly knit muscles, her own legacy from the day her brother had died. Absently she massaged her thigh with the heel of a puppet-clad hand.

"There ye are, Meg," a sweet voice called from the stable doorway. Pulling the door closed, her cousin advanced on them, face flushed, blond braids bouncing against her ample breasts. "Off wi' ye, now. 'Tis near supper time and yer mothers'll be lookin' for ye," Chrissy added, shooing the children along kindly but firmly. When they'd gone, she turned excited eyes on Megan. "They've just sent word up from town. *His* ship's landed, and he'll be here directly."

"Ross Carmichael?" At her cousin's quick nod, Megan put both puppets up to still her suddenly thundering heart. "He came. I—I wasna sure he would . . . not after what happened to Lion." *Poor Lion. Poor Siusan.* Her throat tightened as it always did when she thought of the ill-fated pair . . . her beautiful younger sister and the handsome knight who'd loved her so fiercely. Now Lion was dead . . . and Siusan might just as well be.

"Well, he's here. I just hope things work out better this time." Plucking a piece of straw from Megan's thick blond braid, she tugged on it gently. "Come. We'd best get ye cleaned up."

Even knowing she should change out of the plain russet gown she'd put on this morn to help her mother in the herb garden, Megan held back. "I can scarcely believe he wants to wed me."

"Why shouldn't he? Ye've the face of an angel and a soul to match. 'Tis lucky he is to be gettin' ye," Chrissy said stoutly.

"That wasna what I meant." She knew she was no angel—in looks or otherwise. Her mouth was too full, her eyes too large for her small face, and she was far too spirited . . . according to her very proper mother . . . but that was not what worried her.

She gestured at her left leg, hidden by her skirts, but they both knew what it looked like. "Do you think they told him about *it?*"

Chrissy hesitated, reading fear and hope in one who had had too much of the first and not enough of the second in her short life. "Likely they did," she murmured. At the bedding ceremony, Megan would be stripped naked for inspection by her new husband. Surely the king would not want Megan humiliated by having Lord Ross repudiate her for her imperfection. *Nay, men were not so caring.* But King David *did* want this bond to end the fighting between the two families, so likely Ross had been told the truth about Megan lest he foil his majesty's plans by rejecting her for her lameness. "I am sure Lord Ross knows. He wouldna ha' made this long trip if he didna plan to marry ye."

The worry instantly left Megan's big brown eyes. "Lion said his brother would go wild for me. Remember?"

"Dinna get yer hopes up," Chrissy cautioned.

Megan's smile broadened. "Too late. I'm already countin' on him fallin' deeply in love wi' me. And you've no need to worry that Ross will hurt me. Lion said he was the perfect knight, handsome, strong, brave, clever and kind."

"No man is *that* perfect."

"I'm sorry marriage to Old Fergus left a sour taste in your mouth where men are concerned, Chrissy, but I know Ross is a gentle man. Lion said he doesna raise his voice when he's angry. Can you believe it? Even dear Papa shouts when he's wroth." *Or he used to. Did he still?* The last time her father had come down from his secluded tower, he'd been so quiet and remote she'd scarcely recognized him. Shoving aside the painful memory, Megan added, "I'll wager Ross already loves me as much as I do him."

"Oh, Meg. Dinna rush into this."

"Too late. But fret not. Ross will want me...even if I'm nae perfect." *He had to.* Because she was counting on Ross to secure her future and save Siusan's life. But that was tomorrow's worry. Today's was far simpler. "I canna be perfect for him," Megan quickly added. "But I have been practicin' walkin' wi'out a limp. See..." She clenched her puppets into fists and took one step, then another. "If I go slowly...and concentrate."

The lump in Chrissy's throat thickened so she could scarcely breathe as she watched her cousin. Well she remembered how Megan had looked when they had pulled her from beneath her fallen horse and carried her home. Her leg had been broken in two places, her hip in one. No one had thought she'd ever walk again, though Lady Mary had nursed her day and night. Thanks to her mother's skill, and Megan's own valiant struggles against pain and frustration, she had learned to stand and then to walk. But the muscles in her thigh had never regained their full strength. Seeing her now, gliding across the straw-covered floor, Chrissy wanted to cry. "Ye...ye're doin' very well," she managed when Megan looked back over her shoulder. "And I hope Ross Carmichael appreciates it."

"He will. He isna the sort to repudiate me for my crippled leg." As Comyn had. Her first betrothed had deserted her while she lay recuperating from her accident. *Ross had to want her. He just had to.* Not only because she had fallen in love with Lion's tales of his younger brother, but because Ross was her last hope to have the home and bairns she'd always wanted.

"Meg? Ye moaned. Are ye all right?"

Megan pasted on a smile. "Of course," she lied with the ease of long practice. 'Twas not a lie, exactly; shielding others from her problems was second nature.

"We'd best get inside and dressed for supper, then." Chrissy pulled the heavy stable door open and they both hurried out...directly into the path of a cantering line of riders.

"'Ware!" a deep voice called. Horses screamed; men swore, sawing on the reins as they attempted to avoid the two girls.

Megan tried to dart out of the way, but her left leg buckled and she went down, striking the hard-packed earth with a thud that drove the air from her lungs, the will from her limbs. Dizzy, she watched the horse rear over her, his steel-shod hooves pawing the air so close to her face the breeze fanned it. 'Twas like reliving the accident all over again. Her mouth dry with fear, she lay there waiting for the horse to land on her.

There would be that dreadful moment of impact, then numbness, a black void and pain that went on and on . . .

Bellowing an oath, the rider jerked the horse aside. The beast came down harmlessly, blowing and shaking.

Shaking herself, Megan exhaled slowly. A fine mist clouded her vision; the chaos of shouted orders and neighing beasts added to the ringing in her ears, but she was unhurt.

A man encased in gleaming armor suddenly materialized at her side. "Are you all right?" a deep voice demanded.

Thinking it was Comyn, Megan instinctively recoiled.

"Damn. I mean you no harm." The man lifted the visor and pulled his helmet off entirely, handing it to someone behind him. "Are you all right? he asked again, tossing damp black hair from his tanned face.

Lion, was her first thought. Nay. This man had blue eyes. *Ross Carmichael.*

The air backed up in Megan's lungs. Jesu, he was beautiful as a saint come to earth. Black curls clung damply to his furrowed forehead, framed the sides of high cheekbones and a strong jaw, darkly stubbled. Concern drew his mouth into a flat line, but it was his eyes that drew her, held her. Warm and clear as a summer sky . . . gleaming with intelligence. An intelligent man? Well, Lion had said he was different. And he would need to be shrewd to help her save Siusan.

"Can you speak?" he asked with such gentleness she wondered if he was real.

Megan reached up to touch him, realized she still wore the puppets and tried to snatch her hand back. But he was too quick, grabbing her around the wrist with gauntleted fingers.

"What is this? Some new style in Highland gloves?"

Oh, damn. "L-Lady Fiona." Her cheeks were hot as fire.

His smile sent the fire clear to her toes. "A puppet?"

"I—I entertain the children . . ."

"My sisters would enjoy that."

He had four sisters, Megan recalled. The tiny kernel of hope inside her expanded. She had wondered what it would be like living in the south, near a fancy city like Edinburgh, in a castle filled with people who blamed her family for Lion's death. Now she saw a way to make them like her... "I'd be happy to..."

"Oh, Meggie." The crowd of curious onlookers parted and Chrissy threw herself down beside her. "Are ye hurt, Megan?"

"You are Megan?" Ross asked. "Megan Sutherland?" At her nod, he dropped her hand like a hot stone and leaped to his feet. His soft blue eyes turned cold as the loch in winter, freezing her to the bone. Spinning on his heel, he growled, "Let the Sutherlands see to their own," and stomped off.

Megan moaned and shut her eyes.

"Where are you hurt?" Chrissy demanded.

"It's my heart... it's breakin'."

Chrissy rocked back on her heels. "Stop playactin'."

"I only wish I were." Megan sat up and stared at Ross's retreating back, straight and rigid as an iron poker. "For some reason, I dinna think he loves me," she murmured.

"An understatement," Chrissy amended.

"Yet." Megan straightened her shoulders. Naught could be accomplished sitting about waiting and wishing for a problem to right itself. Recovering the use of her leg had taught her only action accomplished that. "I'll just have to convince him he has made a mistake."

"Good luck." Chrissy extended a hand and helped Megan to her feet. "That one's a hard case," she added darkly.

"But nae impossible." Or so she hoped. Prayed.

Chapter Two

*D*amn his father for raiding, the king for meddling. And damn Megan Sutherland, too, Ross thought, as he rubbed Zeus down.

Damn her sultry brown eyes, her shy, haunting smile and her... her puppets. Whoever heard of a grown woman playing with puppets. He paused, frowning. Was she simple in the head? Was sly Eammon trying to pass an idiot off on him?

Ross curried harder, seething inside. 'Twas just the sort of sneaky scheme that slime would dream up to repay the Carmichaels for their raids. "Force me to wed his dim-witted daughter and breed a pack of imbeciles to sully our bloodline," he muttered, forgetting he had no intention of marrying the lass in any case.

"I do not think Zeus appreciates bearing the brunt of yer anger," Owain wryly observed.

Ross blinked, surprised to see the stallion glaring at him over one shoulder, even more shocked to realize he'd ground the handful of straw he'd been using to dust. "Sorry, lad," he mumbled, smoothing a hand down the sleek hide. The big gray war-horse bred by his English Sommerville cousins did not deserve such treatment just because he was angry at Megan Sutherland.

Nay, 'twas himself he was wroth with, he thought, remembering the pain his rejection had put in Megan's big brown eyes. In that instant, he'd been sore tempted to comfort the very woman he'd come here to scorn. *Because she's beautiful.*

Not beautiful, beguiling. Her almond-shaped eyes tilted up provocatively at the corners beneath high, winged brows, lending an air of sensuality to her delicate face. They were so dark they'd looked nearly black in the fading light of the bailey. Sultry eyes that drew on a man, tempted him to forget about duty and honor and let himself sink into their lush promise.

He'd felt the tug of her lure catch low in his belly, a stirring that rippled through his body, tightening every muscle below his belt. *Lust.* Before he'd known who she was, he'd wanted her. Badly. The swift surge of desire had caught Ross off guard, shocked him. After what had happened with Rhiannon, he'd vowed to control the hot, dangerous streak of passion that made a mockery of his calm, logical side. But it seemed he could no more deny that inbred urge than he could the color of his hair.

"The Carmichael curse," Ross muttered under his breath. It had been thus between their parents and for Lion when he'd met Siusan at that cursed clan gathering. "She makes me randy as a stag in rut," his brother had explained. Then he'd defied his sire, ignored his brother's advice and ridden off to his death.

All for a girl with sloe eyes and a mouth that... Shuddering, Ross steeled himself to resist her, reminded himself that Megan was just like Rhiannon. Though physically they looked nothing alike, he knew they were sisters under the skin. Witches at heart... intent on ensnaring a man for their own evil ends.

Not this time. Ross clenched his muscles against the unwanted spill of heat in his veins, the stirring in his loins.

"The Sutherlands'll be waiting supper on ye," Owain said.

"Let them." It had been hours since their arrival and Ross had yet to step inside Curthill. He shook his head to clear away the image of Megan's captivating face and went back to Zeus.

"Ye'll not break bread with them?"

"Not willingly. Though I fear Lord Nigel'll be by soon to see me to the hall," Ross said. The importance King David attached to this bond he'd use to avoid a war was attested to by the fact that he'd sent his bastard uncle, Nigel, to escort the bridegroom to Curthill. On the sail north, the old man had tried to sing the praises of the bride-to-be, but Ross had closed his ears to these blandishments. He was not wedding her, so there was no need to know aught about her. Though with his lordship peering over his shoulder, it would be that much harder for Ross to find a way out of this match made in hell.

"Strange, Eammon Sutherland was not on the dock to greet us," Owain said, plucking straw from Zeus's swishing tail.

"The first bit of luck I've had." Despite all his fine words about proof, the thought of clapping eyes on the man made Ross's blood boil. "I'm as likely to choke him as not."

Owain's brows rose at the unaccustomed vehemence, but he made no comment. "Why would Eammon kill Lion after agreeing to the betrothal that would link his puny clan of fishermen with the powerful Carmichaels?"

A question Ross had asked himself a thousand times these past months. What had Eammon hoped to gain? "He must be mad, too. No sane man would *want* to make an enemy of Lionel Carmichael. Mayhap Wee Wat has uncovered the answer to that," he added. Since the disastrous Welsh ambush that had cost him one hundred men, Ross had made it a practice to scout an area before he entered. The moment he'd learned he was going to Curthill, Ross had sent the wily little man on ahead to gather information. "I'd speak wi' Wee Wat before I sup wi' my enemy."

As though Ross's command had conjured him up out of the gloom, the wiry Scot materialized in the entrance to Zeus's stall. "Here I am, m'lord."

Dropping the pulverized straw, Ross dusted his hands on the fresh tunic he'd put on after his hasty wash and clapped his spy on the back. "'Tis glad I am to see you, old man."

Wat's thin, leathery face split into a toothless grin. His slight stature and ability to blend in anywhere had made him the perfect choice to come north posing as a traveling tinker. "And 'tis glad I am to be here seein' ye."

"Was there trouble?"

"Of a sort." Wat glanced around warily. "Nae here."

"We're alone." The stable was empty but for the munching animals and the men Ross had handpicked for this mission. Though a man who craved privacy, he had resigned himself to spending the next few days surrounded by a protective circle of soldiers.

"Ye never can tell. Rumor has it Eammon's a bit unstable."

Ross's skin prickled a warning all the while he and Owain followed Wat across the cluttered courtyard. The old crumbling peel towers and the wattle and daub buildings that huddled around them gave Curthill Castle an air of weary neglect that grated on his sense of order.

A family of pigs rooted through a pile of refuse as high as the kitchen shed; carts, kegs and other things he could not identify in the encroaching darkness were heaped about in total disarray. Even the wall they mounted was in an appalling state of disrepair. Had his father been able to land, he'd have made easy work of breaching these puny defenses.

'Twas Ross's first trip this far north, but clearly the tales of Highlanders living like barbarians were true. No civilized people would live in such squalor. How could Lion have ever thought that a woman raised here would one day be fit to rule the splendid estate their parents had worked so hard to build? Because Lion had done his choosing with something considerably lower and less discriminating than his brain.

Fortunately *he* was in no danger of falling into that trap. Seductive as she looked, Megan Sutherland could have the wiles of Circe and he'd still resist her. If he was tempted, he had only to recall where losing himself in Rhiannon's silken flesh had gotten him. Control and moderation had become his motto after that debacle. Thank God, because a level head...and cool blood...were clearly called for here.

Stepping onto the wall walk, Ross dragged in a lungful of air. At least here it was crisp, tangy with salt and free from the stench of humans and animals. And the pounding of the surf on the rocks below would muffle their words. He lifted his face into the breeze, hoping to scour away the apprehension that had assailed him the moment he'd ridden through Curthill's gates. But the space between his shoulders continued to itch as it had when he'd campaigned against the Welsh, where every tree and bush hid an enemy. So it was here. He was glad, suddenly, that he had brought along three knights and fifty men-at-arms in addition to Owain and his score of Welsh bowmen. "What news, Wat?"

Wat spit over the shoulder-high wall. "When Lion arrived here last year, Laird Eammon refused to let him wed Lady Siusan."

"What? Why ever would he—"

"Changed his mind. Rumor ha' it there's been a lot of that goin' on since Eammon's only son died two years ago. Warped him, it did. Eammon's become a recluse. Scarcely ever leaves the tower where he lives wi' his latest whore and doesna even take an interest in his clansmen's well-bein'." A cardinal sin, for the laird was more than a leader, he was the father of his people.

Ross knew too well how the death of a son could change a father, yet he didn't want to feel empathy for his enemies. *Nor desire,* mocked a tiny voice. Quickly closing the door on Megan's haunting image, he sighed. "Knowing Lion, he fought for his woman. This could be the reason why Eammon had him killed."

"Mayhap. A few coins spread 'round and I learned young Lion wasna even wi' the main huntin' party when he died."

"Men can become separated in a hunt," Owain pointed out.

"Only something earth-shattering'd pull Lion from a hunt."

Wat nodded. "They say he was lured away by a message."

"Lured?" The word was ripe with evil. Ross grabbed Wat's bony shoulders in his excitement. "You've proof of this?"

"Nay. The innkeeper had it from a huntsman that just as the deer was spotted a lad came up to Lion, whispered something in his ear. Lion grinned and ride off wi'out a word to anyone. Unfortunately the lad who brought the message is gone."

"Gone." Ross's heart fell, along with his hands. "Dead?"

Wat paused to scratch the thinning hair beneath the woolen cap he wore summer and winter. "Dunno. Two weeks after Lion's death, the lad up and left the village."

Ross's frown deepened. "Who is this mysterious lad?"

"Lucais was page to Lady Megan and Lady Siusan. His Da's a tailor in the village, but when I stopped in to the shop and asked about the lad, the old man closed up like a clam."

So. There was something here. And as laird, Eammon was responsible ... either directly or indirectly. Ross's hand itched with the urge to palm his sword and go after Eammon. But the time was not right, so he curled it into a fist. "Was there any hint that Eammon's behind Lion's death or Lucais's disappearance?"

"Nope." Wat spat again. "Eammon's unpredictable as summer lightnin', but he *is* laird here." And therefore nearly a god. "The people *do* sing the praises o' the Lady Megan, though," the old man added with a sly, sidelong glance at Ross. "Accordin' to rumor, ye'll be takin' an angel to wife."

Ross snorted. *A witch, more like.* A beautiful, beguiling witch. "I'll not be marryin' her." Ignoring Wat's start of surprise, he asked, "Do you think Eammon killed this Lucais to keep him quiet?" If the boy was dead, there went his proof.

"There's been nae hint o' that, but somethin' queer's goin' on at Curthill. I'd wager on it. I've nae been here long enough to find out what. It just feels ... wrong ... in my gut. Ye ken?"

Ross's nape prickled again. "Aye." He'd felt it before ... in Wales. He'd known something was wrong, but he'd trusted Rhiannon's information. Trusted the love he'd thought they shared and ridden into an ambush. "I think we'll take a trip into the village tonight. Owain, see if—"

"Ah, Ross, here ye are," Lord Nigel called out as he heaved his portly body up the last few steps. "They're waitin' supper on ye." He fanned his florid face with the trailing sleeve of his yellow surcoat. Too fat and lazy for fighting, the middle-aged lord spent most of his time at court living off his brother's largess. "I ken ye've nae love for this alliance, but at least the lass is as comely as Eammon claimed. And ye've nae choice."

We'll see about that. All Ross needed was to find Lucais and he'd convince this fat old fool that Lion had been murdered and avoid wedding Eammon's half-wit. "I've my men to settle," he hedged. The thought of breaking bread with Eammon took away the appetite he'd worked up after four days living on sea rations.

"Surely yer captain can see to that." Lord Nigel glanced down at the littered courtyard. "I've nae wish to tarry here. I'd ha' ye sign the betrothal contract after supper and hold the weddin' three days hence.''

"Three days!" Ross felt as though a hand had closed around his neck and squeezed tight. "That doesna gi' me much time."

"Come, come, lad, ye're carryin' on like a virgin bride."

Virgin. The word scalded Ross's pride. Likely *she* wasn't a virgin. Any woman who reached the age of eighteen unwed had something wrong with her. If he could discover this imperfection, he'd repudiate her. "What says my *bride* to this haste?"

Lord Nigel blinked in astonishment. "Why would I ask *her* opinion? By all accounts, Eammon is anxious enough to ha' the deed done. 'Tis all that counts."

I just bet he is. Well, Eammon'd not find him an easy target. He had a small army at his back, and his brain was unclouded by the lust that had done his brother in. "I've no stomach for breakin' bread wi' the man," Ross growled.

"Suit yerself, but Lady Mary sets a fine table, and Eammon'll nae be joinin' us in any case. He's *indisposed.* This Felis of his must be a tasty piece to keep him interested after two years." Lord Nigel hitched up his snug gold belt and turned to leave. "Since ye'll nae be at supper, come down, now, and sign the contract. Father Simon's already witnessed Eammon's mark."

Ross went, feet dragging like a man bound for the gallows. *Three days,* he reminded himself. He still had three days. It wasn't much time, but he'd make do. He'd find this Lucais. And he'd find a way out of this cursed marriage.

"Do you think he isna comin'?" Megan asked anxiously.

Her mother leaned across the empty chair intended for Ross and patted Megan's knotted hands. "Likely he's just washin' up, changin' from his travel garments." The two sat alone at the long table on the raised dais, waiting for the men to join them.

"He refused the bath I had readied for him." Pain and resentment mingled in Megan's voice. She'd waited for an hour on a stool before the fire in the best guest chamber, getting up occasionally to stretch her left leg and add a stick of wood so the room would be warm when her betrothed arrived. He hadn't.

While the water had cooled in the wooden buckets the servants had hauled up the tower stairs, her initial nervousness at bathing her first male had given way to annoyance, then exasperation. A thousand things to do, and here she was waiting on some man's whim. Like her mother, who continued to fuss over her husband, though Eammon had ignored her—along with everyone else—for the past two years.

Finally Megan had sent a maid down to inquire after his lordship, only to learn he was busy with his horse and wouldn't be coming above to bathe. No apology for keeping her waiting.

"Rude, uncouth..."

"Who, dear?" her mother inquired.

Megan swallowed her reply. Thanks to Papa's dalliances and his moodiness, her mother already had a cynical view of men, and Megan did so want everyone to like Ross. "Do southerners wash?"

"Most bathe on occasion," Lady Mary assured her.

"Tell me again what it was like growin' up in the Lowlands."

A gentle smile curved her mother's lips, enlivening her careworn face, hinting at the beauty she'd been before Eammon Sutherland had cast her aside and broken her heart. "Life was...different in Peebles. The people were softer, and the land, too, the hills green and rolling instead of sharp and rocky as the Highlands are, but 'twas nae perfect. Men's rule is as absolute there as 'tis here," she added with a bitterness Megan rued.

Megan recalled the early years when life at Curthill had been sweet, her sire an easygoing man with a ready laugh, not the unpredictable recluse whose orders contradicted everything he had once stood for. That was before the bad times, before the accident that had maimed Megan and killed her only brother. If only Ewan were alive, things might be different. Papa wouldn't have changed. Lion might not be dead, and Siusan wouldn't be hiding in the Highlands waiting, fearing for her life.

'Tis your own fault Ewan is dead. Megan shivered.

"Dinna fash yerself, dearling. Only remember that poor Lion said his brother was a clever, compassionate man."

With eyes like chipped ice. Megan shivered again. "He did jump to my aid in the bailey." And he'd been amused by her puppets... at first. Such a man couldn't be all bad. Somehow, she'd overcome his coolness. She had to.

Lady Mary sighed. "Though you've nae the nature for it, 'tis sorry I am you didna take up the veil as I wanted to but could not. Better cloistered than some man's chattel."

"I am well pleased to be weddin' Lord Ross," Megan said with forced cheer, linking her fingers with those of the woman who had sacrificed so much for her children. Would she feel this same overpowering instinct to protect the babes she hoped to have? Megan wondered. "I will make him a good wife. If he will let me," she added softly.

"He has nae choice but to wed you."

"I'd have him *want* me for his wife." Seeing her mother frown, Megan hurried on. "It began when we first met Lion at the Gatherin' and he described his family. I... I began to fall in love wi' Lord Ross then. And when I saw him..."

"Oh, Meggie."

"He looks just as I thought he would," Megan murmured, lost in her memories of their first meeting. "He is the strongest, most handsome knight in the world. And he has the bluest eyes."

Her mother sniffed. "He'll take your love and crush it beneath his heel. He'll break your heart and dash your hopes."

Megan blinked and looked at her mother's anxious face. "I'm sorry Papa hurt you, Mama. He was a good man before Ewan died."

"I grieve for Ewan, too, but even the death of a son does not condone the things your father has done to me. Lodgin' his mistress in my own home," she said bitterly. "Or the way he's turned his back on the people of Clan Sutherland."

"He may not go out among them as he should, but this trade he's arranged has brought our clan more work and more profit than we've ever made fishin'," Megan said stoutly.

"Aye, and does this profit go to our hardworkin' clansmen? Or into needed repairs to the castle? Nay, it doesna."

Megan patted her mother's hand. Mama did not understand the world beyond her kitchen and herb room. But Megan had felt duty bound to fill the gap left by Ewan's death and
her father's decline. She was much in the village, listening to the
problems of the burghers and fishermen, offering advice and
solutions where she could. "Papa explained that for the moment, most of the money must go back to buy more goods."

"Archie explained . . . Eammon couldna even leave *her* long
enough to tell our people why they were still so poor. And look
at the hall." Her gesture encompassed the dreary room and the
boisterous men who filled it. "I spent years makin' Curthill as
fine and beautiful as my childhood home, but wi' no laird to
keep order, his men abuse it like undisciplined savages."

Megan sighed. What could she say? "I rue the day Comyn
MacDonnel brought Felis here."

"'Tisna dear Comyn's fault. I asked him to bring a skilled
healer from Edinburgh to help after your accident. None of us
could ha' guessed Felis would worm her way into my Eammon's bed."

While her mother was sitting up nights with her. Megan's
stomach tightened with remorse. Still, if she'd been on speaking terms with Felis, she'd have asked for lessons in seducing a
man. The little redhead was obviously quite skilled in that.

"Megan, what are ye plannin'?" her mother asked sharply.

"N-nothing, Mama."

"I know that look, mistress. 'Tis the one you wore as a bairn
when you were about some mischief."

Megan sighed. Adept as she'd grown at hiding her thoughts,
her mother could still sometimes read her. "I was wonderin'
how to go about seducin' Lord Ross," she replied, honestly for
once.

"Megan! Only think what happened to poor Siusan."

'Twas her sister she was thinking of, forced to flee their home
in fear and disgrace to protect her secret. To help Siusan, Megan needed a troop of soldiers and a knight to lead them.
Someone she could trust implicitly. "I dinna plan to let things
go *that* far," Megan replied. She only wanted to bind him to her
so he would wed her willingly and help her family.

"Men are nae so easily controlled when it comes to *that*," her mother said with asperity. "Once roused, they take what they want wi'out a by-yer-leave."

"The way things stand at the moment, Ross is far more likely to reject me than ravish me."

Her mother looked relieved, but only because she did not know how determined Megan was to succeed in this. She was desperate enough to do whatever was required, but had no idea how to proceed. If it had been a matter of choosing the right herb to heal a patient or the right tale to entertain a gathering, she would have plunged in with her usual confident enthusiasm, but . . .

Megan plucked at the skirt of her red gown. The fit was tighter than her usual style, but not skintight as those worn by the whores who frequented the tavern in the village. Hopefully 'twas seductive enough to pique Lord Ross's interest. She'd never been one to fret over what she couldn't change, yet the thought of challenging his icy hatred made her shiver despite the warmth of the hall.

"Dinna fret, hinny," her mother soothed, feeling the tremor that had struck her. "Wi' God's help, things will work out."

Megan nodded, but the coil in her stomach did not ease. Nibbling on her lower lip, she looked out over the noisy hall. It seemed all of Clan Sutherland was here tonight, garbed in their best so the throng fairly shimmered in the light of two dozen fine pitch torches . . . twice what they usually used.

Even the smoke-stained walls of the long, narrow room seemed brighter, and she guessed her mother had ordered them washed down before hanging the best of the wall coverings. Some were a trifle water stained, but in the dimness 'twas impossible to tell. All and all, the place looked quite fine, she thought.

"Well, here's Lord Nigel, at least," her mother exclaimed.

Megan looked up as the graying man threaded his way through the trestle tables, a fortune in gold chain bouncing against round, silk-covered belly.

"Ah, Lady Mary, 'tis good to see ye again," he called as he mounted the dais. Bulbous red nose homing in on the wine flagon, his lordship threw himself into the chair to her right and filled his cup to the brim.

"What of Lord Ross?" Lady Mary asked.

"Not comin'." Lord Nigel hefted the cup and drank deep.

"What?" Megan cried, snapping to attention.

Lord Nigel surfaced long enough to repeat his announcement, then dove in again.

"Where is he?" Megan demanded.

This time Lord Nigel lowered the cup, wiped his mouth on the back of his hand and added, "Eatin' wi' his men."

Megan's hands fisted in the skirt she'd worn with such hope. "When he knows we are here waitin'? Of all the inconsiderate—"

"Likely he is tired from the journey," her mother put in.

"Doesna want to break bread wi' the Sutherlands," Nigel said bluntly. "Seems he shares his sire's opinion o' yer clan, if not Lionel's rashness in attackin' ye."

Megan couldn't breathe for the pain in her chest. Stubbornness alone kept her in her seat as she heard word of her betrothed's absence whispered through the hall. They'd be remembering how she'd already lost one prospective bridegroom. Well, they'd not see her cry this time, she vowed, anger cutting through her anguish, stiffening her spine.

"I got him to sign the contract. Ross'll wed ye... in three days' time, as the king directed." Lord Nigel smiled as though all were settled. "Is that roast boar I smell?"

"Nay, it's my temper frayin'." Tossing down her napkin, Megan turned to Chrissy. "When next I see Lord Ross, I intend to give him a lesson in manners."

"I knew 'twould come to this," Archie Sutherland muttered as he stomped up the steps and crested the seawall that protected the town from the beach. "Ross Carmichael nae three hours at Curthill and *The Black Hawk* comes sailin' in."

As he approached the first row of buildings, a figure stepped from shadows to block his path.

"M'lord." Archie stepped back, tugged respectfully at his forelock. "I didna expect ye here tonight."

"I'm earlier than I'd planned, but I received a message that *The Hawk* was in."

"Aye . . . curse the luck."

"I agree the timin' could be better, but 'tis only a small problem." His lordship propped one hand on the tooled silver at his waist, revealing the gleam of a fine silken surcoat to the pale moonlight. "Tell the men to get *The Hawk* unloaded tonight."

"But Douglas had good huntin' . . . hold's stuffed right full. 'Tis two nights' work at least to empty her," Archie whined.

"Use all the men ye ha' to, but get that ship unloaded. I want her hidden in the cove come morn," the lord growled.

"What o' the next consignment we ha' ready to sell?"

"Tell Douglas to sneak *The Hawk* back into the harbor tomorrow night . . . well past midnight. He's to load on what he can and return for as many nights as it takes to finish the task." Black wool cloak swirling about his boot tops, he turned to go.

Archie shifted nervously. "But . . .

"Now what?" Spinning back, he scowled his displeasure.

"What if Ross gets curious?" Archie grumbled. "Comes sniffin' 'round the village or the storage buildin'?"

"Ha' Douglas's men drive him back to the castle. He's to be lessoned, but nae killed." Not yet. Not unless he could find a way to do it without drawing undue attention.

"But what if Lord Nigel gets word there was trouble?"

"It should surprise no one if Ross is attacked in the very village his sire tried to burn down not three weeks ago."

Archie brightened. "Aye. Ye're right. And the young lordling's an uppity piece, just the sort to get into trouble here for lookin' down his nose at us Highland barbarians."

"Aye. He needs a lesson, right enough. Just see none of our men are recognized or caught and questioned. Understood?"

"Perfectly. All will be as ye wish, m'lord."

His lordship's smile was dimmed by the one part of his plans that had gone awry. Siusan had escaped. He'd find her eventually, but after ten months, even his patience was wearing thin.

Megan knew where her sister was, of that he was certain. Oh, she'd denied it, but Megan was as clever at hiding the truth as she was at weaving a story. Fortunately she was also sentimental. She'd not be able to resist one last visit with her sister before leaving the Highlands for Carmichael Castle. When Megan attempted to contact Siusan, he'd be there.

Chapter Three

"They should rename this cursed town Purgatory," Ross grumbled as he trailed Wee Wat through the maze of rutted paths that passed for streets. It lacked a few minutes to midnight, and there was a storm fast approaching. The air pressed down like a hot, wet blanket, making breathing difficult; the stench of fish made every breath a nasty experience.

Jesu, but he hated fish. Hated smelling them, hated eating them. Lent was truly a time of suffering for him.

Ross pinched his nostrils shut and trudged on. There were no torches set about to light the way through this cluster of buildings huddled at the base of the rocky bluff that led up to Curthill Castle. Despite that lack, they were not the only ones abroad this dark and stormy night. Distant scurryings, muted voices, the occasional thud of a heavy burden being shifted issued from side alleys, echoing off the homes and shops.

"What do ye think is going on here?" Owain whispered, the apprehension in his voice mirroring Ross's.

"Smugglin'... or worse." Ross had briefly peeked into Curthill's hall on their way out and been astonished to find it crammed full of furniture, the walls as thick with hangings as a tapestry seller's stall. He had a few theories as to how the laird had come by the finery displayed so garishly there. But pursuing that must wait. Tonight he was after human quarry... Lucais.

"We're here," Wee Wat whispered.

Ross stopped and peered out of the alley across from the house of George the tailor, Lucais's sire. 'Twas too dark to see much, but a weak light seeping out around the hide covering the window showed they were not asleep. Odd they were up so late. "Owain. Wait here with your men while we—"

"Andrew can wait. I'll watch the back lest our prey escape," Owain amended with the ease of long acquaintance.

Ross nodded. The suggestion fell in with his own plans. Though he'd thought to send Andrew to guard the back, the Welsh were best suited to sneaking about at night. "Agreed. Your Welshmen see like cats in the dark, though you are far too independent," he said without rancor.

"A trait that serves us both well," Owain murmured.

Ross was still grinning when he ordered his men across the street. Of all those who served him, Ross was closest to Owain. When Ross had first hired the Welshman to guide him through the forests of Wales, Lionel had called him crazy to trust one of the enemy. But Owain was himself at war with Rhys ap Dolgollen and only too eager to help Ross...for a price. What had started as a bargain, Owain's sword in exchange for the money the Welshman needed to regain his ancestral home, had matured into friendship.

Ross would miss him sorely when he left, not only the shrewd mind and strong sword arm, but the easy banter. Still, he'd not hold another to an unwelcome duty as he was held to this marriage by his responsibility to his clan.

"The latch is set," Andrew whispered, grizzled mustache twitching over thinned lips.

Ross nodded. "I'd rather burst in unannounced, but needs must. Davey," he called to the fresh-faced new knight who until recently had been his squire. "Knock at the door. Say you've a message from the castle. When they lift the latch, we rush in."

The plan worked to perfection, but when they burst into the hut, they found no coven of plotters, only a startled old woman sitting by the hearth and an equally old man at the door.

"Davey...search the place," Ross commanded before turning to find that Andrew had the old man pressed against the wall, a dirk flirting with the curve of his wrinkled neck.

"We're lookin' for the man who killed Lion Carmichael," Andrew growled before Ross could intervene.

The old man's eyes nearly bugged from his head. Cautious of Andrew's blade, he shook his head so vigorously his white hair flew about. "I didna do it."

"Release him," Ross ordered, glaring so the knight reluctantly lowered the blade and stepped back. "I understand your son, Lucais, was there the day my brother was killed," Ross said to the trembling burgher.

"Aye. But . . . but Lucais didna do it, m'lord."

"I believe you." Ross closed the gap between them, kept his expression calm. "I'd like to ask Lucais a few questions, that's all. Do you know where I might find him?"

"Nay," the old man insisted in a quavering voice. Obviously they expected the worst, for the old woman was praying. Their fear turned Ross's stomach. Jesu, he hated this, yet he could not afford to let them see his weakness.

"I'll take him outside and lesson him." Andrew grabbed hold of the man's thin arm and started to drag him away.

"Stop . . . wait," pleaded the old woman. She threw herself at Ross's feet, but he was the one who cringed. "We dinna ken where Lucais is. He left Curthill months ago and hasna been back. We dinna ken where he went or why."

The last was a lie. Ross read that in the frantic look she exchanged with her hooked-nosed husband. But he suspected that the rest was the truth. "I wish the lad no harm," Ross assured her. "But I'd speak wi' him. Tell me where he is. I swear I'll keep his location from Laird Eammon."

"Laird Eammon? Why ever would he care? He's nae set foot in the village nor taken an interest in us since the bad times began two years past. Just sends his men to collect what we've—"

"Janet!" the old man barked. "Pay her waggin' tongue nae mind," he added as his wife dropped her head, yellowed teeth sunk into her trembling lip.

What the hell was this all about? Ross dragged an exasperated hand through his hair. Jesu, this place was going to drive him mad, he thought. Eammon could have used a go-between to embroil Lucais in his vile scheme, thus keeping his own hands clean, but Ross could prove nothing without Lucais. "Did Lucais leave alone?" he asked.

"Aye," they chorused in unison. Ross knew they lied.

Cursing under his breath, Ross glared at them. "Tell me the truth, and I willna harm you..." He let the threat dangle.

"We canna tell ye more'n we know," Janet wailed. "He woke us one midnight, said he had to leave, and...and we havena seen him since." Burying her face in her hands, she began to cry softly.

Ross exhaled and turned away from the sickening sight. Short of torture, he'd likely not get more from this pair.

"Let me question him," Andrew demanded. When Ross shook his head, the big knight swore. "Ye dinna ha' to watch, if ye've nae got the stomach fer man's work."

"This from the man who taught me not to judge a man by the size of his sword, but the conscience wi' which he wielded it," Ross retorted. As a flush crept across the old knight's tanned cheeks, Ross added in French, "They may know why Lucais left, but not, I think, where he went. We'll set a watch on the house."

"Aye." Andrew subsided, albeit reluctantly.

That done, Ross turned away, still puzzling over what Janet had said about Eammon's men coming to collect. What would they take from a tailor? Cloth? Coin? Frowning, he studied the room he had only glanced at on entering. Now he looked around with new eyes, seeing the luxurious fabric spread on the table, the thread, needles and pieces of trim. Obviously the trappings of a tailor, yet something about the scene grated on Ross. He could not put his finger on what exactly... It was more an instinct. The same feeling of *wrongness* Wee Wat had mentioned.

The feeling intensified when he spotted the chest by the table. Moisture glistened on the oaken lid... as though it had recently come from the sea. *Ah. It fit with the idea he was...*

"No one left this place," Owain said in Welsh, entering through the back door. "And there is no one lurking about, but someone was here recently. There are wet boot tracks."

Ross nodded. "Leave a man to watch who comes and goes," he replied in kind, though he could've given the order in French and not been understood by these simple people.

Once back outside, Ross ordered Andrew and half the men to search quietly through the village while the rest of them followed Wee Wat down to the beach. Here torches had been set in the sand and a guard of two score armed men posted over the boats drawn up on shore for the night.

"A large force to watch a few puny fishin' boats," Ross said, but what really piqued his interest were the empty places here and there that indicated several boats were yet out. In this weather? He shifted his gaze to the sea, restless and churning even in this sheltered cove. A second ship was anchored beside the one that had brought him from Edinburgh and in the water he could make out the shapes of several smaller craft.

What the hell was going on? The fine hairs at his nape stood on end, but it was not the breeze that stirred them. Treachery. Danger. They rode the wind as surely as the rain that would fall any moment, made the air crackle as intensely as the lightning forking through the sky overhead.

One of the guards stepped forward to confront Ross. "Be off wi' ye. The laird dinna allow anyone here at night."

"Surely that doesna include his future son-by-marriage."

"Ye're a Carmichael?" The name came out a curse, and the other men quickly closed ranks with him, faces hard and hate-filled in the hellish red and black of the flickering torches.

Damn. How could he have forgotten his dear sire's recent raid on Curthill? Ross noted a cut above one man's eye, the rent in another's mail through which bulged a bandage. Sand grated, a sword rattled in its scabbard as the eight Carmichaels with him tensed for battle. For one brief instant he regretted leaving thirty of his men up at the castle with Giles. But a wise commander always held some of his troop in reserve, and the men with him were worth three of these any day. Besides, he had talked his way out of tighter spots than this one.

"Aye. I am Ross Carmichael . . . come to wed wi' Megan Sutherland," he announced in a calm, carrying voice. "The king would have peace between our two clans, and so would I." 'Twas the second time this night he'd near choked on his words.

His opponent grunted, looked sideways at his companions.

"There ha' been losses on both sides." *Lion*, his soul cried, but now was not the time for guilt or regret. "'Tis time to put that behind us and get on wi' livin'." *As if he could now that he suspected Lion had been murdered.* "Would you nae rather sleep wi' a lass beside you instead of your swords?"

That brought a murmur of agreement, a relaxing of the callused hands on sword hilts. "We didna start the feud," the captain growled.

The hell you say! A snarl of pure rage clawed at Ross's throat. Shuddering, he suppressed it. "Then let it end here."

The captain nodded grudgingly.

"Excellent," Ross exclaimed as though pleased all was settled. "Well," he added, glancing around with only mild curiosity. "This walk has cleared my head. I'm for bed." Stretching and yawning hugely, he turned away from the soldiers, conscious of the movement at his back that was Owain. Stones scraped as his other men fanned out. They'd be watching the Sutherlands closely while he picked his way up the beach.

"'Tis a den of smugglers we've landed in," Owain commented as they mounted the mossy steps that led up from the water.

"Mmm," Ross murmured. "In another place, I might agree. But what could they be smugglin' out of the Highlands? As far as I ken, they dinna raise enough sheep to be a threat to the wool trade. I canna think of anythin' they produce in abundance..."

"Except lying savages," Owain put in.

"I think they're wreckers," Davey added.

"Aye." Fingering his lower lip, Ross stared thoughtfully back at the sea. Lightning streaked across the heavens, briefly illuminating the trio of small boats rowing in from the ship in the harbor. "If so, 'tis likely Lion found out about it and that knowledge got him killed." He exhaled sharply. Jesu, but he was bone weary. He had not had a decent night's sleep since being ordered to wed a Sutherland. Nor would he get one until he had unmasked Lion's killer and freed himself from this cursed betrothal. It had turned his stomach to sign the document that bound him to that... that seductive Sutherland.

"Shall I leave a man to watch here, too?" Owain asked.

Ross shook off the weariness and the unwelcome memory of Megan's bewitching eyes. "Two. One to watch. One to follow and see where they take the cargo they are unloadin'."

"I do not like reducing our numbers."

"'Twill only be for a short time," he reminded Owain. "We join up with Andrew and the others at the base of the bluff on the far side of the village." Ross glanced at the darkened mouth of the street they must trod en route and felt an unaccustomed pang of apprehension. "Loosen your swords but leave them sheathed," he whispered, and took the lead down the street.

The storm was closing in on them. Wind gusted through the narrow confines of the twisted alleyways they threaded their way through. It swirled dirt into their faces, muffled the thud of their footsteps, and, Ross thought grimly, those of any who might creep up on them.

"Look sharp." He cast a quick glance at the six who followed him. Overhead, thunder rumbled and lightning flashed. The brief bursts washed the buildings they passed in an eerie white light so every shape and shadow seemed about to jump out at them. Soon his eyes ached from the strain of searching for assailants.

"Stick close," he heard Owain murmur.

Mouth dry, nerves humming, Ross inched his sword from its scabbard. Suddenly he heard the thud of booted feet.

"'Ware!" Owain shouted. "Ambush!"

Ross turned toward the cry. Out of the corner of his eye, he caught the flash of lightning on steel as a man leaped at him from a dark doorway. Training and reflexes were the only things that saved Ross. Nimbly sidestepping, he whipped his sword up to parry the rapidly descending blade. He beat back his opponent with three swift strikes, grinning grimly when his final thrust drew a shriek and the man fell.

The triumph was short-lived.

Two more assailants immediately pressed in on him, one wielding a sword, the other a long dirk. Ross slashed at them, the wide arc of his blade keeping them at bay...momentarily. He used the seconds to call to Owain. "How many are they?"

"Too many." The reply ended on a grunt of pain. "One less, now," Owain added. "But there are still two score or more."

For the next few moments, Ross was kept busy fending off the pair who faced him. 'Twas obvious that they were less skilled than he, but sheer superiority of numbers could overwhelm him and his men. And too, they fought in close quarters, on unfamiliar turf and in the dark. His only hope was that Andrew would hear the sounds and come to investigate... before it was too late.

A loud clap of thunder greeted Megan as she stepped from the hut where she'd been summoned to attend a birthing. "Go on ahead, Chrissy, if you wait for me, you'll be caught in the rain."

"I willna melt," her cousin replied.

Megan sighed and arched her back against the ache put there from hours crouching by the poor woman's pallet. "We were lucky to save both mother and babe."

"'Twas nae luck in it. Ye are as skilled as yer mama when it comes to healin'." Chrissy took her arm to urge her on. "Come, now, I've nae wish to get soaked walkin' back."

"'Tis silly of me to refuse to ride. The accident was long ago, and 'twas my fault for racin' along the cliffs, but..."

"Not at all. Ye've reason aplenty to fear horses," her cousin said with typical compassion.

"I hate being afraid...of anythin'," Megan said as they turned the corner from one dark street onto another, the way as familiar to them as the castle corridors. "Fear is so...limitin'. If I wasna afraid of horses, there's so much I could do."

"Like gallop flat out wi' the wind in yer hair?"

"Mmm." Megan lifted her head, smiling as the memories tumbled through it. Siusan, Ewan and herself out riding, racing with each other. Her smile dimmed as she recalled the last ride, shattered bits of sight and sound. The terrified shriek of her mount as it suddenly jerked and bolted. Ewan's panicked cry as he charged after her. The edge of the cliff looming closer, closer. And then they were both flying, out over the brink and into nothingness. But the screams kept on and on, hers and Ewan's mingling with the horses. And the blood...

"Meg!"

Shuddering, Megan let go of the image, found herself standing in the muddy street, her arms wrapped around her waist, tears streaming down her face.

"I didna mean to make you remember," Chrissy whispered, wiping Megan's face with the edge of her cloak.

Numbly Megan nodded. "Someday I'm goin' to conquer that nightmare. I'm goin' to climb on a horse and ride again. Do you know where I'll go first?" she asked a little shakily. "To see Siusan." By now, the babe conceived when Siusan and Lion had met at the Gathering was three months old. She had a niece or nephew she'd never seen. *It hurt, God, how it hurt.* Siusan should have been with Lion, not up in the hills grieving for her lost love, frightened and alone.

"I thought ye didna know where Siusan was?"

Megan winced. *Damn.* You'd think she'd get better at this lying business. "I dinna. But I'm nae likely to find her sittin' about Curthill Castle, am I?"

"I suppose," Chrissy said, eyeing her skeptically.

Oh, she hated lying to Chrissy, but close as they were, Megan dared not reveal Siusan's secret. Siusan had insisted, made Megan swear on their grandmother's soul that she'd tell no one why Siusan had left Curthill or where she'd gone.

"More to the point, why do ye think Lord Ross didna come down to sup wi' us?"

Megan groaned inwardly, not wanting to discuss this, *either.* "Clearly he isna eager for this marriage between us."

"Because he thinks yer father killed Lion?"

"Papa wouldna do such a thing."

Chrissy smiled sadly. "Ye must admit that since the bad times began, the laird's nae been himself. Why, it's been weeks since he's actually come into the hall and when he did join us, he had eyes for no one but that Felis."

Too true. "But he had no reason to want Lion dead."

"Well, Lion did rant and rave when he arrived and learned the laird had changed his mind about lettin' him wed Siusan."

"But Siusan was certain Papa would relent and give his permission if they waited a bit and put no pressure on him."

"I think Ewan's death scrambled his brain. 'Tis the only excuse for half the things he does. I know ye've adored yer papa since ye were little, but 'tis just stubbornness on yer part that ye canna see how he's changed."

Megan sighed. *Poor Papa.* Was she the only one who still believed in him? "I know, but..." But murder? The thought of her laughing, fair-haired father killing someone made her ache inside. Shoulders slumped, eyes narrowed against the dust-laden wind, she followed Chrissy.

Megan was used to navigating these streets at night, for that was usually when illness struck or a bairn decided to be born, but there was something about tonight that made her heart race, her skin prickle with dread. At any moment she expected...

Thunder boomed overhead, shaking the buildings around them. In its wake, a shout split the night.

Megan stopped, turned toward the echo. "What was that?"

"God alone knows." Chrissy's plump arm went around Megan's shoulder as she tried to both shelter her and hurry her. "I heard a rumor that *The Hawk* was in tonight."

Megan's shudder mirrored her cousin's, yet the sound was not the usual one made by drunken sailors. "Hark. I hear swords."

"All the more reason for us to leave."

"Nay." Megan dug in her heels, turning toward the rising clang of steel on steel. "We can at least see what is happenin'."

"Megan, there is naught we can do to aid them."

Her mind knew that, but her heart rebelled. "I must see."

Chrissy muttered a word Megan had not known she knew, but trotted after her toward the battle sounds. What they saw when they rounded the corner stopped them both in their tracks.

A flash of lightning cast white-hot light over the knot of men who writhed and struggled against each other in mortal combat. She had eyes for only one. The tall knight in the red-and-black surcoat. "'Tis Ross Carmichael," she whispered, hands clenched to her stumbling heart. "Oh, Chrissy..." Unconsciously she started forward.

"Meggie! Ye canna just walk into a sword fight."

Megan looked at the battle, then back at Chrissy. "We have to do somethin'." Eyes gleaming, chin up, her braids whipped by the wind, she looked like a throwback to their Viking ancestors.

Though where her courage and eternal optimism came from, God alone knows, her cousin thought. "Meg, what can we do?"

"You must run to the castle quick as you can and bring back men . . . Lord Ross's men. Likely he wouldna trust any of us." She looked again at the man whose blade held a pair of men at bay. Her belly cramped with the need to help him, to protect her man . . . even if he refused to acknowledge he was hers.

"I canna leave ye here!" Chrissy cried.

"I'll nae be here. . .exactly." Megan studied the buildings that formed a backdrop for the bloody drama. "I'll sneak around the other side and wait in Lang Gordy's workshop."

"But they're fightin' on his back doorstep."

"I'll go in the front." She forced a smile. "That way if the men are injured, I'll be close by to lend a hand."

"Ye'll do nae such thing. Ye'll come wi' me—"

Megan shook her head. "I'd only slow you down. Hurry along," she ordered, giving her cousin a shove. "They look to be vastly outnumbered, and no matter how rudely Ross treated me this eve, I'll not be a widow afore I'm even wed."

Chapter Four

Ross grunted as his opponent's blade slipped under his guard and between the chain links of his mail, piercing his left shoulder. He didn't really feel the pain. He was too busy trying to put away this last man. The tide of the battle had separated him from his forces, and he was anxious to rejoin the men because they faced the bulk of their attackers.

The first man Ross wounded had gotten up and run away, but thus far he'd not been able to dispatch this squat, solid swordsman. Arm aching, lungs burning with exertion, he redoubled his efforts. Then he saw the opening he'd been looking for. Lunging forward, he slid his sword down the other man's blade.

The grate of steel on steel filled the air, followed by a keening wail as the man pitched forward. It was drowned out by a loud rumble that Ross took for thunder, but as he turned to look for Owain, a cart shot out of the alleyway, blocking the street.

"Ross!" Owain shouted. "They'd trap you."

"I see!" Ross ran forward, sword high, ready to vault the cart. It exploded into flames just as he reached it. The force of the blast threw him to the ground. Dazed, he struggled to his feet. Owain's cries filling his ears, he made ready to leap the fire, but the heat and black smoke drove him back. Flinging an arm over his face, he stared through the hellish conflagration.

Owain's anguished expression wavered in the intense heat, mirroring the desperation of the situation. He saw his friend start forward, knew Owain would brave even this for him.

"Nay," Ross screamed above the crackle and hiss. "Stay back. I'll find a way around...knock down a door if I have to."

To his left, one creaked on its hinges. Hoping for salvation, Ross whirled, saw stealthy movement, the glint of steel bathed red by the fire. *Reinforcements.* In a few moments, 'twould be his blood staining that blade.

Ross took the only way open to him. Falling to the ground, he rolled beneath the choking blanket of black smoke, aiming for the only other exit, a deep doorway on the opposite side of the little cul-de-sac. Pain rippled out from his wounded shoulder, but he gritted his teeth and kept moving. When he struck the wooden portal, it gave slightly. Needing no more invitation, he shoved it open and scrambled inside. Throat raw, eyes blinded by smoke, he got to his knees, fumbled for the latch. *Had to close it. Had to bar the door.*

"Let me," whispered a voice.

Ross whipped toward the sound just as the door shut, cutting off the wedge of orange light, plunging the room into total darkness. The thud of the bar dropping into place rang like a death knell. Had he jumped from one trap into another?

Crouched low, body compacted to spring, Ross swung his sword in a slow, questing arc before him. Silently he probed the black void around him, but there was nothing to see, nothing to hear. The place smelled of wood and oil...rosemary and lemons.

Rosemary and lemons?

Ross frowned. Where had he smelled that...

"M'lord?"

Ross reached toward the voice, grabbed a handful of fabric and tugged hard. The muffled gasp as his catch thudded against his chest was lost in his own grunt of pain. Despite the agony in his shoulder, he searched out his opponent's vulnerable neck and arched it back. "Who the hell are you?" he demanded.

"M-Megan...M-Megan Su-Sutherland."

Shock made Ross relax his grip...momentarily. Recalling that this was no ordinary woman but the siren who would undo him had him tensing again. "What the hell are you doin' here?"

"R-rescuin' you," she replied. Shaky but pert.

"What?"

"You're beginnin' to repeat yourself, m'lord. We should be movin' away from the door," she added with a wryness he'd have appreciated coming from another and under better circumstances.

He was distracted from her refreshing cheekiness by a thud as something heavy crashed against the outside of the portal. "He must ha' gone in here!" cried a coarse voice. The banging began in earnest then, fists, boots, sword hilts. If they organized and found a battering ram, he'd be done for.

They'd be done for, Ross silently amended. Why had she come to his aid? Or had she? Every frayed nerve in his body screamed *trap*, but they could not remain here. "Is there another way out?"

"Aye," whispered his would-be rescuer. "This is Lang Gordy's storeroom. His shop's beyond. Mind the stuff he's got lyin' about." She squirmed loose of his hold, surprised him anew by taking his hand and tugging him forward.

"I'll take the lead," he growled out of habit and tried to thrust her behind him. "There may be danger."

She elbowed him in the ribs. "Dinna be daft, you dinna ken the way, and I do."

As much as he valued logic, Ross hated hers. He followed grudgingly, sword ready, muscles tense, gut tight with apprehension. Four steps was all the time he had to worry before she lifted another latch. Hinges creaked, a spill of weak light illuminated the stacks of furniture she had led him through.

The room beyond held workbenches and more furniture. His gaze stabbed into each shadowed corner, searching for more of her father's men. 'Twas a carpenter's shop. Empty as far as he could tell. But he did not relax. "You are very familiar with this place," he muttered, shaking off her hand.

"Lang Gordy suffers mightily from the gout, and I often come here to wrap his foot."

"Where is he?"

"Abed and snorin' fit to raise the dead. He drinks a mite." She shut the door and barred it behind them. "There, that should hold them." She dusted off her hands. Cool as you please. Most women would be prostrate with fear.

He tried not to appreciate her bravery, tried to see in it some evil purpose. "You are very sure of yourself, mistress," he muttered suspiciously.

"Would it help if I shrieked and fainted?"

"Nay." Despite himself, Ross smiled faintly. "My thanks for your aid," he allowed.

"Though it wounds your pride to be rescued by a mere woman." Damn if she didn't sound very much like his mother. Too much.

Ross steeled himself to ignore it. "I didna say that."

Her eyes danced. "You didna ha' to."

That she could read so much rankled nearly as much as having to accept her aid. "I said I was grateful," he snapped.

"And gracious, too." Her teasing smile trapped the air in his lungs. "But never mind, now, all we need do is wait—"

"Wait, hell." Ross made for the front door. "I've men trapped in that alley."

"But m'lord. You canna go out there." Somehow she managed to slip between him and the heavy oaken door.

"Step aside," he growled, suspicions rising again.

She shook her head. The hand she raised to his chest trembled, her eyes were wide, beseeching. "'Tis too dangerous. There are armed men everywhere and—"

"What game are you playin'?" Ross snarled.

"'Tis no game. If only you'd wait until Chrissy returns—"

"Ah, you'd keep me here while she fetches more Sutherlands."

Megan blinked, taken aback by his vehemence. "Nay. Chrissy went up to Curthill Castle to get *your* men."

"I dinna believe you." He started to push her aside.

Megan shoved his hand away. "M'lord. We are tryin' to save you," she huffed. Men . . . even this one from whom she had expected better things . . . were dumb as sheep.

"Why would you go against your father to save me?"

"My father?" she exclaimed. "Surely you dinna think Papa is behind this?" She saw from his fierce expression he thought exactly that. Megan laughed. It made his scowl deepen, his mouth thin to an angry line, but she could not help it. "Ach, Papa is nae so daft as that. Granted he's nae the most even-tempered of men these days, but to attack the man who brings us peace—''

"He had my brother killed," Ross roared, fury and anguish rising with his voice.

Megan cringed against the door as his hot words lashed her. "Nay. I swear Papa had nothin' to do wi'—"

"Lies."

"But... but..." Megan groped for the words that would make him believe what she desperately hoped was true. "Papa welcomed the blood bond wi' your great family."

"At first. But when Lion came here and found out what your cursed father was up to, your *Papa* denied permission for Lion to wed, then he had him killed."

"Up to? I dinna ken what you mean."

His lip curled as he gestured at Lang Gordy's workroom with his free hand. "I'm not certain what goes on at Curthill, but 'twasna by honest means that so much fine furniture... enough to grace the halls of a dozen wealthy earls... came to be in this wretched little Highland hut."

Megan blinked. "They came here through the trade."

"Trade? What sort of trade?"

"Papa buys damaged goods, ships it here for our people to repair, then resells it. Lang Gordy does very fine work. Lords as far away as London have bought his things," she said proudly.

He snorted. "Lies. 'Tis nae more than I expected from a Sutherland." That he made the name a curse cut her deeply; that he did not believe her hurt worse.

"'Tis the truth." She stuck her chin out to match the aggressive line of his stubbled jaw. "You want to think ill of us because poor Lion was accidently killed while here to—"

"Bah. Why do I stand here bandyin' words wi' you when Owain and the others are in danger?" He took her arm to fling her away from the door. She grabbed at his shoulder to stop him. He groaned as her hands bit into torn flesh.

She stared at the blood that trickled over her fingers. "Oh, m'lord. You're wounded. Sit down. Let me bind it."

Ross shook off her gentle touch. "I've nae time for that. Nor would I trust you to tend me were I dyin'—"

"Dyin'! Nay, you canna be." She shoved at his chest with surprising strength, caught him off guard and propelled him two steps back. His calves collided with the edge of a chair, and he sat abruptly. "Where else are you cut?" she demanded, running her small hands over his chest, up to his neck.

"Leave off," he snarled, embarrassed at how easily she had manipulated him. Rhiannon had been an expert at it. Furious, he tried to rise, but she stood so close between his spread thighs that he could not move unless he knocked her down and trod over her. *A tempting thought.* Inwardly he seethed with the urge to do just that, but courtesy to women had been ingrained in him from the cradle. "Stop touchin' me."

"I canna assess your hurts if I do that," she replied in the careful, patient tone she might have used with a child.

"I am nae a bairn to be clucked over," he snapped in the voice that had quelled rebellious men on the Welsh campaign.

"Of course you're nae a bairn. I can see now that 'tis just your shoulder that's cut. But we'll soon ha' it set to rights." She smiled and patted his hand soothingly.

Patted it. "Enough, woman!"

That got her attention. She looked straight at him, her magnificent eyes widening. Tears would come next. He steeled himself to resist them. Her lower lip trembled, but she stilled it between even white teeth. Her struggles to compose herself touched him more than a flood of tears would have. Made him feel a monster for yelling at her. After all, she had come to his aid in the alley. "I didna mean to shout so, but—"

"Ha! Men live to bellow, but I expected better from you, for Lion said you didna fall into rages like other men. Still," she rushed on, "'twill do you no good. I am immune to shoutin' and very stubborn. I *will* tend your wound." Despite her brave words, she peered shyly at him through a fringe of spiky lashes. Her midnight brown eyes were nearly black. Dark, mysterious pools that drew him, heightened his awareness of how close she was to him. So close, her breath whispered across his cheek. Rosemary and lemon. Sweet. Seductive.

Ross inhaled sharply, his senses filled with the smell of her skin, the texture of her hair, the pinkness of her tongue as it crept out to moisten her lips. What would it be like to touch . . . to taste? The air around them thickened, but it wasn't the coming storm that made it sizzle; it was desire. A need that turned his blood to fire, his body to stone.

The dim chamber, the rhythmic thudding at the back door, all faded. There was only him. And her. And a craving so strong, so overpowering. He reached for her. Her cheek felt like silk against the back of his hand. Softer even than he had imagined. Her lashes drifted down, her lips parted even as he lowered his mouth to taste what she offered. "Megan. Ah, Megan, I—"

The crack of splitting timber made them both jump, heads turning toward the back door.

Ross hesitated only an instant. "We have to get out." In one lithe, fluid movement, he grabbed her and headed for the front door. Sword in his right hand, the left wrapped around her waist, he paused only long enough to make certain the street beyond was empty, then whirled them outside. She balked when he would have headed to the left, back toward the castle road.

"There's more cover this way." At her urging, they crossed the street, angling right, and slipped between two buildings. They had not gone far when he noticed she was limping.

"Have you hurt your leg?"

Her hand trembled in his. "'Tis naught. I can keep up."

She did better than that, she led. Through a maze of interconnecting lanes and streets, past homes and shuttered shops identifiable by their smells, for the only illumination came from occasional flashes of lightning. The sharp odor of hides put the tanner next to the shoemaker's shop. Fresh-cut wood marked another furniture maker's. As the yeasty scent of the baker's gave way to the waxy tang of tallow, Ross ordered a halt.

Cocking his head, he listened. There, beneath the distant rumble of thunder came the thud of footsteps, the rasp of voices. Many men, running hard. Searching. "It could be my men."

Megan shook her head. "They're comin' from the wrong way."

"All right," he said warily, and started ahead.

"Nay. We must circle around, toward Lang Gordy's shop, for that is where Chrissy will lead your men." When Ross hesitated, wishing he could see her face, judge her honor, she tisked. "Dinna fret, m'lord, I've set my mind on weddin' you, and I'd just as leave have you in one piece when I do."

Her tartness did what a hundred protests of innocence couldn't, eased his suspicions and tickled his latent sense of humor. "Are you always this blunt?"

"When I can be," she said in an odd tone. "When God was handing out temperance, I was learning to be a storyteller."

The puppets, he thought, but there was no more time for banter, because the sounds of pursuit were closer. But as Megan started to take the lead again, she stumbled, would have gone down had he not caught her around the waist.

"Your leg is worse. Dinna argue," he added over her murmured denial. "You point the way, let me do the work." He wrapped his left arm around her and lifted, tucking her tight to his side.

How strong he is, Megan thought. Her feet barely touched the ground as he loped through the night, pausing only long enough for her whispered directions, or to check a street before plunging on. Flashes of white light from the approaching storm cast his face in stark relief, sculptured planes, shadowed hollows, grim determination. He would keep them safe. In his arms, she felt no fear, though she could hear the shouts of the men who hunted them like hounds on rabbits.

Exhilaration sent her pulse racing in time with Ross's booted feet. They moved as one, she and this dark stranger who would soon be her husband. Darting through the village, driven before their pursuers, she felt alive and free, wild as the rain-scented wind that stung her eyes, lifted the hair from her face.

He felt it, too, Megan realized as the tumultuous race ended and they stood in a darkened alley across the street from Lang Gordy's. Panting with exertion, arms still locked around her, he rasped, "You're quite a lass." His grin was a white slash in his shadowed face, bold and reckless as their flight for freedom.

Megan's pounding heart soared, and beneath her hand she fancied she could feel his response through the mail links encasing his broad chest. "You're nae so bad yourself, m'lord," she replied in place of the *I love you* that sang in her veins.

As though he'd heard her, his smile suddenly fled, and she half expected him to draw away. Instead the hand that still rode her waist moved up to trace the line of her spine through her woolen gown. The tingling trail his fingers left on her skin rivaled the jolt of the lightning that crackled across the sky. In the brilliant wash, she lifted her face, studied the one poised so close above hers, muscles taut, blue eyes black, now mysterious and mesmerizing as the night.

"Meg," he whispered. Nothing more. Hushed and hot as the suddenly stilled air, that single word compressed a wealth of need. A longing that matched the one building inside her.

"Aye." Her voice came out an aching sigh. She ached for him, for his touch, his kiss. The heat of his breath fanning her skin was all the warning she had before his mouth swooped down in the darkness to capture hers.

Her first kiss was everything she'd dreamed of and more... much more. His lips were firm and warm, the gentle pressure of flesh on flesh sending a wash of liquid fire through her body. Moaning softly, she went up on her toes, hands reaching to frame his face, draw him closer. An answering groan rumbled through his body as he gave her what she wanted, deepening the kiss, parting her lips with the spearing edge of his tongue. She welcomed the sensual invasion, gloried in the tremor that shook him, the hungry urgency that exploded inside her, leaving her oblivious to everything but this wild rush of sensation.

Too soon, he lifted his head. Breath rapid and ragged, he rasped, "Oh, God. How did this happen?"

The huskiness in his voice made her curl closer. "I knew it would be like this between us," she whispered.

"Nay. It canna be." He started to thrust her away, but she twisted her hands in his surcoat and hung on.

"What is it? Why do you deny the feelings we have?"

"My brother died wi' a Sutherland quarrel in his back, and you ask why?" he growled, peeling her fingers from his clothes.

"Megan!" cried a strident female voice. "Meg, are ye all right? I've brought m'lord's men. Where are you?"

Ross jerked his head up. "Is that your cousin?"

Dazed, Megan managed a weak, "Aye."

"And none too soon." He freed himself and stepped back.

The loss of contact made Megan shiver. Or was it the cold finality of his words? "Nay. It canna end like this," her wounded heart cried. Not after the closeness of their shared adventure.

"It can end no other way," Ross growled. "Andrew? Owain?" he called, moving into the alley.

"'Tis Andrew." The deep, gravelly voice suited the large warrior who hurried to Ross's side, followed closely by a young man carrying a torch. "Did I nae teach ye better than to go wanderin' about yer enemy's stronghold wi' naught but a few men?" the knight chided as though Ross were a wee naughty bairn.

Ross stiffened, and Megan half expected him to knock this Andrew down for his rudeness. "Leave off," he snapped instead. "We've got to find Owain and the others."

"We're here." The tall Welshman came forward, and Ross quickly asked about casualties and prisoners. "We suffered only minor wounds, but we took no captives."

A chorus of masculine swearing greeted that news, Andrew's loudest of all, but Ross merely sighed and started issuing orders. All around them, men jumped to do his bidding. Some trotted off in search of the wretches who'd chased Ross and Megan through the town. Others gathered up fallen weapons, posted a guard and saw to the wounds of their comrades.

How calm and capable he is, Megan thought as Chrissy fussed over her. Inside, she was a mass of contradicting emotions. Pain, confusion and gut-wrenching sorrow. She and Ross were perfect for each other. She'd suspected it a year ago when Lion had first spoken of his brother. Their panicked flight for freedom, the soul-searching kiss they'd shared, had made her certain. Ross Carmichael was the man for her. The only man.

Desperation gave way to rocky determination as Megan watched him direct his men. How controlled he was. The Sutherlands were a rough, unruly lot, given to quarreling among themselves and acting on their own when it suited them. Ross's men looked even larger and more fierce in their steel helmets and gleaming chain mail. 'Twould take a strong man to gain their respect and hold them in line without threat of violence. *Her man.*

A bubble of possessive pride filled Megan's chest. "Is he not wonderful?" she whispered to Chrissy.

Sniffing back tears of relief, her cousin glanced at the circle of soldiers. "He is a man, like any other."

Nay, he is special, Megan started to say, but she knew no way to describe the bond that had sprung up between herself and Ross, drawing them together as they sought to cheat death. Respect, camaraderie, passion, he'd felt all three during those brief few moments. Though he denied it, the searing kiss they'd shared had been graphic proof.

He wanted me, Megan thought again, warmed anew by the way he had stared at her as though she were a ripe peach tart he was about to devour. She wanted more than that; she wanted Ross to love her as she did him. But 'twas a start. All the way back to the castle, Megan planned and plotted ways to bring her reluctant bridegroom to his senses.

Restless as a caged lion, Ross paced to the window that overlooked the sea. The storm had moved off, leaving the air cool and clear, but he'd have preferred the smoky village inn or a room in hell to this cursed bedchamber in Curthill Castle.

The red velvet hangings on the bed reminded him of his brother's spilled blood, the elaborate chairs, the costly silver flagon and cups reminded him Eammon was likely guilty of wrecking, but there was as yet no way to prove it. Jesu, why had he ever thought he liked a challenge?

Still he was not foolish enough to go out again tonight looking for answers. He'd been lucky to escape nearly unscathed. Or had he? "What makes you think the men who attacked us were not from Curthill's garrison?" he demanded, turning on Owain.

Seated across the room, booted feet extended toward the empty hearth, ale cup propped on his lean belly, Owain muttered, "I wish there was another besides Davey to look at yer shoulder."

"I've been tendin' m'lord's hurts for years," Davey declared from his pallet by the door. He had been with Ross for ten years, first as a page, then a squire before his knighting this year. Because his wiry frame and fair, freckled face made him look far younger than his twenty years, he was playing the part of squire again. It meant he could stick to Ross's side all day and sleep in his chamber at night without causing comment. "The wound's nae so bad," Davey added. "The blade slid off yer collarbone. It dug a long, bloody furrow, but the cut's shallow."

Ross scowled. Their casual dismissal of his injury perversely reminded him of Megan's concern. Her fears for his health should not have touched him, but they had. Even now, it warmed him to recall the way she had bullied him into a chair and run her hands over his body looking for other hurts.

Lust. His old nemesis, he told himself and forced her image away. Truth to tell, the ache in his shoulder was nothing to the frustration that mounted moment by moment. "About the attack."

Owain straightened. "Giles and the others ye left within Curthill's walls watched carefully. No one left after we did."

"They could have gone into the village earlier," Ross said.

"Possible, but they were garbed more like sailors than soldiers," Owain readily replied.

"From the ship in the harbor," Ross murmured.

A scratching at the door had all three men reaching for their swords. Davey answered it, and Ross's pulse raced with anticipation when he saw it was Andrew with the Welshman who had been left to watch the boats.

He spoke to Owain in a hill dialect Ross could not follow, so he filled the waiting time by pouring a cup of watered wine. To his disgust, Davey scrambled up, bent on tasting it first.

"Unnecessary," Ross said, and downed a goodly swallow. "Eammon isna stupid enough to poison me wi' the king's uncle here."

"Wreckers," Owain spat. As he went on to list the goods that had been unloaded from the ship in the harbor, Ross traced a circle in the carpet with the toe of his boot. 'Twas not unlike the noose that drew tighter about his neck with each hour he spent at Curthill.

Three days from now, he'd be forced to wed Megan. A fate worse than death, he'd told himself on the voyage here. After tonight, he knew the depths of that hell. *He wanted her.* More than he'd ever wanted anyone before. Even Rhiannon. Nay, he couldn't, wouldn't feel anything for her save hatred. That way lay madness. If she knew, she'd use the knowledge to enslave—

"The booty wasna brought to the castle?" Andrew asked, dragging Ross's mind to a more immediate danger.

Owain shook his head. "'Twas parceled out to the merchants in town. Chests of clothing to the tailor shops, furniture to the carpenters. There are several of each, by the way."

"Passin' strange in a town this small," Andrew growled.

"Agreed, but..." Ross went on to tell them what Megan had said about her father's trade. "Could what you saw have been damaged goods brought into town merely to be repaired?"

Andrew snorted. "In the dead of night?"

"Mayhap the townspeople do this without their laird's knowledge," put in Davey.

"Let us capture one and put him to the test." Andrew fingered his dirk. "Gi' me an hour—"

"Andrew! You're talking like a fool," Ross exclaimed, still smarting over his knight's earlier set-down. "Lady Megan told me about this trade willingly, proudly."

"M'lord?" The Welsh spy straightened away from the wall where he'd been leaning and spoke slowly. "There is one puzzle ... a hut at the edge of the village. It had no windows and but a single door, where two men stood guard. It seemed—" he frowned "—more goods went in than a building its size could hold."

"So." Air hissed out between Ross's teeth. Megan had not told him everything; just enough to allay his suspicions. *Curse the lying little witch.* He pursed his lips and swore he could still taste her traitorous kisses on them. He cursed himself, then, for having been taken in by her seductive wiles.

Chapter Five

"Have ye ever seen the like?" Davey muttered to Ross. Behind them, the Carmichael knights shifted to get a better look. If anything, Curthill's hall looked worse by day and at close range than it had when they'd peeked in the night before.

Seedy as a harlot the morning after. Ross thought that apt considering the folk slumped over the trestle tables looked the worse for a night spent drinking and carousing. The stink of so many bodies mingled with the smoke from the fire roaring in the great hearth made his eyes water.

Signs of wear and tear muted by torchlight yestereve were mercilessly revealed in the stark glare of early morning light streaming in through the open windows. Beneath a thin coat of whitewash, her walls were gray and smoke streaked. The wall hangings stained. With salt water? And the rushes . . .

Ross grimaced at the squishy sounds his feet made as he gingerly stepped into the room, nostrils pinched against the stench of stale ale that rose around him.

"Infernal Highland barbarians," Andrew grumbled, lip curling with loathing as he exchanged glances with Giles Kennedy.

Sir Giles sniffed disdainfully. "These people look like...like ragpickers," said the most fastidious of Ross's men. "Not one of them is wearin' a costume that matches."

Ross nodded. Most of the men sported the typical Highlanders' saffron-colored pleated tunic, yet instead of being bare from knees to boots, they wore hose. Parti-colored hose such as was popular in England and at David's court. They looked . . . ridiculous. Sillier still were those who wore English surcoats, minus the hose, with their rough hide boots.

"'Tis like someone threw a pile of court garb in the middle of the hall and each man grabbed somethin'," Giles said slowly.

"Exactly," Ross spat. These clothes were booty, too, taken from ships the bloody Sutherlands had lured onto their rocky coast and looted. The confirmation of his suspicions strengthened his resolve to find a way . . . any way . . . out of marrying Megan.

"Let's nae stand here all day," grumped Lord Nigel, who'd come himself to fetch Ross for the morning meal. "I see Lady Mary just motionin' for the servants to bring the food." He hurried into the hall with a speed that belied his girth.

"Somehow, I've lost my appetite," Davey muttered.

"I thought it was just me," Ross replied. His head ached, his eyes burned with fatigue and, as predicted, pain gnawed at his shoulder with the ferocity of a ten-pound rat. If his time had not been so perilously short, he might have been tempted to do the unheard-of and lie abed till noon.

"Do ye want to return to yer chamber? I could fetch somethin' from the kitchens." Davey offered.

"Nay. I'll stay." Though the vileness of eating with Eammon would likely make him swallow every bite twice, he had come down to the hall because he needed answers to the questions that bred faster than malicious rabbits.

Just as Ross reached the dais, a thin, pale lady rushed around the buttery screen to intercept him. "We didna expect you down so early. The bread's out of the ovens, but the rest isna quite ready." The speed with which she dropped into a curtsy at his feet made it seem her legs had failed her.

Lady Mary, Ross decided, matching her faded beauty to Megan's. Despite his vow to distance himself from everyone here, he reached down, took one worn, chapped hand in his and raised her up. "That's all right. We do not need much," he said as gently as he would have to his own mother. Though it was doubtful Carina Carmichael had ever been as timid as this poor creature.

Lady Mary stared at him blankly, and he realized he'd spoken in French. "Your pardon," he said at once in Gaelic. "I—"

"'Tis all right, m'lord. I'm a Lowlander by birth and learned the court tongue as a child, but I fear I may be a bit rusty, havin' only Megan and Chrissy to practice wi'."

"Lady Megan speaks French?"

"Aye, and reads and ciphers some, too," the lady said proudly. "I shared my learnin' wi' all my bairns, but what wi' the accident and all, Megan had the most time to read."

Megan had been in an accident? Nay, he did not want to know. Knowing brought caring. And he already cared more than was wise. Last night had shown him a bold, courageous woman, one he might have taken to wife had her name not been Sutherland. "Books are costly and must be difficult to get up here," he said, probing.

"Nay, though Lord Eammon doesna value them, books are sometimes part of the goods that come to us through the trade."

"Megan told me about this trade. Does someone in the village repair the books, too?"

"Nay, 'tis work for monks and we dinna ha' an abbey. We just enjoy them as they are...water stained and a bit tattered."

Because they'd been washed up on shore in a wreck.

"But Megan knows more about the trade than I do," she said.

I just bet she does.

"I'm kept busy wi' my herb gardens and tryin' to keep the hall in order wi' no one to uphold my authority," she said bitterly. "But enough of my problems, do you come sit down. The hot dishes will be out directly."

Why did Eammon not uphold her authority? Ross wondered. Then he remembered Felis, whose exertions kept the laird from his duties. Ross almost felt sorry for the poor lady. Almost. He followed her with the enthusiasm of a man facing the gallows. As they threaded their way through the rows of tables, he looked to the dais at the far end of the hall, half dreading, half hoping to see Megan waiting at the high table.

She wasn't. Was she still abed, recovering from their adventure?

The thought of her curled naked beneath the sheets tightened every muscle below his belt, made him grateful for the long surcoat he wore over his hose. Damn. *He would not want her.* Teeth gritted, he fought the memories of last night's kiss and his own traitorous response to her.

"If you'll sit here, m'lord."

Ross quickly took the chair Lady Mary indicated. On either side of him were empty places. He expected Lord Nigel's royal blood would put him in the one to his left, a high-backed chair upholstered in red velvet. Instead, his lordship sat at the other end of the high table, his face buried in a wine cup.

"'Tis like old times, eh, m'lord," Davey whispered, leaning in to fill Ross's cup with watered wine as he had a hundred times before in his role of squire. "A moment," he added. As Ross reached for the cup, his squire raised it to his own lips.

"Davey." Ross attempted to knock the cup aside.

The lad evaded him, drank deep and lowered the cup to wipe his mouth with a linen napkin. "Owain and I didna really think they'd poison ye wi' Lord Nigel here, still..."

Ross found the Welshman sitting with the other Carmichaels at the table nearest the dais and glared at him.

"To yer continued good health, m'lord," Owain said in Welsh.

"I'll not buy it at the expense of another's," Ross replied in kind. "And you may tell that to the rest of them," he added. Beneath their wool tunics, his battle-honed knights and soldiers wore mail. Each had a brace of dirks in his boots and a sword at his waist. These were necessary precautions but, "I want no unnecessary heroics."

"Nothing *unnecessary* will be done," Owain said. "Ye pay me well to guard yer back. Lord Lionel vowed to have me skinned and hung out to dry did anything happen to ye."

Ross snorted, but his father's concern warmed him, gave him hope they'd come to terms when Lion's killer had been caught. Taking the refilled cup from Davey, he raised it to his lips, winced as pain lanced through his shoulder.

"Should I take another look at yer wound?" Davey asked.

"How came ye to be wounded?" Lord Nigel demanded.

Ross shrugged, but under Nigel's surprisingly sharp eyes and Lady Mary's concerned ones, he was forced to weave a tale about last night's fight in the village. He made no mention of Megan's assistance or his own conclusion that his attackers had come from the ship that carried the wreckers' plunder. Much as he disliked the Sutherlands, he regretted every lying word he uttered.

"Oh, this is terrible," Lady Mary cried when he'd finished.

"Considerin' yer sire's twice attacked Curthill, ye were foolish to wander out in search of amusement," Nigel muttered. "Likely his victims' families wanted to even the score."

Ross let it go at that. Lord Nigel returned to his wine, but Lady Mary pressed for a look at his wound. "The Highlands are much as I expected," Ross said, desperate to change the subject.

The lady sighed, then gave in. "I found Curthill drear and barbarous when I first came north as a bride. But I soon came to value the people. They are independent to the point of wildness at times, but brave and honorable to a fault."

Honorable? Ross nearly swallowed his tongue.

At the back of the hall, a fight broke out between two hairy giants. The thinner one threw a decking punch, then followed his opponent down. Hands at each other's throats, they rolled in the rushes, their growls and grunts nearly drowned out by the shouts of their kinsmen wagering on the outcome of the contest.

Ha! These Sutherlands did not even deal honorably with each other, Ross thought, lip curling. Carmichaels did not behave so.

"You can see, the discipline among the men is sorely lackin' with Eammon so often absent from the hall," Lady Mary said.

"I have yet to meet the laird." *God rot his soul.* "Where has he been keepin' himself?" *Off wrecking?*

Lady Mary flushed, then paled. "He's...indisposed. He's nae been himself since our son died two years ago. Keeps to his rooms and rarely comes down."

Ross cursed himself for prodding, but necessity kept him at it. "Lord Eammon no longer leads his clan?"

"Oh, he still rules here, make nae mistake. Archie brings down Eammon's orders and carries them out wi' the faithfulness of Moses. The trade Eammon devised has been good for our people. Though we're by nae means prosperous," she added. "Archie says that Eammon says the time will come when the people can keep some of the profits instead of usin' the coin to buy more goods."

"Archie?"

"He's captain here. But in all other ways except the trade, 'tis like Eammon has forgotten us, turned his back on us."

"But surely with his own family he is the same."

The corners of Lady Mary's mouth turned down, her eyes glazed as though focused on some distant pain. "For us, 'tis even worse. Sometimes we go months wi'out actually seein' him. Eammon doesna come down from his tower, and we are hardly welcome in it," she said simply, painfully.

"I see." Pained himself, he looked away.

"I doubt it. Eammon has Felis to see to his comfort now, and doesna need me." She was as brave and blunt as her daughter.

Ross found himself pitying them both. His mother would have scratched out her husband's eyes, and her rival's, did he attempt to house a mistress under her roof. But that was because Lionel adored his Carina. In truth, if a man chose to ignore his wife, or shut her up in a nunnery or beat her to death, no one would stop him . . . least of all the holy church. "I am sorry," he murmured.

"'Tis been hard on Megan, too. She worshiped her father and he so loved her that when the old *seanachaidh* died Eammon defied tradition and made Megan bard of Clan Sutherland. The only one my husband seems to care about...beyond *Felis* . . . is Siusan. Scarce a week passes but what he sends men out to look for her."

Out of love, or because Siusan knew too much? Ross wondered. Last night, he'd tried to fit the scraps of information he'd picked up into some logical picture. Lion loved to hunt, would not have abandoned the chase on a whim. But if Siusan had sent Lucais with an invitation to meet her in some secluded woodland glade, Lion would have left quickly, and with the smile Wee Wat's informant had mentioned. There Eammon's men had killed Lion, to keep him from going to the king with the truth about this *trade*. The only question was, had Siusan been a willing party to her sire's evil scheme? "Where is Siusan?"

"Gone." Expression utterly miserable, the lady once more averted her head. "She left wi'out a word."

"She ran off wi' her page," interjected a new voice, and Ross looked up as a stranger mounted the dais. Lean and broad shouldered, the newcomer was dressed as simply yet expensively as Ross in a dark silk tunic, unembroidered surcoat and hose. His fine leather boots were cleaned of mud, and the sword at his side had the gleam of well-honed steel. In appearance, he could have been any one of a dozen men Ross knew from court in Edinburgh...a well-bred nobleman who did not flaunt his wealth.

"Comyn!" Lady Mary exclaimed.

"Cousin." The man bowed over her hand. "May I join ye?" he asked politely. At her nod, he took the chair to Ross's right and turned to face him. "We've nae met, but ye must be Ross Carmichael. I'm Comyn MacDonnel."

"Comyn came here to live wi' us nine years ago...after his sire, a distant cousin, lost his estates," the lady explained. "He's been like a son to Eammon...especially after Ewan died. And a great comfort to me, too." She smiled. "Though I dinna see him as often as I'd like since he's been spendin' so much time restorin' the Highland peel tower Eammon gave him."

"In fact, I've just ridden in from Shurr More," Comyn said pleasantly. To Ross he added, "'Tis sorry I am about Lion's death." The earnest expression on his plain, ruddy face and the genuine regret in the brown eyes that held Ross's so steadily made the sentiment ring all the truer. "Though we didna know each other long, we became friends at the Clan Gatherin' where he met Siusan." He smiled faintly. "I outran him in the foot-race held there, and he retaliated by bestin' me in swordplay."

"That sounds like my brother." As Comyn began to describe the mock battle Lion had won, the stranglehold on Ross's soul eased. Mired deep in guilt and recriminations, the Carmichael clan had not talked about the happy times they'd shared with Lion. It felt good to do so now. By the time Comyn had finished the tale, Ross had decided that here at least was one man with whom he could feel at ease. One he could ask about his brother's death and get honest answers, not lies and evasion.

"Were you here when he died?" Ross asked.

"Regrettably, I was at Shurr More. Ah, and here is our little bride-to-be," Comyn said mockingly.

Despite his vow to remain aloof, Ross's head snapped around, his heart slamming against his ribs. It stopped suddenly, and the air caught in his lungs. Gone was the feisty, rumpled lass with whom he'd shared a few dangerous, exhilarating hours last eve. In her place stood a breathtakingly beautiful vision. He'd wondered what her hair would look like unbound. Now he knew.

Glorious. A molten river of golds and browns, it cascaded over her shoulders and down her back. His fingers itched with the urge to tunnel into her hair and feel its silky weight. Two small sections at her temples had been plaited into braids, drawing the hair back to reveal her high cheekbones, the delicate angle of her jaw, the slender column of her throat rising like polished marble from the neck of a simple red cotehardie.

One look at her breasts straining against the confines of the close-fitting gown, rising and falling with each quick breath she took, made his mouth go dry, his palms slick as an untried lad's. Nay, he'd not give in to the desire that made a mockery of his customary control. He wrenched his gaze upward, determined to resist the provocative challenge he expected to find there. 'Twas how Rhiannon had played the game.

Megan's eyes were warm and soft as his memories of their kiss. Again his heart lurched, and he almost tumbled in after it, pulled into the haunting innocence shining in the depths of her midnight eyes. *Almost.*

She took a step forward, breaking the spell, thank God. Trembling in its aftermath, he noted she paused slightly each time she set her left foot down. She'd injured herself last night coming to his rescue. Instinctively Ross stood to go to her aid.

"M'lord? Is aught wrong?" Davey questioned in his ear.

Damn. Ross sat abruptly, gritting his teeth as pain jolted through his shoulder. Served him right for being so stupid. One

look at Megan and he forgot his vow to avoid her. She had bewitched him. As Siusan had Lion. Not a comforting comparison.

"Comyn, what do you here?" Megan set her tray down on
the table with an indignant thump and scowled at her cousin.

"Why, I've come for yer weddin'," he replied, smiling.

Her frown deepened. "You're nae welcome here. But then,
if you run true to form, you'll nae stay for the ceremony." The
sunlight glinting in her hair matched the fire in her eyes.

"Meg!" her mother exclaimed. "Apologize at once."

"'Tis all right, Cousin Mary. Over the years, I've tough-
ened my hide to Megan's sharp barbs."

Ross looked from Megan's flushed cheeks to Comyn's tight
jaw. *Why would Megan want to alienate so fine a man as
Comyn?* was his first thought.

"But I havena learned to stomach your deceitful ways."

A collective gasp swept the nearer tables, drawing all eyes to
the lass bristled up like an enraged cat. All except Lord Nigel,
who continued to attack the chicken on his trencher as though
he expected it might try to fly away from him.

"Gently. Ye may nae always find me forgivin'," Comyn said.

Megan sniffed and dismissed her cousin with a toss of her
head. "M'lord. I am sorry I wasna here when you came
down," she said sweetly to Ross. "But I made this specially for
you." She whipped the cover off a silver platter and pushed it
toward him.

The strong aroma of the sea slapped him in the face, making his eyes water and his gorge rise. "Fish," he said weakly.

"Baked sturgeon . . . caught fresh yesterday. 'Tis a favorite
dish of mine, and I thought . . ."

He was going to be sick. Ross gagged, swallowed hard and
reached for the wine cup.

"M'lord?" Megan ventured hesitantly.

"It may be a bit early in the morn for those who did not grow
up by the sea." Comyn snatched the fish from under Ross's
nose and took it to Lord Nigel, who dug in eagerly.

"My thanks, Comyn." Ross looked at her dismissively.

Megan shivered. So, he was back to being standoffish. "I got up early to make it especially for you." She could not keep the hurt from her voice.

If anything, his expression grew more remote. "I eat only bread and ale of a morn."

Megan looked from the cheese and chicken in his manchet bread trencher to the mouth that had moved so hungrily over hers last night. This morn 'twas a thin, reproving line. *Why punish me for what you think Papa has done?* She wanted to cry; pride stayed her. "Back to being rude, I see." Goaded by his unreasonableness, she snatched up the trencher and thumped a hunk of plain bread down before him. "There...m'lord grouch." She turned away so fast one slender braid flew out in a circle, neatly clipping the side of his cup.

Thunk. Splash. He had a lap full of wine.

Ross gasped as the cold liquid settled in.

Lady Mary shouted for cloths; the maids scattered to do her bidding. Davey offered to get fresh garments for him.

Ross stonily shook his head, ears hot with indignation, eyes on Megan. Hers were appropriately downcast as she slowly made her way up onto the dais in answer to her mother's summons. Lord, she had a temper quick as his sire's for all she was only a lass. Her slender shoulders hunched inside the red wool gown, shaking slightly. Surely her mother would not beat her for an accident, Ross thought, wishing the idea did not appall him. "Apologize to Lord Ross," her mother prompted.

"I—I am sorry," came the low, choked reply.

"Accepted," Ross said with alacrity, wanting to put the scene behind him, get the answers he sought about Siusan and return to his room for dry clothes.

As she took the chair to his right, she cast Ross a glance that completely shattered his illusions. Her eyes brimmed with suppressed laughter; her lips twitched with it.

The little witch. "Did you do that apurpose?" he hissed.

She started. "'Twas an accident, but...if you could have seen yourself, sittin' there pompous as a bishop at mass, and then the wine spilled, and you looked so..." Her voice cracked.

Ross's hands flexed on the chair arms, tingling with the urge to shake the smile from her lips. How dare she laugh at him.

"Megan, you willna laugh at your betrothed." The expression that entered Ross's eyes stilled Megan's laughter instantly. Disgust. Loathing. Fury. *Dear God.* After last night she'd thought...hoped and prayed, really...that he'd be a little more amenable to the idea. 'Twas not as though either of them had any choice. If he hated all Sutherlands this fiercely, why had he come to Curthill in the first place?

Her painful thoughts were interrupted by a shout. She looked up to see Archie striding into the hall. Everything from the arrogant cast of the captain's thin face as he acknowledged his clansmen's greetings to the swagger of his hips beneath a peacock silk surcoat fine enough for a lord set her teeth on edge. Jealousy. She envied Archie's closeness with her father.

The captain has ideas above his station, Ross thought as Archie stopped before the dais. Though the Carmichaels were not sticklers for such things, none of his father's men would have behaved so, even if he were acting for the laird.

"Laird Eammon willna be down to break his fast wi' ye," Archie announced in his grating voice. "He's...indisposed."

Ross's heart went out to Lady Mary, who made a choking sound and buried her face in a linen napkin.

Megan was shaking, too, her cheeks flaming. "Did he say whether he'd be *well enough* to attend my weddin'?"

Archie smiled arrogantly, lips drawing back from pointy yellow teeth. "I'll see if I can find out."

"After I've eaten, I'll visit Eammon and see how he is." Comyn pulled out the high-backed chair to Ross's left.

Like a flash, Megan was up, grabbing hold of the chair. "Nay. This is Papa's seat."

"I'm sure he'd nae mind Comyn sittin' in his chair," Archie said quickly, flashing Comyn a smile.

"Well I do," Megan snapped.

Comyn's eyes narrowed. Something that looked like hatred flickered in their pale depths, then vanished. "I rode much of the night to get here, and I've a fierce appetite this morn."

"Fine. Eat, but you canna sit in Papa's chair. 'Twould mean you have designs on his place...and his life."

"Superstitious nonsense," Comyn scoffed.

"Traditional beliefs," Megan replied, not backing down. "As *seanachaidh* of Clan Sutherland, I'm expected to uphold them."

Comyn snorted, but Ross felt the stir that swept the hall, knew by the intense expressions he met as he gazed around that Megan was right. No matter that he agreed with Comyn, thought all such old superstitions were nonsense, these people obviously believed in them. Even Archie looked distinctly uneasy. Did Comyn take Eammon's chair, it would be an open declaration of intent.

How brave she looked, standing there defending her father's rights. Last night, Ross had discovered she was a woman of uncommon courage and wit; she seemed doubly so now. Though he had no love for the man she so stoutly upheld, Ross respected her principles. Rhiannon had had none.

You could have heard a pin land, even in the soggy rushes, as the Sutherlands waited.

"Come, m'lord," Archie growled. "We'll go above to Lord Eammon's rooms. He'll nae mind bein' interrupted by *ye*." Pointedly. "He was askin' after ye just this morn. Said he had a matter to discuss wi' ye when ye rode in from Shurr More."

Comyn's eyes held Megan's for a moment longer, a muscle jumping in his cheek as he flexed and unflexed his jaw. Then he turned away and strode from the hall with Archie at his side. If they had not been going to see Eammon, Ross might have followed them for the chance to talk with Comyn about Siusan.

A collective sigh whooshed through the hall, followed by a spate of nervous laughter. Gradually speech resumed.

"A female bard," Nigel sneered, grease dripping from his jowls. "Willfulness, that's what comes o' givin' females the notion they're fit for more than cookin' and bearin' young. Best show her who's master." He saluted Ross with his cup.

"Fortunately I was raised to know my true worth," Megan said tightly. To Ross she murmured, "I am sorry about the fish . . . and the wine. Could I bring you porridge or broken meats?"

"Nay. I've had enough." He stood abruptly, and she knew it was not food, but herself he was done with.

"We could sit in one of yonder window seats," she said quickly, pointing to the wide seat built in below the deeply recessed windows so that they were shielded from the room.

"Nay," he repeated, looking straight ahead as though the sight of her upset his belly as much as the fish had.

Panic made Megan's heart race, her mind scramble. He'd disappear as he had yesterday, and she'd not see him until dinner, if then. "I have things I want to tell you."

That got his attention. "My brother's murder and your sister's whereabouts are the only things I am interested in discussin'." He fixed her with a hard, uncompromising glare.

Megan dragged in a deep breath, held it. "So be it. I will answer your questions about Lion's death." *As many of them as I can without endangering the living.*

Curthill Castle stood alone on the rocky promontory far above the restless, crashing sea, a lonely sentinel standing watch on the site of an ancient Pictish fort. Though her ramparts were in need of repair and bore the marks of battle, including the recent scars left by Lionel Carmichael's fire arrows, Curthill was nearly unassailable. The only landward approach lay over a narrow path that climbed steadily from sea level to the gatehouse beneath the glowering eyes of the tower's arrow slits.

At the base of the cliff, sheltered from the wind by its stark walls, a tiny pocket of grass and a few scruffy trees clung tenaciously to the sandy soil. In that verdant cove, Megan awaited Ross. The sun was warm on her face. The tangy air, fresh and clear after last night's storm, mixed pleasantly with the delicious aroma of meat pasties wafting from the basket cook had prepared, but Megan could not relax.

Somehow she must find out why Ross had turned from her.

"Meet me on the beach," he'd replied to her offer of information about Lion.

"The beach? Why ever—"

"There's less chance we'll be overheard there," he had muttered, scowling at her kinsmen.

"The beach is a bad place to sit. The sand is full of—"

"The beach," he'd insisted.

So she'd agreed, even knowing what was likely to happen. *Not very nice,* her conscience reprimanded. But men seemed to learn best by example, and so pompous a man surely deserved a lesson in humility. When Ross saw what came of not taking her advice, he'd listen to her the next time she offered some.

"You are prompt," Ross called out, crunching toward her across the sand. "'Tis a surprisin' trait in a woman."

"Do you have a poor opinion of all women, or just of me?" The narrowing of his eyes was her only answer. "You'll find I am different from other women," she replied with feigned bravado.

One raven black brow rose. "Indeed. None I know would seek retribution by dumpin' a cup of wine in my lap."

"Or by savin' your life," she countered. He had the grace to flush, but the cheeky reply that crowded her throat was forgotten as she saw six men in dark clothes trailing after Ross, bows slung over their shoulders. They fanned out to take up positions among the rocks. "I thought this was a private talk," she chided.

He shrugged, wincing slightly. *So, his shoulder pained him. She'd been right to bring along her medicines and fresh bandages.* "My bodyguards take their duties seriously," he said.

"Do they even share your bedchamber?" she taunted, then wished she hadn't when he stiffened, drawing himself up even taller so that he towered over her where she sat on the blanket. His gaze was narrowed, but a hot light flickered briefly in their azure depths. Desire, or the sun reflected off the water? Desire, she hoped, remembering the heat of his kisses. Her insides drew tight in anticipation of his next words.

"Nay," he murmured into the hushed, expectant silence. Then he shook himself and scowled. "Dinna look at me like that."

Megan smiled. "I canna help it. You remind me of the tales of the Celtic god, Luga Lamfada...tall and comely, with a face as bright and glorious as the settin' sun."

He turned the color of a sunset. "Are you always so bold?"

"Bold?" She pursed her lips, considering. "I hadna considered it bold to speak the truth."

"Truth?" He raised one mocking brow.

Nor did she pretend to misunderstand that, either. "'Tis a virtue I greatly prize. Mama and Papa taught us always to tell the truth." And she would...unless it meant breaking the vows made to Siusan. His answering snort irritated her. "Would you mind sittin'? Starin' up at you gives me a crick in the neck."

He flopped down onto the blanket, as far away from her as possible without sitting in the sand. His gaze was fixed on the sparkling chop of the bay, as though the sea contained the answer to some great question. Or it pained him to look at her.

"'Tis soothin' to sit and watch the water." Megan pulled out a flagon, cups and several linen-wrapped bundles from the basket.

"Where is your sister right now?" Direct and to the point.

Megan tried evasion. "I dinna know...exactly." Siusan was with their Aunt Brita, but in which room of that ancient tower...

"Dinna mince words wi' me, mistress." His gaze held her to the spot like a trapped butterfly.

She smiled to let him know she wasn't intimidated and poured him a cup of wine. "Why are you so anxious to find her?"

"I'd question her about Lion's murder."

"Papa didna do it," Megan said just as firmly.

"How can you sweetly call him Papa? The man ignores his whole clan and makes your mother unhappy," he exclaimed.

He sounded like a man who cared. "No matter his actions now, Papa was good to me when I was growin' up. When Old Tam came to him and said I had a talent for not only memorizin' the clan stories and legends, but retellin' them, Papa gave me leave to study with Tam and chose me as the next *seanachaidh* when the time came. Papa changed after Ewan died. If he's cool to me, 'tis no more than I deserve." Megan busied herself unwrapping the linen napkin that held the meat pasties. "I challenged Ewan to a race. There...there was an accident, and my brother died."

"Your mother mentioned the accident. I didna realize you blamed yourself." Ross sighed, then said softly, painfully, "Lion asked me to come with him when he wed your sister, but I was committed to fight in Wales."

"Does your father blame you for Lion's death?"

"No more than I blame myself." He looked seaward again.

Megan felt the pain of his guilt, understood it only too well. "You were not even here when Lion died . . ."

"If I had been, he might not have been *murdered*."

"So, we are back to that."

"Always, until I know the truth. Lion was shot in the back, after being lured from the hunt by a message from your sister."

"You think Siusan wished Lion ill? Nay," Megan cried. "Siusan nearly died, herself, after Lion was gone, for she would neither eat nor sleep. She loved him and he her."

"If not guilt, then why did she leave?"

"That I canna tell you."

"Were she and Lucais lovers? Is that it?"

Megan laughed, but it was not a happy sound. "Lucais is thirteen to Siusan's sixteen, and he has a nose even bigger than the beak that takes up most of George's face. Last night you said Papa had killed Lion because of the trade, now this. I think you grasp at straws because you're anxious to make someone pay for your brother's death. I felt that way when Ewan died." She'd wanted to blame it on Comyn, but he'd been away at the time.

"Then why did your sister and Lucais leave?"

Damn. Obviously she was not as skilled at telling lies as she was at telling stories. "She left soon after Lion died." The day Megan had told Siusan about the bairn. Learning that she was carrying Lion's babe had snapped Siusan out of the stupor she'd fallen into after his death, but there was more. A secret so dangerous Siusan had refused to share it . . . even with Megan. "Lucais went wi' Siusan because she needed an escort," she said, covering her fears for her sister and the bairn.

"Where did she go?"

Damn. And double damn.

"You know something." Ross threw down his cup, spilling wine to glisten like blood on the pale gray blanket. "Tell me," he demanded, gingerly flexing his left shoulder.

'Twas tempting, so tempting to share the burden with him. But not yet . . . not until she was certain of his loyalty, positive he'd not hurt Siusan in his zeal to uncover the truth. "I know naught. Your wound pains you. Let me clean and dress it."

"Nay." Crossly. "I dinna believe you."

"Nor do *I* believe *you*. Let me look at your shoulder. I'm accounted a skilled healer and could help ease your discomfort."

"I'm nae in any discomfort," Ross declared, expression stony. "Except that brought on by your family's lies."

Megan shivered under the lash of his tongue. What had started out as two small lies had quickly grown so she was drowning in them. Never had she felt their weight so keenly as with his eyes probing hers. "You should trust me a little. We'll be wed day after tomorrow, and...and I'd ha' trust between us."

"There can be no trust between Sutherland and Carmichael," he said in a hard voice that nearly killed her dreams.

But she had survived far harsher set-downs...from her father and from Comyn. "There can be, if only you will trust me..."

"I trust no woman," Ross snarled.

"Nor do you really want to wed me."

"Nay, I dinna."

She winced, cut to the quick. "Then why did you come?"

"To save my clan from being outlawed, though I doubt a Sutherland would understand such a sacrifice."

Oh, she knew all about sacrifices. Megan sighed inwardly. How much they were alike, she and Ross, though he'd doubtless disagree. She braced for the next volley of questions, but Ross yelped suddenly, swatting at his leg, reminding her of the reason she had not wanted to meet him here.

"Damn, something's bit me," he growled, jumping up and brushing at the immaculate hose above the line of his boots.

"Fleas."

"Fleas," he exclaimed. "I should ha' known that my bed was infested, but they didna trouble me last night."

"Sand fleas." Megan fought to keep her lips from twitching as she watched him dance about, swatting at his legs. "'Tis why I was against your suggestion of meetin' here."

"Then why the hell are they not bitin' you?"

"I dosed myself wi' pennyroyal."

"And none for me?" he roared.

"You've nae shown yourself willin' to listen to any of my other suggestions," she said archly. "So..."

"So you thought you'd teach me a lesson."

"Aye." Megan tried to look contrite, knew by the hard, hostile glare he cut her that she'd failed.

"Sneaky, lyin' Sutherland," he growled under his breath. He spun on one heel and marched off down the beach. The dignity of his retreat was marred each time he bent to scratch his leg. Nor were the men who trailed after him spared. They came off the rocks scratching and cursing.

Megan sighed. What little ground she had gained by saving his life last night had been lost by her stupid joke. How could she have forgotten how jealously men guarded their pride? Worse, she thought as she began to repack the basket, she'd not get a chance to tend the shoulder she suspected was festering.

Siusan's secret was still safe, but Megan felt she had lost something even more sacred... his regard.

Chapter Six

The sound of the surf pounding on the rocks below Curthill Castle barely penetrated the thick walls of the tower that housed Eammon's chambers, two large, interconnected rooms, more lavishly furnished than the rest of the castle. A small fire struggled in the hearth of the room that had served as Lady Mary's solar in happier times.

Sprawled in a high-backed chair, booted feet extended toward the flames, the man who ruled Curthill muttered, "I hear there was trouble in the village last night."

Archie drained his cup of ale and wiped his lips with the back of his hand. "Aye. As we feared, Carmichael and his men were at George the tailor's and on the beach, sniffin' about."

"I trust they didna learn anythin'."

"Not so far's we know. Douglas's men kept them right busy. Hear they fight like devils, fer all they're naught but weak Lowlanders. Douglas lost six men to them."

"What of the cargo?"

"'Twas a fine haul...the best we've made yet. The ship Douglas and his men seized was out of Calais, bound fer London wi' a hold full of Frenchie velvet and Italian furniture bought by some English earl. What goods was damaged are at the merchants', the rest's in the storage hut. Douglas sailed *The Hawk* 'round and concealed her in the cove, as ye ordered. Here's the list of what Douglas sold from our earlier hauls."

His lordship took the rolled parchment, looked through it, then handed it back. "Excellent. See these things are made ready for shipment to London."

Archie frowned, running a filthy finger over the words, picking out the ones he'd laboriously learned ... chairs, tables, several articles of clothing, and some jewelry. "I'm nae certain I know exactly which pieces these are."

"Get Douglas over to help ye tonight. I dinna want to risk bein' seen wi'in a league of the warehouse whilst Ross Carmichael and his men are at Curthill."

"Lord Ross seems as taken wi' ye as his brother was." Archie chuckled. "I dinna think Lion suspected a thing till he saw ye in the glade that day and realized he was about to die."

"Nay. He didna." A faint smile crossed Comyn's plain face, making his eyes gleam with satisfaction. "He never even knew why he died." Comyn almost wished he could have challenged Lion openly, fought him for the woman they'd both wanted. Siusan. There would have been a certain pleasure in besting the big, volatile warrior and riding off with the prize. But Siusan had made her feelings clear when her father had told her ... at Comyn's urging ... that she could not wed Lion.

"If I canna have Lion, I willna wed at all," she'd insisted. "I think of you as a brother," Siusan had added when Comyn tried to press his suit. "And you were betrothed to Megan. I couldna hurt my sister by weddin' the man who repudiated her."

Faced with the ruin of the brilliant schemes he'd put into motion two years ago and nurtured so carefully, so cautiously no one suspected that he, not Eammon, ruled the Sutherlands, Comyn had fallen back on the tactics that had insured his success thus far ... trickery, lies and murder.

"We've come too far to let Ross Carmichael ruin things now," Comyn grumbled. "If he keeps his nose out of Sutherland business, I'm content to see him wed Megan, and good riddance to them both." With her sharp eye and even sharper tongue, Megan had been a thorn in his side from the moment he'd set foot in Curthill Castle. Too bad she hadn't died in the *accident* that had claimed her brother. "If Ross threatens my plans, we'll get rid of him."

"If another Carmichael dies here, old Lionel'll come and take Curthill apart stone by stone, no matter what the king says," Archie whined. "An' next time he'll bring more ships. He'll sink *The Hawk,* and that'll be the end of the trade."

Comyn glared his captain into silence. "Ye sound like an old woman. If it becomes necessary to get rid of Ross, I'll plan things so there's a scapegoat for Lionel to punish."

"M'lord." Felis stood in the doorway of the bedchamber, a vivid study in contrasts. Curly red hair framed brilliant green eyes and a full, pouting mouth set in a face as pale as whey. She was well fed, voluptuous even, her curves seductively delineated by a skintight cotehardie of fine wool. Even used as he was to the sight of her, Comyn felt his loins stir in response to her siren's lure. Small wonder Lady Mary had given up her husband with scarce a struggle. No woman would think herself able to compete with Felis's charms. "Himself's awake."

"And coherent?"

Felis shrugged, the neck of her gown slipping off one shoulder to reveal the swell of her breast. She made no attempt to cover herself. "Come see fer yerself." Her gaze smoldered, lush with promise.

Unfortunately, after two years, her repertoire had become predictable. What he wanted was Siusan. Damn her for having slipped through his fingers after all the trouble he'd gone to to insure she was available. But he had men combing the Highlands, spies in the castle and village. Sooner or later, she'd try to contact her mother or sister, and when she did, he'd have her. "I've nae time for games today, Felis. Tell me what is wrong."

"Ye never ha' time fer me no more," Felis grumbled. "An' I'm sick o' bein' cooped up here night an' day wi' Laird Hammon. Lays there like a stone. Fit fer naught, nae even talkin'."

"If ye're bored, I'm sure Archie'll be glad to oblige."

Archie stepped forward so quickly he tripped, his tongue fair hanging out. "I'll make it good fer ye, Felis. I—"

"Ye disgust me." She dismissed the panting captain with a toss of her hair. "I think ye'd best make time to see *himself.* Fadin' fast, he is. He's sweatin' and his skin's gray like."

Comyn came out of the chair with a roar. "If ye've messed up givin' him his powder..."

"Nay. I've been that careful." Felis shrank back against the doorframe as Comyn flung past her.

"I need him alive another few months." Till he found Siusan and finished the improvements to Sturr More. But when he
reached the canopied bed, Comyn wondered if he'd get even a
fortnight's use out of the pathetic figure huddled beneath the
blankets.

"Megan Sutherland, whatever are ye about?" Chrissy demanded.

Megan started, tried to hide the dingy linen veil behind her
back. 'Twas harder to conceal the fact that she was wearing one
of the maid's coarse russet gowns. "I—I was goin' to the
herb—"

"Ye were not," her cousin snapped, advancing into the small
wall chamber they'd shared since Chrissy had returned to
Curthill a widow two years ago. "Out wi' it."

Megan sighed. "Ross has ordered a bath, and I—"

"Never say ye were thinkin' of sneakin' in there disguised as
a servin' maid?"

"Well . . ."

"Yer mama will have a fit."

"Day after tomorrow we'll be wed," Megan said, determined to brazen this out. "And he'll expect me to bathe him
then."

"'Tis dishonest." Chrissy crossed her arms over her chest.
"Are ye that anxious to get a peek under his clothes?"

"Chrissy! You know I am not." But Megan flushed because
she did want to get Ross out of his clothes.

"Oh, Megan. 'Tis sorry I am that I've given ye a fright of yer
weddin' night. Truly, the pain is not so bad."

"Pain and I are old friends. If I lived through havin' a horse
roll over me, I dare say I'll survive Lord Ross atop me."

"Meg. 'Tis unseemly to joke so."

"'Twasna a jest." Chrissy's tales of her abusive marriage bed
and the pain of seeing her father put aside her mother had made
Megan wary of men, but Ross was different. She'd seen compassion and tenderness in his eyes when they'd first met, witnessed his loyalty to his men last night. Such a man would not
be brutal or faithless. "I love Ross and I am eager to wed him,
but he doesna exactly like me at the moment."

"Oh, Meggie. What ha' ye done now?"

Megan grimaced. Haltingly she told about the meeting on the beach. "I'll soothe his bites by putting some pennyroyal in his bath, but mainly I want to tend his wound. And I know he willna let Meg Sutherland within a hundred yards of it, so..."

"So ye're sneakin' in disguised as a maid."

"Aye." Firmly. "'Tis somethin' I *have* to do." *Because I love him.* Her heart leaped, then clenched painfully. She bit her lip to still its trembling. Somehow she had to thaw his coldness and make him fall in love with her.

"Well, dinna stand there daydreamin'. We've a bath to attend," Chrissy declared.

Megan blinked in surprise but eagerly accepted the unexpected help. Between the two of them, they got her long hair tucked up under the veil and an apron tied over the gown. Megan put her basket of medicines over her arm and led the way. Giggling like naughty bairns, they hurried through a maze of corridors and up the stairs to Ross's tower room, arriving just as the door closed behind the last of the servants laden with steaming buckets of water.

Despite her laughter, Megan hesitated. Did she really have the courage to invade Ross's bath? If he rejected her help, she'd die. But his health came first. Bravely she lifted the latch.

"Wait, Megan. What if he's nak—" Chrissy's words stopped abruptly as the door swung open on a scene that far exceeded Megan's most private fantasies.

He *was* naked.

Or so nearly so that Megan's eyes widened and the air left her lungs in a noisy whoosh.

Sweet Mary, he was... magnificent.

Clad only in thigh-length linen braies, his back to her, Lord Ross conversed with Owain. The light streaming in through the open window gilded the rippling muscles of his shoulders, back and long, heavily corded legs, brought out the reddish cast in the dark hair that lightly furred his big body.

Mist rose from the huge wooden tub, lending an otherwordly quality to the scene. He looked like a pagan warrior about to participate in some ancient ritual, Megan thought. Suddenly she wanted to be part of it. Wanted to go to him, wanted to touch the sweat-sheened muscles of his chest, wanted to feel those strong arms wrap around her. A sweet ache blossomed low in her belly, spreading a melting heat through her veins, until her breasts tingled and her knees turned to jelly.

"Look away." Chrissy grabbed her from behind, spinning her so they both faced the doorway.

"Why did you do that?" Megan grumbled.

"To keep ye from makin' a fool of yerself," Chrissy whispered in her ear. "'Tis nae seemly that ye see him so."

"I didna see anythin'... private," Megan insisted. But her face was hot with the knowledge that she'd wanted to. For the first time in her life, she'd wanted...

"What is the meaning of this intrusion?" Owain demanded, coming to tower over them.

Megan started to answer, but Chrissy stepped in front of her. "We're here to assist wi' m'lord's bath," Chrissy began, but he was having none of that.

"Lord Ross does not require yer services," the Welshman snapped. "Nor does he need an audience," he added to the other men milling about the chamber.

Megan's heart fell as, one by one, Ross's men began to file out. She cast Chrissy a desperate glance. "I canna leave," she mouthed at her cousin.

Chrissy nodded, took hold of Lord Owain's arm and tugged so that he had to turn away from Megan to attend her words. Whatever she whispered made the man frown, but Megan could have kissed Chrissy for her quick diversion. Nor was Ross watching. He'd stepped into the wooden tub the servants had brought and lay back, head resting on the rim, eyes closed in blissful repose.

Surely 'twas a good omen, a sign the Fates were with her. Megan dropped to her knees and scuttled under the bed like a crab, pushing the medicine basket before her. Dust motes billowed about her, making her nose twitch.

Oh, no. Sneeze now, and she'd give the game away. Megan lay on her stomach, nostrils pinched shut, breath held as she fought the tickle in the back of her throat. From beneath the bed, she watched Chrissy's slipper-clad feet march out the door, followed the progress of Owain's booted ones as he approached the tub.

"I think someone should look at that shoulder," he said.

Someone will... as soon as you leave.

"I wouldna trust anyone here to tend it," Ross said in a hard voice that deepened Megan's despair.

"According to Lady Chrissy, the Lady Megan is a skilled herb woman and healer," Owain offered.

"Well, this is a first. You actually speakin' to a Scots noblewoman wi'out bein' forced to."

"'Tis a measure of my concern for you," Owain muttered.

"I've had worse hurts and survived."

Owain's snort reflected Megan's own annoyance. *Arrogant fool.* Did he think he was invincible? 'Twould serve him right if his refusal to trust her led to his wound festering, she seethed, but her newly awakened heart knew it for a lie. She'd not rest till she'd treated his wound.

"I appreciate your concern," Ross went on in that same cool, controlled voice. *Did the man never let down his guard, even with his own people?* "But what I need more than nursin' is to find a way out of marryin' that cursed woman."

Cursed! Her? Megan drew in a sharp breath and with it a mouthful of dust. Tears filled her eyes, partly from fighting the urge to cough, mostly from the pain his words had inflicted.

"Well, the lady is comely and clearly no idiot... as you first feared when you saw those puppets," Owain observed.

An idiot! Anger stifled Megan's coughing.

"Playin' with puppets is hardly grounds to repudiate her," Ross muttered. "But there must be some way out of this." Water sloshed as Ross moved in the tub. "Some flaw or imperfection that would give me just cause to repudiate her."

He did not know about her leg. Megan winced as the old insecurities rose up to taunt her. In her mind's eye, she saw her father's strained expression when he'd told her Comyn would not wed her. "No man can be made to accept a crippled wife," he'd sadly pointed out.

I am not a cripple, she wanted to scream. She was an active, useful person. But men did not see that. Even her father had refused to look on her injured leg. Once she'd been his favorite child, but after the accident he had turned away, from her, from the whole family. That, too, was her fault. Her carelessness had cost her brother his life and her clan their laird. The guilt was nearly harder to bear than the throbbing in her leg.

But she had survived both, like the long-suffering heroines of ancient legend, and as a reward the gods were giving her another chance. They had sent Ross to her. Peeking out from under the bed hangings, Megan stared at her prize. As her gaze swept over Ross's face, the bitterness leeched from her soul. She would make him the best wife. That she still had to convince Ross of this troubled Megan only slightly. She *would* succeed.

"You have men watchin' the storage hut?" Ross asked Owain.

"Aye. And the tailor's, too, in case young Lucais returns."

Megan gasped, her own problems vanishing in the face of this new threat. If Lucais should return and fall into Ross's hands, the lad might be forced to divulge Siusan's hiding place.

Owain headed for the door. "Shall I send Davey to you?"

"In a quarter hour," Ross replied, his voice flat and tired now. "I'd soak this bandage off and have time to myself."

"There are guards posted without. You have only to call and they'll come running."

"Think you some crazed Sutherland will scale the tower walls and leap in through the window?" Ross snapped.

"I'd take no chances."

Ross's sigh filled the silence. "I am sorry, Owain. I'm nae used to being coddled and watched like a helpless bairn."

"Not helpless . . . vulnerable. Neither of us can afford to forget that here we are surrounded by enemies." With those quietly spoken but ominous words, he departed.

How best to approach him? Megan wondered, but the sneeze that sneaked up on her took the decision from her. "Achoo!"

"Who is there?" Ross demanded. Water sloshed; steel rasped on wood. "Come out, or I will come after you."

Damn. Damn. Megan slowly inched from under the bed, praying her disguise would fool him long enough for her to treat his wound and escape.

"You!" He exclaimed the instant she emerged from the enshrouding bed hangings. The sword he pointed in her direction faltered briefly, then rose. "Leave the basket and come here."

Her heart beating against her ribs like a trapped bird, Megan slowly crossed the six steps to the tub, concealing both her limp and her dread. Somehow, she'd brazen this out. "M'lord?" she whispered, eyes downcast as befitted a servant.

"What do you here, Megan?" he demanded.

Her head came up, all pretext of meekness driven out by the memory of his accusations. "I should think 'twould be obvious to one as adept at leapin' to conclusions as you are," she snapped. "Since I've sneaked in here, I must have come to kill you."

He blinked, then frowned. "Dinna be pert wi' me."

"Since you dinna trust me, how can you be certain I didna come to do murder?" she chided, warming to the drama.

"You're nae a murderer."

"Just a cursed woman ... an idiot to be scorned and repudiated?" anger pushed her to say.

He frowned, cheeks red. *How satisfying to bring her pompous lord down a peg.* "'Twas a private conversation."

"Not when *I* am the subject under discussion." Megan clicked her tongue. "For shame, m'lord. I thought you wanted truth betwixt us." His deepening flush was not caused by the hot water. Megan suppressed a giggle. *Oh, this was fun.* "The truth is, we are already contracted to wed and we desire each other. Deny it on penalty of addin' another lie to your conscience," she said when he opened his mouth. "Naive I may be, but I am not stupid. 'Twasna hatred that fueled our kisses last night."

Anger glinted in his vivid eyes as he laid the sword down on the floor. "It takes more than lust to make a marriage."

What of love? her heart cried. Pride stilled it. "What of peace? Is peace for both our clans too high a price to pay?"

"You know it isna, or I wouldna be here at all."

Megan pursed her lips. "There is that, but of greater concern, I think, was provin' Papa murdered Lion." Undeterred by his scowl, she knelt beside the tub. "I want the truth, too. All I ask is that you dinna condemn Papa out of hand."

"He is laird here. If he didna do the deed, he knows who did. And then there is your sister's disappearance."

Megan trembled, bit her lip to keep back the secrets she longed to spill. Not yet. "I canna tell you more than I have, but I promise you Siusan never did Lion any harm." 'Twas just the opposite. Lion's death had put Siusan and their bairn in grave danger. "Mayhap after we are wed."

"If you were so anxious to have a husband, why have you not wed before now?" Ross snapped.

"I was waitin' for you." Truthfully. Her heart ached.

"You didna even know me," he growled.

"I . . . Lion spoke of you, often and wi' great pride."

"He did?" He sounded amazed.

Megan drew strength from the softening of his features. "He told me a thousand stories of your youth together. For instance, you got the small scar under your chin durin' joustin' practice when the quintain swung round and unhorsed you. Lion said you were a man of courage, honor and wit . . . the perfect knight."

His mouth thinned to a grim line. "If I'd been perfect I wouldna have let my brother down." Shadows of regret flickered in the depths of his dark eyes. "If you'll leave."

"Nay." Megan placed a hand on his right arm where it lay along the rim of the tub. "I'd tend your wound." Beneath her fingers, thick muscles knotted and a shiver passed from him into her. Desire chased the ghosts from his gaze, turned it dark and smoky. He might not trust her, but he still wanted her.

His smoldering eyes ignited a spark deep inside Megan. With a wisdom as old as Eve, she knew passion could bind him to her . . . for a time. Logic told her desire alone would not be enough to win so complex a man for all time. To accomplish that, she must conquer his mind and heart, as well as his body.

Still a lass had to work with what she had. And passion was a powerful force. The sound of the surf drifting in through the open window mirrored the sudden, surging restlessness in her own blood. She leaned forward, dazed by what he made her feel.

"Meg," Ross whispered, his brain as fogged as the mist that rose from the water, mixing with the intoxicating scent of rosemary and lemons. She was so close he could distinguish the black pupils in her midnight eyes, watch as they dilated with desire, see the moisture bead up along the tempting curve of her mouth as her lips slowly parted. "We shouldna be here like this."

"But I want you." Her words sighed over him like a caress, leaving his skin tingling for her touch.

"Oh, Meg." The tips of his fingers slid into her hair at the temple, dislodging the veil she wore and releasing a spill of bright hair. Straight and shiny as silk, it tumbled about her shoulders, down her back, a few stands falling into the water to tickle his chest. The blond streaks among the brown glowed like newly minted gold in the shaft of sunlight that surrounded them. "I vowed I wouldna do this again," he murmured, his thumb caressing her soft skin.

"Please." Her eyes drifted shut on a low moan that made his pulse pound all the faster.

"I shouldna want you like this."

"'Tis meant to be." Her small hand moved up around his nape, slender fingers tunneling into his hair. "Kiss me again." 'Twas both plea and command. "We both need that."

"God help me, I crave your taste as a dyin' man does air," Ross growled, fighting the hot, needful fire building inside him. He groaned when she swayed closer, her mouth brushing his fleetingly, making them both shudder.

"Good. So good. I never felt this way before," she whispered across his lips, her scent seductive, tantalizing.

Neither had he, and that was part of what scared him. One brief taste, and he hungered for the whole banquet. "I canna...we canna," he began, voice low, raspy with desire and denial.

"What harm can one more kiss do?" She suited action to words before he could begin to name the dangers. Warm, soft, incredibly stirring, her mouth pressed up against his, lips closed in a childish kiss that should not have inflamed but did. Groaning, Ross gave in to forces beyond his control, wrapped his hand around the back of her neck and sealed their mouths together.

Her lips parted for the questing thrust of his tongue, the soft moan that accompanied her tentative rejoinder more rousing than a harlot's practiced skills. Despite her ready response, here was no whore, he fleetingly thought as she followed where he led. Sweet, so sweet. "I want you. God, how I want you," he murmured, raining kisses over her upturned face. She moaned something, assent, denial, he was past caring, intent on possessing the woman who had obsessed him from the first. "That's it, open your mouth for me," he growled, devouring her, his tongue mimicking the more intimate possession to come.

Soon. Soon. He couldn't wait much longer. Deaf and blind to everything but the primitive drive to possess the woman who'd caught fire in his arms, Ross moved to lift her atop him. His arm slipped, his left shoulder struck the side of the tub. "Damn," he cursed between clenched teeth.

She slid from his grasp in a trice, scrambling around to his left side. "Curse me for a fool," she murmured, face still flushed with passion. "Gettin' carried away kissin' you and I forgot entirely why I'd come in the first place."

"To seduce me?" he growled, trying to avoid her grasp.

It was futile; her grip was surprisingly strong yet gentle. "Mmm. 'Twas nice, but I must see to your wound. Hold still, now," she commanded. Before he could shy away, she grabbed the dirk from her belt and neatly sliced through the wet bandage. Tisking, she dropped the blade and peeled back the edges of the linen. "Just as I suspected. 'Tis putrefying. If 'tis nae seen to at once, you could lose the arm."

Despite the hot water, Ross's blood ran cold. "Nay."

"Let me help you. I can save it," she urged.

"It seems I have little choice."

"Have I ever done you a hurt?"

Ross arched one black brow. "What of the fleas?"

"'Twas not done to harm you. I fear I'm a tease."

In more ways than one. Body still humming with frustrated desire, he fought the urge to match his mouth to her smile. *Damn. He was fast losing the battle to resist her.*

"Dinna be such a stubborn lout. You'll be sorry if you dinna let me help." The warning in her expressive eyes was clear.

"Lout, is it? Oh, very well." Warily he watched her run across the chamber for her basket. Her limp was more evident than it had been earlier. "Your leg still pains you?"

She stopped instantly, turned slowly. "Aye." For once, her bright eyes were downcast.

"I regret you were hurt aidin' me last night."

"'Tis naught." She traced the pattern in the carpet with the toe of her leather slipper.

His Megan disconcerted? Nay, she was not his. But she soon would be. The notion was not as disgusting as it should have been. "Has someone seen to it?" he grumbled.

"You are concerned about me." Her smile rivaled the sun streaming in through the window.

Her open adoration increased his discomfort. *Deceiver.* 'Twas a lie of the worst sort to let her think he cared when there could be nothing between them but enmity. Even had she not been a Sutherland, he could never trust a woman who made him lose control as quickly as Megan did. But he was tempted . . . so tempted. Ross shook his head to clear away that tantalizing, forbidden dream. "I thought you wanted to rebandage my shoulder."

"Aye. Of course." She snatched up the basket and advanced on him, limp scarcely noticeable, eyes bright with eagerness.

Ross steeled himself, as much for the ordeal of having his wound prodded as to muster his defenses against his growing attraction to her. *'Tis only lust,* he reminded himself. *And you've dealt with that before.* Still, there was no denying she was different from any woman he had ever met. *Dangerous.*

"Dinna look so bleak," she chided merrily. "I've yet to lose a patient."

"I'm nae afraid," he snapped.

She laughed. *Laughed.* "I promise nae to tease you, if you promise nae to growl at me."

Ross surprised them both by agreeing. It was her laughter, her cursed smiles in the face of his continued hostility that intrigued him. Aye, for a man who'd lived in shadow for the past year, her sunny disposition was heady as a draught of osquebae.

And about as dangerous.

Head bent over her work, she said, "We really do have many things common, do you nae agree? We both value family and honor. We have both suffered the loss of someone dear and—"

"We are very different," Ross interrupted to stem the warmth building in his chest. God curse his weakness. She scared him as few things in life had. Because the yearning to get close to Megan Sutherland was no longer strictly a thing of the flesh.

Her smile dimmed. "I am nae as brave as you..."

"Ha!" he exclaimed, despite his vow to remain aloof. "After last night, I would say you are braver than is wise."

Untrue. If she had not been so terrified of horses, she would have gone with Siusan to see her safe, could at least have sneaked away to visit her poor sister. "You are the brave one. Valiant and strong as the heroes of legend."

He scowled, obviously uncomfortable with his new status. Her giggle was rewarded by a slow smile. It tugged at the corners of his mouth, easing the tautness from his features. "Ah, you are teasin' again."

So he must have looked as a lad, happy and carefree. She'd do almost anything to make him so again. "A failing of mine."

"Your temper and stubbornness are a failin'. The teasin' is quite...enjoyable. At times," he hastily added.

"Stubborn, is it?" Megan arched a brow and reached for a crock of salve. "I prefer to think of myself as determined." Determined to wed him; determined to win his love. "Determined to convince you that we are honest folk. What say you we go into the town and see what is inside this storage hut?"

"Of all the foolish...dangerous..."

"My people would never deny me access to any buildin'..."

"Suppose the men who attacked us last night are still about? Or are guardin' this buildin'? What then?"

"Of course," Megan breathed. "The sailors from *The Hawk* are responsible for all of this. We have to search that hut and make plans to capture them." She jumped up, made for the door.

"Wait." He stood, realized he was naked and sat with a splash. "What about my shoulder?" Anything to get her back here.

Her stricken look, the haste with which she rushed to correct the oversight made him shake his head. She was as impatient as his sire . . . as Lion had been.

Ah, Lion. He grieved for his brother, yet suddenly found himself hoping Megan's father had not had him killed. For her sake, he hoped it was renegade sailors from *The Hawk.*

Another sign she had already bewitched him.

Chapter Seven

"Try to look less like you expected someone to leap out at you wi' a dirk," Megan hissed as she led Ross on a supposedly aimless tour of Curthill village an hour later.

"'Tis exactly what happened last night," Ross reminded her.

"It makes us look suspicious."

"I *am* suspicious."

"Well, *try* to look less like a thief-taker." Her voice was steady, but her pulse beat as quickly as his own, her small hand riding the back of his wrist in courtly fashion. Unlike the ladies he'd known at court, Megan was gloveless, her slender fingers tanned and lightly callused, and her green wool gown was far simpler than any Edinburgh lady's. He almost believed the guileless picture she presented, eyes wide and curious, face smooth as cream, hair as bright and shiny as a new-minted coin.

Almost. Megan was as good at playacting as any court lady, her smile easy despite the tension radiating from her body into his. Aye, she was more skilled at it even than Rhiannon had been. Wrenching his troubled gaze away from her compelling one, Ross eyed the alleys shadowed by thick gray fog.

Did they conceal the men who'd crossed swords with his last night? "I should have brought more men," Ross muttered.

"Ten men is more than enough. Why, I usually come alone, or wi' only Chrissy. You wouldna want the Sutherlands thinkin' my betrothed was cowardly." She slanted him a teasing glance, leaned closer to whisper, "If you glower so fiercely, no one'll believe you've fallen in love wi' me, m'lord."

Ross's traitorous heart did a slow roll. "Is that what I've done?" He wouldn't. He couldn't. But...

"Aye. Why else would a Carmichael and a Sutherland be strollin' about arm and arm, gazin' into each other's eyes like Tristan and Isolde?"

Why indeed? The answer was as complex as what he was beginning to feel for Megan. Desire, certainly. Respect, grudgingly. But love? Nay, what love he'd had to give had been squandered on Rhiannon. Her betrayal had killed all the softness inside him. What he felt now was white-hot, gut-wrenching lust. That he could control. More difficult, more dangerous was the subtle way Megan clouded his senses. "Romantic nonsense."

"You canna call the folklore and legends nonsense. They are an important part of who we were... our shared past. We Highlanders are a fierce people, too often driven apart by greed, anger and jealousy. 'Tis our past that binds us together."

Ross cocked his head, his eyes narrowed thoughtfully. "I never thought of it that way," he said. "As bard, your stories keep your clan together."

"Tryin' to has been my life's work." Up to now.

"What will happen if you leave?"

If, not when. That hurt nearly as much as the thought of abandoning her duties. "There is a lad—" Lucais, actually "—who has shown remarkable skill as a storyteller. He'll take my place when I leave Curthill. To that end, I have begun writin' down many of the tales." Because Lucais was not here to commit them to memory and she had so much yet to teach him.

"Mmm." Dismissively. *Rude man.* "No wonder you find this... this bit of playactin' so easy."

Megan dragged in a stunned breath. "You're sayin' that I no longer know the difference between truth and fable?" She did, felt too keenly the weight of the two lies she'd been forced to tell him. 'Twas too late to turn back. Too dangerous. Shaking off regret, she said, "Fine, here is the story, then. We fell in love at our first meetin' and are eager to wed." *True, for her.* "I am showin' you about the village. You are glad to meet my kinsmen."

She was good. Very good, Ross conceded cynically. Not a trace of dishonesty tainted her flawless features. Proof that she was a master at the thing he most despised . . . lying.

Obviously the villagers believed what they saw, for they turned out in numbers to greet their lady and her intended. Ross smiled though his gut rolled, complimented the blushing lasses, accepted cups of ale from their menfolk and even kissed a bairn or two. Their little troop finally wound its way around to the other side of the village.

"There is the hut Sim saw the goods going into." Owain gestured toward the small building across the street.

Ross squinted, picking out details through the shifting eddies of thick fog. Perfect for hiding stolen loot. One story, made of stone, the hut sat alone at the edge of the village. Its back abutted the cliff face. A single door opened onto the rutted street; there were no windows.

The back of Ross's neck prickled as the ten men handpicked for this spread out and started toward the building. The tingle became a warning scream when the door opened and two big, burly men stepped out. Beneath their dark tunics, he caught the gleam of chain mail, noted the swords belted low and ready.

"Good day," Megan chirped, shocking all the men motionless as she tripped forward, her skirts held gracefully out of the dirt, a sweet, guileless smile on her face. "I'm Lady Megan. I dinna recall meetin' you before."

The hard-faced pair exchanged uneasy glances. Clearly their instructions had not included dealing with the lady of Curthill. The older one finally grunted a greeting. "Thought ye only came down to heal the sick. There's no one here needs healin'."

"I am showin' my betrothed about the village," Megan said smoothly, then she suddenly cried out as though in pain, put a hand to her head and started to crumple. It happened so quickly Ross barely had time to catch her before she landed in the dirt.

"Megan!" Ross held her close against his stumbling heart. "What is it? Where are you hurt?"

"I've fainted, you dolt," she whispered, eyes closed, lips scarcely moving. "I need to be taken inside and revived."

Ross frowned but played along. "Owain. My lady's taken ill. Open yonder door and I'll carry her within." As he strode toward the hut, Ross brushed past the stunned guards. "You there, fetch wine, cool cloths, the village herb woman." Ross, Megan and Owain were inside by the time the soldiers recovered their wits. "Keep them out," Ross murmured over his shoulder.

Pivoting, Owain tried to close the door in the guards' faces. The older one sputtered a protest and tried to wedge his boot in the doorway. "Ye heard m'lord. Fetch wine and cool water for the Lady Megan." Owain stomped down so hard on the offending foot that the man screamed and hopped back clasping his toes. To the Carmichaels, Owain called, "Let none enter to disturb m'lord."

When Owain closed the door and barred it, Ross released the breath he'd been holding and gently set Megan on her feet.

"See, I told you there was naught here." She turned in a slow circle that took in the table littered with dirty bowls and cups, the pallets on the floor in one corner near a smoldering fire. The place stank of smoke, sour ale and unwashed bodies, but such was usual in peasant huts.

"What is this?" Ross made for the tall wooden cupboard set against the wall opposite the door. "Let's see what's behind it." Putting his good shoulder to the piece, he shoved. It didn't budge, even when Owain lent his strength to the effort.

"Is it nailed to the floor?" Megan asked.

"To a section of wall, more like." Cursing the lack of time, Ross quickly felt along the edge of the cupboard. Near the top, he found the mechanism that released the catch. Hinges groaned, stale air whooshed out to slap their faces as he and Owain swung the heavy piece about, revealing a gaping hole in the wall.

"So, ho!" Owain exclaimed.

Megan gasped and drew closer, apprehension racing down her spine. As Ross stepped through the doorway, she lifted her hand to hold him back, to forestall whatever discoveries lay beyond. *Please, God, do not let us find something bad within,* she prayed.

"Ah, torches. How convenient." Ross's voice echoed as hollowly as the emptiness inside her. Flint grated, light flared, sending pale yellow fingers snaking through the cavern beyond the door, revealing all its secrets.

A treasure trove.

Not just furniture, though there was plenty of that, but casks of wine and salt. Farther inside they found bags of spices, wool and grain. Chests overflowing with silver bowls and golden cups sat alongside bolts of silk, velvet and samite.

"'Tis worth a fortune," Owain whispered.

"Aye," Ross grimly replied, his narrowed eyes reflecting Megan's own deepest fears.

"I dinna understand." But she did. Megan pressed her fingers to her lips to hold back a moan. "These things canna be part of the trade. They're nae the sort who would or could be repaired by the craftsmen in the village."

"Exactly." The torch spilled light and shadow over his grim, determined face. "'Tis wreckers' loot. I'd stake my life on that."

"Nay." The moan clawed at the back of her throat, bringing tears to her eyes. "It isna Papa's doin'." Ross's grunt of disagreement sent her heart to her boots. "What do you intend to do?" *Prove your father guilty.* The words were clear as the blue fury blazing in his eyes. "Nay." Turning, Megan stumbled away.

Ross caught her at the door to the cave, snatched her off her feet. The breath left her in a whoosh, but that didn't stop her from fighting. He grunted as her heel connected with his shin and her pointy elbow plowed into his ribs. "Witch," he growled in her ear. Trapping both her arms with his, he clasped her against the hard length of his body.

Megan shivered in his iron grip, but it was not for herself she feared. She had to see her father, had to get to the bottom of this. He was not guilty. *He wasn't.* Desperation lent strength to her limbs as she struggled to get free. 'Twas like fighting a mountain. "Turn me loose or I'll scream. I swear I—" Somehow he got a wide hand over her mouth, cutting off her words, but not her determination. She sank her teeth into him.

"Damn you!" Ross set his own teeth against the pain. With his thumb and forefinger, he applied subtle pressure to the hinge of her jaw, opening it. She let go for an instant then came back after him. Cursing, Ross grabbed her upper arms and spun her around to face him. "Enough!" He gave her a little shake, trying to ignore the tears welling in her magnificent eyes. "Think what will happen if you run out of here now...like this."

Miracle of miracles, she stilled. He could almost read the thoughts chasing across her expressive face. Shock. Anger. Fear. But not for herself, he guessed. Nay, her thoughts were all for that worthless father of hers. A sigh rippled through her, ripe with sorrow and pain that muted Ross's anger.

"I...I have to see him," she murmured. "Have to know the truth." She looked past Ross to the treasure filling the cave. The fight seemed to drain from her, so she sagged in his grip.

Oh, Megan. If only he could spare her this.

Then she recovered, shoulders squaring. Pure Megan. Shadowed by equal parts sorrow and determination, her eyes lifted to his. "Papa isna responsible for this. Whilst he was busy wi' Felis, the sailors turned his honest trade to evil."

"Lord, you are stubborn." Ross dragged an exasperated hand through his hair. He valued loyalty, but hers exceeded all reason. "No sailors are powerful enough to do such a thing."

"Then it must be Douglas or Archie. Or Comyn. Aye, 'twas Comyn who first brought Douglas's ship here."

"You are as stubborn in your hatred as in your loyalty. Comyn spends most of his time at Shurr More. Just because you dinna like him is no reason to accuse him out of hand."

"You dinna see the evil in him..." *He repudiated me when I lay dying.* "He has the squint eye. Such men are born thieves."

"Superstitious nonsense. We solve naught standin' here arguin' when we both want the same thing...the truth. We will close up the cave, leavin' all as it is and return to the castle as though naught had happened."

"But—"

"Patience," Ross counseled. Though his own was wearing thin, he knew the value of planning, of moving slowly and cautiously. "Do you know where your father keeps his papers?" He felt the shudders that racked her body as she struggled to come to grips with this potentially devastating discovery. "Cry if it helps." He hugged her closer, gently stroked her back.

Beneath his touch, she shivered again, then stiffened her spine. "Nay. Tears willna clear Papa." Drawing in a ragged breath, she raised her head and asked what they were looking for.

Brave. Had he ever known a woman as brave and loyal? "Records showin' where these goods came from." Manifests from the ships Eammon had wrecked. But Ross hadn't the heart to say so.

"Mama keeps the accounts for the castle, since Papa doesna read. I doubt he'd have papers in his rooms. Felis's skills dinna extend to readin' and cipherin'. Wait . . ." She pressed a hand to his chest. "Douglas is our man. He captains the ship that carries the goods back and forth, and those *were* his sailors who attacked you. Besides, he's a big man with cruel, shifty eyes."

"I thought of that. Not the nonsense about his eyes," he added cynically. "When do you think *The Hawk* will return?"

"Normally, it drops off the goods to be repaired, stays in the harbor for a time to take on provisions and those things that are ready for sale, then leaves. The fact that Douglas is gone makes him seem all the more guilty." Hope danced in her eyes.

Worry clouded Ross's. What if Douglas did not return until after the wedding? The marriage itself didn't trouble him as it had before, but once they were wed, he'd have no excuse to linger at Curthill and search for the truth about Lion's death.

"Let us return and lay this before Papa."

Ross shook his head. "We dinna have enough proof with which to confront him. Mayhap when he comes down to dinner, my man could search his rooms."

"I dinna want to confront him, I want him to help us. Besides, he hasna been to the hall in weeks."

Suddenly Ross was anxious to see the man he'd been reluctant to meet. The phantom laird. Something evil was afoot in Curthill, and he had the uneasy feeling that the treasure cave was only part of it. Apprehension trickled icy fingers down his spine. "You must promise to let me proceed at my own pace in this."

"Not if I think you're goin' too slowly."

"This is a dangerous business...men's business," he snapped.

"'Tis my family's business," she countered.

"M'lord. We'd best close up the door and be off before yon guards become more suspicious," Owain interjected.

Ross nodded but didn't take his eyes from Megan's dark, challenging gaze. Her fearlessness frightened him, goaded him into saying, "You are my betrothed wife, and so under my rule. You will do as I say and keep out of this."

"And you will learn that Highland women are nae as biddable as Lowlanders," was all Megan said before turning away.

"It seems ye ha' won another game," Comyn conceded.

"'Twas a hard-fought match, the outcome uncertain until the very end," Ross graciously replied, leaning back in his chair. They were seated before a window in the hall, a cup of ale at their elbows to counteract the warmth of the afternoon sun.

Across the room in a chair by the hearth, Megan gave serious thought to smashing one of the cups over Ross's head. Damn him, what was he waiting for? They'd been back for hours, and Ross had done nothing beyond inquire of Archie if her father was expected down for the evening meal.

Archie had jumped, cast Comyn what seemed to her a suspicious glance. "Dinna ken. But I'll say ye were askin'."

Megan glared at Ross. Smug, pompous male sitting in the sun like a fat cat, lapping up ale cozy as you please with the man who was...to her way of thinking...a prime suspect.

Comyn had squinty eyes and a cynical nature beneath those bland smiles of his. Her mother had claimed 'twas because his family had been killed and he'd been driven from his home, forced to seek aid from the Sutherlands. But there was more to it than that, Megan thought, studying her former betrothed's profile.

The match between Comyn and herself had been made when she was a babe. She'd seen little of Comyn until his family was wiped out by raiding MacKays when she was nine. That he had seemed in no hurry to wed pleased her, involved as she was in learning all Old Tam could teach her about the ancient stories and legends.

Physically he had never attracted her, but now his close-set eyes and lean face gave him a weasely look. But her dislike was more than skin-deep. Inside, Comyn was not a nice person. If he had been, he'd not have discarded her when she was laid low . . . lying abed after the accident, afraid she'd never walk again.

Comyn's predatory gaze was trained on Ross with an intensity that made Megan shiver. He had the look of a beast sizing up a rabbit he planned to kill and eat. That Ross was no weak rabbit brought Megan little comfort. Comyn's expression did, however, stoke the fires of her fertile imagination.

Douglas was not from Curthill. If he was wrecking ships and storing the booty in the village, he'd need the help of someone who was known and respected hereabouts. Someone like Comyn. Aye, she was sure Comyn had taken advantage of her father's preoccupation with Felis to feather his own nest.

Papa should be told of this and never mind his standing orders not to disturb him and Felis. This was more important than his vile obsession with that whore. Mayhap this would shock him into taking an interest in his clan again. Mayhap he'd look at her mother, really look at her, and realize that despite their differences, he'd been wrong to turn aside from his wife.

Inside Megan, the ball of misery eased slightly. She laid the quill across the list of guidwives' tales she'd been writing. *'Tis cruel to draw a straw in front o' a cat,* the old saw read. Wise words, but she was not being led on by false hopes; she was following the truth. All she had to do was sneak upstairs . . .

"I'd expected the Highlands to be cooler," Ross said so sharply Megan's head snapped around. He spoke to Comyn, but watched her closely, a warning glint in his eyes. *Defy me and I'll drag you back by your hair.*

Ha! He was not the violent sort. Still she didn't relish a scene. Much as it killed her, Megan smiled blandly, picked up her pen and began working. *Gang warily,* were the first words her eyes fell on. Go prudently, she would . . . till she could sneak away.

"The clime along the coast is deceptively mild," Comyn said to Ross. "The mountains rise abruptly a short ways from here and there's snow on their highest peaks even in summer. The true Highlands are bleak and stark above the tree line, heavily forested in the passes. 'Tis nae a hospitable land. Many's the traveler—and the invader—who's been done in by it."

"Your warning's duly noted." Satisfied that Megan had understood *his* warning, Ross looked back at Comyn. He had two men watching the hut, a dozen searching up and down the coast for *The Hawk,* and two outside the tailor's in case Lucais came back. There was nothing else he could do until dinner, when Eammon would hopefully leave his tower long enough for Wee Wat to search for a ship's manifests or other papers. "I've no urge to go muckin' about in your wild Highlands. Is your estate up there?"

Comyn snorted. "I've a wee tower on a bit o' scrub land Eammon gave me," he grumbled, picking up the scattered chessmen.

Ross understood Comyn's bitterness ... not because, as a second son, he himself had stood to inherit nothing. Nay, 'twas because he was now heir to the very estate he had loved from boyhood. Cruel fate to give him his heart's wish at the cost of his brother's life. He'd found the price too high.

"Will ye gi' me a chance to even the score?" Comyn asked, and Ross nodded, though in truth he had won twice and MacDonnel not at all. The Highlander played a good game, the outcome hanging in the balance until the last moment. Then Comyn grew impatient, made the fatal error of mistaking Ross's slow style of play for stupidity. Comyn went on the offensive, overextended himself and fell into the trap Ross had set many moves before.

Chess was a good gauge of a man's character, Ross thought. Comyn, for instance, was a more complex man than he'd first seemed, bold and canny, yet an honorable opponent. The longer they played, the more certain Ross became that Comyn was not involved in this wrecking business. The brief flashes of temper when the game did not go Comyn's way hinted at strong passions carefully held in check. This insight pleased Ross, too.

He appreciated the strength it took to control rather than release anger, for he'd developed that skill himself.

Would that Megan had more control over her impulses, he thought, glancing briefly to where she sat, her head bent over a parchment, her quill busily scratching. Committing the clan legends to paper, no doubt. It still seemed a foolish task. Writing down lies to corrupt the next generation.

"Ye're a much more taxin' opponent than Megan," Comyn commented, drawing Ross back to their game.

"Chess is an unusual game for a woman." But then, Megan was unusual in so many ways... not all of them bad.

"Eammon doted on her when she was a child, treated her like the son he feared he'd never ha'."

"I must confess, at first I wasna anxious to meet Eammon, but his continued absence has made me curious about the man. Think you he'll join us for dinner?"

Comyn's hand hesitated over the board, then moved a rook out to challenge Ross's. "Who can say? He's become... unpredictable. What did ye want to know about him?"

Ross shrugged. "Nothin'. Everythin'. It pays to know your enemy," he replied with less than his usual candor, used to keeping his own counsel.

Indeed it does. Comyn scanned Ross's chiseled features. How much had Carmichael seen in the storage hut? Had he gotten beyond the cupboard to the cave? According to the guards who'd come running to Archie, Ross and Megan had only been inside a short time and had disturbed nothing. Still Comyn could not shake the uneasy feeling that Ross knew something.

Archie had gone mad. "We ha' to get rid o' him," the captain had cried, wringing his leathery hands over the news.

"Oh, aye," Comyn sneered. "And bring both Lionel Carmichael and King David down on us like the hounds of hell. Nay, we'd best wait and see how much he knows."

Thus the chess game to feel Ross out. So far, the only thing Comyn had learned was that Ross played a cautiously lethal game. "If Eammon is yer enemy, why agree to wed Megan?"

"To keep the king from outlawin' my clan."

How noble. Comyn's lip threatened to curl. But then, Ross could afford to be noble; he was heir to his sire's vast estates, not an orphan forced to live on the charity of others. Ross had not found himself in love with the younger sister yet betrothed to wed the elder. "Ye'll find Megan a handful," he said.

Ross's scowl took Comyn aback. "Unfortunately a sharp tongue isna grounds for repudiatin' a wife," Carmichael murmured.

Nay, but her lame leg is, Comyn started to say, then realized Ross must not know. Instinctively he weighed the knowledge. How best could he use it? Much as he wanted Ross and Megan gone from Curthill, if she desired this marriage, 'twould be pleasant to snatch her prize away. He owed her that much for keeping Siusan's whereabouts a secret.

Of course, Megan was already paying. Her crippled leg and her anguish over Eammon's withdrawal had been gratifying. All of them were paying the price for having thwarted Comyn . . . without even knowing it. Eammon for having refused to fight the MacKays for Comyn's property, Mary for having saved Megan's life instead of letting her die in the accident staged to remove both Megan and Ewan from the scene and leave Siusan Eammon's sole heir. Comyn hugged that thought to himself. The fact that they did not know they were victims made his revenge all the sweeter. The only fish that had escaped his subtle net was Siusan.

"Comyn, is aught wrong?"

Comyn refocused his attention to Ross's frowning face. Despite Lion's claims that his brother was the canniest man in Scotland, Comyn found him slow and plodding as an old man. And a snoop into the bargain. Ross did not deserve to know about Megan . . . yet. Not unless Comyn saw a way to use it to his advantage.

"Nay, I'm just puzzlin' over my next move." Too true. How to find out if Ross knew about the storage hut? As he lifted a pawn from the board, a Carmichael streaked around the screen separating the hall from the entryway and skidded to a halt.

"M'lord! Lady Megan's gone to see her father!"

Ross's head whipped toward the hearth and the empty chair. "Damn her." Leaping up, he strode from the hall. The two hard-faced Carmichaels who had been lounging in the hall fell in behind their lord, a reminder of how closely he was guarded.

Damn that Megan, Comyn echoed. Seeing years of work and planning in jeopardy, he sprinted after Ross. "I doubt Eammon will see her." Felis had been well drilled on how to discourage visits from Megan and Lady Mary, he thought as they hurried through the entryway hung with the shields of long-dead Sutherland warriors and down the stone steps to the courtyard.

As they neared the newer of the towers, Megan's voice came clear. "Out of my way. You have nae right to detain me."

Comyn surged into the building right behind Ross and found her facing down a pair of Carmichael soldiers and one of Comyn's own mercenaries. "But I do, Megan," Ross growled, hands on hips. Comyn was startled by how much Ross resembled Lion in a rage.

Typically, Megan did not back down. "Let me by."

"Nay." Despite the fire in his eyes, Ross's voice was calm. "I thought we had agreed to do this my way."

"I am doin' what I must to save my clan," she retorted, and in that instant, Comyn knew they'd found his treasure.

"Of all the stupid, childish..." Ross shuddered, fists clenched at his sides. "Be glad you are nae yet my wife. I'd...I'd beat you black-and-blue for your impertinence."

Megan quivered as though his words had been a blow, then squared her shoulders. "You willna lay a hand on me. Not now. Not after we're wed. Think you a wife powerless, m'lord? Nay, a wife oversees the preparation of her husband's food." She smiled thinly. "There are *ways* of punishin' abusive husbands."

"Witch," Ross replied. "Tamper wi' my food, and you'll be worse than bruised. Now, come back to the hall." He reached for her, but she ducked under his arm and bolted up the stairs.

Quick for a crippled lass, Comyn thought darkly. How the hell was he going to keep her and Ross from seeing Eammon? One look at the pathetic husk he'd become, and they'd know...

"Whatever is goin' on?" trilled a feminine voice that seemed to vibrate in the open cavern of the circular stairwell, halting Megan's flight and Ross's pursuit. *Felis.* Comyn could have kissed the bare feet that appeared on the steps above Megan. "Why, it's little Megan," Felis drawled, descending another step, revealing shapely calves, dimpled knees. "Yer Da thought 'twas yer voice disturbed us." Another step. 'Twas so quiet you could hear the sleek, seductive slide of naked thighs brushing together.

Lord. Was Felis completely nude? How inventive, Comyn thought as Megan gasped and drew back, face whiter than the snow that crested the Highland peaks. The guards craned their necks, trying to see what the curve of the stairwell concealed. Even Ross seemed spellbound by the performance Felis was staging.

Not naked, but nearly so, Comyn saw as Felis slipped into view, her ample charms framed by a thigh-length fall of tousled red hair and the wisp of a chemise she clutched to her heart. The nipples of her full breasts peeped through the thin linen shield, the edge of which flirted with the tops of her thighs, allowing tantalizing glimpses of her fiery thatch.

Stupid she might be, but Felis knew well how to paint a carnal picture. Comyn smiled and relaxed fractionally.

"Oh, my." Felis's red lips rounded. "Are ye all come to see Eammon? I'm afraid he's...sleepin'. We've had a busy morn." Through lowered lashes, her exotic green eyes measured each man, lingering at last on Ross. *Trust Felis to single out the man with the money and power.* "Ye understand how 'tis when passion flows hot and sweet, m'lord," she said in a low, husky gush.

If he did not, there were a half-dozen man with tongues fair hanging out who did, Comyn thought, smiling faintly. Much as he begrudged giving Felis a share of their profits, at the moment she was certainly earning her keep.

"*I* understand perfectly," Megan snapped. "Men are as stupid and easily led as any other animal when they're in rut. Tell my father I'll be back later." Head high, she marched down the stairs and left, slamming the iron-banded door behind her.

"If ye'll excuse me, too, m'lords. 'Tis a bit...drafty." Felis's exit was as graceful and sensual as her arrival, all flowing red hair and provocative bits of bare skin.

Ross cleared his throat. "At least that one is honest about her intentions," he grumbled before exiting the tower.

Comyn rubbed his chin thoughtfully. Megan had not exactly threatened to poison her betrothed, but she'd come close enough for his purposes. Here was the perfect way to be rid of Ross and Megan . . . without incriminating himself or Archie. All he needed was to find Megan's medicine chest and select what he wanted.

It would be child's play. When he'd first toyed with the idea of usurping Eammon's power, Comyn had subtly questioned Lady Mary about her potions and powders. Pleased by his interest, she had spilled all she knew, never suspecting that the information would be used to turn her husband into a thrall, a figurehead Comyn could manipulate with none the wiser.

To keep Lionel Carmichael from retaliating, Comyn would conduct a trial in Eammon's name, find Megan guilty and hang her, then send both bodies to the Carmichaels. Why not find her guilty of Lion's murder, as well? 'Twould wrap everything up neatly and leave him free of all constraints. Before she died, he'd have to get Siusan's hiding place from Megan, but he did not doubt he could pry the secret from her . . . mayhap by promising to help her escape the Carmichaels' retribution.

Chapter Eight

When Megan entered the hall for dinner an hour later, her nerves felt as brittle as the silver thread that gave her blue samite gown its stiffness and sparkle.

"What ails ye?" Chrissy asked.

Megan fair itched with the urge to tell her cousin about the treasure and this latest crisis. One look at the lines life had etched around Chrissy's once soft face and she changed her mind. What with her abusive husband and two dead babes, poor Chrissy had suffered enough. Besides, 'twas not Megan's way to burden others with her problems. "I am but nervous."

"Relax," Chrissy whispered in her ear as they made their way through the crowd to the head table. "Likely Lord Ross ha' forgotten all about the incident wi' the sand fleas this morn."

To tell the truth, so had Megan. Their meeting on the beach seemed a lifetime ago, his anger over the fleas tiny compared with the danger they now faced. And she'd only made things worse by trying to see her father. "I hope he can forgive all my transgressions today."

"How was your day?" her mother asked as Megan took her seat.

"Fine." Megan was proud she could keep the turmoil inside from making her voice crack. "And yours?"

"I kept busy wi' preparations for the weddin'." Lady Mary sighed, expression stark as she stared out over the hot, noisy hall. "Other than that, my day went well."

Her mother was lying, too, Megan realized with a start. Nor was this the first time they'd sat together at a meal or over their needlework and fed each other full of falsehoods. Not malicious lies. Half-truths that sidestepped some unpleasant or hurtful subject . . . out of love and a desire to protect.

I do not care that your father keeps a mistress, her mother had said time and again, though the pain showed in her eyes.

I am content to be seanachaidh *of our clan and do not need a husband or bairns,* Megan had said, when, in fact, every newborn she helped birth made her ache to hold her own sweet babe.

Megan had always seen such wee fictions as a kindness. *Why worry Mama?* she'd think and deny that her bad leg hurt. *Mama will think me disloyal if I say I miss Papa,* she'd reason and hide her sorrow. Now Megan wondered if mayhap Ross was right about the evil of a life built on shared lies. "Did you hear about our encounter wi' Felis?" she bluntly asked.

"Megan!" Her mother gasped, put a hand to her heart. "Never speak that . . . that slut's name in my presence."

"But she does exist," Megan said gently. "Mayhap if we talk about her, about what has happened to us since she came . . ."

"You think 'tis my fault he took up wi' her." Her mother's lower lip trembled. "I ken you idolized him, always thought I was too stiff and cold. But you dinna understand what 'twas like to leave everything familiar and come here. Curthill was rougher then than 'tis now, filled wi' half-wild savages. There were no ladies even for me to talk wi', naught but men who lived for fishin' and huntin' and fightin'. Your father loved me well enough at bedtime and ignored me between times. If I turned cold, 'tis only because he left the fire untended."

"Mama," Megan exclaimed, shocked by the outburst. Not for anything would she admit that at times she *had* blamed her mother for the estrangement. "I know how exasperatin' Papa can be."

"Exasperatin'?" Her regal mother snorted. "Even when he deigns to come down, he looks through me like I wasna there."

Oh, Mama. Megan wanted to hug her mother and tell her everything would be all right, but 'twould be the greatest lie of all. Unless a miracle happened, their lives would never be right. "I am very sorry, Mama." For what Papa did and for stirring up this hive of bees. Ross was wrong. The truth could do more damage than a lie. "I—I have nearly finished listin' the Ancient Saws," she said lamely. Anything to change the subject.

"I'm glad something good came of this miserable day." Her mother's eyes glinted with unshed tears. "When I think of Eammon up there in his tower with *her* whilst I am forced to endure the snickers and knowing glances of our guests..."

Megan groaned. Once started, her mother seemed unable to stop, years' worth of bitterness and misery flowing nonstop from her pinched lips. It was going to be a long evening.

"Ah, good eve, ladies." Lord Nigel plopped down in the chair at Lady Mary's other side. From his flushed red face and unsteady hand as he reached for the wine, 'twas clear he'd spent his day drinking. "The laird willna be down for dinner," his lordship added before upending the cup into his mouth.

Her mother gave an anguished gasp. "You spoke wi' him?"

"Nay. Had it from Archie." Lord Nigel gestured to the trestle table a row back where the captain held court with his circle of toadies. They weren't bad men, just weak ones who curried favor by telling Archie how clever he was. Only, Archie was not clever. Strong as the tempered steel of a claymore, but like a sword, he needed direction.

Comyn, on the other hand, was far more than he seemed, Megan thought, her gaze narrowing as she spied her former betrothed slip into the room. Far cannier, far more... sneaky. He did not enter boldly or openly. Nay, he came covertly, gliding through the shadows at the edge of the hall like a snake creeping up on a mouse.

Apprehension slithered down Megan's spine. If there was something evil afoot at Curthill, she'd wager every page in her precious book of stories and legends that Comyn was behind it.

"Comyn, ye are well come," Lord Nigel boomed. "Sit wi' me."

As he complied, Comyn glanced at Megan. The smug glint in his pale eyes turned her apprehension to dread. He *was* up to something, the sly scum. But how to prove it?

"Oh, Meg," Chrissy whispered. "'Tis Lord Ross lookin'..."

"Fit to chew nails or my hide," Megan murmured. Still she could not help but compare his entry with Comyn's. Even though he was a stranger here, Ross strode into the hall like a conqueror, strong, lithe and commanding. The crimson-and-black surcoat he wore over a red tunic was the perfect foil for his ebony hair and tanned skin. How handsome he was . . . and how angry. Somehow she had to find a way to turn that enmity toward Comyn.

"Lady Mary." Ross inclined his head and took his seat, somehow managing to avoid looking at Megan as he sat beside her.

Ire burned away Megan's uncertainty. She'd not let him treat her as her father had her mother. Plucking the small eating knife from her belt, she buried the point in the table a scant inch from where Ross's hand lay open on the linen cloth.

"By all that's holy!" He snatched his hand to safety and flexed his fingers. "Why did you do that?"

"I willna be ignored in my own hall."

His eyes widened. "Are you mad?"

"You wanted truth between us, m'lord," she said, sweet and low, for his ears alone. "And that is the truth."

He opened his mouth, then closed it. His lips twitched with something that looked suspiciously like suppressed humor. "You've a clever mind and a sharp tongue."

"I told you we were well matched."

"Indeed?" The wry smile that spread over his face softened his features, transformed them. Gentleness. Tenderness. What had happened to cause him to hide such things even from himself? Then just as quickly, how could she heal what had hurt him? Mayhap with the truth he valued so highly.

"Indeed." Megan let go the breath she'd been holding. "While you are still in charity with me, I'd apologize," she whispered. "For tryin' to see Papa this afternoon. But—"

"Wi' you, there is always a *but*." He shook his head in exasperation. "Your rashness endangers us all," he growled, low and harsh. "I will handle this."

"*We* will handle this."

"Megan." Under cover of the table, he grabbed her hand. Given his clenched jaw, she expected to have her fingers squeezed until the bones creaked. Instead, he linked them with his. "This is dark, dangerous work. These people are killers."

"But I can help." She tightened her grip on him, her smile never wavering under his scowl. "I know the people, I—"

"Little fool, do you think I want your death on my conscience, too?" he hissed.

"Nor I yours, but—"

"Wine, m'lord?" Ross's squire asked. Megan could have kissed the freckle-faced lad who reached in to fill Ross's cup.

Ross's eyes locked on hers with a determination that nearly made hers falter. "We will continue this discussion later," he announced, and snatched up the wine.

"M'lord, I havena tasted it," the squire sputtered.

"Leave off coddlin' me." He took two swallows, then lowered the vessel and grimaced. "Damn, this stuff is sour as my mood. See if you can find something sweeter." As the squire scurried off, Ross turned his attention back to Megan. His blue eyes stared down at her with blazing intensity. Desire so carefully banked she might not have seen it had she not felt its sensual tug herself. But while she would give hers free rein, his was ruthlessly controlled. At the moment.

Suddenly she felt the urge to test its limits. Glancing at him through her lashes, she murmured, "How is your shoulder?"

Through their joined hands, she felt him tremble. "Dinna look at me like that." His husky voice was at odds with his words; his hand curled protectively around her smaller one.

Megan smiled. "You wanted the truth. I care for you...."

"Nay. You will only end up gettin' hurt." Then lower, "I have naught to give you."

A desperate denial filled her throat, but before she could voice it, he shivered again, released her hand to chafe his arms.

"Does it seem cold in here of a sudden?"

"'Tis hot as blazes, m'lord," his squire replied, coming up behind them. The lad's cheeks were so flushed his freckles had nearly disappeared. "Are ye sickenin' wi' somethin'?"

"I am never sick." Ross passed a hand over his forehead. "But I've a sudden thirst. Where is that wine?"

Megan looked up, her frown meeting the squire's over Ross's black head. She slowly mouthed the word water, sweeping

Ross's face in a single, worried glance. His skin was pale, yet beads of moisture clung to his upper lip. What ailed him? When he'd entered the hall, he'd been as hale and hearty and in command as ever. Now he looked . . . dreadful.

Ross moaned suddenly, shoving back his chair and clutching his belly as he doubled over.

"Owain! Andrew!" cried the squire. "Ross's taken ill."

"Poison! She's poisoned him as she threatened this afternoon," Andrew shouted. Leaping from his chair at a nearby table, he vaulted onto the dais.

"I didna," Megan cried. Yet all thoughts of proving her innocence fled as Ross groaned again. She reached out to help him, but hard hands thrust her aside.

"Away. Leave him alone," Owain bellowed.

"But I can help him." She strained forward, was thrown back so sharply she fell against her chair. Undaunted, she got up, but this time it was Chrissy who restrained her.

"Nay, Meggie. They'll hurt ye."

"I dinna care," Megan cried. "I have to help him."

Her voice was drowned out by the pandemonium that reigned in the hall. Ross's men formed a protective circle around their fallen lord, lifted his writhing body onto their shoulders and carried him from the room.

Megan's heart went with him. If it was poison, she might never see him alive again.

"Do somethin'," Andrew shouted to the three other men clustered around the bed where Ross lay shivering beneath a mountain of blankets that failed to warm him. His face was paler than the pillow, his eyes already sunken and shadowed.

"I do not know what to do," Owain cried, fists clenching and unclenching helplessly at his sides.

"Water," Ross rasped. "Throat . . . afire . . . thirsty."

"Here." Davey quickly held a cup to Ross's lips, but he choked on the first swallow. "He canna even drink."

"He's dyin'," Giles whispered. "We ha' to do somethin'."

Owain trembled. "What? Tell me what, and I—"

"Let me in!" The door swung open and Megan burst into the room, followed closely by a red-faced Carmichael.

"She wouldna stay out," the guard said.

"Murderess!" Andrew charged across the room.

Megan trembled but stood her ground, certain that he'd break off the attack before he reached her. He did. But not by choice. He was barely a foot away when Sir Owain caught his arm and dragged him to a halt. Big body quivering with rage and hatred, Sir Andrew snarled, "If Ross dies, I'll kill ye."

"Fine." Megan glared up at the mountain of muscle towering over her. "All I ask is that you let me help him. If he doesna survive, I'll have no wish to live."

"Pretty words, but can ye save him?" Owain asked warily.

I do not know. She hid her fear and her uncertainty. "Aye. We waste precious time. If I wanted him dead, I'd do naught and wait for the poison to claim him."

"So, ye admit he was poisoned," Andrew snarled.

"A blind man could see that." They followed her gaze to the bed where Ross thrashed about, crying out in pain as Davey tried in vain to comfort him. "But at least I know what he was given. I searched the herb room and discovered the powdered autumn crocus missin' from my supplies."

"Ha! The poison was yers," Andrew cried.

Chrissy stepped around Megan and into the breach. "Anyone in the castle could ha' broken the hasp on the medicine chest and taken the cursed stuff," she replied. "Meg didna do it."

"Enough of this nonsense," Megan snapped. "You can stand over me wi' a dirk to my throat, but I am his only hope."

"Let her by," Owain commanded, and a path was instantly cleared to her patient.

"Is there aught I can do?" Davey asked hoarsely.

Megan started to refuse, then realized that she and Chrissy would not be able to keep a man as large and strong as Ross still while they treated him. "Strip him down to his braies," she ordered the squire. "Then tear into strips some of the linen towelin' Chrissy has and bind his wrists and ankles to the bed." That order brought renewed protests, but Megan did not pause in her preparations to counter them. She merely murmured, "He'll injure himself does he continue to flail about." And he'd not like the things that would have to be done to save his life.

Ross turned his head on the sweat-soaked pillow. His eyes darkened with fury when he saw her. "Witch," he gasped.

Megan stiffened, afraid he'd order her away and his men, in their stupidity, would do as he asked. But even as he formed the words, the convulsions gripped him again, and he doubled over. "Hurry," she urged the ashen-faced knights. She modestly busied herself with the medicines she'd brought while they removed his clothes. Without being told, Chrissy put the pot of herbs over the fire to brew. An infusion of mistletoe to strengthen his heart and parsley to soothe his belly. They'd need it later. Now the most critical need was to rid his body of the poison.

"Hold his head still whilst I pour this down his gullet," Megan said when Ross was decently beneath the sheet.

As predicted, he balked, fighting as much as the bindings permitted. Though his suffering made her heart ache, she brooked no delay. Pinching his nostrils shut, she opened his mouth and poured the stuff in. He gagged, swallowed and glared at her.

"Chrissy, hold this bowl near his mouth. Davey, be ready to lift his head to the bowl when he empties his belly."

"Will that save him?" Davey asked anxiously.

Megan sighed. "I hope so. If we had treated him at once, his chances would ha' been better. As it is ..." She sighed. "We'll do what we can, then trust to the gods for the rest."

The purging was neither pleasant nor painless, but mercifully the herbs she'd given him acted quickly.

"Witch," Ross gasped again when it was over, glaring at her through reddened eyes as he lay weakly against the pillows. "I willna forgive you for this." His lids fluttered shut and he seemed to be sleeping.

"And I'll nae forgive myself if I lose you." The possibilities made Megan quake, but she kept working. "Quick. We must get the infusion of mistletoe into him. 'Twill keep his heart beatin' strong when the convulsions strike again."

"How do ye know so much about this poison?" Andrew demanded.

"'Tis nae a poison in small quantities," Chrissy said with unusual boldness. "It's used to treat the gout but it can also be used to abort an unwanted bairn. Sometimes a woman thinks to hide her shame by treatin' herself and takes too much. A year ago, one of the maids doused herself wi' autumn crocus. By the time Megan and I were brought to her bedside, 'twas too late."

Owain looked down at Ross. "What about Ross?"

"We willna know for hours yet," Megan said gently. Long, horrible hours filled with suffering, if past experience was any measure. *Sweet Mary, she'd spare him this.* Much as she wanted to soothe the sweaty hair back from Ross's forehead, she resisted, unwilling to disturb his rest. "This calm is deceivin', I fear," she murmured. "He'll have belly cramps, convulsions, trouble breathin' and even fevered ravings before the poison leaves him." *If it left him.*

Rhiannon. Beautiful Rhiannon. She danced in the shadows just out of reach, tempting him with brief, provocative glimpses of naked flesh cloaked only in a swirl of knee-length black hair.

Desire turned Ross's mouth dry as dust, lanced through his lower belly as sharp and painful as a sword thrust. "Rhiannon, come to me, love," he rasped. "I need you as never before."

Laughing, she eluded him. "Catch me, and I will fulfill yer every fantasy, yer every need."

Need. Aye, he needed her so desperately he was panting, unable to catch his breath. The knot in his gut tightened, turned to fire. A fire only she could extinguish. "I'm dying... dying wi'out you," he gasped, and started toward her, but his arms and legs were bound. He struggled against the force that held him. "Damn you, let me go to her. Rhiannon!" he screamed.

"She's evil," a voice whispered. Owain's voice. "She seduces ye only to betray ye to her sire's men."

"Nay." But the warning rang over and over in Ross's head.

"Fool." Rhiannon's dark, seductive eyes went hard as flint. "'Tis already done. Look, there."

In the curling gray mist that rose around them, he saw the men who had ridden with him... into the trap sprung by Rhiannon's father. There was blood everywhere and men dying and horses screaming. One hundred men dead or dying.

And all because he had trusted this woman. A hundred souls on his conscience.

"Witch. Murderin' witch!" Ross strained to get at her, his blood fired by hatred now, not passion. But the thongs that held him were stronger than his will, or his hatred. "I'll kill you."

Rhiannon's low, mocking laughter floated around him in the mist. "Nay, ye are too weak-willed to kill a woman."

"I am not." Her image faded, vanished into the mist to be replaced by another, dearer face.

"Come wi' me to the Highlands for my weddin'."

Lion!

"Dinna go," Ross pleaded, the anguish of Rhiannon's betrayal buried by fear for his brother. "The Sutherlands'll kill you."

"Nay. I'll wed Siusan wi' or wi'out Eammon's permission. She's everythin' I've ever wanted."

"Women canna be trusted. She'll seduce you, betray you."

"I'd trust her wi' my life," Lion replied. Then his mouth rounded on a guttural groan, and he pitched forward at Ross's feet, a Sutherland quarrel sticking obscenely from his back. Blood spurted from the wound in a thick, red fountain.

"Lion!" Ross screamed. He reached for his brother, but couldn't bend. Cursing, he struggled fiercely against the thing that held him fast. If only he could push the blood back into Lion's body he could save him. He knew he could.

But his strength was ebbing, and the mist was rising, sucking him down, down into a black void. He fought it, cursing and thrashing until the darkness claimed him.

"I—I think the fever has broken," Megan whispered.

Seated at the other side of the bed, Owain nodded. "Jesu, I'd not want to live through this night again."

"Amen to that." Watching Ross suffer had been hell; hearing him shout his love for another even worse. Who was this Rhiannon? Much as Megan wanted to know, the old habit of dissembling died hard, kept the question locked in her aching heart.

"Ye should both get some sleep," Chrissy said, coming to stand beside her. Faithful Chrissy. Without her help, Megan knew she'd not have made it through the night. As it was, her arms and back ached from bending to apply cool cloths to break his fever or force a cup of foul-smelling brew down his reluctant gullet.

"Go ahead," Megan murmured, rubbing absently at the nagging pain in her thigh. "I'll sit wi' him a little longer to be sure."

"But ye're exhausted," Chrissy said, swaying on her feet.

True. Still, she couldn't leave Ross . . . not yet. Her presence here was essential. If she did not stay and count each breath, his lungs might cease to function. A foolish superstition, Ross would have said, but he was not awake to mock her. When he opened his eyes, she wanted to be near. "Go on to bed, Chrissy."

"A moment. I will see ye to yer room," Owain offered. "Then I'll go down to tell the men Lord Ross is out of danger."

Megan smiled faintly. "Thank you for your help."

"I did little. Ross would be dead had ye not fought to save him, m'lady," Owain said with a directness so like Ross's it brought tears to her eyes. She must be more tired than she'd thought. "Davey is asleep by the door if ye need aught."

Megan glanced at her patient. "Nay, m'lord's sleep is a natural one now. He willna waken for hours."

"I meant for yerself . . . wine, food, anything." Owain's thoughtfulness touched her nearly as much as the tender way he put his arm around her cousin's waist, support Chrissy certainly welcomed, for she leaned into him as they left. Now when had this happened? Poor Chrissy had her work cut out for her. The Welshman seemed even harsher and more unyielding than Ross.

Megan sighed, studying him in the golden wash of the candles set on the bedside table. Ross did not look so fierce and commanding now. Despite the dark circles under his eyes that emphasized the pallor of his skin, his features were relaxed. He looked years younger than the stern, angry man who'd arrived at Curthill two days ago.

Lovingly, her eyes caressed the big body sprawled on the bed, the wide shoulders and deep chest, bare above the sheet that covered his lower limbs. So strong, yet at the moment, so vulnerable. Her heart swelled. Knowing he was out of danger, she welcomed the notion that he'd be weak as a bairn for a day or so. She'd use the time to strengthen the bond between them.

As though her mind had called to his, his lashes suddenly lifted. For an instant he stared at her, eyes clear and unguarded for once, defenses lowered. In their vivid blue depths, she saw the other half of herself and knew beyond a shadow of a doubt that he was the man fate and the gods had intended for her. Here was her mate, her soul mate, her love...

"You," he breathed, and the spell was broken. Down came the shutters; his expression hardened. "What happened?"

"I saved your life." Immodest but true. And she'd need every advantage...fair or otherwise...to win him.

He frowned, and she could hear the wheels turn in that quick mind of his. "*Papa* knows we found the cave and he poisoned me."

Megan sighed heavily. "It could as easily be one of the others. Though I doubt any of them would know mint from marigold. Whoever fouled your wine knew what they were about, wanted to insure you a long, painful death. It can take three days to die from a dose of autumn crocus."

Air hissed out between his teeth, then his mouth tightened. "It seems I owe you my life a second time." Grudging thanks.

She pasted on a sassy smile. "My bride's gown is done and I've a mind to wear it to our weddin' two days hence."

Ross's heart twisted. "Megan, I dinna want to hurt you."

"But the king has ordered us joined, and we desire each other..." Her pained voice echoed the anguish clawing inside him as his feelings for her warred with loyalty to family.

He wanted her. God, how he wanted her. But the idea that he might find joy in their union appalled him. *Guilt.* If he allowed himself to feel anything but hatred for a Sutherland, the guilt would surely kill him and slowly poison her love. Better this unholy need should die now. "It takes more than passion to make a marriage," he said gruffly. "It takes respect and..."

"Trust." Megan threw up her hands. "I save your life...twice, and lead you to that cursed cave. What more must I do to prove myself worthy of your precious trust and respect?"

Nothing. He was the unworthy one. His desire for Megan made him a traitor to his family, his values, his honor. "Meg, 'tis more complicated than just—"

"Nay, I think it is very simple. You would cheat us of our future, because you hold me accountable for Lion's death." Her low, agonized voice matched perfectly the ache in his soul.

"Nay!" Ross struggled to sit; pain kept him flat on his back with her wounded eyes staring down at him. "You didna kill Li—"

"But you hold me responsible for the sins of my father."

Ross dragged in a shuddery breath, muscles clenched against the pain in his gut, in his heart. "Aye."

"And you'll continue to, even after Father Simon joins us in wedlock?" she asked, voice thick with tears she refused to shed.

Ross felt her agony, shared it. "Even if I somehow learned to trust a woman, even if I could live wi' my guilt, my family would never accept the daughter of Lion's murderer."

"Why? I did naught to your brother except love him as one." Despair ripped through Megan. "Is this about Rhiannon? Do you feel guilty because you'd rather wed her?" she blurted out.

He started, eyes grim. "Where did you hear her name?"

"You cried it when you were fevered."

"Never speak it again."

What is she to you? But Megan swallowed the words, afraid of what she'd find out. Mayhap Chrissy could subtly question Owain.

"I am tired." His eyes haunted pools of suffering, Ross turned his face to the wall, effectively shutting her out.

A shudder racked Megan. If they married, her life might be a mirror image of her mother's. She shivered, seeing the rest of her years stretch out before her, bleak, cold and loveless as the windswept moors.

Chapter Nine

"M'lord. Where are ye going?"

Damn. Ross stopped and glowered at the trio clumping down the stairs after him. Owain, Davey and Sim, the guard he'd expressly ordered to stay behind. "To the jakes," he snarled, thoroughly out of temper after a day spent in his chamber.

The three men halted above him and exchanged uneasy glances. "Lady Megan said ye shouldna be out of bed," Davey said.

Owain nodded. "Lady Megan said ye'd be weak, what wi' the wound in yer shoulder and the poison—"

"I am not." Well, only a little, and that because he'd been forced to stay in bed all day.

"Have ye forgotten what happened yestereve?" Owain pressed.

"How could I?" Most of the events after his collapse in the hall were a blur, a nightmare of fear and agony. Of belly cramps and a terrible thirst. Of being unable to breathe. Of having noxious draughts forced down his swollen throat. He'd dreamed about Rhiannon...something he'd not done in months...and about Lion...something he did all too frequently. "I remember," he murmured, thinking of Megan.

She loved him. He'd seen it in her eyes when he'd awakened to find her sitting vigil beside his bed. In that moment, he'd wanted to let himself go. 'Twould be so easy to fall into those warm brown wells of emotion, to wrap himself in the love and light shining there. To hope. To dream. To feel again.

Then cold reason had intruded. What had he to offer her? His family would shun her; he would feel guilty every time he took her into his arms. Brave, blithe Megan deserved better than hatred and remorse. That he already cared for her far more than was wise he accepted. 'Twas his cross to bear. He'd not burden her with it by letting her hope for things that could never be.

Owain's ripe curse cut through his dark thoughts. "The poison must have addled yer wits. What are ye thinking, running about alone with a killer on the loose?"

"Mayhap you are right." Ross raked a hand through his hair and leaned back against the stone wall. It felt as cold as the lump in his chest where his heart used to be. "But one more 'Lady Megan said' and I'll send you all home. I havena forgotten you upheld her threats to tie me to the bed if I tried to get up."

"'Twas for yer own good," Owain said with a shrug.

"I willna be cosseted like a bairn or use the damned chamber pot again. 'Tis humiliatin'." Ross unlocked his trembling knees and started down the tight, winding staircase. Behind him, boots scraped on stone as his men doggedly followed. "I'll be glad to get home where a man may walk about freely."

Murmurs of agreement were buried in a metallic groan as Ross wrenched open the door and stepped outside. The sun had just set and the courtyard was draped in shadows. Here and there, a few torches flickered in the breeze, casting eerie fingers of light and dark over the twin towers and outbuildings.

Ross tipped his head back and stared at the light in the window high atop the newer tower. "Has Eammon been down?"

"Nay." Owain shifted uneasily. "I dinna like it."

"'Tis unnatural . . . even for a man besotted by a mistress."

"Clearly he avoids ye lest ye read the guilt in his face," Davey put in.

"Mayhap." Ross shivered, tried to convince himself it was the cool night air, not the brooding evil he tasted on the wind. "What news from our men while I've been locked up?"

"Naught. No sign of the ship," Owain began. As they headed toward the jakes behind the tower, five dark-clad Welshmen walked on ahead while Davey and Sim dropped back behind. "No one's been near the tailor's or the storage hut except the two men who live there." Owain exhaled, cast Ross a searching glance. "Tomorrow's the wedding and we've found nothing to link Eammon to Lion's murder or prove he's a wrecker. What will ye do?"

"Wed her. What choice have I?"

"Chrissy says her cousin is an angel, devoted to healing the sick and to her duties as bard. Chrissy says—"

"Chrissy, is it?" Ross raised an eyebrow. "Are ye taken wi' the little blond wench?"

"Chrissy is not a wench," Owain said stiffly.

"Soho, that is the way of it."

"Nay, 'tis not. Ye know I cannot wed until I've avenged myself on Dolgollen and gotten back my family lands."

"You are thinking of marriage, Owain?"

"I cannot, though she's sweet as any Welshwoman." High praise indeed. "I fell for her as swiftly as ye did for Megan."

"I havena *fallen* for her." Ross shuddered as the lie tore at his conscience. "I'm forced to wed her to save my clan, and . . . and tryin' to make the best of it."

Owain was not fooled. "I'm that pleased to see ye interested in a woman. After Rhiannon, I thought—"

"Lust. That is all it is. All it can ever be."

"Only if ye will it so." Owain's gaze darkened as he looked into his own unhappy past. "After my Elen died, I had no wish to love again." A slow grin gentled his hard mouth. "But these Sutherland women have a way of sneakin' up on a man's heart."

"Owain." Ross gaped, unable to believe his ears. "Only think what happened to Lion . . . what has befallen us since we came here. Two attempts on my life wi'in two days' time."

"And each time yer lady saved ye." He grinned. "She has the heart of a warrior . . . a lioness."

"She's stubborn, impetuous and . . . and as unpredictable as the wind. She'd make my life hell." Or heaven. *Nay.* He shoved the traitorous thought aside. "And she'd be badly hurt into the bargain." Ross shuddered. "Da's hatred would crush her spirit."

"Ye care for her. Aye," Owain insisted when Ross shook his head. "Otherwise ye'd not give a damn for her feelings."

"I am only grateful because she saved my life...twice," Ross fairly shouted.

"Only a fool lies to himself," Owain said softly. "All I ask is that ye not close yer heart to her because of Rhiannon's betrayal. That one was evil. This one is—"

"An angel," Ross mocked.

"Ross Carmichael!" called a voice that was in no way celestial. Before he could bolt and run, Megan materialized out of the dark. "Whatever are ye doin' down here?" she demanded, hands on hips, head tossed back, eyes blazing in the torchlight.

Magnificent, was his first thought. Then reason reasserted itself. If he softened toward her even a wee bit, he'd be lost. "I am goin' to the jakes. Will you follow me there, too?"

"If you like," she said with a shrug and a half smile. "But we'd best hurry or your dinner'll be cold."

Ross's abused belly winced. "I am nae hungry."

"Stubborn man. You need to keep up your strength." Her smile fled. "The porridge and bread I made will rest easy on your stomach, and Sir Andrew stood at my elbow the whole time to make certain I didna spice it with poison, so 'tis safe."

"How could Andrew think that after all you did to save my life last night?" Ross demanded, indignant on her behalf.

A smile dimpled her cheek. "Your confidence is reassurin', m'lord, but Sir Andrew doesna share it. Even now, he's in your chamber guardin' the food. So if you'd hurry with your ... business." Her delicately arched brow made his face go hot.

Damn. No woman had ever made him blush. "Davey, stay wi' Lady Megan," Ross growled. *She was far more witch than angel,* he thought as he hurried toward the jakes with Owain at his heels. But it seemed more and more certain she'd soon be his little witch. Pain lanced his gut and he was not certain whether it was the aftereffects of the poison or the conflicting urges that clawed at his insides.

Ross cursed and spat, but the bitter taste of failure remained. Barring a miracle, tomorrow he'd wed a woman he desired but could never love and leave Curthill with his brother's death still shrouded in a mystery even darker and more impenetrable than the shadowed tower where the laird hid out.

It lacked a few minutes to midnight when Comyn left Curthill by the postern gate. The sea bubbled like a witch's caldron and stringy black clouds raced across a pale moon. With only that fitful light to guide him, Comyn picked his way down the rocky trail to the beach. Wet sand left by the retreating tide muffled his footsteps as he approached the cliff.

A bulky shape stepped out from the rocks where the shadows were blackest. "'Bout time ye got here," Douglas growled.

Comyn's hackles rose instantly. "Carmichael's men are vigilant. It took time to slip away," he replied.

"Thought ye were takin' care o' him."

"Somethin' got in the way," Comyn said through his teeth, hands balled at his sides in an effort to control his temper. *Megan.* Another score he had to settle with her, and before this was done, he'd find a way. "But Carmichael'll wed Megan tomorrow and they'll be on their way soon after."

Megan would not leave Curthill without contacting her sister. Comyn had men watching her day and night to make certain that when she did, her messenger would lead him straight to Siusan. Soon. Very soon he'd have his due...on all counts.

The captain swore and looked seaward, the breeze lifting lank brown hair away from his fleshy face. "Storm comin'. Need to load the cargo tonight...sail on the tide if I'm to make London on schedule wi' the merchandise Danby ordered."

"Too risky. Carmichael has men everywhere. He knows about the caves, I'd swear to it, but he hasna made a move to use the knowledge, except to post a guard on Eammon's rooms. Which means he must believe Eammon's guilty, but canna prove it. We mustna do anythin' to make Ross think otherwise. The ship stays put until Ross is gone and Lord Nigel wi' him."

"*The Hawk* is my ship. I say where she sails and when," Douglas snapped. "And Danby'll buy elsewhere if we dinna come through with what we promised."

"I dinna care if we lose two orders. We wait."

"Wait all ye like...I'm sailin'."

Toe to toe, they glared at each other. That he stood a head taller than his partner gave Comyn scant advantage. Bardolph Douglas was heavier and meaner. 'Twas rumored he'd once killed a man with his bare hands over a cup of ale. Comyn believed it. The close-set black eyes glaring up at him were hard as flint, remorseless as the gates of hell.

"At least wait until tomorrow ... while everyone's attention is on the weddin'." Comyn hated the pleading note in his voice. He'd begged for his life when the MacKays had exterminated the MacDonnels, sworn he'd never sink that low again.

Douglas grunted and spat into the sand. "What time?"

"The wedding's set for five in the evenin'."

"Fine. I'll begin loadin' then. Sail on the midnight tide."

"Agreed. The townsfolk will be at the castle celebratin' their *dear lady*'s nuptials. Carmichael will likely pull in most of his men in case there's another attempt on his life."

"Good. We'll figure anyone who's loiterin' about in the village is one o' his and shut them up ... permanently."

"And no one'll be the wiser until after ye're long gone." Comyn silently let go the breath he'd been holding. When Douglas sailed, he'd take with him everything that hinted at piracy. The manifests from the sunken ships were in Douglas's cabin. The goods would be in the hold. "Now my only problem is how to get the old man to the weddin'. Eammon's continued absence has worried even Lord Nigel's wine-sogged brain. If the laird doesna appear for his daughter's weddin', there'll be questions asked."

"Opium's tricky. Warned ye when we started. He's been takin' it a long time. Does bad things to a man's insides. Soon he'll be too far gone to be much use to us." Douglas frowned. "My advice's to gi' him none today, then feed him wee bits on the morrow. Just enough to make him alert, neither shakin' wi' need, nor dazed wi' poppy dreams."

Comyn nodded. Douglas was the expert here, the one who'd seen opium used in the East and first suggested it for their purposes. The one who had found a source to buy what they needed to make Eammon their pawn and keep him so. "We're agreed, then."

* * *

Megan's wedding day dawned gray and chilly, but it seemed even the threat of rain could not dampen her spirits. She'd been up at dawn, plaguing the maids with a dozen conflicting requests and flitting about like a scatterbrained chicken.

"I still think ye should wear the blue," Chrissy said, silk whispering as she lifted the surcoat for her cousin's inspection. She and Lady Mary had spent hours stitching the intricate pattern of gold leaves and seed pearls that formed the border at neck and hem. Not that she regretted the work, or the time spent on the close-fitting amber cotehardie intended to be worn beneath. "The gold brings out the blond in yer hair, and the blue turns yer skin creamy as new milk."

"'Tis lovely, but..." Seated on a stool before the fire, Megan frowned. "Let me see the red again." She started to get up, cried out as the wooden comb caught in her damp hair.

"If ye dinna quit jumpin' about, ye'll be snatched bald afore we're done," fretted the stout, gray-haired woman who had been Megan's maid since birth.

Megan slouched down with a long sigh. "Why is everythin' takin' so long today? Why is nothin' goin' right?"

Chrissy looked across the bed she'd shared with Megan since coming to Curthill and exchanged knowing glances with Lady Mary. The coverlet was obscured by a dazzling profusion of bright colors, silken cotehardies and velvet surcoats, dozens of gowns tried on in the hours since they'd risen, agonized over and rejected as being not quite special enough.

Lady Mary put down the crimson surcoat she'd been refolding and smiled faintly. "'Tis just nerves, dearlin'."

"I am not nervous. I'm cold." Shivering, Megan folded her arms over the thin linen chemise that was all she wore. "Do you suppose Ross has yet seen my gift to him?"

"Janet returned an hour past and said she'd personally put the garments into his squire's hands," her mother said gently.

"Mayhap they dinna fit." She nibbled on her already reddened lips. "Or he doesna like them?"

"After you stayed up half the night finishin' it, he'd better," Lady Mary grumbled.

Megan smiled ruefully. "'Twould have been done days ago if I wasna such a poor hand wi' a needle."

"All the more reason he should prize it." Lady Mary sniffed. "But that's men for you...ungrateful creatures. A woman gives him the best years of her life...bears his bairns...cooks his meals...warms his bed...and what happens? Let her get a wee bit long in the tooth, and he tosses her aside like so much garbage."

"Oh, Mama." Megan's eyes filled with tears.

"Megan. Ye must choose a gown," Chrissy said before things could deteriorate further. Bad enough Megan thought Lord Ross did not really want to wed her. She didn't need this, as well. Of course, Owain said his lordship was far more taken with Megan than he'd admit...even to himself. Chrissy sighed, hoping the Welshman had read his lord right. "I favor the blue, myself. What say ye, aunt?"

Lady Mary blinked the moisture from her eyes and nodded. "My thanks, Chrissy," she murmured as one of the maids carried the surcoat over to Megan. "I dinna know what ails me today."

"Nerves. I fear we all suffer from them today."

"Eammon had best have the decency to come down today," her aunt muttered. "If he disappoints Meg on her weddin', I'll never forgive him."

Nodding, Chrissy glanced across the room at Megan's smiling face and sparkling eyes. Her happiness shone like a beacon, even through her nervousness. 'Twould be a crime of the worst sort if Eammon repaid his daughter's fierce loyalty by absenting himself on this special day. "She loves Lord Ross."

"Aye. More's the pity, for he doesna love her."

"He may come to in time. Accordin' to Owain, Lord Ross is confused about what he wants."

"All men want bairns...sons to follow them."

"Oh, aunt. I forgot about *that*." Truth to tell, she hadn't wanted to remember the rest of the damage that accident had caused. Chrissy darted a quick look at Meg. "Will ye tell her?"

Lady Mary shook her head and looked away. "I—I am such a coward. A dozen times I've begun, but she's had so little happiness, and she's been so brave, I...I just couldna..."

"She should be told the truth," Chrissy said gently. "When it seemed unlikely she'd wed, it didna matter, but now..."

"Many women never bear children," her aunt said.

"This isna right."

"Right...what in life is?" Lady Mary asked. "If I told Meg now, she might feel honor bound to tell Lord Ross, who would seize the chance to repudiate her. Think you I want to put Meg through that again? Besides, livin' here, torn apart by the troubles between Eammon and myself, is killin' her. Better she should leave and make her home wi' the Carmichaels."

"What are you two whisperin' about?" Megan called. "Some mischief? Oh, never say you've let cook make naughty marzipan figures of Ross and myself and put them on the weddin' cake?"

"Of course not," Lady Mary said quickly. Too quickly.

"Mama. Is aught wrong?" Ducking the maid's comb, Megan stood. "Is it Papa? Is he nae comin' to my weddin'?"

"N-nay," her mother stammered. "That is, I hope he is."

"'Tis Ross, then. He's ridden away rather than wed me."

"Nay," her mother and Chrissy said together.

Something was wrong. "Mama. Tell me what—"

A knock at the chamber door sent her mother flying to answer it. "Meg. 'Tis from Lord Ross." She closed the door and turned, a small chest in her hands.

"Oh." Problems forgotten, Megan reached for the bride gift. Intricate carvings decorated the top and side of the chest. Inside, it was lined with red velvet, the perfect setting for a gold filigree necklet fine and delicate as a spider's web. "Look, the center stone is amber," she whispered, awed, touched.

"For good luck." Chrissy kissed her cheek.

"I'm so surprised Ross brought me somethin', knowin' how he felt about us Sutherlands and about this marriage."

"Owain believes everythin' will work out."

"Oh, Chrissy, really?" There had been a moment yesterday when she could have sworn he...he cared for her. Then had come all that confusing talk of trust and guilt and Rhiannon. "Did Owain tell you about *her*?"

Chrissy shook her head. "Owain said Ross must tell ye that story, but Owain thinks Ross cares for ye more than he'll—"

"Dinna get her hopes up," Lady Mary muttered.

"You are right, of course," Megan said, returning to the hearth to finish drying her hair. But the hope did not die. It buoyed her spirits through the seemingly endless hours until the horn sounded, summoning everyone to the wedding.

"I thought it would never be time." Anticipation had Megan's feet outracing her heart as she hurried down the tower steps, and out into the courtyard, Chrissy, her mother and a pack of giggling maids in quick pursuit.

The sea of colorfully dressed Sutherlands parted to allow her through, cheering and wishing her well. It was hard to remember to go slowly lest she limp. By the time she arrived at the chapel, she was breathless with excitement.

But where was the bridegroom who should have been beside the door to greet her?

"Do you see him?" Megan asked anxiously, standing on tiptoe to see over the well-wishers. "Mayhap he misunderstood and awaits within." Lifting her skirts, she started inside.

Chrissy caught her arm. "'Tis bad luck to cross the chapel threshold wi'out yer intended."

"Oh, lordy." Megan stumbled back two steps. How could she, the bard, have forgotten? "Will you go look for him?"

That proved unnecessary. Ross materialized in the doorway, looking heartbreakingly handsome in a black velvet surcoat worn over a tunic that echoed the deep blue of his eyes. They widened appreciatively, leaving a trail of tingling skin as they scanned her from crown to toes, then returned to her face. "Jesu, but you are lovely," he murmured.

"Th-thank you for the necklet," she stammered, shy suddenly.

He smiled and 'twas like the sun had come out inside him. Inside her. "The surcoat and tunic you made fit perfectly. Come." He held out his hand.

Dazed, Megan started forward, stopped short. "If you will come out and escort me in..."

"Why?"

"'Tis one of our customs." Damn, she did not want to ruin this good start by bringing up a superstition. Behind her, people laughed, called her a reluctant bride. Megan prayed the ground would open up and swallow her whole, but in the end, help came from an unlikely source.

"If I might explain," Comyn interjected, stepping around Lord Nigel. "There is an old sayin' that the bride who crosses the threshold alone will live out her married life alone."

"Superstitious nonsense," Lord Nigel growled.

Megan eyed the threshold as she would a snake and touched the amber amulet. "I want to please you, m'lord, but..."

The charm must have worked, for he nodded and stepped across the stone threshold. "I believe I owe you a favor or two," he said as he took her elbow and led her within.

Megan blinked, blinded as much by his attitude as by the dimness of the chapel. "Y-you have changed your mind about wantin' to wed?" she whispered. Was the amber *that* powerful?

"'Tis a wise man who knows when to cease fightin' what he canna change." Cool logic, but the fire blazing in his eyes warmed her clear to the toes of her leather slippers. Hope lightened her steps as he escorted her down the aisle.

Now if only her Papa would come, the day would be perfect. But when they reached the altar and she glanced back over her shoulder, the high-backed chair in the first row was still empty. Ah, well, one miracle a day was more than she'd expected.

"Let us undo yer ties," chorused a group of maids from the village. They stepped forward and loosened the silk strips lacing Megan's surcoat tight to her body while an equal number of young lads started on Ross's belt.

Predictably he objected. "My clothes'll fall off," he protested when she explained that this custom showed they were both free of other *entanglements,* and thus the *knot* tied by the church would bind them together for all time.

"They willna untie anything...vital, and they'll see all is reknotted before we start back for the hall," Megan said, and held her breath. Wonder of wonders, he nodded. Behind them, Megan heard a long, drawn-out sigh of approval from her people.

Of the actual ceremony, she remembered little. She stood and knelt when she was told, kept her head bowed and murmured her own prayers. For strength. For forbearance. For luck. She'd need all three if her marriage to this enigmatic man was to prosper.

At last it was done. Father Simon pronounced them husband and wife. "Ye may kiss the bride," he said cheerfully.

Megan dutifully turned her face up, expecting a cool, public gesture. Warm lips settled over hers, moving surely, possessively, swallowing her gasp of surprise, replacing it with a needful moan that echoed her own. "Oh," she breathed when he lifted his head moments later. Too soon.

"I never said I didna want you." His husky words sent awareness shivering down her spine. The incense-scented air around them seemed to vibrate with it, but beneath the desire that darkened his eyes to deepest blue, flickered the guilt he couldn't quite hide. "Come, your people await."

Megan nodded, unable to speak past the lump in her throat. Vision blurred by bittersweet tears, she turned toward the congregation and saw her father sitting in the shadows at the far end of the first pew.

"Papa!" Megan would have run to him if Ross had not had her arm secure in the crook of his. Just as well, she realized when she spotted a smirking Felis at her papa's side. "How dare he..."

"He is laird here," Ross reminded her, voice hard, damning. "But any man who could so disgrace his wife and daughter is surely capable of far worse."

Of murder. For once, Megan lacked the will to defend her father. "I suppose I should be grateful he came."

"I certainly am." While the lads and lasses retied their laces, Ross muttered a few crisp Welsh words to Owain, then, "Smile. Dinna let him see he's hurt you," he said in Megan's ear, his warm breath reassuring.

Megan blinked, touched by the concern in the face so close to hers. "He canna hurt me any longer. Only you have that power."

Only you have that power. Megan's words haunted Ross, weighed on him as the crowd of noisy Sutherlands swept the wedding couple back to the hall.

"I remembered Eammon as being a bigger man," Lord Nigel said as they mounted the dais and took their places.

"He has changed in many ways since our son died," Lady Mary said stiffly. "But, aye, he did look thinner. And...grayer. And he looked straight through me as though I wasna there." Her voice broke. Poor woman. She still loved her faithless husband.

Ross frowned, recalling Eammon's hollowed, flushed cheeks. Strange. As odd as the glint in the red-rimmed eyes that had refused to meet Ross's. Guilt? Remorse? Mayhap, but...

"Papa hasna come in," Megan said, low and sad. "I know 'tis a kindness to Mama that Felis will be absent, still..."

"What?" Ross's frantic glance darted over the high table and around the hall, but Eammon was indeed missing. Half out of his chair to warn Owain or Wee Wat, he saw them stroll through the doorway and sat back down. From their expressions, he guessed they had found something and he burned to know what it was.

"You're up and down like a fly on hot sand. I thought the bride was supposed to be the nervous one," Megan teased.

"Are you nervous?" Ross asked, neatly avoiding a lie.

"I was." Her fingertips reverently touched the necklace, eyes downcast and shy again. "But the amber is a powerful charm. Thank you. I didna expect anythin'."

And that's exactly what she'd have gotten had Owain's words not convinced him he'd be a fool to continue punishing Megan. Problems remained and their future might well be a disaster, but he'd agreed to the marriage. Being sullen and snappish to his bride would not change that. Duty was a thing he understood. That decided, he'd turned the town inside out for a gift. "I know naught of charms. The gold was finely spun as that in your hair."

She smiled up at him, eyes dancing through thick lashes. "You have the soul of a poet, m'lord."

He had no soul. If he had, he'd not have wed her, even to save his clan. *Poor Meg.* She deserved more than he had to offer.

Davey leaned in to pour wine and whisper in Ross's ear, "Wee Wat found some papers . . . says they'll keep till after the feast."

Ross nodded. He glanced over at Megan's shining face, and his throat tightened. *Jesu, he didn't want to hurt her.*

A shout went up, heralding the arrival of the food. Chrissy led the way for an endless parade of servants bearing steaming platters. The offerings were not as fancy as those at Lowland weddings, but plentiful. Roasted boar, sauced venison, fowl of every kind fought for space with stews, baskets of bannocks, pitchers of ale and wine. The forfar bridies, meat pasties, were familiar to him, as was the haggis he declined, but some things were new. "What's that?" he asked, pointing to a pudding.

"Carrageen jelly." Megan dipped her spoon in and offered him some. It looked green, smelled worse. "'Tisna fish," she said when he turned up his nose. "Seaweed, boiled in milk."

Conscious of the cook hovering anxiously nearby, Ross took a small taste, swallowed it twice. "Delicious," he managed.

"So, even you are not above telling a falsehood to save someone hurt," Megan said when the happy cook had moved away.

Ross started to deny it, then sighed. "A few days ago, you'd have called it a kindness, not a falsehood." The laugh they shared was followed by others as the feast progressed through course after course. But Ross found it impossible to relax totally. When he looked away from Megan's smiling face, he gazed out over a sea of rowdy Sutherlands. Though they seemed harmless as a litter of unruly pups, he couldn't forget that somewhere in that boisterous crowd, his brother's killer ate, drank and laughed.

Out of the corner of his eye, he caught Megan watching him, her face soft in the golden candlelight. She loved him. Their joining tonight would seal that bond . . . in her mind, at least. Once she was his, body and heart, she'd trust him with her secrets, lead him to her sister. Much as it went against the grain to use her, he knew he'd do it. *I will make it up to you,* he vowed, shocked to realize how important her feelings were.

Another cheer went up from the increasingly drunken revelers as the dishes were cleared away and the trestle tables pushed against the wall. The musicians who had been playing during the meal gave way to jugglers, knife throwers and tumblers.

"'Tis like the Edinburgh Fair indoors," Davey said, grinning as he leaned in to refill Ross's cup with watered wine. Wine he had purchased himself in town and guarded zealously.

No sooner had the last knife been flung than someone called for a tale from their bard. Megan blushed and refused, but her clansmen were beyond caring and the crowd did not quiet until she stepped down from the dais to take a chair in the center of the room. Her left leg must still hurt her, Ross thought, for there was a slight hesitation in her step. Guilt flared. Damn, he'd been so caught up in his own injuries and problems he'd never asked how she fared.

Then she began to speak and Ross forgot everything but her clear, compelling voice filling the hush that had fallen over the crowd. With her words, her tone, the movement of her hands, the expression on her face, she captured their collective imagination and took them with her on a journey back to the time when gods walked the earth in the guise of men.

When the last miracle had been wrought by Fionn MacCumhail and his giants, her voice died away to a whisper. 'Twas silent then, except for the sounds of sea crashing against the distant rocks, a muted sort of applause that was soon lost under the stomping of countless Sutherland boots.

Jesu, she was something, Ross thought, staring at her proud profile as she acknowledged her kinsmen's thanks. Torchlight caught on her head as she inclined it, set fire to the gold in her hair and at her throat, turned the tears on her cheeks to silver ribbons as she turned to look at him.

Moved as much by her tale as her beauty, Ross rose to go to her, but a delegation of wee lasses reached her first. Squealing and giggling, they set a circlet of flowers on Megan's head, took her hands and drew her off to be swallowed up by the crowd.

"'Tis some sort of pagan rite, I suppose," Ross muttered.

"You dinna approve?" Lady Mary's neck was stiffer than ever.

"I wasna raised wi' such..." *Nonsense,* he almost said, but it no longer seemed so. "Beliefs." That was better.

Lady Mary smiled, her austere face smoothing to show the beauty she'd once been. "I, too, looked down on the Highland ways when I first came here. But these common legends are one thing that binds these fierce, warlike people together."

"They are that," Ross said, but more fondly now. "I could almost come to like these wild, boisterous Sutherlands."

"If it werena for what you think Eammon did." Lady Mary hesitated. "The death of our son changed Eammon, but I know he isna capable of murderin' a man, or of orderin' it done, simply because he didna want him for a son-by-marriage."

Jesu, what was it about Eammon that inspired such loyalty in the very women he'd hurt? "Mayhap there's more to it than that."

"Nay. What could there be? Eammon liked Lion from the first, but when we returned to Curthill, he suddenly changed his mind about permittin' him to wed Siusan." She shifted in her seat. "I am sorry you got hold of some spoiled meat the other night."

Ross blinked. Damn, Megan must have put that lie about to protect her father. Now he was forced to uphold it. "I, er, have recovered, thank you." Vague enough to satisfy his conscience.

"M'lord. If I could have a word," Owain said at his elbow.

Grateful for the diversion, Ross rose, bowed to Lady Mary and stepped down from the dais. As he and the Welshman picked their way through the hall, Ross instinctively looked for his new wife. It unsettled him to not see her golden head in the crowd, but he wouldn't admit it by sending someone to look for her.

Out in the courtyard, Ross drew in a deep breath of cool, salty air and let it out slowly. Overhead, a few early stars peeked out from between high, wind-driven clouds. "I wonder if the Sutherlands fight as zealously as they play?"

Owain grinned. "We may have a chance to find out."

"You found somethin'?"

"Mayhap," Wee Wat stepped out of the night to reply. Rapidly he outlined the quick search of Eammon's tower rooms. "The only thing worth mentionin' was this." He drew a rolled parchment from the sleeve of his tunic.

Glancing around to make certain they were alone in this protected corner of the courtyard, Ross unfurled the paper and leaned closer to the torch Owain held. By its flickering light, he saw a list of merchandise consigned to a Lord Danby, London, England. "The goods are due to be delivered in a week's time by a Captain Douglas of *The Black Hawk.*" He looked up, jaw tight.

"The ship we saw in the harbor our first night here. Our men claim she did not load any cargo that night," Owain said.

"Ah." Ross's eyes narrowed. "But if Douglas doesna sail soon, he'll not make London in time to complete the deal."

"He could be shiftin' the goods tonight," Wee Wat said. "While the villagers are at the castle celebratin'."

"We have men watchin' the hut?" At Owain's nod, Ross raked a hand through his hair. "Have someone check on them. Send men also to the beach. I'd go, too, but I'm afraid I'd be missed."

"Aye. The bedding should be soon." Owain grinned. "Ye'll want to be here for that."

Ross shrugged, but his lower body tightened at the reminder that he'd shortly be abed with Megan. "If you do find somethin', come and tell me at once. This is important enough to disturb even my weddin' night," he added to forestall Owain's rebuke.

"We'll try to gi' ye an hour or two," Owain joked.

With Owain's gibe ringing in his ears, Ross set out to find Megan, anxious to get on to the next stage of the wedding feast. The bedding. The part he'd been looking forward to consciously and unconsciously ever since she'd tumbled across Zeus's path that first day. Desire winding tighter by the moment, he bypassed the great hall and headed for the kitchens. She might be handing out cakes to her wee admirers.

Sure enough, as he stepped outside he saw her standing in the lee of the kitchen building, her back to him. Ross almost cried out a greeting, but something about her hunched shoulders, the way she lurked in the shadows, made his hackles rise along with his suspicions. Darting back into the doorway, he peeked out to spy, watched her hands fly in gestures as expressive as those she'd used earlier to tell her story.

She was upset.

Ross straightened, nerves screaming with the urge to go to her, protect her from whomever or whatever...

Megan shifted suddenly, exposing the person who shared her darkened corner, her secret tryst. A lad, with red hair not even the night could conceal and a face dominated by the largest nose Ross had ever...

Nay, he'd seen that nose before... on George the tailor.

This, then, was the mysterious Lucais. The lad who held the key to Lion's murder.

Chapter Ten

"There she is!"

Megan turned at the shout. Across the courtyard, she spied a horde of brightly clad women stampeding toward her.

"It's time! It's time," they cried.

For the bedding ceremony. Excitement nearly drove out the shock of Lucais's message. Nearly. Instinctively she moved to shield the lad from sight. The merry, wine-flushed ladies posed no threat, but there might be others about. "Hide in the stables. I...I'll come down as soon as I'm able and we'll set about aidin' my sister," she whispered over her shoulder.

"But m'lady. Surely ye canna be thinkin' of bringin' a sick lady and a wee babe through the Highlands alone. We need men to protect us from beasts and reivers."

"My new husband has men, trained warriors." Yesterday, she'd not have trusted Ross to help her. Today was a different matter. He'd been so...so kind, so relaxed and friendly. He'd help her. She touched the amulet for luck. "Get you gone, Lucais, and stay hidden until I come." There was no time to say more before the women pounced on her. As they whisked her toward the keep, she glanced back, saw Lucais had vanished and heaved a sigh of relief.

'Twas short-lived, for ahead of her lay the bedding ceremony, when she'd be stripped naked for her new husband's inspection, her scars exposed at last. Did he care for her enough to overlook them? *Dear God, please do not let him repudiate me.*

"Dinna tremble," her mother murmured as the giggling party crested the steps and started down the upper corridor toward the sleeping rooms. "Lord Ross seems cool and even-tempered... for a man... not the sort to ravish a lass on her weddin' night."

That was the least of her worries. She craved his touch, wanted the fulfillment of the sensual promise that blazed in his eyes when he gazed at her. But... but as usual, her real concerns stuck in her throat. Fear of rejection. Fear for Siusan. Time was running out for both of them.

In more ways than one. No sooner had the ladies reached the bridal chamber... the room that had been her parents' in happier days and was now her mother's... than shouts and the clatter of pounding feet sounded in the stairwell.

"'Tis the men," Chrissy cried.

Amid more giggling and a little soft cursing for their slow fingers, the women set to work. In moments they divested Megan of the garments it had taken hours to put on. They were just tugging the thin linen chemise off over her head when loud shouts and raucous laughter announced the men's arrival.

Megan gathered her hair about her as best she could to shield her nudity, but the tresses that had taken hours to dry this morn suddenly seemed woefully inadequate to this task.

The door popped open, slammed back on its hinges, and scores of drunken men poured in, bearing Ross aloft on their shoulders. They had shucked him of surcoat and tunic and were starting on his hose, bent on rendering him as naked as his waiting wife.

Immediately his gaze locked on her, vivid blue darkening with desire. Megan felt its impact clear across the room, felt her muscles go warm and liquid as his hot eyes moved down her trembling body, palpable as a lover's caress. Inside her, passion bloomed, flared to rival the fire crackling in the hearth. This was it. The moment she'd waited for, hungered for. Swaying, she tossed back her hair, gloried in the way his eyes widened with an expression akin to wonder as they roved over her peaking nipples, moving lower. Lower.

Megan's heart soared, then faltered. He was looking at her hip. *Oh, Lord.* Both of her hands converged on her flank, splayed wide to cover the terrible scars. But it was too late.

"What is this?" Ross demanded. Frowning, he tore away from the merrymakers and advanced on Megan. *Oh. This was worse than she'd imagined.* Oblivious to the startled gasps of the women, she backed up until she bumped into the bed and could go no farther.

"You...you did this the other night?" His concern gave her the courage to speak.

"Nay, I...'twas a long time ago, and..." *And I've tried hard to overcome it. Please, please dinna repudiate me.*

"That's why you limp?" All softness fled his face. "Damn you. I felt guilty. I thought I was responsible for some temporary lameness, and all the while...another lie." Eyes so recently warm with desire went cold, disdainful. "I could repudiate you for this."

Lord Nigel pushed through the crowd. His wine-flushed cheeks heaved like bellows as he stared at Megan. "She's only a wee bit lame. She'll yet give good service. Breed ye up a pack o' sons."

Over the rush of her anguished pulse, Megan heard her mother moan, was vaguely aware of Chrissy sobbing softly. *Damn.* She was a person, not a brood mare or a piece of damaged goods. Anger lent strength to her trembling limbs. Squaring her shoulders, she met Ross stare for stare. "If you plan to repudiate me, do so. I grow chilled standing here in naught but my hair, my *hideous imperfections* exposed to my friends and your retainers."

A muscle twitched in his cheek as he ground his teeth, expression so grim she shivered anew. "Leave us," he growled, dismissing the gawking crowd with a wave of his hand.

"Are ye goin' to repudiate her?" Lord Nigel asked anxiously. Over the nobleman's shoulder, Megan caught sight of Comyn. In a forest of worried, compassionate faces, his stood out, lips curled in a mocking smile, eyes bright with relish. He wanted Ross to cast her aside as he himself had done.

Never had Megan hated him more. Never had she been more certain that he was the villain of this story.

Ross exhaled sharply. "I reserve judgment till the morrow."

"Nay." Megan stamped her bare foot. "I am not some horse you may try out to see if its gait suits you, then—"

"Oh, I am certain your *gait* will suit me," Ross drawled, eyes sliding over her so her skin crawled. "But since you're prone to lies, mayhap I'll find I'm not your first rider."

"Oh!" Megan's furious cry was drowned out by the gasps that swept the room like an ill wind.

Her mother leaped in with the ferocity of a mother bear. "See here. My lass is as pure as the day she was born."

"As if I'd believe what *anyone* here said," Ross snarled. "A greater pack of liars I'd not hope to find in purgatory."

Lord Nigel forestalled Lady Mary's rebuttal with a wave of his beringed hand. "'Tis highly unusual," he mused. "But the king is anxious for the blood bond, and Ross *has* agreed to overlook the lass's lameness if she's a virgin. So be it," he proclaimed. "Come morn, if the sheets are clean and Ross wishes it, he may set aside his wife. Will the church concur?"

Father Simon's close-set eyes narrowed. Behind them, Megan could see the cleric weighing his loyalties. He'd come with Lord Nigel and owed naught to Curthill or to her. "'Tis unusual, but Lord Ross is wi'in his rights to repudiate her for lameness. I can see no harm in waiting till morn to decide the matter."

Some of the tension leeched out of the air. Fabric rustled as the Sutherlands shifted, murmuring to each other, doubtless speculating on tomorrow's chapter of this tale. Ross's supporters were as hard faced and grimly silent as their lord.

"I willna be party to this," Megan's bruised pride replied.

Ross shrugged. "You have no choice." Without even looking at her. "Clear the room," he barked at the gawkers.

"Climb into bed, dearlin'," her mother urged as the others filed from the room. "Damn all men for the rude, arrogant, heartless creatures they are," she added.

Numb, shaking with cold, frustration and pain, Megan allowed her mother to tuck her beneath the covers of the wide, curtained bed on which her parents had consummated their own union. *The ill-fated thing should be burned,* was her last thought before her mother kissed her and drew the bed hangings, enclosing Megan in a dark little world. So must purgatory seem. A black, airless pit where the condemned awaited judgment.

Breath bated, hands pressing the amber to her faltering heart, Megan sat perfectly still. Every pore strained to catch some hint of what her executioner was about, but the room beyond was silent save for the crackle and hiss of the newly laid fire.

Without warning, the curtain was jerked back.

Megan jumped, fought the urge to cringe before the tall, hard-faced man towering over her, eyes blazing with an intensity that dried her mouth, trapped her heart in her throat.

"So, what else have you lied about?" he snarled, strangling the edge of the velvet in a big fist. "About your father's trade? About Lion's death?"

"Nay," she stammered, startled as much by the subject as his vehemence. "I dinna think Papa is involved in anythin', and I—I think Lion's death was an—"

"'Tis a wonder your tongue doesna rot and fall off." Flinging the drape aside, he turned to pace. His stiff-legged stride and the hands balled at his sides were the only outward indication of his fury. Better he ranted and raved.

"At first I assumed you knew about my leg," Megan said, anxious to clear the air. "By the time I realized you didna, I wanted very much to be your wife and thought you...you cared for me, too. I thought—"

"I dinna give a damn about your lameness." The furrows in his brow relented slightly. "Except that you must have known great pain. If you had told me from the start—"

"You'd have repudiated me then and there. You told the whole world so just moments ago."

"Mayhap." Scowl deepening again, he raked a hand through his already disheveled hair. "All women are natural liars, and you Sutherlands have made it into an art. But the time for that is past. I will have the truth. Now." He came to stand over her again, as unyielding as the stone walls. "I swear you willna leave this chamber till you've told me everythin'...startin' with the whereabouts of your sister. She was wi' him when Lion died. She is the key to this, hidden to protect his murderer."

"You are wrong." But was he? Siusan did know something…had fled to guard some secret she dared not share even with Megan.

"Ha. I am on the right trail."

Megan shook her head, tried to smooth her features into guileless lines. An hour ago, she'd have told him what little she knew, trusted him to go with Lucais and bring Siusan and her babe to safety. Poor Siusan, who by the time they reached her might be too weak to travel. *Childbed fever.* Sudden, insidious, deadly. She'd lost a few patients to the ailment herself, Megan thought, stomach clenching in silent denial. Not Siusan. Hadn't she suffered enough? "I dinna know where she is."

"But Lucais does. Save your conscience another lie," he snapped when she opened her mouth. "I saw you wi' him tonight."

In his icy disdain, she saw the shattering of all her hopes and dreams. Later she would mourn their passing, now she must protect Siusan. "My poor sister knows nothin'."

"Your *poor sister* lured my brother here to his death. We willna leave this room until I know where she is." He stalked over and threw himself in one of the chairs that flanked the fireplace. The leaping flames flickered over his unrelenting face, turning it into a mask of gold and black.

Even angry, he was a handsome man, strong and loyal to his family. She understood and appreciated both qualities full well. For the hundredth time she wished they'd met under different circumstances. A dozen *if onlys* churned in her mind. She was just stubborn enough to pursue one of them. "Do you really think I am nae a virgin?" she asked across the heavy silence.

"Does it matter?"

"To me. More than I can say." Megan looked down at her hands, white from clenching the blankets. "There is a way you could prove the point," she said shyly.

"You expect me to bed you?"

"You were eager enough for it before."

If anything, his expression grew angrier. "Like Rhiannon, you'd ensnare me wi' mine own lust. Not this time."

Mention of the other woman's name stiffened her spine. "You'd go back on your word?"

"I never said I'd bed you."

"Aye, you did... when we exchanged weddin' vows. And what of the morrow when the women come to inspect the sheets and find them unsullied. They... they'll think I was impure."

"Let them. All I care for now is findin' your sister and draggin' the truth from her." *So there,* challenged the glance he speared her with. He snatched up the flagon of sweet wine intended for their wedding toast. She measured his fury in the shaking of his hands as he lifted the bottle to his lips.

His threat chilled Megan to the bone, killed all hope of entrusting him with Siusan's safety. Nay, 'twas up to her now. The shudder that racked Megan had naught to do with facing the treacherous journey to her Aunt Brita's, and everything to do with the prospect of having to climb on a horse. But she'd do it.

"M'lord?"

Ross jerked awake, found himself staring into Owain's anxious features. "What?"

"I knocked... you did not answer."

Ross groaned. The steady throbbing behind his eyes meant he must have had too much wine the night before. It was not like him to risk loss of control by overindulging. He frowned, trying to recall what had driven him to...

The wedding. Megan's lies.

Groaning again, he turned his head to the right, expected to see her big brown eyes staring back at him from the other pillow, but it was empty. A slight indentation in the linen marked the place her head had lain. "Megan?" he croaked.

"She wasna here when we came in," Davey said.

"By all that's holy, if she's run off..." Heedless of his aching head, he sat up and threw back the sheet. Jesu, he was naked, yet had no memory of undressing. Worse, an ugly red stain marred the pristine white sheets. *Blood.*

Oh, God. He'd gotten drunk and bedded the wife he'd sworn not to touch. Damn. Damn. Damn. Angry as he was at himself, the sight of all that blood... too much blood... alarmed him. What if he'd hurt her in his rage and unreasoning passion?

Impossible! He could never hurt a woman. Yet clearly he had. Ross bowed his head. The part of him that was drawn to Megan despite her lies and lineage cried silent tears. Maddening as she was with her stubbornness and superstitions, 'twas a crime of the worst sort to have used her so foully.

"Get up. We've work to do," Andrew grumbled, drawing Ross's attention back to the three men who waited at his beside, grim faced and dressed for battle.

"What is it? What's happened?"

"They're loadin' the ship." This from Davey who held a plain woolen tunic in one hand, Ross's chain mail over his arm.

"Fortune smiles on us at last." Guilt and aching head forgotten, Ross reached for the clothes and tugged them on while Owain, Andrew and Davey filled him in on what had been happening without while he had been drowning his anger . . . and his disappointment . . . in wine.

"After we left ye, er, earlier, we went down to the village," Owain explained.

"The two men we'd left on watch were dead," Andrew growled.

"We waited several hours or more before we saw the ship sail in and realized what was afoot," Owain added.

"When was this?" Finding two hours had passed since the discovery, Ross frowned. "Why did you not come for me then?"

All three men looked at the bed, then quickly away. "We thought to gi' ye what time we could," Owain replied.

Would that they had come sooner, Ross thought darkly.

"All is in readiness. Our men left the castle in small groups. Some watch the village from a distance, others are in the rocks above the beach. Wee Wat is waiting there with a boat to row us out to *The Black Hawk*."

"Good. We'd best be off." Belting on his sword, he led the way from the room without a backward glance. The bloodstains were already engraved on his soul. Likely Megan had run to her mother for comfort. Soon enough to face them when he returned. The prospect of trying to apologize was almost more daunting than that of climbing aboard the enemy vessel in the harbor.

"At least there's no moon tonight," Ross said when they were outside. But the darkness made haste dangerous. They crept from Curthill Castle's postern gate, made their way slowly along the edge of the bluff and thence down the winding trail to the beach. A light chop ruffled the inky sea. Not enough to make rowing too difficult, even for landlubbers like them, Ross judged as he stepped into the small craft Wee Wat had purloined.

With Wee Wat and Owain showing remarkable skill at the oars, they moved smoothly around the point of land and into the crescent shaped harbor. Torches flickering on the beach lent an otherworldly quality to the activity there. Men scurried between loaded carts and the line of boats waiting to cast off, carrying bulky shapes . . . furniture, kegs and trunks.

"It appears we're in time. Now if only we can find proof aboard," Ross murmured as they drew nearer the ship. She bobbed at anchor like a queen bee attended by a swarm of worker boats bringing the stuff to fill her belly. That she was being fed on the misery of others turned Ross's sensitive stomach. "Fall in behind that boat there," he whispered. "Row around to the far side of the ship and tie up to the anchor rope. I'll—"

"Ye'll wait here," Owain said, low and sharp.

Ross shook his head. "Nay. I'm the only one who reads English and French." That shut Owain up, temporarily. Though Ross did agree to take Wee Wat along to act as lookout.

With all he'd been through since coming to Curthill, climbing the anchor rope hand over hand taxed Ross's slim reserves. He was panting for breath by the time he reached the rail. A quick look through the slats showed that the men on deck had their backs to him and were absorbed with packing the hold. Heaving himself over the rail, he rolled into the shadowy lee of the aftercastle. A faint thump marked Wee Wat's arrival.

"'Twas a fair taxin' climb," the little man whispered. From inside his tunic he produced a small skin and offered it to Ross.

The *osquebae* burned his throat and lit a fire in his belly that spread quickly, lending vigor to his flagging muscles. Conscious of the passing time, Ross scanned the area to get his bearings. The ship was similar to the cog his cousin Alex Sommerville owned. Having spent a summer aboard her, he knew the small structure atop the aftercastle housed the captain's cabin.

Ross eyed the open space he must cross to get from his hiding place to the short staircase leading up to the cabin. He needed a diversion. Spotting a cask of wine nearby, he plucked out the bung and rolled the keg across the deck. "'Ware," he cried as dark red wine squirted in all directions.

The sailors scattered, then converged on the puddles of burgundy. Some used their hands to push the liquid overboard, others bent to lap it up like hounds.

Grinning, Ross sprinted up the steps and cracked open the cabin door. Empty. A candle burned on a tiny table bolted to the floor. Beside it were a flagon and two cups. The captain had been here recently . . . with company. The reclusive Eammon Sutherland?

Uncertain how much time he had, Ross made for the small desk built into one corner while Wat watched the door. The captain was a messy fellow. Papers littered the desk and spilled onto the floor. Somehow Ross doubted what he wanted would be lying around in plain sight, still he scanned the parchments quickly. Nothing. He tossed them aside and started on the desk drawers.

In the bottom one he found a small chest and picked the lock with the tip of his dirk. The first thing he saw when he lifted the lid was the manifest of the *Fleur de Brittany,* out of Calais and bound for London with a cargo of goods for Lord Danby. The same Lord Danby who was buying from Douglas?

Anticipation quickening his pulse, Ross read the list aloud.

"Wait. Some of those things were on that list in Laird Eammon's room," Wee Wat said. "Those devils, they wrecked the ship, and they're sellin' her cargo back to the original owner."

"Likely. But how did *The Brittany* come to be far enough north to be wrecked on Sutherland shores?"

Beneath the manifest was *The Brittany*'s logbook. The last entry was hurried and nearly indecipherable: *Under attack by pirates. They fly no flag, but the ship is* The Black Hawk. *To any who find this log, know that my men died bravely.*

Pirates. Ross raised his head, the parchment crinkling as his fingers tightened on it. So, this was Eammon's trade. Small wonder no one suspected Eammon of any wrongdoing. *The Hawk* hunted far from Curthill, then brought the ill-gotten goods here to be repaired and resold . . . either to their original owner or to some other unsuspecting noble in far-off London.

White-hot rage drove the fatigue from Ross's body. Bad enough Eammon had pillaged and murdered, but he'd also made slaves of his own clan. Curthill town still retained its worn fishing-village look, with its rutted streets, broken down homes and hardworking people while the laird lived in sumptuous luxury with his expensive whore. Lion had died so that Eammon's trade could remain secret. But it would not remain so much longer.

The budding taste of revenge sweet on his lips, Ross set down the logbook. From beneath his cloak he drew the parchment case that hung from a cord around his neck. Quickly sorting through the contents of the chest, he crammed proof of the plundering into the waterproof leather tube. "In a way, we'll be avenging these dead sailors," he murmured as he dripped candle wax onto the rim of the case to seal it shut.

'Twas but a moment's work to replace the chest where he'd found it. And none too soon, for heavy feet stomped up the stairs toward the cabin. The sound sent Ross diving to douse the candle. Just as it went out, the door opened.

"What the hell's goin' on?" demanded a coarse voice. The large figure filled the doorway for only a moment before lunging toward Ross. "I'll teach ye to steal from Bardolph Douglas."

Hard hands closed around Ross's throat, lifted him from the floor and shook him as a hound would a rat. As stars exploded in his brain, Ross lashed out with both legs. They connected with a satisfying *oof,* but the fingers wrapped around his neck continued to relentlessly squeeze the life from him.

Ross shoved and kicked and bucked, but he couldn't pry himself loose. His throat ached, his lungs burned; the dancing stars were fading fast, crowded out by an endless black void, and Ross knew he was close to losing . . .

"Ach." Douglas shuddered, cried out again, then dropped Ross in a heap. He tottered two steps with Wee Wat's dirk sticking out of his back, then gasped and pitched forward. The whole cabin trembled as he hit the deck.

"I wanted him alive," Ross rasped, rubbing his bruised throat as he staggered to his feet.

"Sorry. 'Twas the only way I could stop him."

"My thanks." Ross sighed. "I needed his confession."

"Ye wouldna ha' gotten word one out o' a hard case like him." Wee Wat wiped his dirk on the captain's tunic and slipped it back into the top of his boot. "We'd best be gone."

"Aye." Ross secured the parchment case under his cloak and jerked open the door. "Come, we need to disable the ship." From his days aboard his cousin's ship, Ross knew what to do.

Leaving Wat to stand watch, Ross crept down the stairs and ducked under the aftercastle. Here the helmsman maneuvered the long wooden rudder by means of a shaft, ropes and pulleys. Since they rode at anchor, the man was not at his post, but just as Ross's blade slashed through the ropes, his luck ran out.

"Someone's done the capt'n in," bawled a voice from above.

"'Ware. We've been boarded," shouted another.

Ross and Wee Wat wasted no time in running to the rail.

"Hope you can swim," Ross shouted over the sounds of pursuit.

Wee Wat spat. "Reckon I'll learn." But the little man's scream followed them down. They hit the water in unison. 'Twas like diving into a deep, black pocket.

Salt water stung Ross's eyes, his nose, the barely healed wound in his shoulder. Disoriented, in pain, he gritted his teeth and kicked out frantically with his legs, praying he didn't come up under the ship. He bobbed to the surface like a cork and was immediately struck in the back by a flailing arm. Turning, Ross snagged Wat by the scruff of the tunic. "How goes the swimmin'?"

"I ain't drowned yet." To his credit, Wee Wat did not panic and grab hold of Ross, though the torchlight reflected in the churning water showed a man who desperately wanted to.

Wat's courage gave Ross the push he needed to fight off his own demons...exhaustion and pain. With one hand he tucked the parchment case more securely under his armpit. "We need to find Owain and the boat."

A row of white faces appeared at the rail. "There they are! After them, lads!"

"Not me. There's beasties in the water at night."

Ross grinned. Here was one superstition he approved of. Before the sailors could overcome their fears, Owain maneuvered the rowboat between the ship and the swimmers.

"Give me yer hand." Owain had them out of the water in a trice, began rowing while his catch lay on the bottom of the boat, gasping like beached fish.

Wat was the first to recover, scrambling up beside Owain and taking an oar. By the time Ross had pulled himself onto a seat, they were straining in unison like a pair of yoked oxen. But they were rowing into the wind and making slow headway despite their valiant efforts. Worse, the rising shouts from *The Hawk* were sure to alert the soldiers on shore. Even as Ross turned in his seat, a volley of arrows from the ship filled the night sky.

"'Ware!" Ross reached beneath the seat, came up with one of the shields he had stored there. He raised it over their heads like the Romans' defensive turtle of yore. The single, metallic thunk as an arrow struck the shield made the tearing pain in his shoulder worthwhile. Two more deadly missiles hit the shield before the tiny boat drew out of range.

Then and only then did Ross make any concession to his screaming muscles. Setting the shield aside, he sagged in the seat, allowed his back to rest against the prow of the boat. "'Twas a close thing, but I got what we came lookin' for." As they crossed the choppy harbor, he told Owain of their find. "Too bad about the captain. I needed him as a witness."

Owain grunted. "Better him than ye."

"I suppose." Ross turned his face toward shore, his thoughts to the next steps in his plan.

Giles and twenty men rose from the rocks the moment the boat scraped on the sandy beach. "We heard the shoutin' aboard ship and feared the worst," the young knight exclaimed.

"We're a bit wet, but otherwise none the worse for the jaunt," Ross replied, the ache in his shoulder dulled by the sweet thrill of triumph. Quickly he sent Andrew and Giles to seize the storage hut and the pirates. "They canna sail away at present, and I want a few of them for Lord Nigel to question."

Ross took Owain, Davey and ten others back with him to the castle. As they passed through the hall, Ross fought the urge to dance and shout his triumph to the soot-stained rafters. He'd not celebrate until the evidence in the case clasped tight under his arm had been placed in Lord Nigel's hands.

"Why here's the bridegroom now," shouted that very lord. Weaving in a chair by the cold hearth, he raised a cup to Ross.

Changing direction, Ross picked his way across a floor strewn with abandoned cups and slumbering bodies. "M'lord, I have somethin' very important to show you."

"Seems to be my night for catchin' young bucks creepin' about," his lordship said. "This one was goin' ridin', of all things." He gestured toward Comyn, perched in the other chair.

"I bring grave news," Ross said. "I fear Laird Eammon is a pirate, a smuggler and a murderer."

"What?" gasped Comyn and Lord Nigel in unison.

"I've proof." Ross broke the wax, drew out the papers and shoved them under the red nose of the king's uncle. "See, here are the manifests, and pages from the logs of three ships, all lost to *The Black Hawk*. Which even now sits in yon harbor."

The old man's bleary eyes widened as he tried to make sense of the documents. "If true, 'tis a grave charge. Come morn, we'll rouse Father Simon and he can decipher these for me."

"Nay." Ross grabbed the old man's arm, stopped just short of shaking him. "If we delay, the bastards'll get away. My men are roundin' up the ones in the village. When you question them—"

Comyn made a choking sound.

Ross turned from Lord Nigel. "I regret distressin' you. I know Eammon practically raised you, but justice must be done."

"Of... of course." Comyn stood, and Ross realized he was dressed for riding in rough wool and chain mail.

"Wherever are you bound this time of night?"

"There's nothin' a Highlander likes better than to ride abroad on a night like this."

Cold and windy with a storm approaching? Strange people. "I am going up to confront Laird Eammon now," Ross told Lord Nigel. "Lest he hears I visited his ship and tried to flee. I'd appreciate your coming wi' me . . . in case he objects."

"Oh, very well." The old man nudged awake the squire dozing behind his chair. "Lend me yer support, or I'll nae make it."

Comyn fell in beside Ross as they left the hall. "I'll come, too. It may ease the laird to ha' me there." His pale eyes glittered with an odd mix of fear and determination.

"You are kinder than he deserves," Ross said, but he understood such loyalty. His own anticipation mounted with every step he took across the dark courtyard and up the tower stairs toward Eammon Sutherland's lair. This was it. The moment when he'd face the man who had ordered Lion's death.

"The door is unbarred," Owain whispered. At Ross's nod, the Welshman eased the iron-banded oak door open and slipped inside. Two more of his quick, silent countrymen followed.

Pulse pounding in his ears, Ross went in after them. Despite the late hour, two tall candles burned in brass wall sconces and the fire leaped high in the hearth. Costly tapestries lined the walls; fine furniture filled every available space. The remains of a meal cluttered a table set for two, but the people who'd eaten the roasted venison and drunk the wine were gone.

A noise came from the open doorway across the room. The breathy, unmistakable cries of two people locked in passion.

So. This Felis really did keep Eammon up half the night.

Ross gestured for his men to fan out. Skirting the outside of the room, they came up on the door from all sides. At the count of three, they burst in.

'Twas dimmer here, but Ross could make out the couple on the bed. The man supine, Felis riding him in all her naked glory. She looked up, got out no more than a strangled gasp before Ross was around the bed, his dirk pressed to the throat of her mount.

"Dinna move, Laird Eammon," Ross growled.

But is was not Eammon Sutherland.

"Archie . . . do somethin'," Felis shrieked.

The captain made a choking sound, eyes wide with horror, his throat moving convulsively beneath Ross's blade.

"What the devil?" Ross exclaimed. He darted a glance at Owain, saw that the rest of the men had filed into the room.

"I can see why Eammon's been locked up in here," Lord Nigel blurted out, ogling the wench with some interest.

Comyn's face had gone dead white; his eyes were locked on Archie with murderous intent. Clearly he took exception to the captain fiddling with the laird's leman.

"Ross . . . look here." Wee Wat had lifted up the bed covers on the far side of the bed. A man lay there, curled up in a tight ball. His eyes were open, but glazed and sightless.

"Is he dead?" Ross asked.

Wee Wat shook his head. "Dead to this world, but alive."

"Who . . ."

"Why, 'tis Eammon," Lord Nigel exclaimed, leaning down to peer into the man's gray, gaunt face. "He looks like death."

"He mayna be far wrong," Wee Wat said darkly.

Ross pressed his blade against Archie's throat, drawing a thin line of blood. "What goes on here?" he demanded.

The captain's squinty eyes went wild. "Nay. I'll not hang alone." He shoved Felis at Ross, toppling them both to the floor.

Felis cried that she'd been cut and went on screaming in Ross's ear while he struggled to get free of her naked, clinging arms and legs. Out of the corner of his eye, he saw Archie scramble off the end of the bed.

"Stop him," Ross shouted. Throwing Felis off, he lunged to his feet, stripped the sword from its scabbard as he swung around the bedpost and launched himself at the captain's fleeing back.

Comyn was there first, meeting Archie with a swift thrust of his own sword that sent the captain staggering back.

"Bastard . . ." Archie hissed. Both hands splayed over the gaping hole in his chest. Blood flowed between his fingers, flecked his lips as he drew a gurgling breath. "I should never ha' trusted . . ." He pitched face first onto the floor, making far less noise than Douglas had. But the result was the same.

"Damn. I wanted him taken alive." Ross came to stand over the man, oblivious to Felis's rising screams.

"Ye said ye wanted him stopped," Comyn pointed out.

Ross bowed his head and groaned in frustration, his mind reeling from the latest turn Fate had taken. It had been a night of ups and downs, of good fortune and bad. But this was most dispiriting of all. To come so close to solving the crime and punishing the guilty, then lose the two men responsible. Dimly he heard footfalls and loud voices drawing nearer. The castle folk came to investigate the commotion. "Owain, keep this room clear till we can sort this out," he ordered. Too late.

Lady Mary rushed in clad in a bed robe and cloak. She spotted Archie's body, checked her headlong dash and swayed. A wide-eyed Chrissy steadied her from behind, but the lady shook off the help, darted forward and knelt to the body. Her hand trembled as she reached to touch the prostrate man. "Oh, Eammon."

"'Tis Archie Sutherland," Lord Nigel said with surprising gentleness. "Eammon lies here, on the bed, but . . ."

The lady was on her feet and beside the bed in an instant. "Oh, Eammon." Tears tracking silver down her face, she tenderly touched his tangled gray hair. "What have they done to you?"

Ross went to join her. The candles Owain had brought into the room revealed much that had been hidden in the dim chapel yestereve. Dear God, was it only last night? It seemed an age ago since he'd wed Megan.

This was his nemesis? Jesu, he'd seen embalmed bodies that looked livelier, Ross thought, taking in Eammon's parchment-dry skin, cracked lips and vacant stare. The centers of his brown eyes were as tiny as black pinheads. The laird hadn't looked this ghastly yesterday, but then it had been dark in the chapel and Ross had had other things on his mind. "Is he alive, Wat?"

"Aye. But his blood flows far too slowly." The little man removed his fingers from the pulse point in the laird's neck and straightened. "I've seen men like this a time or two before in my travels. He's been drugged . . . opium'd be my guess."

"Opium!" Ross's exclamation mingled with Lady Mary's cry as she buried her face in her hands.

Wee Wat lifted a cup from the bedside table and sniffed cautiously. "Aye, there's opium in this, right enough. Ye can smell the stuff. Sickly sweet as a harlot's kiss and twice as treacherous." He lowered his voice for Ross's ear alone. "By the looks, they've been feedin' it to him for quite a while."

Ross blinked, brain scrambling to fit everything together. "So, Eammon wasna behind this after all. Archie kept him prisoner here and let the whole castle think Eammon was enslaved by Felis's charms, yet all the while he ruled in the laird's name."

"I should have known Eammon hadna turned against me, against our family," Lady Mary wailed, stroking her husband's gaunt cheek. "I should have had faith in him...as Meg did." She shuddered violently, then squared her shoulders and dashed away her tears with the bravery she'd passed on to her daughter. "Can we save him?" she demanded of Wee Wat. "Only tell me what to do."

"I dunno." Wee Wat stroked his stubbled chin. "We'd ha' to wean him off the stuff. But 'tis a fearsome business. Dreadful. And even then ... if the mon's nae strong enough ..."

"Anythin' ... I'll do anythin' to save him."

Ross turned away from her anguished expression, certain that Wee Wat would do what could be done. "See if you can calm the whore down and find out everythin' she knows," he said to Owain.

"My place is with ye," the Welshman replied.

Comyn stepped over Archie's body. "Let me. 'Tis a debt I owe Eammon," he added grimly.

Felis's screams turned panicky as Comyn approached her. She tried to run, but he knocked her unconscious with a vicious slap, tucked her under his arm like soiled linen and exited the room with a promise to return when he had wrung from her all she knew.

Ross gritted his teeth. It went against the grain to see a woman treated so...even one such as Felis. Jesu, he'd lacked the guts to kill Rhiannon. She had died nonetheless, in a manner far worse than any he could have devised. Speaking of women ... where was Megan? Why wasn't she here?

Thinking of Megan caused one idea to rise above the others rioting in his tired brain. *Eammon couldn't have killed Lion.* Nay, Archie and Douglas were the villains here. Relief poured through Ross, dizzying him so that the people clustered around Eammon's bed blurred. But they didn't matter. Nothing and no one did but Megan. Megan Carmichael. His wife.

The guilt, the longing, the doubts were gone, washed away by the truth . . . Eammon had not killed Lion. Ross could take Megan home, live with her in peace and . . . and love. They could be together now, as she'd wanted from the start, as he'd come to want with all his body and soul. Aye, he wanted her, in his arms, in his heart. He ached with the need to hold her.

"Megan?" Frantic with the craving to be with her, Ross searched the chamber in a single glance but failed to find his new wife. *God, had he hurt her so last night she was unable to walk?* Nothing less would have kept her from her beloved papa's side. "Chrissy? Lady Mary? Where is Megan?"

The two women exchanged troubled looks. "She . . . she left a few hours ago," Lady Mary said slowly.

"Left? Left for where?" Ross demanded, alarmed.

Lady Mary sighed. "Siusan has taken ill. Megan went into the mountains to fetch her home. 'Twas all she'd say."

"You let her go alone!" Ross roared.

The lady flinched. "Lucais is wi' her. Megan said there was no one else she could trust."

No one she could trust. That was his fault. God curse him for his hasty threats, his lack of faith. But he'd make it up to her . . . if it took the rest of his life.

"Where are ye going?" Owain asked as Ross spun away from the bed and dashed out of the room.

"To find Megan." Behind him, men scrambled to keep up, but panic lent wings to his feet and Ross flew down the steep, winding stairwell at breakneck speed. Dimly he heard Owain urging caution and Davey shouting about the need for mail and helmets. Ross had only one need . . . to find Megan as quickly as possible. Now would not be soon enough.

Owain caught him at the stable door and dragged him to a halt. "Be reasonable. We need trackers, and—"

"Rouse them, then," Ross growled, his breathing as choppy as his thoughts. "But they'd best be quick, because I'm—"

"M'lord..." A Carmichael trooper stumbled out of the stable's dark interior. His clothes were rumpled, blood poured from a gash on his temple. "Yer lady..."

Ross grabbed the man by the upper arms, trembling so hard the soldier shook, too. "What about her?"

"She...she and a young lad left before first light. I was on my way to tell ye, but...but someone hit me from behind and...and I knew no more."

Ross's gut tightened with dread. *Someone else was after Megan and Lucais.* But who?

Chapter Eleven

"There is someone followin' us," Lucais whispered.

"Are you certain?" Megan groaned aloud when he nodded. It must be Ross. That was all she needed. Bad enough she was terrified of falling off the swaybacked mare she'd taken from her father's stables, now she had this new fear to contend with.

"Mayhap we could outrun them and lose ourselves in the forest up ahead," Lucais offered.

"On horseback?" Megan squeaked. Once she would have seized the challenge eagerly, laughed as they raced across the moor to the dark shelter of the thick woods beyond. But that was before; this was now. She shuddered. "You go on ahead."

"Mount up behind me and I'll lead yer horse," Lucais proposed. "That way we can travel faster."

Megan nodded grudging agreement. Though it grated on her pride to be treated like a bairn, her knees ached so from gripping the mare's sides that they scarcely supported her weight when she slid out of the saddle. Cursing her weakness, she tottered over to Lucais, accepted his help in mounting.

"Hold on 'round my waist," he instructed. Odd as it seemed to be taking orders from this skinny youth who had been her page, Megan did as she was told. The year away from home and two trips into the Highlands seemed to have matured Lucais beyond his thirteen years. His hazel eyes were clear and confident as he looked at her down his beak of a nose. "Hang on tight, m'lady. 'Tis bound to be a mite rough."

Rough was a mild understatement, Megan thought as she bounced along on the horse's bony withers. They had left the coast behind and been climbing steadily into the short hills that marked the beginning of the Highlands. Her teeth clicked together with every bone-jolting step the beast took up the slope, her stomach heaved so she was glad she'd not taken the time to break her fast before leaving Curthill. And the ground . . .

Jesu, she dared not even look at it for fear the rocks would suck her down. Ross would have called it a silly superstition.

Ross. Megan's heart gave a leap that had nothing to do with the horse's ragged gait. 'Twas likely she'd never even see him again. He'd have sailed for home by the time she and Lucais brought Siusan down from the Highlands. With any luck they'd make it to Peebles and find shelter with her mother's kin, many leagues distant from Carmichael Castle. Not that Ross was likely to search for her, but . . . mayhap he already was.

She risked a quick look behind them, thought she saw riders crest the last ridge and start across the plateau. The distance was too great to make out any details, but she sensed him out there, his attention focused on finding her.

"We're goin' to circle left, away from the trail we need to take, then sneak back to it when the coast's clear," Lucais said over his shoulder as they entered the forest.

It was cool, sheltering beneath the outstretched limbs of the mighty oak and stalwart pine. "Could we stay here for the night?" Megan asked longingly.

"'Tisna safe."

"And we need to reach Siusan as quickly as possible," Megan finished for him. "Tell me again how she was when you left her?"

"Kinda pale like, and nae very strong."

"The feverfew I've brought will help her throw off the fever. And the rhubarb will strengthen her blood." *Sweet Mary, let it be so.* Her sister had already suffered so much.

Using paths so narrow they were little more than animal trails, Lucais guided them deep into the woods. The brush closed in around them, tearing at Megan's clothes, leaving thin red scratches on her arms. Her lame leg protested the strain; she was cold, tired and miserable. Worst of all was the ache in her heart whenever she thought of Ross and what might have been. If only . . .

Hours passed, or so it seemed. The dim light that filtered through the trees grew steadily darker until Megan wondered if Lucais could see where they were going. "Have we lost them?" she leaned forward to whisper in his ear.

"I think so," came the soft reply. "We've cut back until we're nearly at the trail we must follow up the mountain."

"Do we go on?" she asked numbly. He shook his head, and she was tempted to kiss the back of his grimy neck. "I—I could ride a bit farther if it's necessary." Somehow.

"The horses need rest and so do we. Here's as good a place as any." He dismounted, led the horses through a wee break in the trees and into a clearing scarce bigger than a bedchamber.

To Megan, it looked like heaven. With a groan of heartfelt relief, she slid from the saddle. Her feet touched ground, but her knees buckled so she would have pitched face first into the pine needles if Lucais hadn't caught her under the arms. He half carried, half dragged her over to the nearest tree.

"I hurt in places I didna even ken I had." She collapsed against the huge trunk. "I'll help you wi' the horses in a moment," she wearily promised.

"Seein' to the horses is men's work." He looked disgustingly fresh despite the ride, sounded even more disgustingly like Ross. It seemed she was doomed to be surrounded by arrogant men. "Do ye think 'tis Lord Ross followin' us?"

"I dinna see why my hus—" Nay, she must stop thinking of him as her husband. He'd made it clear enough he did not want *her*. The ache in her chest intensified. "Lord Ross is likely at Curthill sittin' down to supper."

"I suppose. No one seemed to mark our leavin'."

"Except Chrissy and Mama." She'd been forced to rouse them when she had gone to her old room to gather clothes for the trip. Certain her mother would insist on accompanying them, Megan had braced herself for yet another fight. Her mother surprised her.

"I sensed somethin' was wrong. I've been thinkin' about Siusan for the past few days," she had said slowly. "'Tis as though she was . . . was reachin' out to me, you ken?"

"Only too well." 'Twas not the *second sight*, exactly, but the Sutherland family ties were strong, and from earliest days, Megan had been taught to listen to her inner feelings.

'Twas partly for that reason Megan had refused their offers to come with her. Those two were worse riders than she was. The last thing Lucais needed was to be burdened by three horse-shy females. Her mother had squeezed her tightly, then let her go, dabbing at her wet face with the sleeve of her bed robe.

"Was Lord Ross . . . kind last night?"

"Aye." The lie had twisted deep inside her. Megan had pasted on a smile she hoped hid her pain.

"When...when you return, there is something I—I must tell you. Should have told you ages ago, but I . . . I fear that I am a coward at heart, and . . ."

"Nay, Mama, you have the heart of a lion," Megan had interjected. "I only hope that if I am tested as you have been these last years I will act as bravely."

"You already are brave, dearlin'." Her mother had hugged her again. "See how much you've overcome in your short life."

And how much more she had to overcome. *Oh, Ross*. If only things had been different between them. If only. . .

Megan started as Lucais set down beside her the sack containing her book and clothes. She was not brave. If she had been, she'd not be fearing the dawn when she'd have to climb back on the horse and somehow endure another day of terrified misery.

"Are ye all right?" Lucais asked. "Ye moaned."

Megan fought the urge to fling herself on the ground and cry. "I am fine," she said shakily. "Only tired." And sore and frightened and brokenhearted.

"And hungry, too, I'll warrant." Lucais plopped down beside her. "We dare nae risk a fire, but I stole a bit of food from the kitchens this morn." He felt for Megan's hand, filled it with a thick slice of bread wrapped around a slab of fowl. "There's a skin each of water and wine," he added.

To her surprise, Megan found she was hungry. Leaning her spine against the rough tree trunk, she munched steadily. The forest sounds closed round them, the soft whisper of wind through the pines, the cooing of the birds as they settled down for the night in the branches overhead.

An odd sort of contentment seeped through Megan's body along with the warm glow left by the wine she sipped when the bread was gone. Accepting the blanket Lucais handed her, she stretched out on the ground, absently massaging her knotted thigh muscles. In three days, four at the most Lucais had promised, she would be reunited with her sister. Then the four of them would set out for the Lowlands and a new life.

The snap of a twig, the shrill cry of the birds as they took flight was the only warning Megan had before a hard, male body crashed down atop her, pinning her to the ground.

"Lucais!" Megan cried, but from the crashing and thrashing around her, she guessed he had also been attacked. "Ross?" she gasped. "Get off me this instant." The rancid body odor and vile breath of her assailant filled her nostrils. *This wasn't Ross.* She struggled in earnest then, bucking, flailing and screaming for all she was worth.

The trip from the coast to the foothills of the Highlands passed in a frantic blur for Ross. No matter how hard he rode, it was not fast enough. Around every outcropping of rock, he expected to find Megan lying beside the path in a pool of blood.

His teeth ached from grinding them together. His chest ached from holding his breath. His soul ached from the weight of his guilt. He had never felt so...so desperate over another's safety.

"Ease up," Owain called over the thunder of galloping hooves. "Or ye'll kill the horses."

Ross started, felt Zeus's labored breathing between his legs and reined the stallion to a trot, then a walk.

"There's no sense in rushing, ye're near treading on my trackers' heels as it is." Owain pointed ahead to the trio of Welshmen working the trail, heads down like hounds on a scent. Only they sought the bent nail mark made by one of the horses Megan and Lucais had taken from Curthill's stables.

"They've a three-hour lead on us," Ross said defensively. "We shouldna have taken the time to load up provisions."

"That did not slow down our departure," Owain said. Indeed, the minute Ross had shouted his intention to go after

Megan, his men had swung into action like the cogs of a well-oiled mill. Many were veterans of the Welsh campaigns, each had assigned duties and performed them flawlessly. While some readied the armaments and horses, others filled saddle packs with oats, dried meat and water.

"We needed the food," Ross grudgingly allowed. "But the tents werena necessary."

"They're small enough to be carried by packhorses and easily erected," Owain argued. "Lord Comyn warned we'd find bad weather and little shelter in the Highlands. Would ye have Lady Megan sleep on the ground in the rain?"

Ross sighed. "'Tis nae more than she deserves for bein' so foolish as to go after her sister alone." But it was his own stupidity he cursed. He had underestimated both her desperation and her willfulness. A mistake he'd not make again.

"We'll find her," Owain murmured.

For once the Welshman's assurances did not soothe. "Soon, I hope. We're on alien soil with a storm fast approachin'," Ross snapped, worried by the ominous clouds overhead. "I'd find Megan before the rain washes away their tracks."

"We cannot be far behind then now," Owain said.

They made better time crossing the plateau, but the path along the forest was worn from solid rock, and the Welsh lost the trail. Ordering torches lit, Owain bade the men look harder.

"They must ha' gone straight ahead," Andrew reasoned. "Goin' through the woods would ha' slowed them down."

"Agreed." Over Owain's objections, Ross ordered the troop forward, hoping to come across their tracks farther on. The wind picked up, carrying with it the first fat raindrops. Ross was reaching back to draw up the hood of his cape when a scream split the encroaching darkness, echoing off the trees to their left.

Megan. Fear drowned out every concern save rescuing her. Ross wheeled around and spurred Zeus toward the woods.

"Hold. It could be a trap," Owain cried, close on his heels.

"Megan needs help," Ross shouted, as though that excused abandoning his customary caution. The trees closed around him, black as the inside of a cave. He paused only long enough for his eyes to adjust, for his ears to pick up the muffled grunts of a battle being waged up ahead. Touching his heels to Zeus's flanks, he gave him his head, trusted the stallion to pick his way between the trees.

Branches tore at Ross's clothes like hands seeking to hold him back. He flew past them, gut tight with a dread too terrible even to contemplate. *She had to be all right. He had to reach her in time.* The words pounded in time to his galloping pulse.

The scream came again, closer, a high, keening wail that cut Ross to the quick. "Megan!" he shouted as Zeus burst into a small clearing. Scarcely had the stallion halted before Ross was off his back and running. Sword at the ready, he cursed the darkness that reduced the battle scene to a few black shapes rolling around on the ground. "Meg! Where are you?" he roared.

"Here," came a muffled cry from his left.

As Ross turned to her, the other men caught up, crashing through the brush, bearing torches that turned night into day. In the flickering yellow glare, he saw Megan lying in a heap of tangled clothes, a dark-clad figure atop her.

"Fiend! You've killed her!" Roaring his battle cry, Ross grabbed her assailant by the scruff of the neck, pulled him off and tossed him aside. But before Ross could go to Meg, the wretch drew a sword and attacked him.

"Kill them!" the man cried.

A red mist obscured Ross's vision as he parried a thrust aimed at his heart. Never had he felt such overwhelming rage, such an unreasoning need to do violence. He wanted to kill this man and all the others for having murdered his wife. His woman. "Give no quarter!" Ross screamed. He eliminated his opponent with two swift strokes, then swung around to meet the next man.

"Ross! Ross! Lay down your arms. 'Tis done."

"Done?" Staggering slightly, Ross turned from the body at his feet. He cocked his head, images blurring...Owain, Andrew and a dozen others. White-faced beneath their blood-splattered armor, they ringed him at a distance. "All are dead?"

The wary-eyed men nodded in unison.

"Good." Ross lowered his sword. Lord, his arm ached, and his throat was hoarse, but the pain in his heart was the worst. "I must see to Megan," he said dully.

"I'm here." She stepped out from behind Owain but came no closer. There was blood on her cheek, speckling her skirt.

"You're hurt." Ross started forward, hurt anew when she cringed from him. Then he saw the hand he'd extended to her...red from gauntlet to elbow. "Blood?"

"Not yers. Hand Davey yer sword," Owain said calmly. "It wants cleaning and yerself, as well."

Ross glanced down, first at the blood-drenched blade, then at the man on the ground. Men. Two, three, four. "Jesu." The sword slipped from his nerveless hand. "I...I did that?"

"Most of it," Andrew replied, looking paternally proud.

Shuddering, Ross shook his head to clear it. "I dinna remember...except that I was angry."

"Very angry," Owain allowed. "But 'tis past." Turning away, he issued orders that sent the gawking troops scattering. Some went to set up the tent, others to round up the horses and dispose of the battle's grim consequences.

Ross shuddered again. "I dinna understand." He'd never, ever lost control in battle before. "I wanted to question them."

"And so ye shall. We got one of the wretches away..." *Before you could kill him,* hung in the air. "I can question him, if ye like, whilst ye clean up and see to Lady Megan."

"Megan..." Still feeling as if he were part of a waking dream, Ross turned to the only truly important thing here. She stood a foot away, eyes fear-widened in her too pale face. Suddenly the distance was unbearable. "Meg," he groaned. Heedless of everything but the need to hold her, he dragged her into his arms. Her yelp became a sigh as he crushed her close. Or was the sigh his?

"I was so afraid...you canna know how afraid," he rasped, kissing her neck, her ear, her hair. He wanted to do far more than that. He wanted...*God.* Ross dragged in air, fought against the things writhing and clawing at his insides, hot, wild things. Things he could not put a name to, except that they'd been tearing at him from the moment he'd learned she was gone. Lustful demons warred with the primitive urge to protect his mate. And to mate with her. Only in her arms, in her body, could he slake this terrible thirst. "Oh, Meggie mine."

"I am here," Megan murmured. He squeezed her so tightly the rings of his mail bit into her skin. Not that she was complaining. Even stinking of blood and sweat, 'twas heaven to have him hold her as though he wanted to absorb her into himself.

"Are you all right?" he growled in her ear.

"A little shaky." Small wonder. She'd seen men fight in the tiltyard and in contests at the Gathering, but none had shown the awesome strength, the single-minded ferocity of this warrior who was her husband. "Other than a bump on the head when that fiend jumped me, I am fine." Or would be when her stomach settled.

"Ye're getting her bloody," Owain muttered from beside them.

Ross dropped his arms and stepped back, leaving Megan feeling cold and bereft. "What of you?" she asked.

"'Twas a foul deed." He looked at his stained clothes in disgust. "Not even in the heat of battle have I done the like. My only excuse is that I saw you on the ground and thought you were dead. For the first time I truly hated."

"They'd have killed us had you nae come." An armed avenger appearing out of the night to save his fair lady. Just like the legendary heroes in her stories. Megan cocked her head. "I will compose a verse, nay, a whole tale, about this."

"To the one time I lost control?" His eyes widened in horror. "Nay, you willna."

There was that, still she could not condemn his actions. In some odd way, the fact that he'd come after her, fought to save her, made up for last night. "'Twould make a stirrin' tale."

"Jesu, are all Highlanders as bloodthirsty?"

"There is no shame in killin' your enemies before they kill you or your loved ones." His deepening frown cut her to the quick. "Ah, that is the rub." Her bubble burst. "You dinna love me...or even like me. Especially with what happened last night."

If anything, Ross's expression grew grimmer. "Megan." He stepped closer, reached for her again, then dropped his bloodied hand. "There are things I must tell you . . . but not here."

"M'lord. The tent is up," Davey called.

Ross nodded. "Go wi' him, Megan. I'll join you shortly."

And then what? Where did they go from here? Trembling with apprehension, Megan followed Davey to the tent pitched in a clearing above the woods. And not a moment too soon, for a cold raindrop landed on her cheek as she ducked under the tent flap.

Inside, it was small but well furnished, with a table and two stools and a wide sleeping pallet strewn with blankets and pillows. The fire burning in a metal brazier in one corner chased the chill from the tent. Almost as welcome were the soap, towel and bowl of warm water on the table and the bag leaning against it that contained her clothes and the precious book of stories.

"M'lord nearly killed us all gettin' here, but 'tis well worth it to have ye unhurt, m'lady," Davey said earnestly. He gave her a smile she gladly returned, then left to tend his lord.

Despite her aching muscles, Megan was out of her soiled clothes in a trice. There was not enough water to wash her hair, but after scrubbing herself clean, she unplaited her braids and brushed her hair out. Then she spread her soiled gown over one of the stools, donned a fresh shift and crawled beneath the blankets with a cup of the wine in one hand, her book in the other.

There wasn't enough light for reading, but she drew strength from holding the volume. When she'd finished the wine, Megan set the book aside and lay back amid the pillows. The burgundy warmed her chilled veins; the sound of the rain beating on the tent soothed her edgy nerves. Her mind drifted away from the coming confrontation with Ross and into the realm of make-believe.

Tonight she was not a lame, repudiated woman on a lonely quest to save her sister; she was the beloved wife of a brave, handsome knight just home from the Crusades. Their lonely years of separation were about to end in a night of passionate lovemaking that would bind them together for all time.

* * *

Dressed in clean clothes, hair still wet from a chilling dip in an icy Highland burn, Ross headed toward the trio of tents just visible through the fog. The shiver that raced down his spine was not caused by the chill seeping through his woolen cloak; it was the brooding quality of the dark mountains towering over them like harbingers of doom. The sooner they were out of the Highlands, the better.

"The bastard we captured claims 'twas Archie sent him after poor Lady Megan," Andrew growled through his teeth. *Poor* Lady Megan? Andrew's change of heart made Ross smile. "He didna know why, only that he was to capture her and bring her to a meetin' place north of this ridge."

"He'd use her to get her sister," Ross reasoned. "Which must mean that Siusan did witness Lion's murder."

"Odd she did not tell Lady Megan or her mother," said Owain.

Ross grunted. "If Siusan's mind runs in the same path as the rest of the Sutherlands', she doubtless kept quiet to protect them from harm. I've never seen such a family for thinkin' what someone doesna know willna hurt them."

"'Tis hard to say what Laird Eammon was like a year ago, but today he doesn't look capable of murder," Owain said slowly.

"Aye. It must ha' been Archie." After a year of hating Eammon, Andrew sounded confused by the turn of events.

Ross could not have been more grateful. All his problems had been solved . . . well, except that he had to atone to Megan for his behavior last night. Eammon had not killed Lion. The man who had was dead, along with his evil partner, which would put a stop to the piracy. All he needed to do was ride into the Highlands, question Siusan, return her from her self-imposed exile and sail home himself with his bride . . . his wife. Suddenly Ross could not reach the gray tent flying his pennant fast enough.

Halfway there, the sight of Lucais huddled close to the fire brought Ross up short. Here was the chance to get his few remaining questions answered. Changing direction, he hunkered down beside the lad. "You brought a message to my brother the day he was killed, did you not?"

Lucais nodded and shivered, pulling the blanket tighter across his bony shoulders.

"Who was it from?"

"L-Lady Siusan, but she didna mean him any harm," Lucais said in a rush, pale eyes filled with earnest tears. "She loved him."

Ross let go the breath he'd been holding. He didn't want Siusan to be guilty. "She wanted him to meet wi' her?"

Again Lucais nodded, shaking the moisture that clung to his hooked nose. He wiped it away on the back of his hand, sniffed and added, "But he never made it to the glen where she waited."

"Who knew where she would be?"

"Anyone wi' eyes in their head. What wi' the laird sayin' they couldna wed, the two of them had taken to meetin' in secret." The flush that colored his thin cheeks said he knew why, too.

So, Lion had not been able to keep away from the lass. Three days ago, Ross would not have understood such overwhelming needs, had not felt it even in the early days with Rhiannon. But now...

Ross's gaze strayed to the tent where Megan slept. He shuddered, thinking how close he'd come to losing her today. Doubtless thanks to the orders Archie had given before he died. Out of the corner of his eye, Ross glanced at the prisoner tied to a tree at the edge of camp. The wretch had told them all he knew. Come morn, Ross would have to decide whether to drag the man along or kill him for his part in the attack. No matter that the man deserved to die, remorse over his killing of the others stayed Ross's hand. But that was tomorrow's problem.

"Was Lady Siusan wi' Lion when he was killed?"

Lucais started. The Adam's apple in his throat bobbed as he swallowed. "Nay, but she found him soon after. When he didna arrive for their tryst, she went lookin' for him. He...Lord Lion died in her arms. When neither of them came back to the castle, Lady Megan sent me to find them. I...I came upon her a league from the glen, still cradlin' his head to her breast and keenin'." Tears glistened in his eyes. "Keenin' and rockin'. She . . . she loved him so much, she'd nae leave him, even after the Lady Mary came and tried to draw her away so the men could take him." The lad choked on a sob. "Lady Mary gave her somethin' to make her sleep. Even then, she wouldna release him. Finally they had to carry them back together, still entwined in each other's arms."

The lad's tear-streaked face blurred, and Ross looked away from the truth mirrored there, struggled to master the tears filling his own eyes. "Did Lady Siusan say anythin' about what happened that day?" he managed past the lump in his throat.

"Said 'twas her fault." At Ross's startled gasp, Lucais hurried on, "Nae, she didna loose the arrow that felled him, but she told Lady Megan that if she hadna been such a blind fool, she'd ha' seen the danger and saved Lord Lion."

"You mean she saw who shot him?"

"I canna say. But she knew somethin'."

"Did she tell Lady Megan?" Anger coursed through Ross. Had Megan lied to him about that?

"Lady Siusan denied she knew anything but...the ladies love each other well and sometimes they...they think to help by..."

"Lyin'. In a good cause." Once he'd have sneered the words; now he saw Siusan had reason to hide the truth. She must have known Archie was the real power at Curthill, knew he'd find a way to kill her, too, if she accused him of Lion's murder. Thank God she had *not* told Megan. That little firebrand would have stopped at nothing to punish Archie.

The image of Megan facing down Archie and that hulking brute, Douglas, rocked Ross to his very soul. A wave of possessiveness swelled inside him, nearly choking him. His eyes flew to the tent, and it was all he could do not to follow them, snatch Megan up and crush her to him, protect her with every fiber in his being. *Protect? Hah.*

He wanted to do far more than that. Fists clenching, Ross put aside his own desires as he had so many times before. "How soon after Lion's death did Lady Siusan leave Curthill?"

"'Twas a week or so," Lucais said, his gaze shifting away from Ross's as they had at first.

"Because Lion's killer threatened her?"

"There was a mite more to it than that." The lad shifted uneasily. "But I promised Lady Siusan and Lady Megan I'd not say more, so I canna tell ye, m'lord...even do ye threaten to break both my legs and cut out my tongue," he insisted, narrow shoulders squaring beneath the thin blanket.

Jesu, these Sutherlands were as fiercely loyal to one another as the Carmichaels, Ross thought, smiling faintly. Much as he wanted to press for every last detail of Lion's death, he had had enough of strife for one day. "Your steadfastness does you credit. My thanks for explainin' what you could, lad. I'll leave you to your rest."

Ross stood and turned toward the tent. He had his own trials to face and waiting till morn would not make them any easier.

Chapter Twelve

Anxious as he was to see Megan, Ross hesitated at the tent flap, torn between scratching on the leather and barging in as was his husbandly right. Rights be damned. At the moment, he felt more like a beggar at her gate. What was he to say? How did a man unused to being in the wrong explain away the many he'd done her?

His insistence that her father was a murderer was the easy part, given the circumstances. And 'twould be a pleasure to tell her she'd been right to have faith in Eammon. But how did Ross excuse his rape of her last night? A momentary burst of insanity?

More like a not-so-momentary burst of lust.

Damn and double damn. But he'd solve nothing standing here. "Megan?" Ross called softly, pushing open the tent flap.

Wonder, not indecision, stopped him in his tracks. Lord, she was beautiful. The candlelight set her hair ablaze, a golden banner unfurled across the pillows. Her lively features were soft in repose, one hand curled against her cheek like a sleeping bairn's. But the swell of her breasts rising against the sheer linen of her shift was all woman. His woman. His wife.

Desire kindled deep inside him, fed by days of wanting her, of watching her. His hunger was that of a starving man faced with the feast of his dreams. Nay, he thought as he moved closer, his need for her went beyond the passion that turned his blood to liquid fire, his loins to aching, twisted coils only her touch could ease. Not love; he had none to give. Yet what he'd come to feel for Megan was stronger, more overwhelming than mere desire.

Like a wildfire, it burned through his doubts, turned his memories of Rhiannon to ashes. This was Megan, brave, clever, loyal, laughing Megan. Like a lodestone, she drew him to kneel beside her pallet...the pallet they would share. He wanted. Jesu, he wanted to rip away the blanket that shielded her from his gaze, fall on her and sheathe his aching flesh in hers.

As though sensing the greedy need building inside him, she shifted, lips parting for the kiss that trembled on his lips, on hers as he brushed their mouths together.

"Ross..." Her lashes fluttered. "I've missed you." Her arms slid from under the blanket and around his neck, slender silken bands that drew his head down for another kiss.

Slowly. Dimly Ross remembered he should go slowly, but when her mouth opened beneath his, his control slipped a notch. Groaning, he took what she so sweetly offered, his tongue spearing in to taste, to explore, to tangle with hers as she shyly followed his lead. The honesty of her response humbled him; the feel of her fingers tangling in his hair as she sought to get closer threatened to burn away his good intentions.

Gasping, Ross tore his mouth from hers, closed his eyes as he battled the overwhelming rush of desire that surged through him. Hot. Relentless. Like nothing he'd felt before. But this was not the time to let his needs run rampant. She'd been ill-used last night and was exhausted now, surely deserved better than to be taken quickly by a man who'd turn animal in an instant.

"Ross...?" Her eyes opened, dreamy with sleep and passion. "Come, lie wi' me."

Ross needed no more invitation than that to strip off his tunic, hose and boots. On a moan of pure pleasure, he slipped beneath the covers, glorying in her answering sigh as she pressed against him, soft, warm and welcoming. What need for words when with his actions he could make amends for last night? he thought. Gritting his teeth against the driving urge for completion, he fought for control, found a measure when she shifted and winced. "What is it? Where are you hurt?"

"It's been years since I rode."

"Your leg?" he guessed, heart contracting as she ducked her head. "Let me massage it." He got the hem of her shift up before she could object, ignored her attempts to evade his hand as it closed on her waist. The murmured protests faded to a sigh as he massaged the upper swell of her hips. The sigh became a whimper when he explored the curve of her thigh. He flexed his fingers into the firm, resilient flesh and wrung a moan from her that neatly covered his own sound of pleasure. "Good?" he rasped.

She stubbornly held her tongue, but the way her body melted into the blankets with every sweep of his hands was answer enough. It was also pure torture to watch her, to touch her, to feel her quivering under his hands. A torture he richly deserved.

It was heaven, Megan thought. The cramp had left her more completely than ever before. Her blood sang and her very bones had turned liquid beneath his magic touch. How could the same ritual her mother and Chrissy had performed a thousand times since the accident feel so... so wonderful performed by him? Because he was her mate, her destiny.

"Megan? Are you asleep?" His breath fanned the side of her face, tickling the skin behind her ear. She wanted him to kiss her there. He did and her whole body, her whole being, came alive. *Oh, joy.* Somehow between last night and this he'd mellowed toward her, become the man in her stories, her dreams... warm, loving, a lover. "Ross... oh, Ross."

"Mmm?" In one fluid movement he was leaning over her, eyes dark, smoky pools of sensual promise.

She wanted them fulfilled, yet her quick tongue suddenly turned shy. "I dinna know how to tell you."

"You, at a loss for words?"

Megan licked lips suddenly gone dry. The hungry way his gaze followed that simple movement gave her courage. "I—I need you."

"And I you, but you are in pain."

The cramp in her leg paled beside the gnawing fire in her belly. "I need you. And you need me, too." More than he realized. Deep inside, he carried scars far worse than hers. Together, they could heal each other. If only he would let her...

"I do need you." His husky words slid down her spine like molten honey. "But this may not be the best time . . ."

She put her fingers over his lips and shook her head, drew strength from the shudder that racked his big body. "Now is definitely the time. I love you," she said simply.

"Meg." Ross groaned, turning his face into her palm. "How can you say that after all I've done? The ways I've hurt you?" *Jesu, she didn't yet know the truth about her father.* "Meg, I—"

"Shush. You've healed me, too." That he had not repudiated her for her leg meant more than she could put into words. Her nails rasped on thick stubble as she stroked his cheek. 'Twas like the man himself, prickly on the outside, soft inside. "There has been too much of violence and bloodshed and hatred. Come, let us find peace in each other."

One look at the hope that made her face glow in the candlelight and he knew he couldn't shatter her transient happiness by telling her that although her papa was not a murderer, he might well be a dead man ere they returned. Galling as it was, Ross decided to lock the truth up . . . for the moment. "Hot as things are between us, we'll be more likely to burn down the tent than forge a peace pact," he teased. His reward was in the slow, supremely female smile that set twin flames blazing in her eyes. The small stain on his soul was worth the price.

"I've dreamed of this." Megan twined her arms around his neck, drew his head down. The moment their mouths met, she felt a rightness that brought tears to her eyes. "This is even better than my dreams," she murmured in the instant before he took control of the kiss.

Deep, hot, demanding. The kiss was as different from the others they'd shared as a tranquil sea from a turbulent one. Where before his lips and tongue had coaxed, guided, now they swept her along in a sensual storm of feelings and sensations. Megan gave herself up to them without fear, glorying in the urgency with which his hands stroked her back through the blanket, molding their straining bodies together.

"Jesu!" Ross wrenched his mouth from hers, but instead of pulling away, buried his face in her hair. He should leave her, should stagger outside and stand in the cold rain until he had mastered this surging, white-hot lust. But he couldn't. Mayhap if he hadn't nearly lost her today, hadn't felt the provocative resiliency of her flesh beneath his hands, hadn't been surrounded by the scent of herbs and woman that was uniquely Megan, he'd have had the strength to resist, to let her sleep.

"Ross. Oh, Ross. It feels so good."

"What?" he croaked.

"Your arms around me." She snuggled closer, her hip nudging the rigid, sensitive length of him. "Does it feel good to you?"

"Too good," he managed.

"Silly. There's no such thing as too good." She laughed, the sunny sound rippling from her body into his, muting his passion as nothing else could have. It reminded him that despite all the sorrows she'd known, she could still laugh. That gift was as precious to him as she was. He'd not steal it from her by frightening her in his unbridled haste. She deserved better.

"Too good," he repeated, but this time the words were low, muffled as he nibbled his way down her slender throat.

"Oh." Megan moaned as his lips moved from her neck to her collarbone and lower, leaving a trail of fire in their wake. They brushed the upper swell of her breasts, and she arched closer. Beneath the shift, her nipples peaked, waiting, wanting. *Hurry. Please hurry,* she silently urged as he slowly pulled off the linen that kept her from him. Her legs shifted restlessly, trying to ease the pressure building at the juncture of her thighs.

"Beautiful," he whispered. His breath feathered across her breast in the instant before his tongue gently touched the tip, making her start in surprise. "Easy. You'll like this." He laved the sensitive peak, watching through lowered lashes as the flush of arousal turned her pale skin rosy in the candlelight. "Good?"

"Aye. Oh, aye." Heat exploded, radiated out from the hot rasp of his tongue, turned her blood to fire. Her senses came vividly alive, heart pounding, pulses throbbing with needs she couldn't begin to describe. Moaning, she tunneled her fingers into his thick black hair. The moan became a full-throated groan when he responded by taking her into his mouth. The wet, rhythmic tugging on her sensitive nipple sent chain lightning streaking deep inside to tighten the coil in her belly.

She wanted. Sweet Mary, she wanted. Just what, she was not sure, but he seemed to understand her need, for his magic hands roamed over her body, finding pleasure points she had not known existed, rousing them and her to a fever pitch. She cried out when at last his long, clever fingers reached the focus of her passion, slipping inside to send her senses soaring.

Ross echoed her cry as Megan arched against him, hands clutching his head to her breast, hips moving in a dance as old as time. With trembling hands he ripped off the linen braies he'd worn to bed. He wanted those legs wrapped around him, wanted her clinging to him as he buried himself deep, deep inside the lush wetness his fingers had found. And he knew she wanted it, too. Wanted it with an innocent passion that nearly matched his own.

Innocent. Eyes closed, Ross fought to regain some measure of control for her sake. For her sake, he forced his fingers from the softness he craved more than his next breath. "Easy, love. Easy." He stroked one hand down her thigh, felt the change from satiny skin to scarred and everything inside him froze. *Jesu, her leg.* How could he have forgotten? "I may hurt you."

"Only if you stop." She smiled, but her lip trembled. Stop now, and she'd think herself unwanted. Mention her leg, and she'd think it the cause.

"I want you." As proof, he matched the empty cradle of her thighs to the power throbbing in his. "But I'm too wide."

"I'd say the mare's back is wider than your hips, m'lord. If I managed to ride her, I dinna see the problem."

"Oh, Meg." He dropped tiny kisses onto her nose, her eyelids, her temples where the fine hair was pale as sunlight. "What am I going to do wi' you?"

She slanted him a teasing glance. "I hoped you'd know that."

He chuckled, the sound rusty, but growing less so the longer he was with her. He'd coupled...more times than he could count, but suddenly he could remember none of the women from his past...not even Rhiannon. "Strangely, I feel new at this myself."

"We'll find the way together." She leaned closer, kissed the square edge of his jaw, shivering again as her breasts brushed the crisp hair on his chest. A throaty growl shook that chest and Ross's arms closed around her so fiercely it drove the air from her lungs. Breathless, giddy with happiness and desire, she dared to explore. Her hands moved hungrily up his corded arms, across impossibly wide shoulders and down his massive chest. Beneath warm, satin skin, his thick muscles rippled and bunched. So strong. So solid and secure. This was what she wanted.

She stilled, overwhelmed by the sensations rising inside her like a great bubble. Passion, certainly, but more, much more. She felt...cherished. Cherished and protected. When his grip on her eased, she whimpered, "Nay. Dinna let me go."

"I willna...not ever," Ross whispered against her mouth before taking it in a possessive yet tender kiss. Silently he told her what mere words could not...how much he cared. She opened to him, sweet as a flower offering nectar, a prelude to the hotter, deeper joining to come. She trusted him, believed in him, loved him, he felt it in her touch, knew it in the depths of his bruised and battered heart.

"Ross!" Megan cried. Her legs twined with his, slender and delicate, hips shifting as she sought relief from the fire he'd kindled in her. The feel of her coming apart in his arms burned through the last of his restraint.

Groaning, Ross rolled her onto her right side to spare the left. Her thighs parted, openly seeking the mating that had been inevitable from the moment they'd met.

"Ross!" Megan cried again, the sobbing sound ending on a moan of pure pleasure as he sheathed himself in her heat. What pain accompanied that initial, swift thrust was lost in the wonder she felt as the power in his body surrendered to the softness of hers. "Now I am truly yours," she whispered.

"Mine." He said it over and over as they moved together. Slowly at first, then faster until her pulse was racing in time to the thud of his heart beating with hers.

"This is what I was born for," she gasped.

"Aye. I need you the way I do air, water." His voice gritty with barely leashed hunger, he nipped at her lips, her throat, her breasts, tiny, biting kisses that fueled her desire.

Suddenly she could not get close enough. Wrapping her legs around his lean waist, she took him deeper. He took her higher and higher. She soared, driven by the fevered pace he set, they set. The flames inside her spread, grew hotter and hotter until the fiery coil shattered.

Melding two into one.

I will never be alone again, was Megan's last coherent thought before wave after wave of ecstasy washed through her....

And into him. Ross groaned and buried himself in the core of the spasms convulsing up from their joined bodies, pouring himself into her, heart and soul.

Drained, satiated, Ross lay still in the wild, shivering aftermath, his senses filled with the scent of her hair, the soft puff of her breathing across his sweat-dampened skin. Never had he thought to find such pleasure, such oneness with a woman. 'Twas a miracle, thought this man who'd never believed in them. A miracle named Megan. His arms tightened possessively around her.

"Mmm." She snuggled closer, head tucked under his chin, one arm thrown over his chest, legs entwined with his. "Let us stay right here, just like this, for the rest of our lives."

Ross chuckled, planted a kiss on the top of her tangled hair and urged, "Go to sleep, lass. You've had a busy day."

"One that started badly, but ended—" she kissed the hollow where his pulse beat "—wonderfully. I like being your wife."

"And I like havin' you to wife." Mindful of the things left unsaid, Ross's smile dimmed. Tomorrow would be soon enough to taint her happiness with news her father was enslaved by opium.

Near sunset of the worst day of his life, Comyn rode out of Curthill. The thud of his horses' hooves on the wooden drawbridge echoed the hollowness in his gut. *Destroyed*. Years of careful planning and canny scheming, destroyed in a few minutes by a man he'd thought too slow and plodding to find his own butt.

Midway to the woods that bounded the castle on the west, Comyn paused to look back. A light shone from the window of Eammon's chamber where Lady Mary and that bedeviled gnome of a man, Wee Wat, worked to save Eammon's miserable life.

"Ill luck to ye," Comyn muttered and spat three times on the ground to seal the curse.

"Ye require somethin', m'lord?" asked one of his men.

"Ross Carmichael's death," Comyn growled. "And Megan's, as well." Aye, a slow, painful death to all those who'd crossed him. And he had the weapon to do just that, he thought, glancing at the twenty soulless mercenaries who rode in his tail. Ten more would be at the meeting place ... holding Megan and Lucais trussed up like piglets bound for slaughter. An apt description.

"What if Sir Giles discovers we havena gone into the village, as ye said we would, and comes after us?" Hakon asked.

"Let him." An evil smile split Comyn's face. "There's only a dozen Carmichaels, and I'd ha' killed them where they stood if it hadna been fer Lord Nigel's presence. Let them come."

"Aye, we'll slit their throats and dump them in a gorge so deep not even the beast of the night'll find them."

"That's the spirit. Come, we've a rendezvous to keep." Comyn kicked his horse into a trot, but just as he entered the woods, an animal streaked across his path.

"Jesu, what was that?" one of his men exclaimed, drawing rein so sharply his mount screamed in protest.

"I didna see ... a cat, mayhap," Comyn replied. "Come ..."

"Nay. I think it was a fox," someone cried.

Twenty deep voices groaned in horror. "'Tis an ill omen to ha' one cross yer trail when ye're startin' on a journey. We ha' to find it and kill it afore we can go on."

"Stop actin' like a brood o' bairns," Comyn snapped. But his fearless men, heartless hulks who'd been hired because no task was beneath them, milled and muttered, victims of their stupid superstitions. "I willna wait to search this vast forest for some beastie we wouldna recognize if we caught it," he declared. "Stay, and ye'll find yerselves a new lord. Come now, and I'll double what I offered to pay."

Amid much grumbling about dire consequences, all twenty men fell into line behind Comyn. "A bonus to the man who reaches the meetin' spot first," he said. It broke the spell fear had cast over them, sent the men crashing through the dark night.

Megan awoke with a start as an icy draft invaded her warm nest. "Where are you goin'?" she sleepily inquired.

A gentle hand smoothed the hair from her face so an equally tender kiss could find her lips. "The sun has long been up. 'Tis time and past we were on our... Jesu, I made you bleed again."

Megan glanced down, gasped and dragged the blanket over her soiled thighs. "'Tisna really *again*." As his frown deepened, she added, "That first night I got chicken blood from the kitchen and spilled it on the bed so that in the mornin' the ladies would see and not think I'd been impure... or unwanted."

The wobble in her lower lip as she said that last was Ross's undoing. He sighed and his anger drained away, too. "You shouldna have pulled such a low trick. Still, I am glad I didna hurt you... What of last night? You didna cry out...."

Her cheek dimpled. "What little pain there was, was naught compared wi' the pleasure you gave me."

"The pleasure we gave each other." But she noticed that he didn't return her smile.

"What is it? What's wrong?"

"Meg... there is something I must tell you." Apprehension raced down her spine as he stretched out beside her again. He drew her into the crook of his arm as though his embrace could deflect the blow. "Much happened after you left me on our weddin' night," he began, caressing her back as he told her about his middle-of-the-night visit to *The Black Hawk*.

"Piracy!" Her eyes narrowed. "I knew it was Douglas."

"Well, he is dead now, and Archie, too, though I wish I had been able to question them both about Lion's murder."

"Archie is dead? Why? How?"

"He was the mastermind behind this evil scheme."

Megan snorted. "Archie hasna the brains to plan his way out of a dark hole on a sunny day."

"Well, we caught him red-handed. In a manner of speakin'." Picking his words more slowly, holding her more closely, Ross related what they'd found in her father's tower rooms.

"Archie was abed wi' Felis?" Megan said. "But I thought..."

"That she was your father's leman." Mayhap Felis had been Eammon's at one time, but such speculation could only add to the hurt. "Nay, 'twas Archie we found in Felis's, er, arms."

"Oh, Mama must have been that happy. Where was Papa while all this was goin' on?" The hope shining in her eyes was so precious, knowing he must shatter it so painful.

Ross swallowed. "Damn. There isna an easy way to say this. Meg, your father was there, in the room wi' them, yet he wasna aware of them. Nor did he see me and my men come in, or hear Felis's screams. He... he is enslaved by opium."

She blinked. "Enslaved? What does that mean?" The dazed look left her, gradually replaced by panic as he told her what Wee Wat had said. Trembling, she asked, "Papa is goin' to die?"

"No one knows. Your mother is a skilled healer, and I left Wee Wat wi' her, for he has some experience in these matters." Her breath came in shallow gasps; her fingers dug painfully into his chest, but he'd not deny her whatever support he could give. "Let it out," he crooned, rubbing her shoulders, torn apart by the shudders that ripped through her slender body. "Cry, and when your tears are spent, we will decide what to do."

Megan shook her head, nearly choking on the lump in her throat. "I cried a river of tears when Ewan died, and again when I broke my leg. They dinna help. Oh, poor Papa. I knew... I should ha' done something. I should ha..."

"Shush. Dinna blame yourself. Archie planned shrewdly. He made it seem your sire was besotted with Felis so that no one would think his absences odd. The presence of a leman in your father's chambers kept you and your mother from intrudin', too."

Megan tipped her head back and looked him square in the eye. "You give Archie credit for more brains than he has...had. How came he to die if you wanted him alive for questionin'?"

"He caught us by surprise. One minute he was lyin' under Felis, the next he was up and fleein'. Comyn was forced to—"

"Comyn." Every suspicious pore in Megan's body went on alert. "Of course...it must ha' been Comyn behind this."

"Nay. Just because you dinna like him, is no reason to—"

"Ha. Comyn fooled you wi' his false smiles, but the truth is, he repudiated me for my lameness."

"Repudiated?" Ross blinked. "You were betrothed to him?"

"Aye. I see your *friend* didna tell you about that."

"Nor did you," he reminded her in frigid tones.

Megan shrugged, but there was nothing casual about the fear and anger roiling inside her. "'Twould have meant tellin' you about my leg, and I couldna risk bein' repudiated...again. I was contracted to Comyn as from childhood, but he never fancied me. He cast me aside while I lay recuperatin' from my accident."

"Surely you exaggerate," Ross murmured. "Comyn wouldna..."

"Just because he is a man? Oh, you make me angry." She punched him in the chest she had recently clung to. "Damn. What did that Rhiannon do to make you doubt women so, even me?"

Ross stiffened. "I willna discuss her."

"Ha! Knowin' how rabid you are for the truth, I wager she lied about some tiny thing and now you tar all women wi' that—"

"Cease." His hands tightened as though he'd like to shake her. Indeed, he was trembling with anger, but he controlled it. "You've had a shock. For that I excuse your outburst."

"Decent of you, indeed," she snapped.

His jaw clenched, but he held his tongue. "I even forgive you for not tellin' me about Comyn. Rest. We can stay here as long as you like, then return to Curthill. Andrew and some of my men can go wi' Lucais to bring your sister home."

"Nay," Megan said quickly, reminded of other duties. "Much as I want to go to Papa, Siusan's need is greater. I've brought medicines to treat her, but childbed fever is a tricky thing. And too, your men couldna cope wi' a sick woman and a bairn."

"She has a bairn?" He looked like he'd swallowed his tongue.

Megan damned her own loose one. But what was done was done. "Siusan swore me to secrecy, but..." The memory of his tenderness eased her concern. "I suppose now that you are my husband..."

"Whose babe is it?" Ross demanded.

"'Tis Lion's, of course. And there is no need to be angry."

"Angry! Angry!" Ross leaped up like a scalded bear, began to pace the confines of the tent like an enraged one. "My brother sired a bairn and you never told me? Even knowin' how much it would ha' meant to me...to my parents. How could you keep such a thing from us?" Then, before she could reply, "'Tis...'tis unconscionable." He stopped and turned on her, eyes narrowed to cold, furious slits. "Mayhap it isna Lion's."

"Wretch." Megan scrambled to her feet. Gathering both the blanket and her wounded dignity close about her, she faced him down. "Get you gone, then. Lucais and I will continue alone."

"The hell you will," Ross growled, coming to tower over her, not surprised that she yielded not an inch, only thrust her chin out to challenge his. "I will see this bairn for myself, then decide what must be done."

Dread prickled across Megan's skin. "What do you mean?"

"If the bairn is Lion's, I'll take it back to be raised among the Carmichaels."

What about Siusan? What about me? Megan couldn't breathe, couldn't think for the fear and misery pounding through her. "But you dinna understand how dangerous it was, how—"

"I understand. Another Sutherland lie." He made the name a curse. "Be ready to ride as soon as we've eaten." With that announcement, stark and forbidding as his expression, Ross threw a cloak on over his hose and tunic and stalked from the tent.

As the flap closed behind him, Megan's brave front crumbled. Sinking to her knees in the bed where they had made love only a few hours before, she closed her eyes and prayed for strength.

"What will he do?" she whispered through numb lips. And more important, what could she do to save Siusan and the bairn from this new threat?

Chapter Thirteen

"'Tis goin' to rain again," Andrew said sourly.

Ross started. Torn from his reverie, he turned his eyes skyward to find that though it was just past noon, the sky was once again dark as night and crowded with ominous black clouds. "We canna afford to stop," he muttered. If things had been different, he'd have ridden back and apologized to Megan for the soaking to come. As things stood, he doubted he could speak to her without shouting. And who could blame him?

"Lady Megan may have had good reason to keep the babe a secret," Owain murmured from Ross's other side.

"The best. A lie comes most readily to her lips." Ross sank his chin into the folds of his cape as the wind picked up. Last night he'd thought they'd made a start, forged a bond that would link them as closely as his parents were, but this morn that dream had been ground to death by her lies.

Ross's mood deteriorated along with the weather. As they crested the steep hill they'd been climbing all day and started down the other side toward the next one, the storm pounced on them. It began to rain, and the wind rose from a stiff breeze to a howl in seconds. Perversely, his first concern was for Megan.

Squinting against the icy spray, he turned to see Davey drape a blanket over her head and shoulders. It billowed about her while she struggled to wrap the edges close, and he knew she'd be soaked to the skin ere she got it round her. Damn. The sight of her slight figure battling the fury of the storm tore at something deep inside him. He wanted to go to her, take her up before him on Zeus and shelter her with his own body. 'Twas a feeling unlike any he'd had before, the nearly overpowering urge to nurture her, to care for her, to protect her from any and all.

"We'll stop here," Ross shouted into the teeth of the gale.

"Here?" Owain yelled.

"Impossible." Andrew's gesture encompassed the land around, the rocky, inhospitable glen they traversed, the steep slope ahead. Neither offered a scrap of shelter from the elements.

Lucais sidled his horse closer, cupped his hands to Ross's ear. "We canna stay here. The rains'll turn this wash into a ragin' river in no time. The woods begin again at the far side of yonder ridge," he offered through chattering teeth. "There's a weaver's cottage a mile or so within the woods. I've sheltered there before. The old woman's oft away from home, but she always has a fire laid and food put by. Said I was welcome to stay whether she was there or not. If we canna ride so far, there's a wee cave in the hills 'twixt here and the forest."

Ross nodded. "Take the lead. I'm goin' back for Megan."

"Aye, m'lord. Best take her up on yer horse," the lad shouted over the storm. "Since the accident, she's been that scared to ride. I worry about her keepin' her seat in this."

Afraid to ride. The phrase rang over and over in Ross's head as Zeus scrambled toward Megan. Dear God, she'd asked to ride with Lucais and he'd refused, thinking they meant to escape. He had seen the fear in her eyes and ignored it. Because he was afraid. Afraid of giving in to her, of losing control.

Davey made no comment as Ross transferred the lead rope from his horse to Zeus, but Megan glanced up at him when he swung his stallion in beside her mare.

"Af-fraid I'll escape in the r-rain?" she stammered through blue lips. Huddled under a wet blanket, water dripping off her nose and stubborn chin, she should not have looked appealing. God knows, she was more waif than beauty, but her attraction went past the delicately shaped face, the soft, vulnerable mouth, the silky, sun-shot hair. The wide, dark eyes staring up at him were mirrors to her soul, a soul as bright and clean as a child's, despite the burdens of pain and duty she'd borne.

Ross's heart stopped, contracted painfully, then started again with a lurch that made his whole body tremble. Oh, God. He loved her! Nay! He couldn't. He wouldn't. Shuddering with the force it took to shut the door, deny what he felt, he growled, "Aye. I've come to personally make certain you dinna escape."

Ignoring her fear-widened eyes, he tugged sharply on the lead rope and pulled her horse after him. They slid down the side of the hill, then joined the mad scramble of horses attempting the steep face of the next one. Mud obliterated the trail, turned the rocky hillside slippery and treacherous as greased slate. The line of march broke as every man and beast sought his own way up out of this wet, oozing hell. One man-at-arms went down, screaming as his horse faltered and the two of them rolled back into the gushing brown torrent that now filled the glen.

Ross paused, his commander's instinct urging him to leave Megan and help the fallen man, but in seconds the thick river washed its first victims down the mountain and out of sight. There was nowhere else to go but up.

"Hang on," he shouted, wishing he had Megan across his lap, in his arms, but realizing this was not the time to make the transfer. Her face was gray with fear. He gave her a smile that held far more confidence than he felt and prodded Zeus in the ribs. Beneath his thighs, he felt the stallion's powerful muscles bunch and knot as the war horse bullied his way up the slope, dragging the mare in his wake.

They popped over the crest of the hill like a cork drawn from a keg. To his left, Ross saw a black smudge in the rocks that he supposed must be the cave. Farther away to the right, marched the line of trees that marked the forest. Too far. The horses were done in, his men scattered. Tempting as the thought of the cottage and a warm fire were, they'd make for the cave.

"This way, Megan," Ross shouted, gesturing to the left. He caught a brief glimpse of her frightened face in the instant before her horse suddenly pulled away, snapping the line that bound them together. "Megan!" he screamed at her retreating back. But the wind and rain shoved her name back into his mouth.

It was her worst nightmare revisited.

One minute Megan had been in control, frightened by the headlong dash up the mountain, but definitely in control of her horse and her fears. The next her horse shrieked in pain, tore the reins from her numb fingers and bolted. The wind ripped the blanket from her grasp, exposing her to the drenching rain, but the icy deluge scarcely penetrated her panic.

A silent scream lodged in her throat, Megan grabbed hold of the horse's flowing mane, buried her face against its straining neck and hung on for dear life. For what seemed an eternity, the mare scrambled over the uneven ground as though the hounds of hell pursued them, then they burst into the woods and she momentarily checked her headlong dash.

"E-easy, lass." Megan straightened, ran a shaky hand down the blowing, trembling beast's neck and encountered something alien. "What?" A flash of lightning gave her a quick glimpse of the hard, slender object protruding from the dark hide and a sticky wetness that wasn't rain. "Blood?" Megan's hesitant touch made the mare scream, roll her eyes and take off again.

Branches and brambles snatched at Megan's clothes and hair as the horse dashed headlong through the black forest. Mouth dry, hands white where they gripped the pommel, she tried to stay aboard, but a low hanging limb whacked back, caught her under the left arm and lifted her clean off the horse. She sailed through the air, landed with a thud that drove the air from her lungs. Black dots danced before her eyes, sucking her down... down...

"Megan! Megan!" The hard, insistent, blessedly familiar voice jerked her back from the void. "Where are you hurt?"

She groaned. "Everywhere."

"Your head? Does your head hurt?" Ross caressed her forehead, her cheek, brushing away the wet hair that clung there. "Open your eyes, love."

Despite the pain, the endearment and the panic in Ross's voice intrigued her. She lifted her lashes slowly, saw a shadow crouched over her. Instinctively she recoiled. "Dinna . . . dinna let the horse roll on me."

"Your cursed mount ran off." She was alive and coherent. Ross swallowed hard, but the leaden taste of fear did not lessen. She was soaking wet, shivering uncontrollably and God only knows how badly hurt. The need to get her someplace warm and dry tightened the knot in his gut. "I'm going to lift you."

Her soft moan as he took her up in his arms, the blood that welled around her teeth where she bit her lip went through him like a lance. Never had another's pain seemed so like his own. "Steady," he said to her as much as to Zeus as he mounted.

That her eyes drifted shut again increased his concern, but mayhap it was better if she could escape the pain. With Megan cradled in his arms, Ross kneed the stallion into a slow walk. Despite the thick canopy of leaves overhead, the rain filtered down in a steady stream. Ross hunched his shoulders and gave his precious burden the protection of his body, keeping one eye peeled for the weaver's cottage. He nearly missed it in the dark, would have if Zeus had not stopped suddenly, perked his ears and looked to the right.

"What is it, lad?" Working one hand free, Ross drew the dirk from his belt and shifted Megan's inert form so he could use it if he had to. He hoped the stallion had heard Owain coming to look for them, yet was not disappointed when a thinning of the trees revealed the small cottage.

No light showed around the hide-covered window; no smoke rose from the chimney in the thatched roof, still he approached slowly and cautiously. A flash of lightning illuminated the area, making it apparent that the only inhabitant was a goat tied in the lean-to beside the cottage. Ross relaxed his guard, put his blade away. The empty stall beside the goat could have held a pony, if so, then the weaver was away.

"Damn," Ross whispered, his breath a puff in the cold, damp air as he looked down at the woman in his arms. He had no idea how badly she was hurt, nor how to help her. Why was she constantly placing him in situations that made him feel totally inadequate? The corners of Ross's mouth tightened. Nay. He was the one at fault. If not for his cursed pride, he'd have

asked about her accident, learned she feared horses and had her
ride before him where he could keep her safe.

Wet leather creaked as he dismounted, but Megan didn't stir
as he carried her to the door, lifted the latch and shouldered his
way into the cottage. As he ducked through the low doorway,
another flash of lightning gave him a chance to get his bearings. Fireplace to the left, pallet on the floor beside it.

Nonetheless, he bumped his hip on the table as he walked
blindly toward the pallet. When his feet kicked the straw-filled
mattress, he bent and laid his precious burden down upon it.
With the aid of a few more heavenly bolts, he found the flint on
the mantel, lit a thin taper and used it to ignite the twigs laid in
the tiny hearth. Watching the flame catch, he gave silent thanks
to the mountain woman's foresightedness, then set his mind to
the things that had to be done.

'Twas a moment's work to get Zeus into the lean-to, divest
him of saddle and the trail pack that held Ross's supplies. "I'll
be back to rub you down soon as I've seen to Megan, old
friend." He gave the stallion's rump a pat of gratitude, then
moved on to tasks far less familiar than bedding down his
horse.

Inside, the fire burned brightly, though it gave off little heat
as yet. Megan lay where he had left her. Frowning, Ross bent
and touched her throat. The feel of her cold skin, the faint,
unsteady beat of her pulse beneath his finger increased his
alarm. Damn. She had to be all right. She had to. He stripped
off his cumbersome chain mail and tossed it in a corner. Ignoring his own wet clothes, he divested her of hers with more
speed than skill. Her simple woolen gown laced up the back,
and when the strings knotted, he cut them with his knife.

The sight of her naked body, which last night had inspired
passion, tonight brought terrified concern. Jesu, her skin was
blue! All but the angry purple scar that cut her left leg from
hipbone to just above the knee. The pain she must have suffered.

Heartsick, he covered her with the weaver's thin blanket and
rubbed gently. Her body felt fragile; the way she moaned,
tossing her head from side to side on the pillow, made his gut

clench with renewed fear. Her hair was so wet it looked black in the dim light. Damn. He had to get her dry.

The worn linen towel he found on the table with the washbasin was barely adequate to dry hands much less Megan's thick, waist-length hair. Ross threw it down in disgust and ransacked the cottage like a madman. Beside the loom at the far end of the cottage's single room, he found bolts of fine wool.

Ross grabbed up the top two and hurried back to the fire. He swaddled Megan's body in a length of soft blue, wrapped her long, wet hair in coarser brown. It took nearly the whole bolt to get her hair dry. His hands were cramped by the time he'd finished, but he did not care.

Rocking back on his heels, he surveyed his work with a sense of pride. She was dry, and her lips looked less blue, now if only there was nothing damaged inside... Nay. He'd not think of that. Firelight glinted on the gold strands as he ran his fingers through her hair, trying to comb out the tangles.

"Ouch!" Her eyes opened, filled with reproach.

"Megan! Are you all right?"

She blinked rapidly. "Where am I?"

"In a weaver's cottage. I got you out of the rain, and—"

"Something stinks of wet sheep."

Ross grinned and touched a finger to her wrinkled nose. "I'm afraid that's you. There was naught but fresh-woven wool to towel you off wi'." He leaned closer, smile fading. "Tell me you are all right," he commanded.

"I... I canna move."

"Oh, God." Ross's stomach heaved. "Oh, Meg..."

"Some fool's bound me up like a corpse," Megan muttered, wriggling in an effort to get free.

Ross looked at the blanket and let out a sigh of relief. "Dinna move till I make certain you've naught broken." He gingerly touched her through the thick swaddling.

You'll learn naught that way, Megan nearly snapped, but his ashen features, the concern that darkened his eyes squelched the words. Sweet Mary, he looked worse than she felt. Gone was the cool, pompous Lord Ross. In his place sat a flustered man in wet, muddy clothes, face grimy, hair standing on end where his fingers had raked it. Over his shoulder Megan caught the gleam of chain mail dumped in a haphazard heap and winced.

He jumped back as though she'd screamed. "Oh, Lord. I hurt you. Is your arm broken?" He lightly touched it again.

"Nay." His concern chased the chill from her body faster than a fire. "I dinna think I've broken a thing, but if you'll loosen the blanket, mayhap we could better tell."

He unwrapped her with the care reserved for spun glass, stopping every second to ask if he'd hurt her. Each time, Megan shook her head and smiled encouragement. In truth, she did not think anything was broken, but his attention was so dear... "Is this the first time you've tended a wounded person?" she asked.

"Nay. On the battlefield, we often see to each other's hurts, but it's never been so... I've never felt so..."

"Helpless?" At his brisk nod, Megan's smile broadened. He still cared about her. More than he'd admit. She just wished she felt a little better in honor of the occasion. Her head hurt, every muscle in her body ached, especially her left leg where a cramp threatened. "I... I probably look like a drowned rat."

He scowled. "Why do women always worry about their looks? You should be glad you're alive."

"I am." Still it would have been nice to be wearing her best blue gown with her hair combed and her face clean. Megan sighed silently. "I am grateful. The last time I fell off a horse the results were much, much more painful."

"How did the accident happen?"

"I dinna remember the details too clearly. One minute my sister, brother and I were riding along the coast, the next my mare bolted. I—I tried to control her, but she was terrified. Too terrified to stop when we came to the gulch. We tumbled over the edge and she...she landed atop me." And Ewan's neck was broken.

"Jesu." Air hissed out between Ross's teeth.

"'Twas worse for the mare," Megan said lightly, hating the pity that had replaced his concern. Pity was the one thing she did not want from her knight.

Brave. She was as brave as any woman he'd ever met. He respected that even more than her wit or her beauty. "I'm glad you were not hurt this ti— What is it?'' he cried as a violent shudder shook her.

"I'm cold, of a sudden,'' she murmured, teeth chattering.

"I'll get another length of cloth.''

"On the inside. I'm cold on the inside.''

Oh, God. She was broken somewhere deep inside. "What . . . what can I do to help?''

"Something hot to drink.''

"Something hot.'' He leaped up and looked around as though he expected a servant to thrust a cup into his hand.

Men. How helpless even the strongest of them were at such times. Despite her aches, Megan smiled and turned her head toward the hearth. "If there is water in that black pot, set it over the fire. A cup of hot water will do if the weaver does not have any herbs with which to flavor it.''

He found water in a bucket, splashed some in the pot and put it on to boil. Lifting the candle he'd set down beside Megan, he prowled the room, muttering under his breath. After a moment, he rounded on her. "I feel the veriest idiot,'' he confessed. "I havena the slightest idea what I'm lookin' for.''

Nay. But he was trying so hard. A suggestion or two from Megan led him to a large basket tucked away in the chest atop the woman's few garments. He brought it over, sat cross-legged beside Megan as he poked through the basket.

"Gently,'' Megan admonished as he pawed at the crocks and sacks of herbs. "Take each one out and see what it is.''

He dutifully lifted out a crock and held it toward the light. "There's naught written on it.''

"I doubt the woman can read and write,'' Megan said dryly. "Try sniffin' them.''

Both black brows rose. "Fat lot of good that'll do.''

"Let me, then.'' Megan started to sit. White-hot pain lanced through her left leg. Groaning, she flopped back down.

"Meggie.'' Ross's frowning face hovered over her. "I'm goin' to look for Owain. He knows about healin' and such.''

"You'll do no such thing,'' Megan said, conscious of the rain pounding against the cottage. She'd not risk losing him in this foul weather. "We can manage. 'Tis just a cramp in my . . . my bad leg. Hold the packets beneath my nose.''

The fourth one proved to be chamomile. It took two cups of the stuff to warm her up.

"Better?" Ross asked as he laid her head back down on the pillow. At her nod, he polished off the cup she'd insisted he have. "'Tis not *osquebae*, but I do feel warmer myself. Has the pain eased? Can you sleep, now?"

Megan nodded, though her leg had knotted up like the fibers of a hemp rope, and she knew she'd not sleep until it eased. If Chrissy or her mother had been here, they'd have found a salve and massaged her leg, but...pain of a different sort twisted through her as she recalled the way Ross had looked at her leg on their wedding night. She couldn't go through that again.

Closing her eyes, she set her teeth against the agony and feigned sleep. She was very good at this, had had much practice over the years in avoiding others' pity by hiding her feelings. After a few moments he folded another layer of wool over her, rose and added more wood to the fire. His feet made little sound on the hard-packed earthen floor, but she felt him come and stand over her again. He smoothed the hair from her forehead with such gentleness tears stung the back of her lids.

"I'll be right back," he whispered. The latch clicked and a wave of cold, wet air entered the cottage as he left it.

The breath hissed from Megan's body in an agonized groan. Abandoning all pretense of sleep, she loosened the folds of wool and began rubbing frantically at her tortured thigh. No good, she realized after a moment. Pain robbed her fingers of their strength. Sobbing, she somehow wriggled out of the confining cocoon Ross had wrapped her in and struggled to stand. The room swam, the lump on the back of her head throbbed. She ignored it all. She had to walk in order to loosen the corded muscles.

Hopping two steps to the table, she leaned on it while she caught her breath. Fists clenched, head bowed against the inevitable, she transferred some weight to her left foot. "Oh." She threw her head back, shuddering as pain lanced through her, but she did not ease up, knowing this was the only way.

The door opened and Ross blew in on a gust of rain and wind. "What the hell!" The door slammed, he advanced, dripping water and scowling like a thundercloud. "What are you doing up?"

"I...have...to...walk. My...leg...cramp..." Her left leg chose that moment to fold, pitching her forward into his arms.

Swearing, Ross swung her up and carried her to the pallet. "Lie still. Let me get out of these things ere I drown you." He tore off everything but his hose, then knelt to her where she writhed on the blankets.

"Nay. Dinna look at it," Megan cried, trying to shield her scars with trembling hands. "'Tis foul and ugly..."

"Silly lass." He brushed her hands aside, closed both his over her knotted flesh and began kneading. Still she fought him, and Ross's conscience ached. 'Twas all the fault of his stupid outburst on their wedding night. Now was not the time to explain the inexcusable. Later, when he had eased her pain, would be soon enough. "Mayhap the weaver's basket has something for pain."

"Nay. I'll take no opiate," she cried hoarsely.

Ross understood instantly why she feared that which enslaved her sire. "Hush, hush," he crooned. "I'll force naught on you."

"You are. You are touchin' me, and I dinna want it." Her nails raked the backs of his hands, drawing blood.

Ross winced, but his steady, deep massage never faltered. "Hurt me if it helps. God knows, I've hurt you."

Instantly she sheathed her claws. "Nay. I dinna want to hurt you, but..." She tossed her head on the pillow, eyes shut tight.

"That's it, fight the pain, love, not me. Let me help."

"I'm...not...your...love."

"You are more to me than you realize. More even than I realized," he said, low and quiet, yet she heard.

Her struggles ceased; her eyes popped open. So dilated with pain they were black, they met and bored into his blue ones. "Nay." She wrenched her head aside. "I dinna want your pity."

"I know." And he did, for he hated the pity that sprang into his mother's eyes whenever the Welsh disaster was mentioned. 'Twas not pity he sought, but the truth about what had happened that terrible day. He owed Megan no less than the truth.

"'Tis nae pity I feel for you," he began softly, his thumbs and fingers still working to ease the coils of misery from her flesh. "Empathy, mayhap. I know what it is to be struck by a pain so deep and sharp you would kill to be relieved of it."

"Y-you do?"

He smiled bleakly. "Aye. When this passes, I will share my scars wi' you." The visible ones, at least. The others. The private, personal hell within himself, he showed to no one.

"You were injured in a battle?"

"Of a sort."

His cryptic reply, the grimness of his expression, drew Megan from her own problems. "What does that mean?"

"Later. Later when you are well."

Megan sighed. She would never be well. Oh, the pain would pass, but her leg would always be as it was. Ugly. Imperfect.

Pain ripped Megan from a restless sleep to utter darkness. Dazed, disoriented, she whimpered.

"Shh. It's all right. I'm here," Ross whispered. His hand came out of the night, found her brow unerringly, touched it gently. "The candle must have burned down. Do you hurt again?"

She nodded against his hand. "N-nae too bad, though."

"Dinna move. I'll be right back to help." Wool rustled and she realized he'd been lying beside her, separated only by the individual lengths of cloth each had been wrapped in.

Reaching beneath her own covers, she rubbed at the dull throb in her thigh. As she shifted, she became aware of aches in other places, her left hip, shoulder, and her rump. She heard Ross rebuilding the fire and wished he wouldn't. Though the room was cold, flames meant light. Illumination that would reveal her ugliness. It had been bad enough before, when the pain had been so severe she'd been forced to let him help. "I'm fine, really."

"Then you'll be even better when I'm finished." He sat down beside the pallet, stuck a fresh candle in the spiked iron holder on the floor and pulled the medicine basket closer. "Mayhap there's something in here that would help. No opiates, I promise," he added when she opened her mouth to object. "How about this?" He held a little pot under Megan's nose.

"Rosemary," she murmured.

"I thought so." Candlelight softened the harsh planes of his face as he smiled at her. "It reminds me of you."

"I—I put it in my clothes to freshen them," she stammered, baffled by the changes in him, the softness, the openness.

"Mmm." He replaced that pot, opened others until he found one that she admitted might chase the dull ache from her thigh.

"But it isna necessary," she insisted, clinging tightly to her woolen cocoon as he unwound it.

"Megan, I've already seen your leg."

"I know." Miserably, the brave eyes that had so often challenged him averted so the shadows hid their expression.

His heart ached for her. "Did I not make the pain go away before?" he asked, gentling her as he would a wild thing.

"Aye. But . . . but 'tis nae so bad now. I can manage it."

"I dinna want you to have to *manage it*," he growled. "Why do you have to be so cursed brave? Why can't you just give in?"

She blinked, but he saw the tears. "I-it's ugly."

"The only ugly thing about your scar is the pain it caused you when it happened . . . continues to cause you now."

"I-it repulses you. I saw the look on your face."

"On our weddin' night." Cursing under his breath, he stared at the fire. "I came to you already angered by the sight of you whispering in the dark wi' Lucais. To discover you'd lied about your leg . . ." He shuddered, squeezed his eyes shut. Opening, they caught the firelight, glinted with emotion. Pain. Rage. Remorse. But not a hint of loathing. "I said things I deeply regret."

"About repudiatin' me," she managed to whisper.

"Aye. But for your lies, Meg. Never for your leg," he said so earnestly she wanted to believe him. *Dear God, how she wanted to believe.* But . . . "I dinna think of you as crippled." As though sensing her doubts, he suddenly snatched the cloth from her leg, bent and pressed his lips to the ugly, knotted ridges.

"Nay," Megan cried, and tried to scramble away. His wide, warm hands pinned her to the pallet securely yet painlessly. His mouth rained scalding kisses on her scarred flesh. Nay, 'twas, not his kisses that burned, 'twas . . . *tears?* She stilled instantly, raised a trembling hand to touch the dark head bent over the leg she could barely stand to gaze upon. "Ross?"

His face, when he lifted it, was a thing of terrible beauty and silent suffering. Candlelight glinted on his wet, spiky lashes, intensified the blue fire blazing in his eyes. "We all bear scars, Meg, some more visible than others, but I can never, ever think of you as crippled in any way."

Megan made a little strangling sound, as though she'd choked on his words. *Believe,* he willed her. And she must have heard the truth behind them, for a single tear slid from the corner of her eye and down her cheek. He caught it before it reached her hair and wiped it away with the pad of his thumb.

"You are the bravest, most beautiful woman I know," he whispered. Her tears came in earnest then. Great, gulping sobs, as though she'd held them in too long and now couldn't hold them back. Tucking her trembling body into the curve of his, Ross held her until the storm inside her tapered off to wee wet sniffs. "Better?" he asked as he wiped her face with the linen towel.

"I doubtless look red and swollen as a pig."

"That's on the outside. Inside, you feel better."

That got a watery smile. "You could at least deny 'twas so."

"Nay," he said, his own grin fading. "I'd have the truth between us . . . from now on. So swear you?" he asked.

"Aye." Megan met his gaze squarely. "Siusan made me vow I'd tell no one about the babe . . . not even Mama or Chrissy."

"And certainly not your brute of a husband-to-be."

"There were times, when you werena bein' a brute, when I wanted to tell you, wanted to share the burden. Oh, Ross, when I heard Siusan was sick, I wanted so much to ask for your help."

Ross, too, recognized the truth when he heard it. "Till I stormed into our bridal chamber, shoutin' and makin' threats."

"'Twas a bit off-puttin'." A dimple flirted with Megan's right cheek. "'Tis a good thing you dinna lose your temper often, m'lord, for you've a right fierce look about you when you do."

"You're no cool cup of broth yourself, m'lady." He raised his right hand, palm toward her. "Pax?"

"Gladly," Megan said, fitting her hand to his. She sighed and wiggled her whole body closer when he linked their fingers together. All the tension seemed to drain out of her, even her leg felt better. She was content to lie there in his arms, her head on his chest, listening to the steady beat of his heart, the soft patter of rain on the thatch. If only they could stay right here safe and secure, for the rest of their lives.

Chapter Fourteen

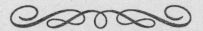

A dark shape slipped between the rocks and ducked under the ledge where Comyn crouched out of the rain. "Well?" he asked.

"Nae sign of Carmichael and the lady," Hakon growled, water running down the nasal of his helmet and into his matted black beard. "I swear my arrow struck her horse, but where she and the lord went to after the bloody thing bolted is anyone's guess."

"Of all the cursed luck," Comyn muttered.

"'Tis that fox what ran across our path. The lads were sayin' we should ha' found it and killed it ere we set out."

"Ye're a superstitious old woman, Hakon."

The bulky giant ran a grimy finger down the scar that bisected his left cheek, drawing his lip into a perpetual sneer. "That may be, m'lord. But things havena been goin' our way. First Carmichael kills the men ye sent to capture the lady." They'd had that tale from the soldier Ross had let go. "Then this storm comes upon us just when we'd finally found their trail."

"Storms are common this time of year," Comyn grumbled. "And they're held up same as we are. Tomorrow we resume our hunt."

Hakon's eyes gleamed maliciously in the sockets of his helmet as he fingered his sword. "I look forward to gettin' my hands on the ones what cut up our lads."

"Find Megan and Lucais for me, and ye can do whatever ye like wi' the Carmichaels," Comyn promised through clenched

teeth. Damn and double damn. He should have had Siusan by
now and been halfway to Sturr More. Instead he was hiding out
like a runaway serf, cold, miserable and hungry. "They should
be made to pay."

"We'll make 'em that sorry they set foot in the Highlands,"
Hakon snarled. "Lord Ross was a fool to leave some of his men
and a knight at Curthill. Now there's only five and thirty of
them to our fifty. 'Twill be like shootin' fish in a barrel."

Ross opened his eyes to find the room still in shadows, the
fire burned down to a faint glow, the candle about to gut in its
own juices. A few hours yet before they had to crawl from their
warm nest and set out to find Owain and the others. Not
wanting the night to end, he tightened his hold on Megan, loving the slide of her smooth legs as they tangled with his muscular ones.

"Ross?" The pale head on his chest stirred, lifted. "What is
it?" she asked, blinking owlishly at him.

"Naught." He kissed her nose. "Go back to sleep."

"Mmm. Dinna want to." In the dimness, her eyes glowed like
the banked coals in the hearth, kindling an answering heat deep
inside him. *Too soon,* he cautioned himself, but the slender
fingers that trailed over his chest made mockery of the warning. "You are so furry... and warm."

Hot. He was hot and getting hotter. "Nay. We canna," he
rasped. "You're new to this, and I wouldna hurt you."

He could never hurt her... physically. His tenderness last
night had proved that, but subtlety was called for here, not his
much overvalued truth. "Is there any of the ale left?"

"Aye." Looking clearly relieved, he rewarded her with a
quick kiss that warmed her to her toes. He untangled their
limbs and rose with a litheness that was as wholly Ross as the
whorls of dark hair that covered his tanned body.

Graceful as a big cat, she thought as she watched him pad to
the table and pour a cup of ale, seemingly unconcerned with his
nudity. It fascinated her. Never had she thought she'd stare at
a man so greedily, devouring him from his wide shoulders to his
narrow hips as a starveling would a feast.

"Look at me like that, and you'll find yourself playin' with fire," Ross growled as he hunkered down beside the pallet.

Megan sat up to take the cup, ignoring the slight ache in her left thigh as she had countless other times. There was an ache of a more pleasurable sort blossoming low in her belly. That she would not ignore. "Fire is very . . . warming," she murmured. Sipping the ale, she slanted a provocative glance at him through a veil of lashes that did not obscure the stirring of his body.

"Witch." His voice was low, husky, free from censure.

"Oh, I canna be a witch, or I wouldna have survived the fire you roused in me last night." With a shrug of her shoulders, she set the cup aside and dislodged the swathe of blue wool he'd wrapped around her earlier. His eyes followed the falling cloth, desire warring with good intentions as they swept down her throat to the swell of her breasts. She shivered in anticipation; her nipples peaked to meet the dark promise glittering in his gaze.

"Meg." He reached out, brushed a sensitive tip with the backs of his fingers, smiling when she moaned and leaned closer, pressing herself against him. "You *are* fire, my beautiful little wife." He filled one large, warm hand with her breast, wrapped the other around her nape and drew her into a kiss that went on and on. His mouth devoured hers while his fingers molded and shaped her aching flesh.

"You burn through my control like wildfire," he rasped when he let her up for air. Face taut with desire, he laid her back in the warm nest of blankets. The smile he gave her when she reached for him sent sparks chasing over her skin to rival the flashes of lightning that seeped in around the cracks in the door.

"Oh, Ross. I love you so," she blurted out, pride drowned by the heady feelings surging through her.

"I know." He wanted to say more, but he was afraid, she realized. Never taking his eyes from hers, he lowered himself into her embrace, yet kept his weight from her. "Oh, Meg." He tunneled his hands in her hair, nuzzling her neck, bathing her in kisses that silently said what he couldn't in words . . . he cared.

'Twas enough...for now. Megan arched up to meet him. "I want to feel you warm and solid above me," she murmured. But when she tried to tug him down atop her he resisted.

"I wouldna hurt you..." The words ended on a strangled groan as she traced his lip with her tongue. "Temptress," Ross whispered, glorying in the quiver that shook her as he deepened the kiss. She tasted of spring ale and rising passion, clean, delicious and heady. As his hands closed on her satiny flanks to lift her closer, his fingers brushed the scar on her hip.

Megan stilled instantly. Her mouth trembled beneath his; her heart stumbled like a cornered rabbit's.

"Steady, love," he murmured, though his own heart was far from it. "Your skin is soft and supple, even where 'tis scarred."

She relaxed. "Mama worked goose grease into it every day."

"I see then where you came by your dedication to healin'." He ran his fingertips down to her knee, slowly up the inside of her leg, and across her flat belly, feeling his own desire build as the delicate muscles fluttered beneath her warm skin. "Am I hurtin' you?" he asked as a moan rippled through her.

"You know you couldna," Megan whispered. Leg forgotten, she arched up to meet his hand as it slipped lower, lower. "Oh," she gasped when he found the spot that had been aching for his touch.

"This time we'll take it slow and easy," he promised, slipping a finger in to explore and tantalize. "Slow," he said again, lowering his mouth to her breast, suckling it so sweetly she sank her hands into his hair to hold him there while the dark, syrupy heat melted her bones. "And easy..."

Ross suited actions to pledge, tempering her greedy haste with seductive patience. Holding his own soaring need carefully in check, he wooed her with provocative words and lush caresses. He nipped and nuzzled and kissed his way down her body, lingering in the special places that wrung sharp cries of pleasure from her, made her twist and strain and reach for him.

"Now, love," she begged, low and husky, her small hands closing around him, threatening to burst the remnants of his control with the hunger he'd built in her. In them.

"Meg," he groaned, her name both surrender and victory as she drew him to her. The soft planes of her body rose up to meld with the hard planes of his, to take him, sheathe him with such open wonder, he groaned again. "Meg. Oh, Meggie mine." *She did love him.* Love shone in the passion-darkened eyes looking up at him from a frame of tumbled golden hair.

He tasted it on her lips, felt it as she came apart in his arms, trusting him with everything she was, teaching him to trust in return. In this woman. In this moment. Her cry of completion shattered his restraint as nothing else could. He gave himself up to a force that went beyond their physical joining. To Megan. The woman who had made him feel and hope and dream again.

When they finally settled back down to earth, Ross gradually became aware of her right leg trapped under him and stirred.

"Dinna move," she pleaded.

"What is it? Where do you hurt?" he demanded.

"Nowhere. But I'd not be parted from you so soon."

"Nor I from you, but I'm crushin' your leg."

"Nay." She snuggled closer. "I like the feel of your arms around me, and 'tis said that a woman who lies still after couplin' stands a better chance of getting with child."

He snorted. "Sounds like a guidwife's tale to me."

"Mayhap. But then, many of those old wives are mothers."

"Jesu, I've barely gotten used to being a husband and you'd make me a father."

Megan tilted her head to study his frown in the dimness. "Surely you want bairns . . . sons to follow you?"

"It would please my sire, something I've had little luck doing in this past year."

"How could he not be proud of you?" Megan demanded.

My valiant defender, Ross thought, smiling faintly. It was oddly pleasant to have one, more pleasant still to lie here stroking her satiny back while she curled close. "He's a hardened warrior who doesna appreciate some of my less militant skills."

"Like readin' and cipherin'?"

"Among other things." The cool tone bespoke another mystery.

Megan frowned. Lion had spoken of their sire with love and a respect that had bordered on worship. Was there trouble between Laird Lionel and his second son? she wondered, and as quickly, how could she heal the breach.

"Sleep, Meggie. We've a long ride ahead of us."

Megan closed her eyes, but long after Ross's breathing settled into the slow patterns of sleep, she remained awake, pondering her new life. With Lion's death no longer an issue between them, she should be at peace, but there were still obstacles to be faced. Siusan's health . . . and her father's.

Thinking of her poor papa brought to mind her mother's cryptic words that last morn. What secret did she hide that made her avert her eyes and call herself *coward?* 'Twas likely nothing, Megan thought, not wanting anything to intrude on her newfound happiness. But the knot in her stomach refused to ease. Suddenly chilled, she curled closer to Ross. His warm, solid presence was a talisman to ward off evil. She hoped.

"If we carry on the way we did last night, we'll be knee-deep in bairns before the year's up," Megan said the next morning as they broke their fast on oatcakes and dried apples.

Ross looked away from her shining face, unwilling to taint her happiness with his worries. Women died in childbed. Well he remembered his father's fears as his mother lay laboring to bring another Carmichael into the world. He'd only just found Megan, had yet to know an hour's peace in which to savor the joy and wonder she'd brought into his life.

"Speaking of babes, Lucais says wee Kieran's hale and healthy, has a set of lungs to rival a smith's bellows."

Ross looked up from the oatcake he was crumbling. "How old is your sister's bairn?"

"*Lion*'s son is three months."

"Point taken," Ross conceded, but he'd not truly believe the bairn was Lion's until he actually laid eyes on it.

Megan knew it, too. Frowning, she limped over and plopped into his lap. "Ross, Siusan was faithful to . . ."

"Your leg bothers you this morn."

Now it was Megan's turn to stiffen. "'Tis fine."

Ross heaved a sigh and raked a frustrated hand through his hair. "You canna prickle up every time I mention your leg."

"I willna be coddled because of it. I can do anythin'—"

"I know you can," Ross said gently. "You've proven that time and again, but I canna stand to see you in pain, Meggie mine." He smiled inwardly as the endearment drained the fight out of her. Despite her brave front, she still felt unworthy... because of her leg. He'd cure that. "You are very important to me." More important with every passing hour. He wrapped his arms around her, enjoying the way she snuggled into his embrace. "When I think how close you came to gettin' hurt last night." He hugged her tighter. "'Tis plain I must teach you to control your mount before I let you ride alone again."

Megan's head snapped up, clipping him in the chin. "I'd like to see the person who could control a horse that's been shot."

Ross stopped rubbing his chin. "What do you mean?"

"Someone put an arrow in my mare last eve."

"Impossible. 'Twas dark, stormin', you must have imagin—"

"I didna imagine the arrow stickin' from her neck."

"It could ha' been a branch that—"

"A branch wi' feathers?" Megan crossed her arms over her indignantly heaving chest. "Why do you always doubt my word?"

"I believe you're tellin' the truth." *As you know it.* "But who would shoot at you in the middle of a storm? And why?"

"To capture me and force me to lead him to Siusan."

"Archie and Douglas are both dead."

"Comyn isna."

"Comyn is at Curthill helpin' Giles keep order," he snapped.

"And I think he isna! I think he is out there somewhere, stalkin' us. But you willna believe me." Megan turned away.

"Meggie." Ross caught her chin, brought her gaze back to his. "What possible reason could he have for—"

"Greed. He wants more than the small tower Papa gave him. And for revenge, too. He was furious because Papa wouldna attack the MacKays who killed Comyn's family and burned their castle."

"I can understand that," Ross said in a hard voice that reminded her of his fierce need to avenge Lion. But...

"Nay, you dinna understand. Comyn's clansmen had been raidin' the MacKays for a while. Not the sort of reivin' that's near a way of life for some Highland clans, liftin' cattle and such, but senseless burnin' and lootin'. When they fell upon an unprotected village, raped the women, killed the men and razed the place to the ground, the MacKays retaliated in kind."

Ross nodded. "'Tis to your father's credit that he didna seek reprisals and embroil his clan in a war to avenge such soulless men," he said, pleased anew that the matter of Eammon's guilt no longer tainted their marriage. "But that doesna mean Comyn is cruel or evil."

"Oh!" Megan punched him in the chest and jumped from his lap. "You are the stubborn one, unable to see Comyn for what—"

Zeus's sharp neigh, clearly audible through the cottage's thin walls, cut off her retort.

Ross whirled toward the sound. "Visitors." He leaped up, buckling his sword on over his hose and tunic. "Wi' luck, 'tis Owain and my men. If not..."

"You canna go out wi'out your chain mail," she cried as he made for the door.

"No time. Bolt the door behind me and stay here. I mean it," he ordered, giving her that I'm-in-charge look she hated.

He was gone before Megan could call him foolish. Shivering with dread, she wrapped the blanket more securely about her and grabbed her eating knife from the table. If he thought she was waiting here for him to be killed, he had another think coming. Just as she reached for the latch, the door sprang open.

"Where the hell are you goin'?" Ross demanded. His big body filled the doorway, eyes blazing with righteous male anger.

Megan let go the breath she'd been holding. He'd not be angry with her if there was danger. But she was in no mood for one of his lectures. Reaching up, she plucked a handful of thin air and mashed it into his broad chest.

"What was that for?"

"I'm catchin' your temper. You seem to be losin' it again."

"Only where you are concerned." He glared at her, but his mouth twitched with wry humor. "What am I goin' to do wi' you?"

"Well . . ." She let her gaze rove over him. "I can think of a thing or two you showed me last eve that—"

"Megan! Mind your tongue or you'll embarrass yourself before our hostess." He stepped aside to reveal a small, gnarled woman swathed in a black cape made of fine, closely woven wool.

"Love ha' naught to be ashamed of," the weaver said. Winking at Megan, she hobbled over the threshold. "My, my, ye've made yerselves right to home." Her eyes, black as two raisins in a wrinkled pudding, danced as she spied the nest of rumpled wool where they'd made their bed.

Megan's face went hot. "Oh, I'm sorry," she began, looking to Ross for support. His gaze was on her, vivid blue, blazing with the memories they'd made in the cozy cottage. "We . . . we can repay you for the cloth we ruined, can we not, Ross?"

"Aye," he said slowly, looking at her with an intensity that made her heart pound, made her wish the weaver woman was miles away and they had hours in which to feed the carefully banked fire gleaming in his eyes. "I've a mind to keep the wool. 'Twas soft—" his smile deepened "—and warm . . ." The glowing embers burst into flame, searing her to the soles of her bare feet. "What say you, Meggie, shall we buy the wool as a keepsake?"

This from the man who did not believe in love? Megan was tempted to say, but she nodded instead, content to feast on his roguish smile and laughing eyes.

"Ah, to be young and in love," the weaver woman muttered before introducing herself as Dame Isla Sutherland.

"I am Megan Sutherland of—"

"Megan Carmichael." Ross slipped a possessive arm around Megan's waist, squeezed her when she leaned into him.

"Ah, the lady *seanachaidh*." Isla dipped her head in tribute. "Young Lucais sang yer praises when he visited, said ye were the most skillful bard in all the Highlands. The village of Larig lies two miles distant, and they've a fine *tigh-ceilidh*. I'd gladly gift ye the wool if ye'd come to the entertainment house tonight and bring a few of the old legends alive fer us."

"Oh, I'd be honored," Megan said, but her smile died when she looked up and saw Ross's grim expression.

"We need to locate Owain and press on."

"There's men in the woods," Dame Isla warned.

Ross smiled. "My men, they're doubtless lookin' for us."

"These men are lookin', right enough, but I dinna think they're yer men." Her eyes probed his with an intensity that made Ross flinch, made his skin crawl with thoughts of witches and second sight. What she saw within him apparently pleased her, for she released him with a blink of parchment lids and said, "Ye couldna be one o' them. These creatures who crash through the forest wi'out regard fer beast nor bracken are *Cruithneach*...cruel, bloodthirsty trolls in league wi' the devil."

More superstitious nonsense, Ross thought. Yet deep inside him, ancient instincts stirred, raising the hair at his nape, sending icy fingers crawling over his skin. *There is no such thing as a demon.* Still... "Come, Meg," he said gruffly. "The sooner we find my men and leave this place, the better."

"A moment," Dame Isla said. "Ye'll need a bit of luck if ye're to pass through the woods unscathed." She ducked outside and returned with a stick the length and breadth of Ross's middle finger. "Rowan," she said, holding it out to him. "I cut it from the tree by my door. 'Tis a powerfully good charm."

"Thank you," Megan said gravely. Elbowing Ross in the ribs to cut off his derisive snort, she reached for the stick.

Dame Isla evaded her grasp and instead stuck the piece of wood in the sheath that held Ross's dirk. "He'll ha' need of this before ye're done."

"Done?" Ross eyed the woman skeptically.

She smiled. "I ken ye're a Lowlander and dinna believe as we do, but keep the rowan branch wi' ye just the same. Call it an old woman's fancy, if ye like."

What Ross did not like was the way her piercing gaze raised the hair on his arms, his nape.

The storm had blown itself out, leaving the air cold and damp. Wisps of fog clung to the wet earth of the forest floor. Eerie and mysterious, they added to Megan's sense of disquiet, made her nerves vibrate. Any moment, she expected something or someone to jump out at them. For all his cool logic, Ross sensed it, too, holding her tight against his chest as

he guided Zeus through the dark, silent woods. Just as the trees
began to thin enough to see daylight ahead, he drew rein.

"Why are we stoppin'?" Megan whispered.

"There's the cave we were makin' for when your horse...
bolted." Ross pointed to a black hole in the rocky cliff on the
other side of the clearing, but all Megan could see was that he
still didn't believe someone had shot her horse.

His lack of trust saddened her anew. "I dinna see any sign of
the men," she said tightly.

"Nay. The storm was too bad for them to search for us last
night... for which I'm grateful." He hugged her briefly. "So
likely they've gone lookin' this morn." Dame Isla's warning
hung in the air, thick and ominous as the thickening fog.

"Lucais could have led them to the cottage," Megan said.

"Mayhap we missed them in the woods." Calmly said, but
the steely arm around her tightened protectively.

Megan shivered. "The person who shot my horse could have
captured Lucais."

"Megan." Exasperated. But not half as much as she was.

"Fine. Fine. Don't believe me." It wasn't fine, but she'd not
argue the point though her heart was heavy. "Do we go back?"

Ross nodded, turned Zeus and began the trek through the
woods. "'Tis not that I dinna believe you, Meggie," he said
after a lengthy silence. He stroked her back by way of apology, warming her through the mended gown and the blanket
she wore as a cape. "Mayhap you confused this time wi' the
time of your accident."

Megan frowned. "There was no arrow then."

"Last night you told me there was."

"I did? But... but..." The memories that had eluded her for
two years suddenly rushed in, swamping her. Dragging her back
to that bright summer's day. Laughter floating on the
wind... hers and Ewan's. A whoosh, a thunk, a scream. The
mare rose up, pawing the air, her gray hide splattered with
blood. So much blood and at its center, a slender wooden shaft.

"Oh, my God." Megan's lips trembled. She brought her
fingers up to still them, but the shudders were coming from
deep inside her. "I didna remember until now..." Dazed,
horrified. "There was an arrow. I... I saw it strike my mare.
She bolted. Rocks and trees flew by. Then *we* were fly-

ing...nothing but sky beneath us. Until we landed." Sobbing, she buried her face in Ross's chest.

"Easy, love, easy." Ross hugged her close, found comforting her as natural as breathing, as natural as loving her. "'Tis all right. I willna let anythin' hurt you ever again, Meggie mine."

Typically her tears were soon spent, but his conviction that this revelation had settled the matter vanished the minute she raised her head and tilted her pointy chin at him.

"I may ha' forgotten what happened two years ago, but I didna confuse the two incidents," she said, drying her cheeks on the blanket. "'Twas light the day of my accident and my mare was gray. Last night was dark and stormy, and I saw the arrow stick out of the horse's wet black hide. *I wasna mistaken.*"

Ross searched her eyes, startled by the conviction and the anguish in their depths. He felt her pain as though it were his own, as though last night had somehow bonded their two souls together. She had given herself to him then without reservation, without question, trusting him not to hurt her. Could he deny her his trust? "I believe you."

The breath left Megan in a soft sigh; her eyes filled with tears of gratitude. Never had he felt more humbled by another's emotions. "Thank you," she murmured. But her next words shattered their rapport. "It must have been some of Comyn's men who—"

"Megan. Stop blamin' Comyn for everythin'. 'Tis likely that either the men Archie sent to capture you are still about, not realizin' that he's dead, or 'tis bandits."

"Next you'll be sayin' 'tis Dame Isla's trolls," she snapped. "Just because Comyn's a man—"

"That has naught to do wi' it," Ross said through clenched teeth. Damn, he'd lost his temper more since meeting her than he had in his entire life. "I like him. Lion liked him . . . hell, everyone likes him."

"Everyone but me." Megan pleated the blanket with fingers that shook, her heart and mind in turmoil. Could she be wrong about Comyn? Could that sixth sense inside her that made her more sensitive to the forces of good and evil be wrong this time? *Nay.* "This is all the fault of that Rhiannon . . ."

"Meg," Ross growled. "I've told you before—"

"That you willna discuss her. Granted this isna the place." Her eyes flicked to the dark woods where someone, or something, searched for them. "But when we are safely back home wi' this adventure behind us, I think you owe me the truth."

Ross sucked in air, exhaled sharply. He'd never shied away from the truth before, but it hurt even to think of Rhiannon and the one hundred men who'd died for his stupidity. "We shall see," he said woodenly. "First we must find Owain and the others." Unsheathing his sword, he laid it across Megan's lap and urged Zeus ahead, his body as tense as the tempered steel.

"Are we goin' back to the cottage?"

"Nay, to the village where Dame Isla said she sheltered from the storm last night." Though he didn't believe in trolls, the hushed, brooding air seemed to close in around him. Heart pounding, senses alert to every nuance, Ross's eyes darted ahead of them through the forest, searching for enemies behind every tree trunk, every rock.

It seemed to take forever to ride the two miles to Larig, a motley collection of mud and wattle huts huddled in the lee of a rocky hill. Megan's feeling of foreboding grew as they rode deeper into the village. Here the huts were built so close together they formed a solid wall of stone and dab on either side of the rutted road. Both the shuttered windows and the closed doors were banded with iron. "I dinna like this," she whispered.

"Nor do I." The prickle in Ross's neck had become a screaming itch. The road curved just after the last of the stone cottages. Rounding the bend, they came face-to-face with a tall wooden structure that stretched from one side of the mountain pass to the other, blocking the way.

Trapped.

Chapter Fifteen

Cursing under his breath, Ross wheeled Zeus. *Too late.*

A dozen armed men stepped out to block the trail. The trolls Dame Isla had said were in the woods? These men looked fierce and barbarous enough to deserve the Pictish name, *Cruithneach. Bah, listen to him.* There must be something in the air that had stolen his logic. They were Highlanders, dressed in saffron shirts overwrapped by six-foot lengths of thick blue wool. The *plaids* served as a combination surcoat and cloak during the day and blanket at night. "What is the meanin' of this?" Ross demanded in Gaelic.

The largest of the men, a hairy devil who Ross guessed would top him by a foot, stepped forward. "If ye've a mind to pass, there's a little matter o' the toll, m'lord."

Megan leaned forward. "See here, we are..."

"Hush," Ross growled in her ear. To the Highlanders he snarled, "I havena been raidin', so I owe you no black mail in exchange for passage over your lands...if they are your lands."

Thick brows knotted over the man's beady eyes. "These are Sutherland lands. But 'tisna black mail, 'tis a toll, fer passin' through Larig gorge."

Greedy Highland devils. "I gave what coin I had to the weaver woman in the forest in exchange for a night's lodgin'."

"I'll take yer horse, then," the giant declared. His men laughed and stepped closer, reaching for their prize.

Ross gave Zeus the signal to attack, and the stallion lashed out with his front hooves as he'd been trained to do in battle. The villagers screamed and scattered, scrambling up the wooden barricade like sailors climbing the shrouds. From the top of the heap, the giant called, "The woman, then."

Ross felt Megan tremble, clutched her closer and whispered, "I'll keep you safe, dinna fear." To the thieving bastard he growled, "This is my wife. Touch her and you die."

"Oh, shut up," Megan snapped. "I'm not some bone for you two to squabble over like hounds." Feeling Ross start, seeing his opponent blink, she tossed the blanket back from her head and lifted her chin. "I am Megan, *seanachaidh* to Eammon Sutherland."

"So ye say," grumbled the giant, but the scrawny little man at his side tugged on his sleeve.

"Dame Isla said Eammon had a woman bard, Jock."

Jock stroked his yellow beard. "How do we know she's her?"

"I'll prove I am by tellin' a story. What say you, a tale of ancient valor in exchange for passage through your gorge?"

"We havena got time for a story," Ross grumbled.

"But we do have time for a fight?" Megan replied.

Ross looked at the hard-faced Highlanders surrounding them and groaned again. "Jesu, if my father hears I let a lass get me out of this predicament by telling a tale, I'll . . . I'll never live it down," he muttered.

"Ah, better you should die fightin' them," Megan snapped.

"Meg," Ross warned, but another female voice interrupted.

"She's Meg Sutherland, right enough," a woman called, swinging all eyes to the women and children of the village who crept from hiding, faces alight with curiosity. "Lady Siusan sheltered wi' Dame Isla on her way north near a year ago. She was the spittin' image of this lass and spoke proudly of her sister, Megan, who was the bard to Eammon Sutherland, of Curthill."

"*He*'s a Lowlander, Mairi," Jock quickly replied.

"But he is wed to me, so that makes him a Sutherland."

"And Sutherlands dinna take from their clansmen," said the tall, red-haired Mairi.

"Noble sentiments for a band of brigands," Ross muttered.

Jock's scowl deepened. "Dinna call us thieves. Ye Low-landers charge a toll for passage o'er yer roads an' bridges, too. 'Tis nae more'n we're tryin' to do here."

True, but Ross wasn't giving an inch. "And if we canna pay?"

"Payment isna necessary between kinsmen," Jock grumbled.

"My thanks." Megan slanted Ross an I-told-you-I'd-take-care-of-this look. Ignoring the low growl that said he didn't appreciate her cheek, she asked, "Have any strangers but ourselves passed by in the last day?"

Jock shook his head. "The pickin's ha' been slim."

"Heard men in the woods this morn," muttered one man.

"That must ha' been what roused my dog," put in another.

"How many men?" Ross asked. "Where were they headed?"

The first man shrugged. "Dunno. Thought they was daft bein' out so early." Further questions revealed that the man lived north of the woods and had actually heard two mounted parties thunder by, one a short while after the other.

"Owain and my men," Ross murmured. But were they pursued or the pursuer? And who were the others? "We'll be on our way."

Just as the villagers made to move the barricade, a man ran down the center of town. "Jock. Jock, come quick." He stopped to catch his breath, then added, "There's a fierce battle goin' on over to Larig ridge. A band o' Highlanders ha' cornered some knights...English or Lowlanders, by their trappin's. I've never seen such grand horses and armor. The way they're goin' at it, 'twouldna surprise me if they killed each other."

"'Tis my men," Ross exclaimed. Sensing his tension, Zeus screamed and strained to be off. Ross drew back on the reins and the destrier pranced in a circle. The momentary distraction gave him time to make hasty plans. "If you'll direct me to the ridge," he said to Jock. "And keep my wife safe."

Megan protested long and loudly when he lifted her down into the arms of the Sutherland women. "Take me wi' you!" she cried, reaching for him though Mairi held her back.

"A battlefield is no place for a woman," he said gruffly, heart aching for one last kiss, one last chance to hold her. He wheeled away before he could weaken and drag her into his arms. But he couldn't resist a final glance over his shoulder.

The image he carried away with him into what might be his last battle was of Megan standing in the center of Larig surrounded by her kinswomen. Head unbowed, pale hair gleaming in the sunlight, she looked as fiercely determined as her Viking forebears. *Please don't let her do anything rash,* he prayed, before turning his thoughts to the coming fight.

It took less than a quarter hour to reach the ridge. To Ross, it seemed an eternity. As he approached the crest of the mountain, he heard the clash of steel on steel above him and stopped. Tension boiled in his veins as he dismounted and crept around a rocky outcropping. What he saw made his blood run cold.

The terrain was as wild as any they had traveled, a narrow shelf of land that fell away on one side to create a deep gorge. His men were a short distance away, their backs to that precipice, surrounded on three sides by a host of hairy men in wool, skins and mail. Every muscle in his body vibrated with the urge to rush down the trail and fall upon those who threatened his clansmen. But caution was too deeply ingrained.

Jesu, what now? Ross ducked behind the rocks to think. He was only one man, well armed and mounted on a war-horse trained to slash and fight, but still only one man. The element of surprise would give him an advantage for only minutes. If he had a few men . . . six or eight men-at-arms would make all the diff—

Behind him, Zeus neighed, and Ross swung around, sword sliding from its scabbard.

A dozen sturdy garrons, the short, shaggy Highland ponies, scrambled up the trail and stopped beside Zeus. The men were from Larig village, fully armed and smiling hugely.

Ross sheathed his sword and slipped through the rocks to meet them. "Why are you here?"

Jock swung down from the lead pony. "We've come to gi' ye a hand, m'lord." A muffled shout of agreement went up from the other men, and they waved their seven-foot spears in the air.

Ross swept the assembly with a commander's eye, his admiration for their bravery growing. Lowland knights rode into battle encased in metal, the men-at-arms in chain mail. The Welsh wore stiff leather jerkins as armor. These men had only their thigh-length saffron shirts, low leather boots, conical helmets and round shields for protection. "Your help is well come," he said, hope rising for the first time since he'd topped the ridge and gazed upon the battlefield. "My men are outnumbered—"

"We Sutherlands fight wi' the strength of two men."

Ross grinned. "Let's have at them, then."

"A moment." Jock turned to call forward the last man in the group, and Ross realized someone rode pillion behind him. "We'd best leave the bard here," Jock added.

"Megan!" Ross exclaimed as she peeked from around the man's shoulder. "What the hell . . . !"

"I came to tend the wounded," Megan hedged with far more courage than she felt. *Sweet Mary, he was angry.* She'd make him truly wroth did she admit she'd risked riding onto a battlefield for the same reason she'd refused to leave his bedside the night he'd been poisoned. She knew . . . in her heart of hearts . . . that if she let him out of her sight, he'd die.

"Of all the stupid . . ." Ross tore off his helmet and advanced on her, face taut, big body trembling with a force that made her want to step back. "If I wasna so pressed for time I'd . . . I'd . . ."

He loved her. She saw it blazing beneath the fury in his eyes. That knowledge gave Megan the courage to stand her ground. Going up on tiptoe, she pressed a kiss to his hard, disapproving mouth, felt it soften briefly. He *did* love her. "Go wi' God, my love," she whispered. "I'll be here, in the safety of the rocks, waitin' for you, prayin' you come back safe to me."

Ross groaned and squeezed his eyes shut. When they opened, resignation had doused his fury. "Jesu, you try my patience." Jaw clenched tight, he stalked to Zeus and mounted. "Megan, I am orderin' you to hide among these rocks. Dinna come out until I return for you. I'll be less than worthless in this fight if half my mind is on whether you are in danger."

"I promise, on my mother's soul." That seemed to satisfy him, for he nodded and turned toward the Sutherlands.

"Come, we will give these bastards a nasty surprise."

"Aye," came the soft roar as the Sutherlands threw off their encumbering plaids and drew their weapons.

Megan started as a horrible cry rose from Ross's throat and was picked up by his makeshift army, echoing off the mountains as they charged from behind the rocks. In spite of her promise to stay hidden, she was drawn after them. She stood with her body pressed against a boulder and watched the drama unfold.

Ross's men swept across the plateau like a vengeful yellow wave, swords and spears glinting in the afternoon sun. The attackers were so stunned by the swiftness of the assault that two were killed where they stood. The others turned to face this new threat, forgetting their original quarry. A roar went up from the Carmichaels, and they immediately fell on their tormentors. Caught between the two forces, the enemy screamed and broke, fleeing the scene in total disarray.

The two men leading the retreat caught Megan's eye. One was big, a hulking brute who towered over the other men. The other was smaller but more richly dressed. *Comyn,* was her first thought. Comyn and that mercenary captain of his. What was his name? Haken or Hakor or something like that. He'd come to Curthill a time or two, though he usually remained behind to defend Shurr More in Comyn's absence.

Damn, but she wished she could sprout wings and fly after the two fiends, detain them long enough for Ross and the pursuing Sutherlands to catch and unmask them. Nothing less would convince Ross of Comyn's guilt.

She shifted and strained against the rock, tension bubbling in her veins as she silently urged Ross on, but alas, 'twas not to be. The pair she'd marked disappeared down the side of the mountain and into the trees. Wisely, or so it seemed to her, Ross turned his men back from a possible trap in the woods and made for those few knots of men still writhing in combat.

Shivering, Megan turned away from the rout, the relief she felt at the victory dulled by new fears. Her eyes scanned the distant mountains, picked out the tall peak that was her goal.

Siusan waited there, alone and vulnerable, trusting her sister to save her. Yet Megan could not shake the feeling that time was running out . . . for Siusan . . . for Ross and herself.

"'Tis quiet," Owain observed as Ross joined him by the fire.

"Too quiet." Apprehension slid down Ross's spine as he swept the camp hastily set up beside a burn on a grassy knoll below the battlefield. His eyes probed the darkness beyond the circle of light shed by a ring of smoking torches. Beside each torch stood a Carmichael soldier, back to the light, alert and ready for trouble. It was out there. Ross did not need whatever heightened instincts Megan possessed to sense their enemy lurking close by.

"We killed a goodly number of them," Owain said.

"Aye, but we didna come away unscathed." Ross looked to the tent where Megan toiled to aid his men. Fearful as it made him to have her here, he grudgingly admitted they had need of her skills. "Seven men have minor cuts and gashes, Lucais is still unconscious, and Andrew's arm is cleaved to the bone. Davey says he's like to lose it."

"Ah. Jesu . . ." Owain frowned into the fire.

"If only I had reached you sooner," Ross whispered.

"We should not have attacked them as we did. I tried to tell Andrew 'twas foolhardy, but you know him."

"Impatient. Anxious to even the score."

"He thought they were common reivers, but the bastards were too well armed for that. All wore helmets and had chain mail beneath their shirts . . . English-style mail, and the big brute who led them had steel armor. Most carried swords and shields instead of the Lochaber axes and spears your villagers favor."

Ross frowned. "Mercenaries, then." But in whose pay? His eyes strayed to the single prisoner they'd taken alive. Well, mostly alive. They'd bound him, but like poor Lucais, the man had yet to regain his wits. "Tell me all that happened." What with collecting the wounded and making camp, there'd been little time for conversation since the battle.

"Lucais led us to the cave. The storm was at its height, and it took time for everyone to straggle in. Lucais said Lady Megan's horse had bolted, so we expected you last of all. When you didn't come, I wanted to look for you, but Lucais convinced me you had likely taken refuge in a weaver's hut."

"We did," Ross said, perversely glad his men had not found him that night.

Owain leaned forward to poke the fire. "Just past dawn, the rain stopped and I could wait no longer. I took Lucais and the bowmen to look for you. Inside the forest, we found Lady Megan's horse." He set the stick down, turned troubled eyes on Ross. "The beast was dead . . . of an arrow in its neck."

Air hissed past Ross's teeth. "Megan said as much, but . . ."

"Ye did not want it to be true, because that would mean someone had tracked us through the storm."

Shamed by his lack of faith in Megan, Ross urged Owain on.

"Barely had we stripped the horse of the saddle and packs, when the bastards attacked us. Andrew heard the noise and came to our aid, whereupon our assailants fled. When we reached the plateau, I urged Andrew to draw back, sensing a trap, but . . ."

But Andrew had not fought with Ross in Wales, had not learned its bitter lessons. "He knows only one way to meet an enemy. Head-on." Ross glanced at the tent where even now Andrew might be losing an arm, and with it his life. For the old warrior would curl up and die if he couldn't fight.

"Aye. We charged," Owain went on, "had them with their backs to the gorge. They melted down the sides of it as suddenly and craftily as any Welshman, then crept around behind and turned the tables on us whilst I was trying to convince Andrew and the others to leave rather than look for them. Thank God ye came when ye did, or we'd have been done for."

"'Twas the Sutherlands from Larig who made the difference," Ross murmured, his opinion of that clan turned completely around. They were more unruly than Lowlanders, but every bit as brave and loyal. "Could the men who attacked you have been from Curthill?"

"Ah, more of the men Archie sent. Nay, I knew them not, but armored and helmeted, one man looks much like another."

Which was why warriors riding into battle wore their clan badge or carried banners to recognize friend from foe. Ross moved on to a more difficult task, relating Megan's accusations, including the news that MacDonnel had once been betrothed to her. "She insists he's guilty...says he has the squint eye. More of her foolish superstitions, but..."

"I was raised with such beliefs myself," Owain interjected, reminding Ross that the Welsh beliefs did not differ that much from the Scots Highlanders'. "And found many had a basis in fact, not that I've seen any evidence of treachery in Lord Comyn."

"Nor have I. He hasna done one suspicious thing, other than not tell me he'd been betrothed to Megan."

"He did kill Archie," Owain said, stroking his chin.

"And Wee Wat killed Douglas," Ross retorted. Jesu, he felt weary of a sudden. Tired of planning and plotting and worrying about things he could not come close to understanding.

"Wat acted to save yer life. Comyn need not have used the point of his sword to stop Archie from fleeing the room. And too, we do not know what happened to Felis after she left with Comyn."

"You accuse Comyn of killin' her?" Ross made a disgusted sound. "You're as bad as Megan, seein' evil where there is none."

"And ye call her stubborn." Owain shook his head. "Whoever attacked us wanted Lucais. The man who knocked the lad on the head tried to drag him away, though he's no rich ransom prize."

Ross looked toward the tent where the boy lay. "In hopes he'd lead them to Siusan. Which brings us back where we started. Who is stalking us? Men sent by Archie? Or brigands? Or—"

A harsh, agonized scream tore through the night, dragging men from their blankets, turning the guards at their posts. The cry came again . . . from the tent containing the wounded.

Ross was on his feet and running before the sound faded away. Thrusting aside the flap, he lunged inside, sword drawn. What he found stopped him in his tracks.

A brace of torches sent light and shadow dancing over a scene straight out of hell. The air was thick with smoke, leaden with blood and fear. Andrew lay in the center of the tent. Na-

ked to the waist, drenched in his own blood, he writhed to escape the two people struggling to hold him down.

"Dinna just stand there like a great lump," Megan gasped.
She was draped over the knight's chest, a bloody cloth pressed
to his upper arm. "We ha' to keep him still ere he bleeds to
death."

Ross sheathed his blade, motioned for Owain to help Davey
hold the legs and knelt at Andrew's head. As he braced his
hands on the warrior's shoulders, the man's lashes lifted.

Fear, raw and wild, glittered in Andrew's eyes. "Better dead
than maimed. She's goin' to take my arm off."

"What?" Ross lifted his head, gaze locking with Megan's as
she continued to apply pressure to the knight's arm. The compassion he saw there muted his fury. "Meggie?" he asked.

"I'd save it, if I can. But he refuses to take a draught for the
pain." She nodded to the cup overturned on the ground. "And
I can do naught for him while he thrashes about so."

"Ha' to stay awake," Andrew rasped. "Canna sleep...wake
up and find it . . . gone."

Ross understood completely, yet he also trusted Megan.
Swallowing the lump in his throat, he gently squeezed the
heaving shoulders of his old friend and mentor. "If Meg says
she willna take it off, she willna."

"I've given her reason to dislike me," Andrew murmured.

Ross looked up in time to see sadness tighten Megan's lips.
"In that you are not alone, but fortunately for us, my Meggie
has a forgivin' heart. Your crimes against her are less than
mine, yet she saved me from the poison. You can trust her wi'
your arm." Beneath his hands, Andrew relaxed. "Davey, fetch
us another cup of that stuff, and help him to drink it," Ross
said.

Megan gave Ross a small smile of thanks . . . and not just for
the help in calming her patient. His support warmed her, gave
her the courage to face the grim task that lay ahead. Over her
shoulder, she asked Davey to fetch needle and thread from the
pack hastily assembled by the women of Larig.

Andrew's eyes were closed, but he winced when the needle bit
into his flesh. Megan flinched herself, 'twas her least favorite
form of stitchery, yet he'd bleed to death did she not close the

gaping wound that laid him open from shoulder to elbow. 'Twas an ugly gash that bled despite the belt tied around his armpit to staunch its flow.

Her hands shook, her stomach rolled with doubts. Samples were her strength, dosing the sick with herbs and birthing babes, not treating battle wounds. She felt woefully inadequate to the task, dreadfully afraid Ross's trust in her was misplaced, yet when she raised troubled eyes, he met them with a faint smile.

"Do your best, love. 'Tis all anyone can ask of you."

Love. Aye, that really was love that gleamed in Ross's eyes, not the reflection of the torches. It steadied her hand. This time, Andrew did not move when her needle sank in. Blessedly, he'd either fainted or the opiate had done its work.

Faithful Davey sat to one side, blotting the cut so she could see what she was doing. Ross never left her other side the whole time. His presence was like a rock from which she drew strength during the long ordeal. From time to time, he wiped the sweat from her brow and rethreaded the needle.

When at last it was done, the wound closed, packed with nettle leaves to lessen the chance of infection, and bandaged, Megan sagged back on her heels. Instantly Ross was there, slipping an arm around to support her back. She let him take her weight, murmured a protest when he began washing her hands.

"Easy, love. Let me get you clean." His touch, as he washed away Andrew's blood, was as tender as it had been last night when he taught her about men and women. 'Twas so easy to lean into the curve of his strong body and let him care for her. But when he dried her off and picked her up, she stiffened.

"I have to tend Lucais." The lad lay as he had since they'd carried him in, eyes closed, face so pale his freckles stood out like dots of cinnamon. She'd washed and bandaged his head wound, but he had not regained his wits. She feared he never would.

"Davey will sit wi' him," Ross assured her. "You've done all you can for tonight."

"But..." She tried to wriggle free.

Ross held her fast, caressed her face with his eyes to take the sting from his actions. "I mayna have your skill at healin', but I know that do you nae get some sleep, you'll be of little use to yourself or the wounded come morn."

She sighed, all the fight draining out of her. "All right."

That she gave in so easily worried Ross more than her extreme pallor or the mauve shadows below her eyes. She felt fragile and vulnerable in his arms. As he ducked under the tent flap and out into the cold night air, he held her close against his chest, wishing he could absorb her into himself, keep her safe always. Only, none of them were safe, he thought, eyeing the bandages on the men who stirred in their blankets as he passed through the camp and entered his own tent. Nor would they be until this hellish journey was completed.

The fierce need to protect her, even from herself, took him by surprise. *He loved her,* Ross thought, looking down at his precious burden. 'Twas a hell of a time to realize it, with their situation so precarious. Yet oddly fitting, for nothing about their marriage was normal. *He loved her.*

"Ross?" He started, shaken from his reverie to find her staring up at him. A small smile tilted her mouth, chased the shadows from her dark eyes.

"I canna breathe," she murmured fondly.

"What? Oh." Flushing, he eased his grip...fractionally. Yet was still loath to let her go.

Reaching up, Megan brushed her hand over his stubbled cheek. "Thank you. For your help. For your trust."

"'Tis I who should thank you, Meggie." He shifted her, lowering her legs and aligning their bodies so they touched from breast to knees, male to female, hard to soft. "Oh, Meggie. I..." *I love you.* The words hovered on the tip of his tongue, but old fears died hard. He loved her, yet dared not give her that much power over him. Mouth buried in her neck, dragging in great gulps of air, he trembled like a horse that had run too far, too fast.

Megan twined her arms around his neck and clung. Never mind that she still couldn't breathe. *He loved her.* She knew it, felt it in the thunder of his heart against hers, in the shaking of his hand as it stroked up her back and tunneled into her hair. A man like Ross Carmichael did not quiver for just anybody.

"Oh, Meg." He raised his head, eyes soft as a summer sky, expression full of wonder. "I...I..."

"You love me." Framing his face with her hands, she kissed him full on the mouth, tasted surprise and fear.

"A lady usually waits to be told such things," he grumbled when she let him up for air.

"I'm nae known for my patience." Despite her uncertainty, she slanted him a teasing glance. "I wasna certain how long it would take you to forget that Rhiannon and admit you loved me."

He stiffened, and she cursed her hasty tongue. "I'd not—"

"Speak of her, I know," Megan said softly. Though part of her feared hearing about this mysterious woman, she knew they could not be happy till all was in the open. "But she is like a disease festerin' below the surface of our marriage, poisonin' us. Can you not tell me what she did to make you hate all women?"

He exhaled sharply, the anguish in his face nearly making her want to recall the question. Nearly. His arms tightened around her, and he began to speak, low, harsh words that sounded as though they'd been dragged from him. "I met Rhiannon a few days after we crossed the mountains to fight in Wales. She..."

"Was very beautiful?" Megan asked unhappily.

A cynical smile twisted Ross's lips. "She was dark, exotic and practiced as a spider at lurin' stupid fools like me into her web. 'Twas from her I learned holy church was right, women are natural-born liars and deceivers."

"I resent that," Megan huffed. "What lies I've told were spun to save others hurt."

"There is no such thing as a good lie, but Rhiannon's were the worst of all. She duped me into trustin' her, then betrayed me to my enemies," he growled through clenched teeth.

"Can you nae forget—"

"Forget that her lies led us into an ambush that cost the lives of one hundred of my men?" he snarled, the anguish in his face unbearable.

"Ross." She drew his head down, pressed her cheek to his. "How awful for them...for you. I wish I could ease the pain."

"You have. In so many ways." He turned his head, brushed her mouth with the softest of kisses. "Time and again, you've come to my aid, little warrior. Though I wanted to beat you for puttin' yourself in harm's way, had you not brought the Sutherlands today, my men and I could well have perished."

"'Twas my kinsmen who saved you," she replied, for it was not his gratitude she wanted.

"Aye, and I owe them a debt for that, but..." He kissed the tip of her nose. "Your brave heart led them."

At the moment, Megan didn't feel brave, she felt as though she teetered on a precipice, one step away from having the ground yanked out from under her. "D-do you still love Rhiannon?"

"Love." Ross snorted, and she pulled back so she could see his face, startled by his grim expression. "Whatever I felt for her withered under the dyin' screams of my men and was buried wi' her. Nay, I didna kill her," he added when she flinched. "'Twas the Welsh commander wi' whom she'd been sharin' her...favors...and her information about me. Rhys ap Dolgollen decided her usefulness had come to an end, and he gave her to his men."

"Oh, Ross, how dreadful." Megan wrapped her arms around him, knowing of no other way to ease his grief.

"Aye." Ross dragged in a cleansing breath and with it the scent of herbs and woman that was uniquely Megan. It wrapped around him like a healing balm. No matter that this subject must be painful for her, too, her first thought was to help him. Could he do less? "'Tis in the past, and I'd put it behind me."

She tipped her head back, eyes shimmering with unshed tears that magnified their color, their compassion. "Can you?"

Ross released the air in his lungs and with it went a large measure of the hatred trapped there, too. "Wi' you, I think I've already made a start." He'd expected a smile, but his brave little warrior promptly burst into tears. "No greetin', lass. Like my sire, I'm undone by the sight of my wife's tears."

"'Tis j-just that I'm s-so happy," she managed, sobbing.

"Shush, now." Feeling a bit like crying himself, Ross scooped up his quivering wife and laid her down on the cot in the corner of the tent. With a tenderness that was new to him, he undressed her and tucked her under the blankets, but she refused to quiet until he'd stripped off his own clothes and climbed in with her. "Sleep," he crooned, stroking her tear-drenched face.

"Hold me close," she begged, clinging to him with surprising strength considering all she'd been through these past two days, nor was she satisfied until she had him just where she wanted him. "Ah." She sighed when he filled the emptiness inside her with his own aching need. "This is where we belong," she whispered, setting a pace that made him groan in ready agreement, left him trembling and crying her name as the world spun away.

This was exactly where he belonged.

Chapter Sixteen

Ross was feeling far less contented the next morning when young Lucais opened his eyes and saw Megan.

"Oh, m'lady. I feared ye were dead," were the first words out of the page. "I saw the arrow in yer mare's neck and—"

"Ha!" Megan glared at Ross. "I told you that the horse had been shot. Why do you groan?"

Damn. This was why he never lied, he thought, squirming under her irate frown. "Someone told me about the mare."

"And you did not share the *truth* wi' me?"

"You never asked about the beast and I've had other things on my mind since yestereve when Owain told me of the—"

"Humph." Her gaze softened as she looked back at Lucais. "How do you feel?" The lad admitted to feeling as though he'd been run down by a herd of Highland cattle; Ross felt worse. Nor did it help that his wife treated him like a leper, ignoring him as she moved from blanket to blanket, checking on her patients.

All save Andrew were alert and capable of riding. Davey sat beside the older knight, dutifully cooling his brow with wet cloths and giving him opiates at Megan's direction.

"Because of what happened to Papa, I feel terrible keepin' Sir Andrew in a stupor," she said. "But the pain would make him thrash about and mayhap pull out the stitches."

Ross nodded glumly, laid a hand on Andrew's shoulder for whatever comfort it gave, then followed Megan outside.

She sucked in a cleansing gulp of early morning air, let it out slowly as the tent flap dropped behind them. Eyes on the ground, shoulders hunched against the dawn chill, she walked slowly up the trail to the tumble of rocks that marked the edge of the ridge on which they'd camped.

Lost in his own unpleasant thoughts, Ross followed her. The wind was light, carrying with it the clank of equipment, the stirring of horses, the rumble of men's voices as they went about the business of breaking camp. Though he'd have preferred to linger here a few days, 'twas too dangerous.

"Could we leave your men here and go on alone? Just the two of us?" Megan asked, turning so suddenly Ross bumped into her.

He caught her by the shoulders to steady her. "Absolutely not," he exclaimed when he saw she was serious. "We may have driven those devils off yesterday, but 'tis nae guarantee they've given up. I want to be far away from here if they finish lickin' their wounds and decide to come after us again."

Megan's lips tightened. "I understand. But do you nae see, they'll follow us to Siusan."

"I am capable of protectin' one more woman," he huffed.

"And the babe?"

Ross had a sudden, horrible image of Megan and Siusan standing in the middle of a battle, clutching wee Kieran between them while all hell broke loose. "I'll pay the men of Larig to go wi' us, and buy more men if need be."

"What of the wounded?" she hedged. "Andrew canna travel."

"Agreed. I'll leave him wi' the women of Larig. By the time we've seen your sister, he should be mended enough to travel." Or he'd be dead, but Ross didn't want to think about that.

"We're nae facin' ordinary thieves," Megan said darkly. "They have made two attempts to capture Lucais and me."

"I can protect you. Warfare is men's work. Leave it to me." The shadows had hidden Ross's expression, but his exasperation rang clear in his voice.

Perversely it fed her own. "'Tisna your skills as a warrior I doubt. God knows, I've seen ample proof of them," she snapped, irritated and frightened. "But your pride could be the death of Siusan and Kieran if Comyn follows us—"

"Comyn!" Ross spat, raking both hands through his hair. "Jesu, I am sorry our prisoner died this morn, or nae matter how it turns my stomach, I'd ha' tortured him till he gave us the name of his leader."

"Comyn." Fear for her family outweighed his anger. First chance she got, she was drawing Lucais aside and going on al—

"And no sneaking off on your own," Ross growled, fingers biting into her shoulders as he gave her a little shake. "Promise me you willna even attempt it."

Rage gave her the strength to break free of his grasp, or mayhap he let her go. "Are you nae afraid I'll give my vow, then break it," she snapped before whirling away from him.

The crunch of footfalls on stone was all the warning she had before his steely arms wrapped around her from behind. "I believe you'd honor any pledge you made to me," he said softly. Despite her struggles to resist, he tucked her into the curve of his body and rested his chin on her head. "You are much like this land, Meggie mine, wild, beautiful and difficult to conquer."

Megan glanced out over the plain they must cross to the mountains beyond, great purple peaks silhouetted against the rosy gold of the rising sun, but righteous anger kept her silent.

He sighed, ruffling her hair. "'Tis like standin' in the clouds wi' the whole world spread out at your feet. Makes a man feel small in comparison. A humblin' experience," he added softly. "A bit like lovin' you." He hugged her tighter. "I'd much rather make love wi' you than quarrel."

As close to an apology as she was likely to get from this proud man. Still she was stubborn enough to want to press the point. "Does that mean you've reconsidered our goin' alone?"

"Absolutely not." His arms became a vise.

"I didna mean we should march boldly down the trail for all to see," Megan began, desperate to make him understand and agree. "I thought your men could march out as usual, wi' another wearin' your colors. We'd wait until they'd gone...likely drawin' our enemy wi' them, then we'd sneak off in the opposite dir—"

"Meg . . ." A warning.

Damn. Double damn. She hoped Rhiannon was suffering in hell. Nor did she regret the un-Christian thought. The woman deserved to pay, for those who'd died in her trap, for the scars she'd left on Ross. "I know you think it a lyin', womanish trick, but..."

"I see naught of the sort. I know you are desperate to keep Siusan and her bairn safe. Dividin' our force isna the way to accomplish that goal. What if we dinna fool these *brigands* wi' the ruse and they follow us instead?"

Shivering, Megan turned in his embrace, wrapped both arms around him and buried her nose in his woolen tunic. "If any harm comes to Siusan or Kieran, I'll never forgive myself"

"Dinna be afraid. I'll keep you all safe. I swear it." He kissed the top of her head to seal the vow, and Megan knew he meant it. But there were some things that were beyond even Ross's steely control. Comyn, for one.

He was still out there, watching and waiting. Megan felt it to the depths of her soul. All she could do was remain strong and vigilant herself . . . and pray that when the time came for the final confrontation, good would triumph.

"Look. There is Kilphedir," Lucais announced.

From the confines of Ross's hard embrace, Megan nodded and breathed a sigh of relief. 'Twas late in the afternoon and she'd feared they'd not reach her aunt's tower before dark.

"Ah, we made it wi'out further incident," Ross said, looking down his nose at her. She was tempted to punch him in that pompous feature and remind they had yet to get safely home with their two precious charges. She preferred not to think of the challenges that awaited them back at Curthill. Her mother was a skilled healer. Together she and Wee Wat would cure her Papa. She had to believe that or go mad dwelling on the alternatives.

"'Tis easy to see why they named it Kilphedir, *the rock*," Owain muttered, bringing Megan's attention back to the tower.

'Twas as rough as Lucais had warned, rising from the rocky cliff like a great black fist thrust into the darkening sky. As they drew closer, Megan saw that its strength was an illusion. The wall surrounding it was a flimsy pile of stones intended more to keep the cattle and horses inside the barmekin than to protect the peel tower from attack. Kilphedir's real defense lay in the fact that there were no doors or windows on the ground floor.

See why I was worried? Megan asked Ross with her eyes.

I will see to it, he replied in kind. Yet his gaze turned grim as it traveled over the tower.

Except for the faint light shining from the windows, it seemed Kilphedir slept. But as they approached the wall, a score of helmeted heads appeared behind it. Their spears glinted dully, dangerously in the fading light.

"State yer name and business," a gruff voice demanded.

Ross gave his name and rank. Before his words had died away, four men appeared in the upstairs windows, bows drawn and a dozen more materialized at their backs.

Enough of this nonsense. "'Tis Megan, Aunt Brita."

Instantly two bowmen were shoved aside and a gray head appeared at the window. "Megan! Dinna stand there, ye great gapin' fools, let the lass in," Brita bellowed.

Ross raised one brow. "A formidable woman, Aunt Brita." Nor did he change his mind a moment later when the old woman flew down the ladder and met them coming into the barmekin. She had Megan off the horse and into her arms before he could blink.

"Let's ha' a look at ye," she commanded after a hug that made her niece wince. "Ye're a mite worse for wear." Aunt Brita's sniff of disapproval was doubtless as much for Megan's wrinkled gown as the harried expression Ross wished he could case. "Who's he?" Her grizzled head jerked in Ross's direction.

"M-my husband."

Ross did not like the uncertainty in her voice one bit. He was her husband, dammit. "Ross Carmichael," he announced, swinging down from Zeus's back and bowing to the old woman.

Another sniff, and he found himself waiting with bated breath as she looked him over like a stallion brought to market. "Handsome as sin and twice as strong, I'll wager. Probably hell in bed, too, like my own dear Dugan," she added, winking as Ross's cheeks went hot with embarrassment. "See to yer men whilst I set the cook to heatin' up a bit o' food."

"I want to see Siusan," Megan began, but her aunt would not hear of it until they'd eaten.

Something was wrong. Air hissed through Ross's teeth and his nerves sizzled as Aunt Brita herded her niece up the ladder, snapping orders right and left as she went.

"You'd best mind your manners," Owain remarked with a grin.

"I'd say we'd all better." Ross frowned up at the tower. Shortly he'd be face-to-face with the woman who...at least inadvertently...was responsible for Lion's death and with the son she'd birthed. Equal parts dread and anticipation washed through him. He had a long time to worry about it, because Siusan did not join them for dinner.

Kilphedir's hall was as plain and rough as its lady. A large square room with a smoky hearth at one end, a stairway leading up to the second story at the other. Despite the fact that they'd likely eaten hours ago, Brita's people packed the hastily reset trestle tables. Partly to catch the news and partly to keep an eye on him, Ross guessed from the many wary glances slanted in his direction as he dug into the thick stew and brown bread.

If Megan sensed their scrutiny, she did not say a word, but merely poked at the food in her wooden bowl with a weariness that tore at Ross. For the first time in his life, he cared more for someone else's welfare than he did his own or even his family's. It scared the hell out of him. And scared men were not the sanest, he'd discovered. All the while he'd been defending his ability to protect Megan, he'd been wondering how he'd live with himself if the unthinkable happened and he somehow failed her.

Under cover of Brita's chatter about her late husband, Ross reached for Megan's hand. She started but did not protest when he laced his fingers with hers. "I am sorry, Meggie mine."

"Sorry?" she whispered back.

"For shouting at you this morn. I promise to make it up to you when we're alone." He winked.

She blinked. "Are you flirting wi' me?"

"I guess I am," he admitted, as surprised as she was. Such foolish behavior was not like him at all, but... Their gazes locked, held. The sounds of eating, the hum of voices, even Brita's strident one, faded. The air between them was suddenly charged, as though a storm had swept in on them, full of thunder and lightning. Aye, their lovemaking was as wild and explosive as a fierce summer storm. Yet the feelings it left behind were as fresh and beautiful as a rain-drenched landscape after the storm had passed. She felt it, too, Ross saw by the catch in her breathing, the flush that crept up from the neck of her gown.

"Ask your aunt where our room is," Ross murmured, eyes lowering to the tempting curve of her mouth.

Mcgan's smile flattened to a thin line. "Nay. I—I need to see Siusan first." Turning away from his disappointment, Megan tugged at her aunt's sleeve. "Where is she? Where is Siusan?"

Aunt Brita's smile went the way of Megan's. For the first time in Megan's memory, the woman whose visits to Curthill had always resembled happy, laughter-filled invasions looked uncertain. "I...I had thought to wait till morn when ye'd be rested and—"

"What's happened?" Megan clutched her aunt's fleshy arm.

"She isna dead." Quickly. "But..."

Megan was coming to hate that word. "I'd see her."

"Ye havena finished yer supper," Aunt Brita hedged.

"I couldna eat another bite." Clutching the amber amulet, Megan leaped up and stepped over the bench. Scarcely aware of Ross's hand supporting her, she stumbled up the stairs in her aunt's wake, entered the chamber in a haze of dread.

Every effort had been made to make the room cozy and comfortable. A fire burned in the hearth, candles on the chest beneath the window and on the table beside the bed chased the shadows from the corners. On that same table sat a cup containing a spray of white heather for freshness and luck.

Megan barely noticed any of these things, her gaze pouncing on the woman in the tall, curtained bed. Siusan's face was as pale as the linen pillowcase beneath her lank blond hair. Her body made a pitifully small mound in the bed covers, one small hand lying limp atop the blanket.

Uttering a cry, Megan darted into the room and took her sister's hand. Through a veil of tears, she saw Siusan's lashes lift to reveal glazed eyes. Sunk deep in mauve rimmed sockets, the agony and unspeakable weariness in them made Megan cry out, "Oh, Sius..."

"Meggie?" Siusan blinked, smiled faintly, the shadows in her eyes lifting briefly. "I knew you'd come..." Her voice trailed off as her eyes moved past Megan, widening. "Lion..." she whispered, voice aching with hope, wonder.

A strong, tanned hand reached around Megan, closed over the limp hand she held. "Nay. 'Tis Ross."

"Ross." Siusan's thin smile crumpled. "He's dead. I...I couldna save him... arrived too late."

The word ended on a sob that settled Ross's lingering doubts. Siusan had loved his brother. "Hush. 'Tisna your fault."

Siusan shuddered. "I should ha' known he'd be in danger." She started, gaze darting around the room. "Did you come alone?"

"I brought my men..." Ross began.

"But not Papa... or Comyn." Her fear intensified, eyes darkening to haunted black, hand trembling beneath his. "Tell me you didna bring them here," she begged.

Ross shifted uneasily, exchanged a worried glance with Megan. Had she been right about MacDonnel after all? "Nay. They are both back at Curthill."

"Thank God." Siusan's eyes squeezed shut.

"What is it? Did one of them kill Lion?" Ross asked, even knowing this was not the time to push. He'd come so far, waited so long, yearned so desperately for the truth...

"Ross!" Megan exclaimed. "Can you nae see she's...sick?"

"'Tis all right," her sister said faintly.

Dying. It hit Ross then that Siusan Sutherland was dying. And she knew it. 'Twas plain in the stark, unbearably sad look she gave Megan. *Nay,* Ross's heart cried, aching for both of them. The word broke from Megan's lips as the truth hit her, too.

"'Tis all right," Siusan said again, softer still. "I want to be wi' Lion. I...I only waited until you came. I need you to care for Kieran, to protect him as though he was your own."

"I will. I swear it," Megan said thickly, eyes brimming with tears. "But once we get you to a warmer clime, you will be—"

Siusan tossed her head. "Too late...has been since Lion...since Lion died in my arms. Dinna greet for me." Her hand slipped from Ross's grip, traced the path the tears had taken down Megan's pale cheek. "I want to go...need to be wi' Lion. But I hate to leave Kieran..." Her dark, anguished eyes moved past Megan to the cradle by the hearth.

"'Tis the one Uncle Dugan made years ago for the babes Aunt Brita lost. For a time I feared I might loose Kieran, too, but he is strong, like his sire." Siusan's gaze fastened on Ross again. "He's all that's left of Lion and me. Keep him safe for us?"

"Aye. I'd do anything for Lion's son," was all Ross could get out past the choking fullness in his throat. *God.* Lion had a son and he'd never even seen him. The enormity of it drove Ross to his feet and across the room. His legs failed him when he looked into the cradle and saw the tiny black-haired scrap of humanity lying there. "Lion's son." Dropping to his knees, he hesitantly touched the downy head.

The infant stirred, raising fine black lashes. Violet eyes stared solemnly up at him, so familiar that the ache of recognition drove the air from Ross's lungs, pierced his heart. How much it would mean to his grieving parents to know that Lion had left a piece of himself behind. "Why did you not send word to us?"

"I was afraid." Siusan's voice was so faint it barely carried the length of the room. "Afraid that if *he* knew I was carryin' Lion's bairn, he'd kill us both."

"He? Do you know who killed Lion?" Ross demanded, unable to contain the question that had haunted him for nearly a year.

Startled by his outburst, Kieran started to cry.

Megan leaped up from the bed like a scalded cat. Pushing past Ross, she picked up her screaming nephew. "There, there, lamb. Aunt Meg's here. She won't let the loud man hurt you. This can wait till Siusan is stronger," she hissed at Ross.

One look at Siusan and Ross was very much afraid she'd never be stronger, but neither could he bring himself to hound this frail woman. "I'll go below, then, and leave you to your rest. We'll talk of this on the morrow."

Brita sighed as she eased her bulk into the chair beside Ross's and stared at the fire leaping in the hall hearth. "At times like this, I miss my Dugan. Oh, I'm capable of protectin' what he left me when he died five years ago." She glanced at her clansmen bedded down with Ross's on the floor at the far end of the room. "A Highland lass learns defensive tactics alongside her stitchin' and cookin'. Still, 'tis nice to have a strong man to see to postin' the night watch and such things."

Ross nodded, eyes on the fire, mind above with Megan.

"So, what do ye think of the Highlands?" Brita inquired, stretching her booted feet toward the warmth.

Ross grunted. "I've not found them exactly hospitable."

"And marriage to my niece?"

His hold on his ale cup tightened. "Even more of a..."

"Challenge?" Brita supplied. "I hear 'twas a forced marriage. Do ye hold that against her?"

"Nay," Ross snapped, head whipping around to confront the old harridan, only to find her smiling. "I did at first," he grudgingly admitted. "But I've come to..."

"Love her," Brita supplied with that maddening habit of hers. "She's a braw lass. Her heart's suffered much pain." Her eyes strayed to the stairs and the worry lines at their corners deepened. "But losin' Siusan'll come near to breakin' her."

"I'd ha' come months ago to take Siusan and Kieran somewhere warmer and safer, but they kept the truth from us."

"Wi' good reason."

"There's never a good reason to lie," he snarled, nostrils flaring as though he'd smelled something foul.

Brita pursed her lips. "When ye've lived as long as I ha', ye'll discover that there are times when a lie is kinder than the truth." At his snort, she added, "Ha' ye never been forced to bend the truth to spare a loved one pain?"

"Never. Lies are dishonorable."

"Yet sometimes what a person doesna know canna hurt them." Brita held up a wide, callused palm to forestall his argument. "The truth is, yer family wouldna ha' welcomed the daughter of Eammon Sutherland. Nor is it the cold wet weather or childbed fever that will take Siusan. She's pinin' fer her man."

"She's willin' herself to die?" he asked, shocked.

"Siusan doesna ha' Meg's strength of body or will. When she fell in love wi' Lion, 'twas for all time. She gave him her heart, and when he died, he took it wi' him. She must follow."

"But what about her responsibility to Kieran?"

"She knows Megan'll look after him. From the day she sent Lucais for Meg, Siusan's been hangin' on by a toenail, waitin' for her sister to come . . . so she can go to Lion."

Nay, Ross wanted to cry, but he knew 'twas true, and he ached for Siusan, for Megan, for the wee bairn who'd grow up not knowing his father or his mother. He shook with the force of his rage and sorrow. "At least the men responsible for Lion's death have paid wi' their own lives."

"They have?" Brita exclaimed and smiled broadly, but the corners of her wrinkled mouth turned down again when Ross told her how Archie and Douglas had met their end. "This makes no sense. They werena even there when Lion died."

"What do you mean?"

Brita glanced quickly around the hall full of sleeping men, then dropped her voice. "When Siusan reached Lion, he was . . . he was dyin'. As she held him in her arms, she thought she saw two men skulkin' in the shadows at the edge of the woods."

"Were they the ones who killed Lion?"

"At the time, she was too overset to care for anythin' but tryin' to help Lion, though Mary tells me he was grave wounded and likely wouldna ha' recovered even if she or Megan had been there to help, but . . ."

"Did she recognize these men?"

Brita sighed. "Aye, later, when she'd come to her senses, she realized 'twas Eammon . . . and Comyn she'd seen."

"Both of them?" Ross breathed. "But which one killed . . . ?"

"She doesna know who murdered Lion, mayhap he didna either. He was shot in the back."

"But when she got back to Curthill, did she not confront her father and Comyn wi' what she'd seen?"

"Nay. At first she was too overcome by the loss of her Lion. I understand Mary had to gi' her somethin' to make her sleep before they could even pry her loose from his body. She spent the next week in her room, face to the wall, grievin' so she made herself sick." Brita cleared her throat. "Megan suspected Siusan was pregnant wi' Lion's child. That, at least, pulled Siusan from her misery. She had lost her love, but she had his bairn."

"That would ha' comforted my parents as well . . . had they known," Ross said sharply. "If only she'd come to us . . ."

Brita snorted. "Somehow I canna picture the mon who defied the king to attack Eammon welcomin' his daughter."

True. Lionel's pain had been deep, unreasoning, then. And now? Would he welcome Megan when he learned that a Sutherland had been there when Lion died? Somehow he had to find out which one had really killed Lion. "Did either Eammon or Comyn threaten Siusan? Is that why she left Curthill?"

"Nay. Accordin' to what Siusan told me when she got here, she was sore afraid. She could barely stomach the sight of either her father or Comyn. And too, she feared she'd somehow let on she suspected them and they'd kill her and the babe."

"Did Megan know all this?" Ross asked tightly. The quick, negative shake of Brita's gray head eased the coil in his chest, slightly. At least Meg had not lied about that. "Close as they were, why did Siusan not confide in her sister?"

"If ye can ask that, ye dinna know our Meg very well. Much as she loves her father and hates Comyn, she'd ha' confronted MacDonnel right off."

"Aye." Ross absently massaged the back of his neck.

"If ye want the truth, I think Comyn *is* guilty. He had an odd way of starin' at Siusan when he thought no one was about."

Ross slumped back, air hissing through his teeth. "If only there was some way to know for certain."

A child wailed inside Kilphedir tower.

Hidden in the shadows of the puny barmekin wall, Comyn paused in his scrutiny of the defenses, followed the shadow cast against the hide covering the second floor window. Back and forth it paced. A woman, with something clasped to her breast.

A child at Kilphedir? And not a maid's brat, for that would have been in the servant's quarters.

It struck him then, with the same sickening force as the knowledge that he'd lost Siusan to Lion... 'twas Carmichael's.

Comyn's lip curled, his blood ran cold with pain, then hot with fury. *Carmichael's spawn.* The cursed seed must have been planted at the Gathering, soon after they'd met. He gnashed his teeth, hatred growing, fed by the image of his Siusan, naked in another man's arms. Months he'd planned and plotted the death of his rival. The perfect crime. Only he had not been quick enough.

The babe cried again, and Comyn's expression hardened, eyes narrowing to angry, glittering slits. There it was... tangible proof that Siusan had been seduced by Lion. Sight unseen, Comyn hated the thing. When Siusan was his again, he'd drown it.

Ducking his head behind the wall, Comyn slunk around to the back of the tower. Here the ground fell away, increasing the distance to the top of the wall. There would be fewer guards here, because the defenders would think it less vulnerable.

Comyn smiled as he slung the rope from his shoulder and peeled the wool from the iron claw attached to one end. Grappling hooks were indispensable to a pirate intent on snaring a ship at sea. Yesterday his men had found them useful in climbing up the cliffs near Larig to entrap the unsuspecting Carmichaels. He found this one every bit as helpful in scaling Kilphedir's wall.

Balancing atop it like a cat, he found himself over the sheep pens. Better and better. They scattered, bleating, when he dropped among them, but provided cover while he crept up on the guard who'd come to investigate the beasts' sudden fright. And an excellent place in which to hide the dead man's body.

'Twas child's play from there. Comyn waited in the sheep pen for a few moments to make certain the coast was clear, then he raced across the barmekin and sank the hook into the sill of a darkened window in the back of the tower.

The brat had quieted by the time he reached the corridor, but the layout of the tower was similar to the one Comyn had been raised in, so he had no trouble finding the right room.

Megan was bending over the cradle when he opened the door. She whirled on him, eyes widening. "How did you get in here?"

Comyn shrugged. "I've been hoppin' in and out of peel towers since I was a lad. Where's—"

"Comyn!" Siusan sat up, white-faced as though she'd seen a ghost. Indeed, she looked like a haunt herself.

Bearing Lion's brat had done this to her, Comyn thought, hatred increasing as he noted her translucent skin, the dark shadows under her beautiful eyes. "I've come to take ye away."

"Nay." She swayed where she sat, one trembling hand rising to keep him at bay.

"Siusan. We were meant to be together..."

"You... you killed Lion," Siusan gasped.

"He didna die by my hand," Comyn said firmly, indignantly.

"Leave her alone. Leave my sister alone." Megan launched herself at him, pounding, kicking and scratching like a wild thing. He barely felt her efforts through his mail and leather, but her screeching was bound to attract attention.

He felt a certain primitive thrill as he slammed his fist into the side of her head. She hit the floor with a satisfying thud, lay perfectly still, eyes closed, a trickle of blood flowing from one corner of her mouth.

"Oh, God. You've killed her, too."

Good! Megan deserved as much. But he did not want her death to come between himself and his prize. "She's just stunned," he lied smoothly. "Come, we've a long ride ahead of us."

"Nay." Siusan ducked under his arm, scrambled off the bed and headed for the cradle. She was so weak she could barely stand, but she flung herself between Comyn and the babe.

"We can take it wi' us if ye like," Comyn growled. Anything to get her away without a fuss. He could always get rid of the little bastard later. "Ye'll like what I've done wi' Shurr More."

She shook her head, breathing quick and panicky. "Dinna touch me," she warned when he stepped close.

"Siusan. I love ye...I always ha'. Everything I've done ha' been for ye...for us. But I havena got time for this non-sense." He grabbed her arm, startled to discover how thin she was.

"Murderer. Murderer," she gasped, twisting and turning like a wild thing caught in a trap. "Get your bloody hands off me."

"Quiet." Comyn gave her a shake. It shuddered through her. The strangest look came over her ashen face. She shuddered again, pressed her hand to her heart.

"Lion," she cried in a strangled voice. Her eyes rolled back in her head; she sagged in his grasp.

Nay. It couldn't be. Comyn laid her on the floor. With trembling hands he smoothed the hair from her face. "Siu-san?"

"Lion." Her whisper ended on a sigh. Her pinched features relaxed into an expression of pure bliss, and she was gone.

Chapter Seventeen

"Oh, God. She's dead." Callused hands stroked her face.

The anguish in that familiar male voice made Megan want to open her eyes, tell Ross she was all right, but her lashes were so heavy, the pain in her head so sharp...

"She's alive." Aunt Brita, sounding old and quavery. Poor woman, first Siusan takes sick, now her other niece is laid low.

Megan stirred, wanting to reach out and comfort her aunt.

"Meggie! Talk to me. Say somethin'...anythin'." Ross.

"But..." she teased. He didn't laugh. Scooping her off the floor, he hugged her with a fierceness that made her ribs creak.

"Jesu, you gave me a fright. What happened?"

"'Twas Comyn. He was here...in this room." She tightened her grip on Ross's shoulders, willing him to believe her. "Do you not see? He must have been the one behind the attacks. Did you capture him? What of Siusan and Kieran?" She craned to see the bed around his big body.

He laid her down, glanced quickly at her aunt. "Meggie..."

"'Tis Siusan, isn't it?" At his nod she groaned, stuffing the knuckles of her right hand into her mouth to keep back the screams of anguish that filled her throat. "Did Comyn...?"

"I think her heart gave out," Aunt Brita said gently. "There's nae a mark on her, and her face is sweet and serene as an angel's. She's wi' her Lion, now."

Great shuddering sobs tore through Megan. "Sh-she wanted that more than anything. More than stayin' to see her babe grow into a man." Battling tears and her own shattered emotions, she turned toward the cradle. "Poor Kieran. He's alone now. Bring him to me, please.'' She extended her empty arms for Ross to fill.

Ross's expression grew even grimmer. ''By the time we got here, Kieran was gone,'' he told her. ''The guards heard a bairn cry, saw someone go over the back wall.''

''Comyn has him? Mother of God!'' Megan sat up, swayed dizzily. ''We have to go after him.''

Ross caught her close, hugged her. ''My men are already preparin' for the journey. You're stayin' here wi'—''

''Nay. I'm goin'.'' Megan leaned back in his embrace, ignoring the ache in her temples. ''You'll need me to care for Kieran.''

Ross shook his head. ''You're exhausted, hurt.''

''I promised Siusan I'd care for him, yet Comyn stole him.''

His arms tightened around her; a muscle in his cheek jumped as he flexed his jaw. ''Tis my fault,'' he shocked her by saying. ''If I'd believed your accusations about Comyn, Siusan might be alive and Kieran here safe and sound.''

''Oh, Ross, I didna mean that I blamed you.''

''I blame myself.'' He freed her from his grip and stood, face hard, eyes bleak. ''I'll nae risk you, too. You'll stay here where your aunt can tend you.'' To that hovering woman, he said, ''I'd appreciate the loan of a guide who knows the mountains.''

''I'm goin'.'' Megan got to her knees and no farther, restrained this time by her aunt's wide hand.

''I'll see to the lass,'' Brita said. ''Twenty of my best men'll go wi' ye to lead the way and lend a hand if it comes to a fight. Likely he'll make fer Shurr More, about ten leagues east of here, through some of the wildest country in the Highlands.''

Ross nodded curtly. ''It doesna matter if I have to go through hell, I must take Comyn before he reaches his tower.'' *Or he'll shut himself inside and we'll never get Kieran out.* Megan heard the words as plainly as if Ross had shouted them, read, too, the anguish in the dark eyes he turned on her. ''Keep safe,'' was all he said before striding from the room, but she had felt the force of his love move over her, through her.

''I canna let him go alone,'' she cried, clutching at her aunt's arm. ''I just know something bad will happen if I'm not there when he meets Comyn.''

"He's much like my Dugan," the old woman mused. "Strong, honorable and too damned proud fer his own good." Releasing her hold on Megan, she climbed stiffly to her feet. "Come, we've much to do and not much time before yon knight'll be ridin' out to save wee Kieran."

Megan agreed readily, submitted to her aunt's skilled treatment of the bump on her head and dressed for the journey in a thick leather tunic and a pair of woolen trews.

"Wore them when I was younger and slimmer," Aunt Brita confided. "Just the thing for goin' reivin' wi' yer mon."

The loose-fitting hose did indeed promise greater comfort and fewer drafts than her gown. Under different circumstances, she probably would have enjoyed the freedom of movement they provided. As it was... "About Siusan..."

"The maids ha' laid her out in her room," Aunt Brita said with a softness that would have surprised those who did not know that beneath her rough exterior beat a heart of pure mush.

Not unlike Ross, Megan thought as she followed her aunt down the corridor. Only, when he found out she'd defied him, he might never again show her that gentle side of his nature. Outside the door to her sister's chamber, she paused, wishing he were here to hold her hand now, then slowly entered.

Siusan did look peaceful and happy for the first time in over a year. She wore the gown she'd made for her wedding, deep red velvet that accented the gold in her hair, lent a rosy glow to her cheeks. "Oh, Sius..."

Aunt Brita's arm came around Megan, offering warmth, support, comfort. She longed to collapse into that promised haven, but already she heard Ross below, shouting for his horse. And somewhere in the night, Comyn fled with his trophy.

"I'll bury her on the hill, wi' Dugan and our babes," her aunt promised, tears trickling down her wrinkled face.

Megan kissed that wet, leathery cheek and looked her last at Siusan. "I'll miss you, sweet sister," she whispered. "And I swear on your soul that I'll find Kieran and raise him as though he was my own bairn."

* * *

Agonizing hours later, Megan wondered if she should not have followed Ross's orders and remained behind with Aunt Brita. Though she rode well back in the pack of riders, a pair of Sutherlands glued to either side by their lady's command, she felt vulnerable as a leaf swept up by a strong current.

The pace the Sutherland outriders set was a brutal one, considering the narrow, rocky trails they traveled through the mountains. Her fear of riding had long since faded, dulled by the numbness in her rump, the knotting in the muscles of her bad leg from gripping her mount's sides.

They stopped once to water their horses in a gushing stream. Megan drank greedily from the cup handed up to her, bit off a hunk of dried meat and let it soften in her mouth. She did not accept her guard's offer to dismount, afraid she'd collapse in a heap. Ross was some distance away, talking quietly with Owain, but she dared not cause any stir that would provoke his interest in the lad who rode with the Sutherlands.

Instead, she leaned her wind-chilled cheek against her horse's sweaty hide and closed eyes that ached from searching the blackness ahead for some sign of Comyn.

And Kieran.

Tears welled against her lids. He was so small, so vulnerable. *Please, God, keep him safe till we find him.* And even afterward, Megan amended. In her mind's eye, she saw the two forces meeting, swords drawn, spears flashing. Men, even one as dedicated to saving Kieran as Ross was, would concentrate first on defeating their enemy, not realizing how fragile a bairn was. At three months, he was too young to avoid the horses' hooves if he fell to the ground—even supposing he survived the fall—or dodge a stray blow or...

Megan groaned, sickened by the myriad horrible possibilities. 'Twas why she'd come. To keep Siusan's babe safe even from those who would rescue him.

Fear for the babe straightened Megan's spine when moments later Ross gave the order to ride on, lent strength to her weary muscles and flagging spirits as night yielded to the pale gray tentacles of dawn.

Ross was nowhere near as tired as Megan, but he was fully as worried as she was, muscles knotted from straining forward, trying to ride faster, see farther. He fancied he could hear wee Kieran's cries on the night air, but 'twas only his guilty conscience. Damn. If he'd put more faith in Megan's suspicions about Comyn, the poor babe would not be in mortal danger.

It was full light and they'd been eight hours in the saddle when one of the scouts thundered back down the trail with word their quarry had been spotted.

"None too soon," exclaimed the Sutherland captain. "By my reckonin', we're scarce a mile from Shurr More."

"Forward," Ross ordered, tensed for action. "Try to encircle them, cut off their access to the tower." As they rounded a curve in the mountain, he spotted Comyn's men cantering across the moor that led to the next rise. Ahead of them, set into the sheer face of the cliff, rose the black towers of Shurr More.

Impregnable.

The word flashed through Ross's mind, sent apprehension racing down his spine as he dug his heels into Zeus's sides. To hell with caution, speed was essential. If Comyn reached his stronghold, they'd not get him out for years. And the devil alone knew what that madman intended to do with Kieran. Behind him, Ross heard the thunder of hooves as his men scrambled to keep up.

Comyn's men heard it, too. The rear guard turned back. "'Ware," they cried. The warning echoed off the mountain, spurred those ahead into a full gallop. But momentum and the element of surprise were with Ross, carried him around the enemy's right flank. The first man he passed stared open-mouthed, then reached for his sword. Too late. Ross was by him, blade at the ready, energy focused on sweeping to the head of the column.

'Twas a little like herding sheep, he thought, having watched the sturdy sheepdogs work a flock as he was attempting to work Comyn's MacDonnels. Never once did he look behind to see if his own men were keeping pace. He trusted on faith that when he came abreast of Comyn and tried to turn him, Owain and the others would be strung out in his wake, waiting to draw the noose around their prize.

Two more men to go. One more. Suddenly he was racing neck and neck with Comyn. As though sensing him, the Highlander glanced over. The pale eyes that had good-naturedly challenged Ross over a chess board widened, then narrowed furiously.

Why had he not seen the potential for violence in this man? Ross wondered fleetingly. Because he'd been so certain the Sutherlands were guilty; because Rhiannon's deceit had blinded him to Megan's integrity. Aye, Megan had the right of it; he had trusted Comyn on sight because he had more faith in men than in women.

Leaning low over Zeus's neck, Ross silently begged the weary horse for one last burst of speed. Beneath him, powerful muscles bunched as the stallion faithfully obliged. Raising his sword, Ross angled closer. Mayhap he could end it here and now...

That thought died as Comyn shifted. The folds of his cape whipped back to reveal Kieran encased in a sack slung around Comyn's neck so that only the tiny face showed. It was red, so swollen from crying the eyes were mere slits. The sack beat a ragged tattoo against Comyn's chest with every jarring step his horse took, and Ross felt the vibrations shudder through his own body.

"Bastard," Ross roared through clenched teeth.

"That he is," Comyn shouted back. "And he'll be treated as such," he added ominously. His glance shifted ahead, no doubt gauging the distance to his tower and safety.

"The hell you say." Acting on pure instinct, driven by fear and rage so strong it nearly consumed him, Ross turned Zeus directly into Comyn's path. He murmured an apology to the stallion as the two horses collided. Both beasts screamed. War trained, they tried to lash out at each other with their hooves, but the close quarters prevented any blows from landing.

Kieran continued to cry, and Ross's heart ached for the babe, yet having the bairn strapped to his chest made it difficult for Comyn to draw his sword and fight back.

Checkmate.

Roaring an oath, Comyn dragged on the reins, attempting to move away, but at Ross's command, Zeus crowded closer.

It was turn or be trampled. Stop or be ground to dust.

That realization made Comyn's eyes bulge with unholy fury in the instant before he pulled his horse to a stop.

Behind them, all hell broke loose as Comyn's men tried to bring their own mounts to a halt and failed, skidding into one another. Men shouted, horses screamed and bellowed as they collided. When the dust settled, they were surrounded by a ring of Carmichaels and Sutherlands, swords drawn.

"Attack, Hakon," Comyn shouted. "I'll double yer pay."

The leader of the mercenary troop eyed his opponents' superior numbers and growled, "Dead men canna spend aught. Besides, the luck's against us...has been since that fox crossed our trail when we left Curthill."

Another Highland superstition, Ross mused, noting the other men's unease. One he didn't understand but did approve of.

Comyn was not about to give up without a struggle. "Fools!" Pulling the dirk from his belt with his left hand, he held it to the squalling infant's throat. "Let me go, or the brat dies."

"Let you go, and he dies." Ross hid the sickening fear that swept him as the blade flirted with Kieran's soft baby skin.

"Nay!" cried a high, female voice. "He's a bairn, nae some war prize for the two of you to squabble over."

"Megan!" Ross and Comyn exclaimed together.

"Aye." She took advantage of Comyn's surprise to swing her horse next to his and reach for the dirk.

On instinct, he moved it out of range, right into Ross's outstretched hand. "Drop it." Ross seized Comyn's wrist.

"Nay." Their eyes locked as Ross applied pressure, squeezing tighter and tighter, watching the determination in his opponent's expression drown under the pain. Just as he felt the bones shift, knew they were near to cracking, the dirk clattered to the ground. Ross's shout of victory was short-lived.

"Back off, or I'll snap his neck," Comyn threatened, his right hand encircling the babe's throat.

"Ross," Megan murmured. Over the short distance that separated them, her fear-darkened eyes beseeched him to comply to save her sister's son...his brother's son.

Jesu, it was bad enough he had Kieran's safety to consider, now he had her to worry about, as well. He told her so with a hard, castigating look that should have sent her scurrying back to the Sutherlands.

Instead, she glared at him. "Do as he says," she ordered, "or he'll hurt Kieran."

Did she think him too stupid to realize this?

"Checkmate," Comyn snarled, grinning.

Only if I let it be, Ross thought. He gave Megan a hard look. *Keep your tongue between your lips no matter what I say or do,* he silently warned. To Comyn he said, "Take the brat, then."

Comyn raised a sandy brow. "Ye'd give up Lion's bairn?"

"Is it his?" Ross fought to appear unconvinced.

"It has black hair," Comyn exclaimed, but his grip on Kieran eased as he tried to get a better look at the bairn's face.

Ross let go half of the breath he'd been holding. So far, so good. Now if he could only lure the man a step farther...

"Mayhap she had other black-haired lovers." He ignored Megan's squeak of outrage. Easy to do, since Comyn's roar drowned it out.

"My Siusan wasna like that."

"Mayhap the bairn is Lion's, then," Ross allowed, shrugging.

"If ye're nae certain, why did ye come after it?"

"Because Megan fancies raisin' it, and you know how stubborn she can be when her mind's set on a thing."

This Comyn did not dispute. "I've my own plans fer *it.*"

The wealth of loathing in that single word sent raw panic clawing at Ross's innards. Jesu, what did Comyn intend? Struggling to keep his voice calm, Ross offered, "Why do we nae settle this dispute like knights?"

"What do ye mean?" Comyn demanded.

"Single combat. You and me."

"Agreed." Comyn smiled, an ugly, predatory showing of teeth likely intended to make Ross feel like a mouse in a trap. Obviously a few of Andrew's doubts about his lord's fighting skills must have reached Comyn's ears.

"Oh, Ross," Megan wailed, raising a hand as if to forestall the battle. The fear in her voice broadened Comyn's smile.

"Hush, woman," Ross said sternly. "I know what I'm about. Let her hold the babe, and—"

"Ha!" Comyn insisted Hakon do the honors. Ross countered by demanding another of Comyn's men. One who was unarmed and stood in the clear, well away from the tower and Comyn's troops.

'Twas the best he could do under the circumstances. Yet he saw by the stubborn set of Megan's chin that she had plans to better the odds if she could. No telling what she would try. Jesu, he did not need this, on top of everything else.

While the men dismounted and took their places for the contest, Ross stomped over to Megan. "Stay out of this, Meg," he growled as he lifted her from the saddle. She folded the minute her feet touched the ground and would have crumpled into a heap if he hadn't caught her. "Meg?" Concern drove out anger. "Is it your leg?" At her nod, he swung her into his arms. "Little fool. The pace was too hard on you. Owain—"

"Nay. You'll need him to watch your back," his supposedly pain-stricken wife whispered.

Ross looked down into eyes bright with determination, not dull with agony. "Meg? What are you about?"

"Helpin'."

"The hell you are. I want you back out of harm's way and..."

She groaned loud enough to wake the dead a league away and writhed, drawing every eye to the way she thrashed and gripped her left thigh. "My leg," she cried. "Put me down."

Ross started toward Owain and Davey, but was brought up short by a sharp tug on the hair that escaped his helm.

"Set me nearer to where that fiend stands wi' Kieran," Megan snapped. Had he no sense at all? It seemed not, for Ross insisted that he did not want the two most vulnerable members of the party sitting together, and dumped her on Davey. Literally.

Quivering with equal parts frustration and indignation, Megan waited until Ross and Owain had gone forward to meet with Comyn and his captain halfway between the two groups of fighting men.

"Davey," Megan whispered as the squire carried her to safety. "'Tis too rocky here. Do you take me over there." She pointed to a spot a few yards from where Comyn's hard-faced man stood over Kieran. When the lad hesitated, she added, "We willna be able to see m'lord fight otherwise." Typically, the thought of missing the action overcame caution.

Megan groaned in earnest as her much-abused rump met the cold, hard ground. The mercenary guard glanced at her, then back at his leader, clearly dismissing her as a possible threat. Her leg was sore, and she massaged it through the wool trews, one eye on the now silent infant lying in the grass a short distance away, the other on Ross and Comyn as they took their places.

Neither man had slept the night before, but she knew Ross had been through hell these past few days because she'd been by his side most of the way. As though to lend weight to her fears, Comyn hefted his huge, two-handed claymore, swung it easily over his head, drawing the attention of their audience. The blade fell suddenly, in a swift, gleaming arch aimed directly at Ross's chest. Megan's scream strangled in her throat as Ross raised his weapon and deflected the blow.

Ross shuddered as the impact of Comyn's blade jarred down the length of his lighter weapon, numbing his hands and arms. Though nearly matched in height, the Highlander had the advantage in reach and upper body strength. Which meant Ross would have to be smarter and quicker if he wanted to win.

Much quicker.

To spare Zeus the weight, Ross had left his plate armor behind and wore only mail beneath the woolen surcoat, now wet with the sweat of his exertion. Heavy and unwieldy the claymore might be, but it was capable of cutting through his chain mail like butter. Knowing that full well, Comyn attempted to beat him back with a furious hail of blows.

Ross gave ground, the shouts of his men rising above the thunder of blood against his ears. Megan's cry penetrated most sharply, reminding him of her presence when he could least afford the distraction. Damn her impetuous hide. Though her intervention had led to this chance to save Kieran, he heartily wished her safely back at Kilphedir with her aunt.

Closing himself to all save the man he faced, Ross ducked clear of Comyn's attack and skipped backward. Comyn followed like a trained bear, ponderous and feral. They parried and feinted, testing each other with steel as they once had with chess pieces. Their harsh, labored breathing filled the silent clearing, punctuated by the clash of metal on metal. Just as he had over the chess board, Ross drew out each move, not letting his opponent guess his mind was several strokes ahead of his blade. Refusing to go on the attack, Ross maintained a defensive posture, probed Comyn's fighting style, looking for the weakness Andrew had long ago assured him every man had.

And there it was. The greatest sin a knight can commit . . . overconfidence. Assuming his opponent was slow, not careful, Comyn grew sloppy.

Calmly Ross slipped in under that lax guard. Steel shrieked as his sword slid down the leading edge of Comyn's claymore, reversed and neatly stripped it from the Highlander's grasp. "Check," Ross cried as the sword flew through the air and landed a body length away. "I'll take my nephew now."

"The hell ye will." Deep in the sockets of his helm, Comyn's eyes narrowed to furious slits. "Strangle the brat," he bellowed.

"Of all the dishonorable . . ." Ross turned to countermand the threat, even knowing none of his men could reach Kieran in time. But Megan already had. Snatching the babe from between the guard's feet, she made for Ross. Face white, strained, eyes and mouth wide with fear, she limped over the uneven ground, Kieran clutched tight to her breast, the guard in quick pursuit.

She wasn't going to make it. Oh, God. She was not fast enough. Screaming her name, Ross started across the field toward her even as Comyn roared an obscenity and launched himself into the fray. Before either of them could reach her, Megan's left leg gave out. She stumbled, lurched and went down. Rolling to spare Kieran her weight, she landed on her back.

The guard was there before Megan stopped moving. Drawing a dirk from his boot, he put it to her neck. "Stay back!"

Ross's mouth went dry, heart dropping even as he jogged to a halt and lowered the tip of his sword. "Give it up, Comyn. My men have yours surrounded," he said, even knowing 'twas futile.

Comyn threw back his head and laughed as he stepped in to take the knife from his man. "That may be, but I ha' yer pawns in check." The last rays of the setting sun glinted wickedly on the blade as he tossed it from hand to hand.

"What now?" Ross asked to keep the man talking. Out of the corner of his eye, he had seen Davey inch around the cluster of men, angling toward the terrible drama unfolding before their horrified gazes. Given a little time...

"I've nae use fer Megan. Ye may take her and ride away. But the brat stays wi' me."

"Nay!" Heedless of Comyn standing over her, Megan sat up, one hand on her bad leg. Across the distance separating them, Ross winced, feeling the pain that cramped her left leg, longing to go to her. "I willna leave Kieran." She hugged the whimpering babe closer. "You'll need me to tend him, Comyn," she argued.

"Meg!" Ross cried, aghast, starting forward.

Comyn held him off by grabbing Megan around the waist and hauling her to her feet. His blade flirted with the underside of her stubborn little chin. "Stay back," he warned. "And yer squire, too," he added, head whipping around to confront Davey creeping up from the right. "All I want's the brat."

"Meg, hand Kieran to Comyn and come to me," Ross said, words thick, gritty with anguish and futility.

Megan felt it, shared it. More than anything, she wanted to do as Ross asked and run to the safe haven of his strong arms. Comyn hated her...had for a long time. She was afraid, so afraid of what he'd do to her when he got her inside his tower, alone and vulnerable. But she could not let Kieran go alone, either.

Careful of the dirk, she tilted her head so she could see Comyn's face. Deep in the sockets of his helm, his eyes blazed with the unholy lust for vengeance. Mad. Only a mad man would seek to make tiny Kieran pay for the wrongs he imagined Lion had done him. She could not temper that seething hatred, but mayhap she could use it to her own use. "Think you 'twill be satisfyin' to torture a three-month-old infant?" she forced out.

Comyn blinked, obviously shocked by her bluntness. "What..."

Across the space that separated them, she could feel Ross watching her. Growing darkness and the shadows cast by his helmet hid his expression. But his anger was a palpable thing, clear in the tense lines of his body as he stood there, sword poised, head high. A predator ready to strike. If he had not hated her for her lies, he'd hate her for this, her final betrayal.

Ross watched her, but he remembered Rhiannon. Only *her* crime was so much worse. Rhiannon had cost him the lives of one hundred men. *She* would cost him the one life that meant more to him than his own. *I'll keep him safe, no matter what,* she had vowed.

Lifting her eyes, she confronted Comyn's demon gaze. "He's too young to appreciate the fact that you make him suffer for his father's sins." *Forgive me, Kieran, Lion, Siusan.* "And he willna grow any older wi'out a woman's care." She bid a silent farewell to Ross and calmly stepped through the gates into purgatory. "You need me to keep him alive...."

A smile curved the lips beneath the nasal of his helmet. "Ye'll be at my mercy, too, Megan." The smile spread, a cold, cruel promise of things to come. He felt her shudder and laughed.

Oh, God. She could not go on. Inside the bundle of blankets she held, Kieran stirred. His tiny fist slipped into the neck of her tunic. Cold as ice, it sought the warmth of her flesh. He whimpered, mouth rooting about at her breast for nourishment.

The small, weak sound, the feel of his fingers clutching at her, went through Megan like a jolt of lightning, rousing instincts she'd not known she had. *He was hers.* Given into her care by her beloved sister. Blood of her blood. She'd not turn him loose this side of hell. And she was very much afraid hell was where both she and Kieran were bound.

Chapter Eighteen

"He's gone mad," Davey whispered to Owain. "Watchin' that bastard take Lady Megan and the babe away has driven m'lord mad."

Owain sighed and cast a concerned eye over Ross. He stood apart from them in the center of the grassy moor. Head bowed by grief and despair, sword dangling forgotten in his hand, he was still as a stone statue. Aye, and deaf as one, too, for he'd ignored Davey's offers of food and drink, as well as Owain's attempts to interest him in planning their next move. Any move.

"We can not continue thus." Owain stalked across the brittle grass, stopped beside Ross and gently touched his arm. "Ross..."

"Leave me!" the calm, logical Carmichael heir shouted.

"Ross, be reasonable..."

"Reasonable!" He turned on Owain, body trembling, eyes red-rimmed pools of anguish glaring from the sockets of his helm. "How can I be reasonable when he has them both. Foul, mad bastard, he has them both and there isna a bloody thing I can do about it. Jesu, 'tis all I can do to stand here when every muscle in my body screams wi' the need to run up the hill and batter down the walls of that damn castle...wi' my bare hands if need be." His breath spewed out in sharp, harsh puffs that frosted in the cool air like dragon's breath.

"Fine," Owain said evenly. "We will come with ye. Fifty pairs of hands will make quicker work of the task."

Ross blinked, shook himself like a man emerging from a dream... or a nightmare. "But 'tis hopeless, stupid..."

"Nonetheless, if ye think it the best way to free Lady Megan and the babe, we are with ye."

Ross glared at Owain, the dazed look in his eyes easing. "Dinna do this to me, Welshman. Dinna make me responsible, for my wits are scattered, my heart sunk deep in misery."

"Ye'll do what's best for yer lady," Owain replied, his own pulse steadied by certainty that Ross was himself again.

"Best!" Ross's head snapped toward the dark, brooding mass of Shurr More set out like fretwork against the dusky sky. "Best was if the fool woman had stayed home where she belonged."

"Yet 'tis thanks to her that the babe is not in there alone, unloved and untended," Owain softly reminded him.

"Nay, thanks to her rashness, Comyn has two of them to torture." Ross looked away from the fortress. "He hates her. Dear God, why did I not see it? Why did I not believe her?"

"Because Rhiannon had poisoned yer mind."

"Small comfort that is," Ross snapped. "'Tis my fault she is in there." He dragged in a ragged breath. "But regrets willna change what has happened." Squaring his shoulders, he sheathed his sword. "Come. Bid the men mount up. We ride."

"Ride?" Owain exclaimed, but he spoke to thin air. The statue had come to life and was hurrying toward the horses. "But . . . but we can not leave Lady Megan and the babe," he protested, trotting along at Ross's side.

"We can do naught here."

And that was that.

Opulence. From the moment she'd been hustled inside Shurr More, Megan had been wrapped in it, choked by it.

She could not bear to look at the fine tapestries lining the walls of the chamber Comyn had thrust her into hours ago. Could not bear to sit on the ornately carved chairs flanking the fireplace, or lie down on the immense canopied bed at the other end of the room. More of his bloody pirates' booty.

So she paced. The soles of the boots Aunt Brita had given her a scant four and twenty hours ago beat a muffled path across the thick carpet from window to door and back again. The constant movement had worked the worst of the cramps from her leg, but done little to ease her fears.

She was alone. More alone even than she'd bargained for when she'd decided to take this terrible gamble.

Ross and his men had gone...left her here to Comyn's mercy.

Megan groaned and pressed her forehead against the cool window glass, a rarity even in Edinburgh, for which Comyn must have paid as dearly as he had for all of these luxuries. But her thoughts weren't on her captor, they were on the man who had stood on the plain below a few hours ago. The man she loved with all her heart. The man who'd claimed he loved her yet did not trust her.

With her eyes, she'd beseeched him to understand what she was doing and why. Kieran was important to both of them. Surely he must know that she couldn't let the tiny babe go alone into Comyn's stronghold.

The sound of a key grating in the lock jerked Megan from her morbid reverie. Turning, she felt the hair rise on her nape as Comyn strolled in. At his heels trailed the maid who had brought her wash water, swaddling cloth and barley gruel for Kieran. Dry and full, the babe had promptly fallen asleep on the bed; the intervening hours had not been as kind to the maid.

"I see ye've noted her split lip and black eye," Comyn grumbled. "She'll get worse the next time she defies my orders and helps ye coddle the bastard."

"The bairn willna live long if you starve him," Megan pointed out. "I'm sorry," she murmured to the maid, who averted her eyes, set the tray down on an oaken side table and fled. So much for gaining the lass's aid in caring for Kieran and eventually escaping from this luxurious pile of horrors.

"I want him to live...but nae in comfort." Comyn prowled the room, touching a silver candlestick, the velvet drapes framing the window. Lastly he stood beside the bed, looking down at the sleeping infant. The savage twist of his features made Megan rush forward, hands outstretched to snatch the babe to safety.

Comyn backhanded her, sent her reeling against one sturdy wooden post. "Carmichael's bastard doesna deserve comfort. This bed was to ha' been Siusan's. I dinna want him in it. Keep him off the bed and out of my sight. If I see or hear him, I'll kick him down the stairs." He paused, fingered his stubbled chin. "A crippled slave wouldna be as quick, but 'twould be amusin' to watch him stumble about the place the way you do."

Megan ignored the gibe. "But where will he sleep?"

"He'll ha' a basket in the kitchen ... like a dog. And when he's old enough, he'll fight them for scraps from my table."

"But ... he'll starve ..."

"Nay. He willna. I survived on the scraps yer sire gave me."

Megan straightened, indignation burning through her fear, giving her strength. "Papa took you in, gave you a place at his table, valued you above his own son. And you turned on him."

"I did what I had to do to survive. Eammon was a coward. He refused to help me punish the MacKays fer stealin' my birthright, refused to fall in wi' my scheme to make us rich."

Oh, Papa, Megan silently cried. If only she had not been involved in her struggles to regain the use of her leg, she might have saved him from the opium.

"He gave me a pitiful tower, I turned it into a castle fit for a king."

"Paid for wi' the blood of those whose ships your men sank."

"They were naught to me. *An eye for an eye,* I say. I ha' but regained what the MacKays and yer father stole from me. From here I'll rule my kingdom."

"Kingdom? You have only fifty mercenaries." And a score of servants whose cringing manner as they slunk out to greet their lord bespoke cruelty. Not surprising, but the audacity of Comyn's next words took her breath away.

"I've coin enough to buy an army wi' which to take back what's mine...and more besides. The Highlands first, then..." He smiled, eyes alight with greed. "I may be in a position to challenge the king. But I'll start wi' the Sutherlands. Brita first, fer keepin' my Siusan from me. Then I'll settle wi' the Mac-Kays. After that, Curthill. Eammon should be dead by now..."

"Nay. He canna be."

"Fer two years now his body's fed on the opium I bought him. Accordin' to what Douglas told me, Eammon'll nae survive its loss." His smile widened. "And a nasty death it is."

Oh, Papa. Horror-struck, Megan swayed, then caught herself. Her mother would save her father. She had to believe that... or go mad. His next words nearly drove her over the edge.

"And then there's what I owe ye."

"Me? What have I ever done to make you hate me so?"

His lip curled. "Yer very existence ha' been a thorn in my side. If not for ye, I could ha' wed Siusan years ago." He raked a hand through his shaggy hair. "Jesu, ye didna even ha' the decency to die when ye should ha'."

"You. You did shoot my horse from under me," Megan gasped, skin tingling with fear and loathing. A nasty smile was her only answer, but the truth was a feral light in his eyes. "And Ewan?"

"And Ewan. One wee accident was to ha' brought me all...a fittin' punishment for yer father, Siusan for my wife, Curthill as a base for my trade."

Fiend. Bile filled her throat, but she had to keep him talking, had to find a way out for Kieran and herself. "Why did no one find the arrow in the horse's neck?" she managed.

"Why, because Hakon volunteered to go down and bring up the poor beasts and Ewan's body. He retrieved his arrow then." Comyn crossed his arms over the gold chains on his chest. "Ye ha' to pay, ye realize," he said as calmly as though they were discussing a bolt of cloth she'd purchased.

"Bein' shut inside your stronghold is torture enough," she said with feigned calm. If she could lull him into giving her the freedom of the castle, she could find a way to escape.

"Nae enough." Comyn stroked his chin, candlelight intensifying the mad glint in his eyes. "Ye're a proud bitch. Bard of Clan Sutherland," he sneered. "A few nights locked in the barracks wi' my men'll bring ye down a notch or two."

"Nay." Her heart thudding so loudly she could barely hear Comyn's lewd laughter, Megan worked her way around the bedpost.

He stalked her, expression sharp, predatory. "Mayhap I'll use ye first." His lips peeled away from his teeth in a wolfish grin. "Recall the time ye caught me tormentin' the hounds in their kennels? Yer sire didna believe yer tale, but he did wonder how one came to be missin'. 'Tisna only hounds I like to tie up, Meg. Ye'll learn things in my bed ye never did in Ross's."

Sweet Mary. Frantically Megan eyed the distance to the door. Too far for her lame leg. Nor could she leave Kieran.

They were saved by the sudden pealing of bells.

"What the hell!" Comyn stalked to the window, threw it open and stuck his head out. "Smoke, from the kitchen and stables. 'Tis Ross's doin'. I thought he gave up too easily, but he willna burn this place down around my ears like the Mac-Kays did my parents'. I'll be back to deal wi' ye," he snapped before hurrying out.

The clunk of the iron bar settling into place echoed off the stone walls of the chamber with dreaded finality. Shivering, Megan sank down onto the edge of the bed. Escape was her first instinct, but how? She was alone, on the third story of a tower inside her enemy's stronghold, with the door barred from outside.

She'd go out the window.

Megan leaped up, lifted the sleeping Kieran and limped over to the hearth. Setting him on the floor a safe distance from the fire, she stripped the linen from the bed and tied it into a makeshift rope. There should be enough to reach the roof of what she guessed was the chapel and from thence to the ground. If Ross had somehow gotten inside Shurr More, he'd find her much more quickly if he didn't have to search the entire castle.

Bloody hell! Megan had gone out the window!

Ross's hand tightened on his sword as he stared down the length of knotted bed linen to the roof below. It was full dark, but the glow from the burning buildings turned night into a hellish sort of day. In the bailey below, he saw figures dashing to and fro, trying to put out the fire, trying to flee the Carmichaels and Sutherlands who had followed Ross over Shurr More's walls. But no frightened woman and babe sat on the roof. "Why could she not have waited here to be rescued, like any normal woman?"

The first servant he'd encountered, a maid with a split lip, had been only too glad to tell Ross where Comyn had housed his lady prisoner and the babe. Relieved to know they were all right, Ross had sent the rest of his men to subdue the Mac-Donnels while he raced up the tower stairs in search of Meg. Now this.

Scowling, Ross hurried away from the window. He opened the door a crack, heard voices drifting up the stairwell. "Stand guard above and kill any man who tries to free the lady." *Comyn.*

Ross grabbed the first thing that came to hand...a five-foot wrought-iron candle stand...and jammed it into the brackets intended to hold a metal door bar. Not a second too soon. The latch wiggled and someone swore. Heavy blows rained against the door as Ross sprinted for the window. Hand over hand, he let himself down the knotted linen, wondering how Megan had managed the climb with a babe strapped to her chest.

Jesu, she was something else, he thought, furious, proud and terribly worried. What if Comyn's men caught her? What if...

"There he is. Stop him," Comyn called from above. The linen line jumped and twitched as someone sawed on it.

Ross dropped the last few feet to the roof, landed with his knees bent to absorb the shock, slid down the slick slate and over the edge. A dirk followed him, bouncing harmlessly off his helmet as he squatted in the gravel beside the chapel. A second, sharper blow from behind made his ears ring. Cursing, he surged up and grabbed the lurking figure, pinning it against the rough stone of the chapel. "Yield," he growled.

"Gladly," came a soft, pert reply.

"Meggie?" Ross's hands trembled as they tunneled into her silky hair, turning her pale, dirt-streaked face into the light. "Oh, Meggie mine."

"Ross." Her single, hope-filled word ended on a squeak as his hug drove the air from her lungs.

"Oh, Meggie." His mouth was on her neck, her cheek, in her hair; his hands were clutching, kneading her back.

Blindly she rooted around until her mouth found hers, sealing them together in a kiss that warmed her from head to toe. "Oh, Ross. Are you angry wi' me?" she gasped, moments later.

"Furious." The shadows couldn't disguise the fire blazing in his midnight eyes. Part anger, part fear, all love. It went a long way to healing the wound his leaving had caused. "When I heard you put yourself in that madman's hands, I...I..." Words obviously failed him.

Megan had no such problem. "I couldna let Comyn take wee Kieran off alone," she said in a rush.

Ross's expression hardened. "You could have trusted me to save you and the bairn."

"But—"

"No buts. Not this time. Where is Kieran?"

"Here." Megan stepped around the corner, retrieved the small, blanket-wrapped bundle and settled it in the crook of her arm. "He's been so good," she whispered, folding back a corner so Ross could see the sleeping babe.

"As you have not. You will cease actin' so rashly and never put yourself at risk again," he growled.

"Aye." Meekly. "Thank you for comin' for me . . . for us. When you said you didna think Kieran was Lion's, I was afraid—"

Ross snorted. "See what comes of lies? I fancied that if Comyn thought I didna really value Kieran, he'd leave the babe."

"You tried your hand at playactin'?" Unbelievable.

"Fat lot of good it did." He kissed her again, then buried his mouth in her neck. "Jesu, Meggie, I died a thousand deaths when you rode off alone wi' Comyn."

"I felt the same when I thought you'd deserted me," she said in a small voice.

"Never." He kissed the lone tear that tracked down her cheek. "But . . . Jesu, I begin to sound like you. I judged it wiser to leave, then sneak back, thought 'twould go easier on you if Comyn did not know you were my life, my heart."

Sweet words, indeed. Megan allowed herself to bask in them and the warmth of his strong embrace for a moment before reality intruded. "Ross, it isna enough to get Kieran and me away from here, we have to stop Comyn." Briefly, quickly, she told him what MacDonnel planned to do with his ill-gotten wealth.

Ross clenched his fists, lip curled in pure disgust. "Is there no end to the man's perfidy?"

"Nay. He confessed to stagin' the accident that killed my brother and I'm positive he is the one who killed Lion, too."

"Given the way he felt about Siusan, it does seem likely." And he knew Meg didn't want her father to be the guilty one. "But now is not the time for such speculation." Ross gently covered Kieran's face and herded Megan away from the chapel.

"First things first. I must get you and Kieran away from here. Once you two are safe, I'll come back and deal wi' Comyn."

"How did you get inside the castle?"

"When he stole Kieran, Comyn left behind a rope wi' a hook on one end. It looked a useful thing, so I brought it wi' me. Came in handy for scalin' his back wall."

Megan stopped. "You came alone?"

"Nay. Owain and the others are here, subduing Comyn's mercenaries." Keeping close to the wall where the shadows were thicker, he headed her toward the back gate.

"And you scold me for taking chances." The shiver that iced her skin had little to do with the coldness of the stone beneath her fingers as she felt her way along the wall. *Did he think himself invincible?* "Where are Comyn's men?" she whispered.

"We knocked out those who were on sentry duty. The rest were in the hall noisily celebratin' their lord's victory. Now they're fightin' the fire and my men." He paused at the corner. "Wait here while I make certain the way is clear."

It seemed an eternity until he guided her out into the open. A light breeze lifted the hair from her face. Tendrils of smoke eddied across the ground like gray snakes. At the other end of the courtyard, the fire crackled and hissed. Leaping skyward, it formed an orange backdrop against which black figures writhed in silent combat. Sutherlands, Carmichaels, Comyn's mercenaries.

"What if someone gets hurt?" Megan fretted.

Ross sighed. "You canna worry about everyone," he grumbled, hustling her in the opposite direction. Keeping her safely tucked behind him, Ross led them from tower, to smithy, to back wall. The few people they encountered were servants cowering in the dark. Still, he did not relax even when he spotted their goal. "There's the postern gate." He pointed across the deserted garden to a door in the stone wall. "Just a little farther. You've done well keepin' Kieran quiet."

Megan patted the warm lump. "He feels safe wi' me."

"I know the feelin'." Ross's smile was a white blur in the night, but as he stepped from the protective wall of the kitchen, a dark shape moved to block their path.

Comyn.

Megan gasped as firelight glinted off his upraised blade. The sound became a low groan of fear as it swept downward. Steel shrieked on steel as Ross's sword met it halfway.

"Run, Meg!" Ross shouted. He had no time to see if she obeyed, because Comyn was on the attack.

Megan stumbled back out of the way, limped around the two men as they circled and parried. Ahead of her, the way was clear to the gate and the freedom it promised. Conscious of the precious weight against her chest, she desperately wanted to take the chance Ross had bought them. But...

Heart in her mouth, Megan watched Ross fight for his life, for theirs. All too well she remembered the outcome of the last battle between these two. What if Comyn tried some other dastardly trick? She should be here to see, to warn Ross. But...

Kieran stirred, whimpered as though her turmoil had invaded his sleep. She had promised Siusan she'd look after him. Where did her first duty lie? To the man she loved, or the bairn she had come to love as though he were her own?

"Leave, Meggie," Ross called, and she realized that her very presence was a danger to him.

She pressed her fingers to the amber resting in the hollow between her breasts. "Keep safe, love," she whispered, and fancied the stone warmed in silent promise. Clutching that hope nearly as closely as she did wee Kieran, she turned and ran for the gate, heedless for once of whether her limp was noticeable.

Ross heard Megan leave, and it was like a great weight had been lifted from him. He'd expended too much energy worrying about whether Comyn would try to capture her again. Now he could turn the full force of his attention to their fight.

In seconds, 'twas clear Comyn had learned nothing from their earlier match. He still dropped his guard when he went on the offensive. Ross only hoped he was not too tired to take advantage of this slight advantage. A second night without sleep had taken its toll in weary limbs and sluggish responses. He countered the exhaustion by recalling what was at stake here... not just the lives of Megan, Kieran and the other Scots Comyn would enslave given the chance, but his own quest for vengeance.

Ah, sweet revenge. Conjuring up his brother's image lent the strength of rage to Ross's flagging muscles. "This time, I've got you," Ross goaded, sword flashing as he went on the attack.

Comyn blinked, stunned by its fury. He retreated two steps, three, then recovered and drove back. "I'm the better swordsman."

"The more devious, mayhap, but..." He chuckled at his use of Megan's word. "Not better." To prove the point, he slipped under Comyn's sword and drove for his shoulder. The tip bit through the silken surcoat, but skidded harmlessly off mail links.

"Forced to wear chain mail even inside your own castle?"

"I thought you gave up too easily."

"Did my brother give up easily?"

Comyn missed a step, groaned as Ross's sword caught him in the left thigh, sundering padded leather and striking flesh. Swearing viciously, he gripped his leg and drove hard into Ross. "I didna kill your brother."

"Siusan said you were there when he was murdered."

"I wasna certain she saw us." Comyn's lip curled. "She went a wee bit mad when he died."

"Seein' someone you love cut down does that to a person."

"Love!" Something ugly glittered in Comyn's eyes. "I hated seein' them together, hated knowin' he'd touched her." Rage painted bright flags on his cheeks. Studied swordplay gave way to sloppy, wild strokes as his fury at Lion grew. And then there it was, the opening Ross had been waiting for.

"For Lion," Ross said softly, his voice drowned out by the grating of his blade as it slide down Comyn's. He aimed for the vulnerable joint at the elbow, turning the point so it slipped into the groove and found tender flesh.

Comyn cursed and his sword thudded to the ground. Eyes rounded with astonishment, he stared at the blood trickling down his arm then, "Ha. 'Tisna a mortal blow," he sneered.

"Nay. I'd see you dragged to Edinburgh in chains to face the king's justice," Ross said with real satisfaction. Victory was within his grasp. "I'd see you pay for murderin' Lion."

"Me?" Comyn laughed, the sound harsh and mocking. "But I didna kill yer brother...Eammon did."

"Nay!" Ross took hold of the man's bloodied surcoat and shook him. "Sutherland had no reason to murder Lion. You did. I want the truth."

Comyn smiled, eyes glittering with savage pleasure. "Told him Lion had his opium. Told him if he wanted it, wanted to stop the demons clawin' at his gut, he'd ha' to kill Lion. Damn good shot it was, considerin' the way his hands were quakin'."

"Eammon killed Lion?" *Nay. It could not be.*

"I couldna come to Siusan wi' Lion's blood on my hands," Comyn said in that madly sane voice of his.

"Jesu, this is terrible." Dazed, Ross tried to come to grips with the sudden, horrible revelation.

Comyn used the distraction to his advantage. Jerking the dirk from his belt, he sprang at Ross. The momentum carried them both to the ground where they rolled around battling for possession of the long, wicked knife. This time it was Comyn who had the advantage of surprise. He used it to bring the blade to Ross's throat. "Now ye'll pay..."

Ross fumbled for his own dirk and came up empty-handed. Dimly he recalled using the knife to silence one of the guards at the back wall. But wait... there was something. A smooth, slender length of wood. The rowan twig Dame Isla had given him. For luck.

In that instant, Comyn's ran out. The sharp stick found the only unprotected spot on Comyn's armored body...his eye. He cried out in surprise. Air wheezed past his lips and he was gone.

Ross fancied he heard the gates of hell creak open to gobble up another evil, soulless fiend. One whose acts would reach beyond the grave to poison the living.

Chapter Nineteen

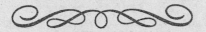

"There it is! I see Curthill in the distance."

Davey's excited shout lifted Megan's gaze from the face of the bairn sleeping in her lap. Sitting taller, she eagerly drank in the sight of the familiar stone towers, her nostrils flaring to catch the briny tang of the sea. *Home.* "We're home," she murmured, twisting to look up at the man who had brought them safely through the wild Highland passes. By day, Ross's arms had sheltered her and Kieran from cold and rain and harm, by night his big body had warmed them while they slept. "We're safe."

"Aye." He lifted the visor of his helmet to reveal a face as taut and guarded as though they were still deep in the mountains. Though Comyn's MacDonnels were locked up in Shurr More under watchful Sutherland eyes, beasts and brigands had posed a real threat. But no more. So why...?

"Is it Andrew?" She craned her neck to see down the line of riders. The older knight still scowled his displeasure at being in the center of the troop with Sim as nursemaid, instead of at the front leading it, but he sat upright in the saddle. Spying Megan, he raised his left hand and kneed his horse forward.

Megan groaned and faced front. "Oh, here he comes."

"M'lady, ye wanted aught?" Andrew asked, drawing rein.

"Nay. I was but lookin' about."

"If ye need anythin'... anythin' at all, ye ha' only to ask, Lady Megan." He looked down at his right arm, thick with bandages, bound tightly against his chest, but whole and healing.

"Your recovery is all the thanks I need," she insisted for the hundredth time since they'd arrived at Larig and found the knight recuperating and anxious to make amends.

He grunted, expression obstinate as chiseled marble. "I'll be wi'in hailin' distance, all the same."

"You have to speak to him...make him realize he isna in my debt," Megan said to Ross when Andrew had ridden back.

"We are all in your debt," Ross said a little stiffly.

What is wrong with you? Megan wanted to shout. But 'twould do no good. He refused to discuss the canker that had eaten at him since Shurr More. "I'm sorry you had to kill him," she ventured softly.

"Comyn deserved to die." Hard and cold as his expression.

"But nae by your hand."

"Better mine than any other."

Damn his stubbornness. "Ross! Talk wi' me ...''

He looked at her then, tenderness chasing the shadows from his eyes as they caressed her face and moved on to wee Kieran in her arms. "What would you have me say?"

"Is it Papa?" she asked, and the knot in her stomach coiled tighter as the shutters came down over his eyes once more. "Are you afraid he's dead?"

"Dead?" He started as though the possibility that had made her jumpy as a trapped bird, hopeful one instant, apprehensive the next, had not occurred to him. "Nay, I . . . ah, here's Giles."

Megan shoved aside her own concerns to greet the troop that rode out from Curthill, an exuberant Giles in the lead.

"I was nearly to the point of sendin' out search parties," the handsome knight called, stopping at Ross's side.

"All is well?" Ross asked his grinning man.

Giles's smile faded. "Lord Comyn's gone missin'. I feared he'd been set upon by the pirates, yet found no evidence of—"

"Comyn met a fittin' end," Ross growled. "'Tis a long tale, and the tellin'll wait till my lady is wi'in."

Ordinary words, yet Megan felt the tremor that moved through Ross's body as they rode over the drawbridge. What was there at Curthill to make such a brave man shake? One glance around the courtyard and she forgot the question.

"Sweet Mary," she murmured, eyes round with wonder as Ross lifted her down from Zeus's back. "'Tis…'tis as clean and orderly as it used to be, before the bad times."

Even Ross smiled. "Giles, you've wrought a miracle."

"'Twasna my doin'. When they heard how their laird had been kept a virtual prisoner in his own castle, the Sutherlands were so ashamed they'd not seen what was happenin', they fair tripped over each other tryin' to set things right again." Still Giles's chest puffed out with pride as he led them inside the keep.

In the hall, the changes were even more dramatic. Gone were the wet, soggy rushes, the scarred tables, the pack of unruly men who'd used Archie's friendship as license for debauchery. The scent of sweet herbs rose around them and even the tapestries looked brighter, Megan thought as they braved the crowd of laughing Sutherlands.

"Meg!" Lady Mary paused in the doorway, lifted her skirts and ran the length of the hall with the agility of a woman half her years. Cheeks flushed, eyes shining, she reached them quickly. "He's alive. Your father's alive."

"Alive!" She'd been afraid to ask. Relief turned Megan's knees to jelly, but Ross steadied her from behind. Good thing, because her mother's fierce hug sent her back two paces.

Caught between them, the sleeping Kieran roused and protested loudly.

"What's this?" Lady Mary stepped back, gaze widening as Megan peeled aside the edges of her cloak. "Oh, 'tis a bairn."

"Siusan's son. But I wasna able to save her," Megan said, whereupon, all three burst into tears. The noise attracted Chrissy and the other women, who promptly began to cry, too.

"Jesu, 'tis fair deafenin'," Lord Nigel grumbled, coming to stand at Ross's side. "Wi' Eammon out o' danger, I'd expected smiles. What ails them now?"

"They're grievin'," Ross said, wondering if he'd forever be.

"Chrissy, could you see to wee Kieran?" Lady Mary said, dabbing at her wet face. "I'd take Megan up to see her father. I'd rather we didna say anythin' about poor Siusan's passin' till he's stronger," she added.

"You know best, Mama, but if he asks for her, I willna lie," Megan said slowly, her eyes on Ross. "I'm through wi' lies."

Would that he were, Ross thought grimly, the secret he'd kept shut deep inside him eating at his gut, his soul.

Megan grabbed his hand. "Come wi' us. I want you to meet Papa." She tugged him across the courtyard toward the laird's tower. "He's alive." She squeezed his hand, eyes dancing with joyous relief. "He's a long way from well, but he's alive." She started up the steps.

Ross hung back, not certain if he could face Lion's killer. "'Tis late. Mayhap we should wait till morn to visit . . ."

"I need to see him." She turned, expression grave. "I need to see him with my own eyes. And when the time's right, I need to explain about Siusan."

Jesu, he ached for her. For them. "Siusan's death wasna your fault. You did your best to help her." More than her best. She'd braved her fear of horses and her fear of Comyn.

"As you did for Lion?" Megan asked.

"'Tisna the same," Ross grumbled. "I let my brother down by not coming here wi' him." And by withholding the truth about his murder. *Damn. How could he live with that?*

"Determined as Comyn was to have Siusan, do you really think you could have saved Lion from him?"

Ross sighed. "Mayhap not, but I should have tried."

"Comyn was mad," Megan said as they reached the tower stairs. "If he had not succeeded that day, he'd have tried again and again until he had what he wanted. Your being here wouldna have stopped him, and mayhap you'd have been killed, as well."

Little healer, Ross thought sadly. But the scars of his last meeting with Comyn went too deep even for her skills.

Seeing Eammon Sutherland again was an ordeal, but not of the sort Ross had supposed. The old man in the curtained bed looked as frail and insubstantial as a ghost, face white as the pillow under his head. Beneath the blankets, his limbs shifted restlessly as though seeking an escape from the demons that had turned him into a gaunt husk. Only the demon was inside him.

"Oh, Papa," Megan gasped. Her hand tightened in Ross's till his bones creaked in protest, but he did not draw away, unwilling to have her face this fight alone.

"Meggie?" Eammon's parchment lids lifted. "Ah. Ye're a sight fer these tired eyes." The dark eyes he'd bequeathed to

Megan drifted from her face to Ross's. "Lion?" A faint smile tugged at his dry lips. "'Tis good to see ye, lad. I had a terrible dream...thought something bad had happened. Couldna bear that. Come closer..." He raised a hand; it fell back on the bed. "Ha' to ask ye a...a favor. Pirates. Cursed pirates. Tried ta stop them... Failed. Not strong enough. But ye are." Again his hand twitched.

On instinct, Ross reached over and took it, grasping the bony claw in a tender grip. "'Tis all right, sir."

"Nay. 'Twillna be all right till they're stopped. Say ye'll do it...stop them, fer my people," Eammon pleaded, eyes tearing.

The backs of Ross's own lids stung, and he heard Megan's sobs, felt her shuddering through their joined hands. "Consider it done," Ross said gently.

"Ah." The old man sagged into the bed. "Knew the minute I saw ye that ye were the man fer my Siusan...the man to save my people." His eyes drifted shut. "Nasty business...canna think how it started. Tired...too tired to fight Comyn."

"Shh," Megan soothed, voice thick with tears. "Everythin' is taken care of. You concentrate on getting well."

"I ha' to...my Mary says she'll kill me if I dinna."

As her father drifted to sleep, Megan turned and buried her face in Ross's tunic. "Thank you for pretendin' you were Lion. Tomorrow, if he's stronger, we'll tell him the truth."

Truth. The word lanced through Ross like a hot blade. "We'll wait till he's stronger," Ross said slowly, stroking her back. His own muscles were so tight no amount of massaging would loosen them. Duty warred with desire, truth with love. If he told the truth, he risked hurting Eammon, who was as much a victim here as Lion, risked hurting Lady Mary and the rest of Clan Sutherland just as they were struggling to put their lives back in order.

And what of Megan? Their life together was just beginning. How could he doom that bright hope? And what of wee Kieran? Would his family welcome the bairn if they knew that in his veins flowed the blood of his father's murderer?

Jesu, he wanted to scream and rant and rail against the Fates for thrusting upon him this terrible burden. Aunt Brita had the right of it, the truth was not always a good thing. Would that he had never heard Comyn's confession. Would that he had gone on thinking Comyn had shot the arrow, for he truly *was* the guilty party here, no matter who had pulled back the bowstring.

"Ross. You're shiverin' with cold and exhaustion," Lady Mary said, laying a concerned hand on his arm. "I ordered a bath brought to the chamber you and Megan shared on your weddin' night. Do you go ahead. I'd...I'd speak wi' her for a moment."

Dimly Ross realized that his mother-by-marriage was disturbed about something, but he was too grateful for a few private minutes in which to explore his own hell to wonder what demons inhabited hers.

"Mama, I am glad to see you, and I would like to talk wi' you, but I must see if Ross needs anything. And Kieran, though he's been so good through this whole ordeal, may be fretful surrounded by so many strange faces." Megan made to leave.

Her mother thrust a cup of wine into her hand. "Please sit a moment...here by the fire." She perched on the edge of a chair drawn close to the hearth in her sewing room.

Megan sank into the other chair. "Something is wrong."

"Well." Her mother swallowed, looked away.

"Mama, this dreadful mess has taught me to value the truth. If Siusan had told us she suspected Papa or Comyn had had a hand in Lion's death, things might have turned out differently."

Lady Mary shook her head. "Nay, you would have defended your papa and ordered Comyn strung up from the nearest tree."

Megan nodded. "Exactly the right things, too."

"That is, if Comyn didna kill you first."

Megan sighed. "We'll never know. The point is, Siusan might be alive if she hadna lied to us and run away. You must tell me whatever it is that is botherin' you so we can deal wi' it."

Lady Mary looked down at her knotted hands. "'Tis possible that you mayna be able to have children."

"What?" Shock held Megan frozen for an instant, then she leaned forward to grab her mother's arm. Her grip tightened as her mother repeated the horrible words. "How can that be?"

she asked, dazed, aching. Dimly she was aware of her mother explaining about bleeding and internal damage, about the midwife called in to confirm her suspicions, but the only thing Megan truly heard was the sound of her dreams crumbling.

"Ross," was Megan's first thought. "He'll be devastated."

"Why tell him?" her mother said, frantic fingers digging into Megan's arm. "He could yet repudiate you for this."

"He has a right to know his wife is...ba...ba..." She couldn't get it out, could scarcely think it. *Barren.* Why this, on top of everything else? Why this, just when it seemed their troubles were behind them? "I...I must tell him." But how?

Ross lay back in the tub, eyes closed, tight muscles and turbulent thoughts momentarily eased by the hot, soapy water. He need decide nothing right now. Surely after supper would be time enough to destroy those he loved. Or even tomorrow. Aye, he'd visit Eammon again on the morrow and take things from there.

The ringing of the chapel bell sounded the first call to dinner, Reluctantly Ross opened his eyes and sat up. Megan would have to hurry did she want to wash before they went down to eat. The bell came again, louder, more strident, and as the pealing died away, heavy feet pounded down the corridor.

"Ross!" Owain burst in, sword in hand, helm in the other. "A ship! A strange ship's sailed in, set *The Black Hawk* aflame and is starting on the town."

Ross was out of the tub in a flash, wiping a towel over his dripping body. As he pulled on his clothes, he peppered Owain with questions. But no one knew the answer to the most pressing...who was attacking them? He was more or less dressed by the time Davey rushed in with his armor. The rest of his men were waiting at the foot of the stairs.

"Andrew, stay here with half of the castle garrison. Raise the drawbridge, man the towers and for God's sake, dinna let Lady Megan outside these walls. Wee Wat, stay and look after your patient. The rest of you, come wi' me."

Half the town was afire by the time Ross and his men raced down the winding road from the castle. Purgatory, he'd once called it. Now it more resembled a scene from hell. The streets were clogged with crying women and bairns, singed livestock and confused men struggling to save their homes. A few shouted commands from Ross brought order out of chaos.

"Sim, take any who canna fight to the storage hut and hide them in the caves," Ross shouted over the pealing of the bells. With his fighting force divided into thirds under Giles, Owain and himself, Ross headed for the beach.

The sun had just set, but the plume of black smoke rising from *The Black Hawk* turned the sky over the harbor dark as night. No flames were visible. Hopefully those aboard had extinguished the fire, Ross thought as he turned his attention to the enemy ship making for shore. Her unfurled sails flapped like the wings of a giant bird swooping down on some unsuspecting prey.

"Bowmen to the fore," Ross shouted. "Form a turtle over them wi' your shields."

None too soon, for the sky suddenly rained arrows, a few of them tipped with fire. As soon as the shower ceased, the men dashed from shelter and began stomping out the burning shafts.

"Pick up the spent quarrels and return fire," Ross bellowed. "See how they like being trapped aboard a flamin' ship."

They did not like it at all. Most of the arrows fell short, hissing into the water, but a pair struck the flapping canvas and caught hold. Two angry orange flowers took root, sending hungry tentacles streaking over the sails. Howls of rage drifted across the harbor as the captain of the ship sent men aloft to cope with the sailor's worst nightmare.

The voice sounded oddly familiar.

Owain thought so, too. Casting a sidelong glance at Ross, he said, "Their leader has a bellow like..."

"Da." Ross started forward. A deadly whine from on high had him throwing his shield over his head. "Damn him for rushin' in before he knows what's goin' on."

"How are we going to let him know it's us before he's killed us?" Owain shouted over the thunk and twang of falling arrows.

Ross solved the problem the minute the *rain* stopped. Shield at the ready, he threw back his head and let go the Carmichael battle cry. Around him, forty voices picked up the call.

"A Carmichael. A Carmichael." The Sutherlands joined in, so the cry swelled to a wave of sound, ringing off the cliffs below the castle, rolling over the water.

Ross raised his hand, and the wave crested, fell off to leave total silence in its wake. It hung there, heavy as the smoke from burning pirate ship, taut as Ross's breathing as he waited. If that was his father, would he think this a trick? If it wasn't, would the enemy try to trick them? Then it came, the roar he'd not thought to hear for a week at least.

"Ross? Is that ye, lad?"

Lad? How many men called their five-and-twenty year-old son lad? "Aye, Da," he called back, grinning. "'Tis me."

"Are ye well?" With a quaver at the end that turned Ross's smile poignant. "Ye were gone so long, we feared ye were dead."

"I'm alive, Da, but tired and hungry. If you've a mind to conquer us, hurry it up so I can get back to my bath."

"We'll be in directly," came the subdued response.

Giles and most of the Sutherlands left to assess the damage to the town while Ross waited for the ship to furl sail and anchor. Scarcely had the weight splashed into the inky water before a boat was lowered over the side. It made straight for Ross, his father sitting in the prow. The minute the hull struck stone, Lionel waded ashore, still dressed in full battle gear but minus the helmet, his long black hair tangled with sweat.

"Ross!" He threw both arms around Ross and squeezed the air from his lungs.

"What are you doin' here," Ross gasped, ribs creaking.

"Yer mother was worried." Lionel released Ross and stepped back, looking him up and down with a critical eye. "Ye've lost weight and yer color's nae so good."

Small wonder. "I've been chasin' about the Highlands." And he hadn't slept easy since Comyn revealed the truth.

His father grunted, cast a damning glance at Curthill's lighted towers. "Did ye catch the bastard that killed Lion?"

"Aye." Slowly, painfully.

"Ah." His father smiled, the deep lines bracketing his mouth eased, his eyes squeezed shut briefly. When they opened, peace shone in their violet depths. "And the woman?"

Ross braced himself. "I married her."

"Ah. Then I expect ye'll be givin' me a grandson before the year is up," he mused. "Good work...on all counts." He clapped Ross on the shoulder. "What is it? Why'd ye wince?"

"Old wound," Ross said.

"Lionel Carmichael! How dare ye leave me on that ship?"

Ross started, turned to see his mother being helped from a second boat. "Mama? You brought Mama wi' you to wage war?"

"Brought?" Lionel rolled his eyes. "I *brought* Hunter. Yer Mama and sister stowed away," he grumbled. "Can ye credit it?"

"Easily," Ross replied, thinking of Megan.

"Ross. Oh, Ross." His mother flung her arms around him. "Oh, ye've lost weight." She stepped back. "And ye look a fright."

"Comes of havin' only just returned to Curthill and bein' called from the first bath I've had in a week by the news that *The Hawk* was aflame and the town under attack."

"That's the same ship that nearly sank me last time," his sire growled defensively. "I thought it had done ye in."

"'Tis in friendly hands now, Da," Ross assured him.

"Did ye catch him?" Elspeth demanded, poised at their sire's side, eyes hard with hatred. "Did ye catch Lion's murderer?"

"Aye," Ross said, and the path he must trod opened clearly before him. It was not the path of his choosing. And mayhap living a lie for the rest of his life would doom his soul, but better everlasting damnation than the alternative...a living hell for those he loved. "Comyn MacDonnel was his name, and Lion wasna his only victim." As he stood on the smoky beach and briefly sketched the tale for his family, one that changed only the name of the man who'd sent the arrow into Lion's heart, the ache in his own chest eased.

This might not be the truth, but it was right.

"Oh, Ross," Elspeth exclaimed when he'd finished. Leaving their father, she came and wrapped her arms around him, leaned her forehead against his chest. "I'm sorry I doubted ye."

"'Tis all right, poppet. There were times I doubted myself." But no more.

"Now, where's this new daughter of mine?" Lionel grumbled. "And did ye mention food? We've had naught but cold fare and a cramped bed this past week."

Ross chuckled, gave Elspeth a squeeze and set her from him. Or tried to. She kept her hands around his arm. "Megan and supper await at Curthill, but there's a third surprise." The tears that greeted news of Kieran's existence set the seal of his decision. Now at last there would be peace.

"Gone? What do you mean, Megan is gone?" Ross demanded of Lady Mary. "Tired as she is, if she's gone down to the town to treat Lang Gordy's gout, I'll ... I'll ..."

"She ... she had to leave," the lady replied. Fingers twisting in her skirts, she looked away from the window embrasure where she'd drawn him for a private word. He followed her gaze to the chairs around the hall hearth where his family cooed over Kieran.

"Does this have something to do wi' the babe?"

Lady Mary shook her head, but her face went whiter still.

"M'lady. Wi' all due respect. I've had a hellish week, topped off by my sire's rescue, and I'm that exhausted. If you'll just tell me straight out where Megan has gone, I'll go and fetch her back or stay wi' her till she can return."

Lady Mary dragged in a ragged breath, stuffed a knuckle into her mouth to silence her sobs. "She ... she's gone because she canna b-bear you a babe."

"What nonsense is this? Married a week and she already fears she's bar—?"

"Sh-she is barren," the lady choked out. She filled in the rest between sobs.

When she finished, Ross took her by the shoulders. "How can you know for certain?" he demanded, half mad with grief. Not for himself, but for Meg, who had so wanted bairns of her own.

"I ... I dinna, but I've seen the like before. Women who are hurt so they bleed have trouble conceivin' and ofttimes dinna bear any babes at all."

"Sometimes isna *always*. Why did you even tell her, dammit?"

"Because she insisted on knowing the truth."

The truth. Ross rolled his eyes skyward. So, this was his penance for what Megan had called his rabid obsession with the truth. He was doomed to a lifetime of nasty revelations. "Tell me where she has gone," he demanded.

It took another few moments to coax the information out of Lady Mary and several more to reach the stables and a horse. Not Zeus, who had given his all and was asleep on his feet, but a chestnut gelding who covered the distance from castle to town in a wild, reckless plunge that matched Ross's needs exactly. Moments later, he was pounding on the door to George's hut.

"Who's there?" the tailor called timidly.

"'Tis Ross. I've come for Megan." Over the thundering of his pulse, he heard frantic whispering and scuffling. "I know she's in there, so open up and let me in," he demanded in his best lord-of-the-castle voice.

"A moment," George replied, but several passed before the latch scraped and the door creaked open to reveal three startled faces . . . George, his wife and Lucais. The latter looked so guilty Ross didn't have to scan the room to know Megan had fled.

"Where is she, lad? And speak quick."

"I . . . I canna tell ye." Lucais looked as miserable as Ross felt, head bent over the book that lay open on the table.

Megan's book of stories and legends. It had seen a few adventures of its own. The edges were tattered from tossing about in her pack, the ink on some of the pages was smeared by the rain that fateful night he'd almost lost her, by her tears. He'd be damned if she'd cry any more.

Ross crossed to the table and snatched up the book, closed it and clasped it to his chest. "I have to find her . . . now. She's hurt, lad, and she needs me to heal her."

A crooked smile transformed Lucais's plain face, made his eyes dance. "Lang Gordy's, m'lord. And good luck in yer quest."

"Quest? Ah, my quest to win the fair maiden's heart." He already had that, 'twas her stubborn mind he had to conquer. Ross hugged the book a little tighter and smiled himself. The notion seemed not at all foolish. Nor, when he stepped outside and saw the rowan bush growing beside the house, did it seem silly to pluck a twig and stick it in his belt. For luck. Only a fool ignored something that had worked in the past.

They'd come full circle, he thought a few moments later as he crept up on the carpenter's back door. 'Twas here the adventure had begun. Breath bated, he lifted the latch, stole through the storage shed and into the house. All was quiet, save for Gordy's rhythmic snoring coming from the bedchamber. The only light came from the small fire in the hearth. By its golden glow, he saw Megan lying on a pallet in the corner. The sight drew him like metal filings to a magnet.

She slept on her side, body curled into itself beneath a single blanket. Exhausted as she was, her lids twitched restlessly. The soft whimpers that came from her parted lips brought him to his knees beside her.

"Meggie." Laying the book aside, Ross touched her hair.

Her eyes flew open, lashes fluttering like startled moths. "Ross." Her smile was warm enough to melt lead, her eyes dark pools of love and longing. She reached for him, then remembered. With a groan of pure anguish, she turned away.

Ross was having none of it. Gently but firmly he grasped her upper arms and rolled her onto her back. "Meggie." She cried out, struggled to escape him. "Easy, lass. You'll hurt yourself." But pain had driven her beyond reason or logic, and he was forced to resort to desperate measures himself. Pinning her milling legs with one of his, anchoring her arms with his hands, he trapped her beneath him, saddened to feel her heart thud against his like a snared rabbit's. "'Tis all right, love," he crooned, wondering how he could make it so.

She stilled, eyes wide and wounded. "M-Mama told you."

"Aye, she did." *Curse the woman, could she not have lied just this once?*

Megan averted her gaze. "Then you know what you must do."

Aye. He did. Woo her.

"Ross, stop nibblin' my ear and listen," Megan said, but her breathless words lacked conviction. The dark, tantalizing word he whispered back turned her blood to molten honey. "Nay, we canna," she said weakly. "We have to . . . you have to repudiate me."

"Too late. You've bewitched me. You're stuck wi' me." His tongue teased a fiery path from her ear to her collarbone.

Megan shivered. She shouldn't want this, couldn't want this. She had to stay strong. "I canna give you bairns."

He raised his head, gave her a dazzling smile. "You've already given me Kieran."

"But . . . but he isna yours."

His smile never faltered. "He's the babe of my heart. Of our hearts, precious to us because we both loved his parents and fear we failed them. We will love Kieran as we loved them. We will take him and raise him as our own."

Tears blurred the face hovering so close to hers. "Oh, Ross," she said, throat too full to say more.

His mouth closed over hers, warm and possessive yet infinitely tender. On his lips she tasted the salt of their mingled tears and knew she'd never loved him more.

"I love you," Ross murmured over and over between kisses.

How she'd longed to hear those words, but not like this with things gone so tragically wrong. "Oh, you stupid man. Why can you not see that you'd be better off wi' someone who—"

His hands tightened and he gave her a wee shake. "Think you I could bed another woman? Nay, but you've spoiled me for that. Refuse me, and you doom me to a life of eternal misery."

Megan blinked, eyes widening as he went on, raving about the bleakness of unrequited love. "Ross?" she said at last. "Either you've taken leave of your senses, or—"

"Did you know that Clan Carmichael has no bard?"

"The way you're goin', you could claim the post."

"I think 'tis catchin'." He released her arms and stretched out beside her, head propped on one hand. "I even stopped to pick some rowan for luck." He took the twig from his belt and tickled her nose with the leaves. "Come lie wi' me and be my love and true happiness we will find."

Megan gave a watery chuckle. "That doesna even rhyme."

"I fear I have a lot to learn." He dropped the rowan and tunneled a warm, wide hand into her hair, his thumb tracing lazy circles on the sensitive spot beneath her ear. "You taught me to dream, to hope, to love. Come home wi' me and teach me the rest." His expression sobered. "Miracles do happen. That you came into my life is proof of that. Mayhap we will have bairns of our own," he added, not wanting to give her false hope, but Lady Mary and the midwife were not God. "If not..." He shrugged. "Truth to tell, I'm not eager to risk losin' you to childbed fever or some such. Kieran will keep you plenty busy, and what wi' sickness and fightin', there always seems to be an orphaned bairn underfoot at Carmichael Castle. You could foster them."

"It... it isna the same. I wanted... I dreamed of havin' my own." Megan's lower lip wobbled and she could not say more.

"I know." Ross held her close as two people could get. Mayhap someday they would. "But we will have each other, and Kieran. Can that not be enough?"

"I suppose it will have to," Megan said sadly.

Ross kissed her nose. "I feel like last prize."

"Oh, nay. Never that." She framed his face with her hands and kissed him with all the love pent up inside her. "You are the only man I have ever wanted." He waited for the but. It never came. Instead, she tipped her head back and smiled. "I love you."

"And I you, Meggie mine." He leaned his forehead against hers and sighed. It was going to be all right. "What say we go back up to the castle? Wi' any luck, we can sneak up to your room while our families are playin' wi' Kieran."

"You dinna want me to meet your parents?"

"Later." He kissed her, his heart in his eyes. "Much later. I've yet to make love wi' my wife in a bed. A real bed."

Megan smiled, cheek dimpling as she snuggled closer. "It couldna be any better. But..."

Epilogue

September thirtieth, the day after Michaelmas, dawned clear and bright, the nip in the air a warning that summer was indeed over and winter would soon be upon them.

Ross drew in a deep breath, let it out slowly. Usually he dreaded the long months of inactivity when the harsh weather kept a man indoors with little to do, but the thought of being cooped up inside Carmichael Castle with his wife of two months appealed.

"Tired, lad?" his father asked as they walked under the portcullis whose iron teeth guarded Carmichael Castle's inner bailey from the outer.

"Aye," Ross admitted, but 'twas the pleasant sort of weariness that came of long hours supervising the harvest. And a bountiful one it had been. The hedgerows had been plucked of hips, berries, nuts and apples. Barley and oats filled the storage bins, ale fermented in the big kegs in the brew house. Such animals as were judged ready had been slaughtered, salted and smoked. The rest had been turned out to fatten on what grain remained in the stubbled fields.

"Ye did well to put in the windmill," Lionel muttered.

That stopped Ross in his tracks. He and his father had argued long and hard about installing a windmill to turn the grist mill when there wasn't sufficient water in the stream.

"Ye needna look so dumbstruck. I own up to a mistake...on the rare occasion when I make one," his father grumbled.

Then why haven't you installed me as heir? But much as he valued the truth, Ross feared the answer to that question. So he went through the motions of being the next chief of Clan Carmichael and tried to turn a blind eye to the doubts in his kinsmen's. Yesterday, when all the Carmichaels from near and far had gathered to celebrate the harvest, he'd half expected... nay, he'd hoped, dammit, that his father would make the announcement.

"'Tis a grand sight, seein' our clan gathered together," his father said, drawing Ross's attention to the outer bailey. The keep had been built upon a knoll, so from their vantage point they looked down on the large, grassy field of the outer ward. Enclosed by the castle's stout walls, it housed the stables, barracks, smithy and tiltyard. 'Twas here the visiting clansmen had erected their city of tents. Bright pennants flew from atop each one, showing the Carmichael red and black along with the personal device of each cadet leader. Ross's chest swelled with pride. "I thought most of them would have started for home by now."

"Heavy heads ha' slowed their departure, most like, for they feasted far into the night. 'Twas a grand time we showed them, dancin', drinkin' and storytellin'. Speakin' of which..." Lionel craned his neck to scan the colorful patchwork of tents and people decked out in their brilliant best. "Where's our Meg?"

Our Meg. The bubble of joy in Ross's heart expanded. How quickly and easily his family had taken to Megan. Of course, there was naught not to like. She was bright, clever and loving. Her unflagging optimism, her tremendous capacity for healing, had blown through Carmichael Castle like a cleansing wind, scouring out the grief and guilt that had divided them since Lion's death. Aye, he'd been right to keep silent about what had really happened, Ross thought. With every passing day, the weight of that lie grew less. "'Tis usually easy to spot her by her *tail*."

Lionel chuckled. "Aye, a Highland chief ha' his bard, his henchman, his tattler and his harper to follow him about. Megan ha' a *tail* of wee ones a league long." He glanced sidelong at Ross. "Speakin' of which..."

"Da." Warningly.

His father flushed and looked away. "Her leg's mended so ye can scarce tell she limps. Likely her innards healed, as well."

"'Tis in God's hands," Ross said sternly. At times like this, he regretted having been honest with his parents. He'd only done so to keep his father from harping on the subject of babes and breaking Megan's heart anew each time he did.

Lionel grunted, then brightened. "Ah, there are our womenfolk." He set a brisk pace downhill toward the area where the trestle tables had been set up for the Michaelmas feast.

Ross hurried after him, surprised to note that the huge cook fires nearby had been lit again. A haunch of beef turned over one; another held the wild boar he'd killed in the hunt two days ago. "Whatever can Mama be thinkin'? There's no need to serve up a feast again today, wi' everyone likely to leave by noon."

"A man's got to eat," his sire replied, eyes dancing with suppressed excitement. *His father was up to something.* But before Ross could question him, they reached the cluster of Carmichael women. "Ah, there's my wee bard," Lionel exclaimed, grinning at Megan, who held court at the nearest table. A dozen bairns sat in a circle at her feet while her puppets performed for them.

That Megan had charmed the children was not nearly as surprising as finding Elspeth glued to her new sister's side. "She's tellin' the tale of how Loarn and his brothers established the ancient kingdom of Dalriada," his sister said. "They were fierce warriors, and I think we are descended from them."

"Could be." Lionel rocked back on his heels and grinned as Carina drifted over from the cook fires to link her arm with his. "What say ye, love? Have we Loarn's blood in our veins?"

"Some of us do." Face flushed, eyes sparkling, Carina looked round the circle of Carmichaels, gaze falling last on wee Kieran asleep in his wet nurse's arms. Her smile faltered for a heartbeat, then recovered. "Ross most certainly does."

"Me?" Ross shifted his attention from the babe to his mother, acutely aware of the rustling noise behind him as his clansmen drew nearer. Inside the blue velvet surcoat Megan had insisted he wear today, his flesh shrank in anticipation of his father's caustic comment. It never came.

"I've a tale I'd ha' told," his father said instead.

A story? Lionel Carmichael was a man of action, a man whose deeds became legend, but who seldom listened to the ballads commemorating them. Ross looked at Megan, found her staring up at him so intently he feared something had happened. "What is wrong?" he demanded, starting forward, but his mother shoved a cup of wine into his hand and bade him sit on the blanket someone had spread on the ground behind him. 'Twas one of many. In fact, it seemed all of Clan Carmichael now encircled Megan, cups in hand, faces alight with anticipation.

"They've certainly taken to this storytellin'," he muttered as Andrew squatted down beside him.

"And why not?" the older knight huffed. "Yon lass's got a silver tongue and the heart of an angel."

Ross raised one brow. Effusive praise, even from Megan's most ardent admirer...next to Ross himself. Two months wed and he was more in love with her than ever. But he knew her. "She has the heart of a lioness, and she's up to somethin'." He only hoped that whatever it was didn't spoil the surprise he'd planned for later when the guests had departed.

"I'd hear the tale of how Ross killed Comyn MacDonnel." Lionel's bellowed request set off a wave of cheers.

"Nay." Ross's startled eyes locked on Megan's calm ones. Her reassuring smile didn't chase the knot from his gut. He couldn't relive that terrible day, he couldn't, but as silence fell and she began speaking, Ross realized the story had been stripped down to the basic facts and then embellished with new ones.

Comyn was twice as dark and evil as in real life, his attempts to best Ross by trickery played up so they were only exceeded by Ross's brave, honorable struggle to right the terrible wrong that had been done to his beloved brother. Ross's triumph, the final twist that made the lucky rowan shaft the instrument of Comyn's destruction, wrung shouts of approval from the crowd. Nor was there a dry eye in the field when Megan told how wee Kieran had been saved from death at the hands of the madman who had made him an orphan.

"Ross! Ross! Ross!" the assembled Carmichaels chanted.

Red-faced with embarrassment, yet oddly moved to tears, Ross stood and waved to his people. Then he started toward Megan, uncertain whether he wanted to kiss her or shake her.

Andrew took the decision from him by grabbing his arm. "Come. We've a bit of unfinished business to attend to." The crowd parted as the knight led Ross to the edge of the tiltyard.

Ross's soaring heart sank when he saw his armor lying on the grass and Davey waiting to arm him. "I willna fight you."

"There's been enough of that," Andrew agreed.

"Then what . . . ?"

"'Tis a ceremony of sorts," Megan whispered, slipping her hand in his and squeezing.

"Is this your doin'?" he demanded warily.

"I did mention it when I was talkin' wi' Da, but . . ."

"Into yer armor," his father cried. "The lads are gettin' that tired of standin' around wi' the stones."

Ross blinked, belatedly realizing that each of the Carmichael men had a large rock, either in his hands or at his feet. "You are goin' to stone me?"

"Silly." Megan kissed him on the cheek and withdrew while Davey, Owain and even Andrew hustled him into his armor.

"Well?" Ross demanded when 'twas done, feeling silly indeed standing there in full battle dress. The feeling persisted only as long as it took his father to pick up a veritable boulder, carry it a dozen paces and put it down.

"I, who set the seed, place the first stone," his sire said solemnly. "Let it be the foundation from which the next laird of the Carmichaels one day rules."

Sunlight glinted on the tears in his eyes as Lionel strode back to stand with his wife. The other men quickly followed, laying stone after stone until they'd built a shoulder-high, triangular-shaped mound. Lastly Megan stepped forward with Kieran in her arms. In his tiny fist he carried a pebble, which she helped him release to join the others.

"For Kieran, who stands as heir to Ross," she said, her voice as thick with tears as Ross's own throat.

If the Carmichaels thought it odd that Ross had named his brother's son to follow him instead of one he might someday have, it didn't dim their roar of approval. Surging forward, the men lifted Ross onto their shoulders and set him atop the pile of rocks. Giles and Davey stood on either side to steady him while Andrew handed up the sword Lionel had carried into battle.

"Let it be known, from this day forward," his father shouted, voice ringing off the castle walls, "that Ross Carmichael is my acknowledged heir, and will be yer chief after me.'' The last was nearly drowned out by the cheer that swept through the assembled Carmichaels.

Overcome by emotion, Ross swayed, would have fallen had Andrew not lent his support. The sea of faces beneath him blurred, all save the closest one. Megan looked up at him with love in her eyes, tears streaming down her cheeks. She was still there, clutching Kieran and smiling, when his clansmen set him back on the ground.

''I'll get you for embarrassin' me so,'' Ross hissed, kissing her brow to take the sting from his words. Truth to tell, he was more touched than he could put into words without breaking down.

''Dinna blame the lass,'' his father boomed, slapping him on the back and nearly toppling him over. ''She but mentioned such a ceremony for confirming an heir was used in the Highlands. I...''

Leaped on it like a starving trout, Megan thought, hugging Kieran a little tighter in her happiness. The ceremony had proved a graceful way for Lionel to acknowledge Ross as his heir without admitting he should have done so a year ago. And Ross...

His dazzling smile, the serenity of his gaze, blue and unclouded as the autumn sky, made her scheming well worthwhile. But...there was an odd glint in those same eyes whenever they chanced to meet hers that had Megan just a wee bit worried. By the time the meal had been consumed and Ross's good health toasted by every Carmichael over the age of ten, she had nearly nibbled a hole through her lower lip.

The shadows were lengthening, the air definitely cooler by the time Megan walked up to the castle to check on Kieran. Gazing down on his sweet face, downy black hair framing chubby cheeks faintly pinked by the sun, her heart turned over. *Oh, Siusan.*

''Dinna grieve for them, love,'' Ross whispered, arms stealing around her waist and pulling her back into a tender hug. ''They are together, as they wanted, and we will keep Kieran safe.''

''Aye, we will,'' Megan said softly. Turning in his embrace, she twined her arms around his neck. ''Are you angry wi' me?''

His smile chased away any lingering doubts. "How could I be, since you have given me what I wanted second most in life?"

"'Twas your father's doin'," she demurred.

"Liar." Gently and without censure. "Still I canna complain too greatly, since I have a surprise for you."

"You do?" Megan giggled and snuggled closer. "I liked the one you gave me this morn," she murmured, eyes warm with the memories of how she awakened near dawn to the feel of his fingers caressing her intimately, stealing her reason.

"'Tisna *that* kind of surprise."

"Too bad." She walked two fingers up his chest. He nipped at the one that brushed his lips. "'Twas a nice way to wake up."

"I can think of an even better one."

"Impossible."

"What say you to a few days in Edinburgh?" he proposed. "My father has a house there, and I've a mind to visit . . . just the two of us." He wiggled his eyebrows, making her giggle again. The sound went to his head faster than strong wine. More than anything, he wanted to make her happy, to erase the ghosts that flickered in her eyes from time to time when she remembered the one thing that was denied her.

"What of Kieran?"

"Kieran has his nurse, my mother and three sisters at his beck and call. Besides, you will have your hands full in town."

"I will?" she asked, clearly intrigued.

"*The Hawk* is due in from Curthill wi' a load of goods to be sold, and I'll need your help checkin' the manifest." The trade had resumed. This time as Eammon had originally intended, with the Sutherlands turnin' out honest product for the southern markets. Ross had agreed to act as factor on the exchanges.

"There'll be news of Papa, then." His recovery had been slow but steady. Though he'd likely never regain his full strength, he was at least restored to his family. "And if he's much better, Chrissy may come for a visit."

"Owain will be almost as pleased to see her as you."

Megan's smile dimmed. "Do you think they'll wed one day?"

"Time will tell," Ross said, though he doubted 'twould happen until Owain had regained his estates. He regretted his choice of words as soon as they left his mouth, for Megan shuddered and averted her gaze. Damn. He'd used that phrase when she brought up the subject of bairns of their own, and he refused to let her dwell on it. "There is another reason you'll be busy once we reach Edinburgh," Ross said slyly.

"Oh." She rallied swiftly, raising a questioning brow.

"A kinsmen who lives there wrote Da to say he'd lost his sister and brother-by-marriage in a fire. Their infant daughter was spared, but . . ."

"Oh, she was burned?" Megan cried.

"Aye. Her back, neck and one side of her face were badly burned," he said, touched by Megan's horrified gasp. "The physician who was called in says there's no point in tryin' to save her, for she'll be scarred and—"

"Physicians." Megan made a rude noise. "They know naught." She wiggled out of his arms and started from the room, then turned back. "What are you waitin' for? We'd best hurry."

"Owain and Giles will have the men ready to ride by the time we change clothes, and I set the maids to packin' hours ago," Ross replied, crossing to take her hands in his. "The babe mayna live, but if she does, she'll need a home, special care . . ."

"And lots of love. I know how people treat those who are . . . flawed," Megan said scathingly. "What is her name?"

"Flora . . . little flower."

Megan frowned. "You dinna mind . . . takin' her in, I mean?"

"The chief of the clan is the father to his people," Ross said gravely. On the trip back from Curthill, he'd vowed he'd give her as many bairns to love as he could, whether of their bodies or not. "I dinna want *all* of them livin' wi', but . . ."

"There is room for one more. Oh, thank you." Megan drew his head down and kissed him soundly. "I love you," she murmured when he let her up for air.

"And I love you," Ross said huskily, folding her close, glorying in the wild thudding of her heart against his. "Together, we will lead our clan . . ."

"And raise our bairns." The eyes she raised to him were moist, yet free from the shadow of grief, bright with hope for the days to come. His own spirits soared.

This was the way it was meant to be.

*   *   *   *   *

MORE ROMANCE, MORE PASSION, MORE ADVENTURE...MORE PAGES!

Bigger books from Harlequin Historicals. Pick one up today and see the difference a Harlequin Historical can make.

White Gold by Curtiss Ann Matlock—January 1995—A young widow partners up with a sheep rancher in this exciting Western.

Sweet Surrender by Julie Tetel—February 1995—An unlikely couple discover hidden treasure in the next *Northpoint* book.

All That Matters by Elizabeth Mayne—March 1995—A medieval about the magic between a young woman and her Highland rescuer.

The Heart's Wager by Gayle Wilson—April 1995—An ex-soldier and a member of the demi-monde unite to rescue an abducted duke.

Longer stories by some of your favorite authors. Watch for them in 1995 wherever Harlequin Historicals are sold.

HHBB95-1

Fifty red-blooded, white-hot, true-blue hunks
from every State in the Union!

Look for MEN MADE IN AMERICA! Written by some
of our most popular authors, these stories feature some
of the strongest, sexiest men, each from a different state
in the union!

Two titles available every month at your favorite
retail outlet.

In January, look for:

WITHIN REACH by Marilyn Pappano (New Mexico)
IN GOOD FAITH by Judith McWilliams (New York)

In February, look for:

THE SECURITY MAN by Dixie Browning
(North Carolina)
A CLASS ACT by Kathleen Eagle
(North Dakota)

You won't be able to resist MEN MADE IN AMERICA!

Harlequin® Historical

Why is March the best time to try Harlequin Historicals for the first time? We've got four reasons:

All That Matters by Elizabeth Mayne—A medieval woman is freed from her ivory tower by a Highlander's impetuous proposal.

Embrace the Dawn by Jackie Summers—Striking a scandalous bargain, a highwayman joins forces with a meddlesome young woman.

Fearless Hearts by Linda Castle—A grouchy deputy puts up a fight when his Eastern-bred tutor tries to teach him a lesson.

Love's Wild Wager by Taylor Ryan—A young woman becomes the talk of London when she wagers her hand on the outcome of a horse race.

It's that time of year again—that March Madness time of year—when Harlequin Historicals picks the best and brightest new stars in historical romance and brings them to you in one exciting month!

Four exciting books by four promising new authors that are certain to become your favorites. Look for them wherever Harlequin Historicals are sold.

On the most romantic day of the year, capture the thrill of falling in love all over again—with

Harlequin's

Bachelors

They're three sexy and *very single* men who run very special personal ads to find the women of their fantasies by Valentine's Day. These exciting, passion-filled stories are written by bestselling Harlequin authors.

Your Heart's Desire by Elise Title
Mr. Romance by Pamela Bauer
Sleepless in St. Louis by Tiffany White

Be sure not to miss Harlequin's Valentine Bachelors, available in February wherever Harlequin books are sold.

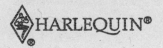

HARLEQUIN®

Don't miss these Harlequin favorites by some of our most
distinguished authors!
And now, you can receive a discount by ordering two or more titles!

HT#25577	WILD LIKE THE WIND by Janice Kaiser	$2.99	☐
HT#25589	THE RETURN OF CAINE O'HALLORAN by JoAnn Ross	$2.99	☐
HP#11626	THE SEDUCTION STAKES by Lindsay Armstrong	$2.99	☐
HP#11647	GIVE A MAN A BAD NAME by Roberta Leigh	$2.99	☐
HR#03293	THE MAN WHO CAME FOR CHRISTMAS by Bethany Campbell	$2.89	☐
HR#03308	RELATIVE VALUES by Jessica Steele	$2.89	☐
SR#70589	CANDY KISSES by Muriel Jensen	$3.50	☐
SR#70598	WEDDING INVITATION by Marisa Carroll	$3.50 U.S. $3.99 CAN.	☐
HI#22230	CACHE POOR by Margaret St. George	$2.99	☐
HAR#16515	NO ROOM AT THE INN by Linda Randall Wisdom	$3.50	☐
HAR#16520	THE ADVENTURESS by M.J. Rodgers	$3.50	☐
HS#28795	PIECES OF SKY by Marianne Willman	$3.99	☐
HS#26824	A WARRIOR'S WAY by Margaret Moore	$3.99 U.S. $4.50 CAN.	☐

(limited quantities available on certain titles)

	AMOUNT	$
DEDUCT:	10% DISCOUNT FOR 2+ BOOKS	$
ADD:	POSTAGE & HANDLING	$
	($1.00 for one book, 50¢ for each additional)	
	APPLICABLE TAXES*	$_____
	TOTAL PAYABLE	$_____
	(check or money order—please do not send cash)	

To order, complete this form and send it, along with a check or money order for the
total above, payable to Harlequin Books, to: **In the U.S.:** 3010 Walden Avenue,
P.O. Box 9047, Buffalo, NY 14269-9047; **In Canada:** P.O. Box 613, Fort Erie, Ontario,
L2A 5X3.

Name: _____

Address: _____ City: _____

State/Prov.: _____ Zip/Postal Code: _____

*New York residents remit applicable sales taxes.
 Canadian residents remit applicable GST and provincial taxes.

HBACK-JM2